STANTON ADORE

T L SWAN

ALSO BY T L SWAN

My Temptation (Kingston Lane #1)

The Stopover (The Miles High Club #1)

The Takeover (The Miles High Club #2)

The Casanova (The Miles High Club #3)

The Do-over (The Miles High Club #4)

Miles Ever After (The Miles High Club – Extended Epilogue)

Mr. Masters (The Mr. Series #1)

Mr. Spencer (The Mr. Series #2)

Mr. Garcia (The Mr. Series #3)

Our Way (Standalone Book)

Play Along (Standalone Book)

The Italian (The Italians #1)

Ferrara (The Italians #2)

Stanton Adore (Stanton Series #1)

Stanton Unconditional (Stanton Series #2)

Stanton Completely (Stanton Series #3)

Stanton Bliss (Stanton Series #4)

ACKNOWLEDGMENTS

I would sincerely like to thank my dear friends who have read Stanton Adore and offered endless encouragement, I would not have had the confidence to do this without you. If I have given this book to you to read, I dearly value your friendship and know that you know... Deep down I am crazy.

My very trusted first round of readers. Jo, Emma, Vicki and Andrew. You read my chapters as I wrote them, I will forever be in your debt... Thank you.

A special mention to Andy who has never read a romance novel before, let alone one of an erotic nature. I cringed every time I clicked the send button to you. You surprised me every time with positivity and grace.

My second round of readers who read the book when it was finished. Brooke, Selena, Jolene, Rachel, Renee, Anne, Carly, Gia, Nicole, Mel, Bridget, and Bee.

My wonderful three children and husband who have watched me type for hours every chance I got and who still loved me anyway. They all told me continually that they love my book, when they had never read a single page.

To my Mum and Dad, I am who I am because of you. I only hope I can be half the parent that you have both been to me, my sisters and brother as we grew up. I love you both dearly. Thank you.

A special mention to my beautiful Mum who has read the book nearly as many times as I have. Your support and love of the story has made it all worthwhile.

Thank you and I love you.

Xxx

GRATITUDE

The quality of being thankful;
readiness to show appreciation for, and to return kindness.

DEDICATION

To my husband
I would marry you again in an instant. Thank you for being you, I
love you.

ADORE

Have you ever had a moment?
A specific moment in time.
When you know the next decision you make
is going to change the course of your life.
And if so, do you go forward or walk away,
knowing that heart break is imminent?
This is what I'm trying to decipher.
This is my story.
I'll let you be the judge.

MEMORIES... strange things that they are. Every human brain has millions upon millions of these, however it chooses only certain ones to recall in your conscience. To put into your psyche. How does it decipher which ones to wipe and which ones to forget, and which ones to replay again and again? And does the human brain have the ability to exaggerate memories? Make the highs higher, the lows lower, passion more tender, the orgasms stronger?

Think about it. Which ten memories are poignant to you? Good or bad, they are usually connected to life–changing events. Moments in time that stand still and, in course, change the direction you are headed within your life.

My name is Natasha Marx. As a clinical psychologist, I spend my days dissecting people's minds, dealing with their memories. Mostly trying to erase them or at least repress them. Help them move on from the shadows of their souls.

I blow out a breath and I shake my head, staring into space as once again the movie screen that is my brain replays the motion picture. Dredging my heart out with it on its way. Captivating an audience of one to a tender erotic time of my life.

A time when choices were made easily and unguardedly. A time when the side effects of my actions held no consequence for anyone concerned.

A time of innocence and betrayal.

CHAPTER 1

Natasha

HIS BREATHINGS LABOURED, like he's gasping for air. My heart races out of control as anticipation of his next move thrills, excites and petrifies me all at the same time. I sigh gently, and my eyes close as I roll my head to the side to allow him greater access to my neck.

"So beautiful," he whispers. My God, if someone had told me two weeks ago that I would be here, doing this with him in the middle of the night, in a tent with both sets of our parents only thirty meters away, I would have thought they needed their head examined I can't believe it myself. What the hell am I doing? I am way out of my depth.

He smiles into my neck, "Precious girl, can you feel me? Feel how ready you are for me?" He gently and slowly adds another finger into my sex and tenderly takes my erect nipple into his mouth between his teeth and draws his head back. The wet sound of my arousal hangs thick in the air. I take a deep breath as my legs instinctively open wider. My knees bent high, my back arches and my hips gently rotate. My body takes over as I start to ride his strong thick fingers. I bear down, needing more. My wet center is blessed with yet another burst of creamy arousal. His fingers ease in and out stretching me open, preparing me as he gently runs his open lips back down my neck. His breath is shaking as he tries to control the raging hormones that threaten his undoing. He leans up onto his elbow and looks down at me. "I need this...please...let me make love to you." He runs the tips of his four fingers over my swollen flesh in a circular motion grazing my clitoris. My body jerks in response. His forehead rests against mine and his eyes bore into me, then my breath catches as my eyes close. "God, I want you Tash... please..., I've never wanted anything so much." He grazes my neck again with his teeth. My senses are under assault, my brain ceasing to operate.

Mechanical meltdown. "Josh, you feel so good," I whisper. I grab his face with both hands and slide my tongue into his mouth. He flicks his fingers against my wet clitoris and my breath catches. My body convulses and I moan in a husky voice that is unrecognizable to my ears.

"I can make it feel better, precious...let me." I place my hand on his forearm to feel the muscles flex as he rides me with his hands, strong, able pleasure–giving hands. His palm circles on my outer lips as his fingers delve deep to massage the front wall of my vagina, a place only he knows where to find. My eyes roll back in my head and I bring my feet up and place them flat on the ground to bring his fingers deeper. I'm panting, the orgasm so close I can taste it.

"No," he whispers and removes his fingers.

"Josh, no," I whisper. "Don't stop, baby, please I need this."

"No, Natasha," he whispers. He only uses my full name

when he's accentuating his point, forcing his will on me. He tenderly kisses me again, his tongue melting my resistance. "We've been doing this every night for a week. I'm giving you multiple orgasms." He gently bites my neck as I smile.

"Hmmm," I whisper. "Is there a problem with that?"

"No problem, it's just...tonight... I need, I need," his breath catches, "something...something more." His breath quivers as his fingertips find that spot on my clitoris again, circling with precision. I moan involuntarily and my neck arches, throwing my head back into the pillow. "How does the word penetration sound?"

I giggle into his neck. "Did you really just say that?" He smiles.

I know he's teasing me. "Penetration, really."

"Ok, would you rather I say I'm going to fuck you into next week? Fuck you so hard you won't be able to walk for a week? Push into that beautiful tight little pussy of yours with my hard cock?" He growls into my neck as he hears the crude words he's just spoken. They turn me on beyond words and ignite my already boiling blood. That's it, the last of my control dissipates. I know I will do anything he wants.

He removes his hand again and dips his tongue into my mouth, kissing me tenderly, loving me. "Presh," he pleads. Both of our breathing is labored. I close my eyes and make the decision I know is wrong. It's one that my physical being won't let me refuse, one that is out of my hands. I crossed that line in the sand over a week ago. Moments pass... more passionate kissing. Every fiber of my body is screaming at me, demanding. I desperately want this beautiful man, needing this connection as much as he does. I mentally kick myself as I hear the words slip from my lips.

"Make love to me, Josh... I need you, too." He kisses me possessively as he growls acceptance.

"Are you sure?" he asks.

I smile into his kiss. "I'm yours, Josh, take me."

He bites my neck and digs his hands into my behind. "Fuck, you're beautiful," he whispers. Goosebumps scatter over my body. "I will make it good for you, baby, you know that don't you?"

I nod nervously. His hand slides down my body. Back between my legs, he skims my pubic hair with the backs of his fingers. Gently he bites my shoulder as he eases a finger inside me. I groan with overwhelming need and hunger. His other hand rises to my breast as he gently squeezes my nipple. I'm under assault. Losing my mind. My breathing is now in pants as he adds another finger in and out in a circular movement, stretching me, teasing me. My body oozes another rush of cream.

"That's it, precious girl, can you feel how wet you are for me?" He gently adds another finger.

"Oww, Josh," I tense.

"Sh, sh, baby. Relax." He kisses me deeply as he uses three fingers to gently probe and stretch my tight opening. It gives me a pleasurable burn. "Oh God, you're so ready for my cock." His crude words push me over the edge. "Do you have any idea how much I fucking adore you?" he whispers into my ear, and I bring my hand down to feel him. His hard shaft is oozing pre ejaculate. I give him a long stroke and then swipe my thumb over the slippery, engorged head. Feeling every vein on his thick length that I now know from memory.

"Don't, baby," he pulls away. "I don't want to come," he whispers. I sit up on my knees to take him in my mouth. The temptation too great, I need to taste him. "Stop... now." He pulls me off him and pushes me down. He moves his weight onto his elbows as he positions himself over me. Slowly sliding the side of his shaft backwards and forwards through my swollen wet lips.

The intimate kissing continues. "We were meant for each other; you know that don't you?" I nod and smile. I do know this, without a doubt in my mind. He nudges the opening of my sex with his large length. His breath quivers and I know he's trying to hold himself back, so he doesn't hurt me. He goes in a little way. Ahh, I tense. "It's ok... it's ok," he whispers. He kisses me again and I relax. "That's it, baby, you're doing great." His voice is strained but just the sound of it calms me. Shit, this hurts! He pushes again and I tense, oh fuck, this really hurts. "Take me," he whispers. "Relax, baby, and take my body, it's here for you, I'm here for you." I slowly start to relax as he pauses to allow my body to adjust to the hard intrusion while running his open mouth up and down my neck. Our mingled breathing sounds like we are running a marathon. I can hear the quiver in his breath as he inhales. God, this is just so unexpectedly intimate. I can't control my feelings any longer. I blink quickly to try and stop it. But it's too late, a tear escapes onto my cheek.

"Baby, no," he whispers, mortified that he's hurting me. It's not the physical pain that I'm unable to cope with, but the emotion I feel for this man. The love I have for him. It's overwhelming, it's too much. He whispers again, "Take me, beautiful girl," and kisses my ear. Wanting desperately to please him I force my legs to open further and he thrusts deep with one lunge. He's entirely in. Oh shit, he's big. "I'm sorry, precious," he whispers. "Sshh, sshh, it's ok, it's ok, I'm in."

I hold my breath, unable to speak, shocked to my core. This really fucking hurts—*what the hell!* "You feel amazing," he whispers as he stares into my glassy eyes. He stays still, deep inside me, allowing my body to adjust to his brutal length. Kissing me gently, he swipes his tongue through my lips, and I feel my arousal slowly rise back up.

He leans up onto his elbow to look at me and gently wipes my hair off my face. "Do you have any idea what you mean to me?" he whispers into my ear. I gradually relax. Slowly he withdraws and gently slides into me again. I breathe out, overcome with emotion and unable to hide it any longer.

"Josh," I whisper. His eyes are closed, he's breathing heavily.

"Yes, baby," he answers, his lips against my cheek.

"I love you," I whisper. His eyes fly wide open.

———

"Been a big week, hey?" My eyes fly up nervously to Simon in my office doorway. I nod and quickly rearrange the papers on my desk. I try to rein in my now pounding heart, guilt written all over my face. Bloody hell. I need to stop thinking about this shit when I'm at work.

"It has been a big week, Simon. I'm tired. Do you still want to go for that drink?"

He frowns and shakes his head. "Don't try to weasel out of it. We do this every Friday."

I give him a resigned smile. "We do. Give me a minute to freshen up, will you?"

He smiles. "Sure, meet you out front."

I wander over to the large arched window overlooking the park. It's just on dusk. Large magnolia trees surround the manicured lawn, which has four stone benches in the center An old man is reading the paper on one of them. It's a beautiful haven in the middle of a city. I'm lucky to have this view from my office. I blow out a breath as I take out my ponytail and redo it.

What are you doing now, Joshua? Who are you with? Why do I remember him in technicolor but live my life in black and white? I drag myself up and change my clothes. I feel like going out like a hole in the head. Why do I constantly agree to do things I don't want to do?

———

Saturday at Mum's is always the same. Bridget, my younger sister, who also moonlights as my best friend, goes on and on about her dickhead boyfriend. Mum and I always sit and listen while she vents or at least we pretend to listen. We drink coffee, eat cake and read the papers, roll our eyes at each other and occasionally add our two cents' worth. Which goes unnoticed I might add. It's a Saturday morning ritual, an excuse to catch up.

"Oh," Mum claps her hands in excitement. "I got my outfit for the wedding."

"Oh yes," I answer, blowing out a deep breath as I brush the crumbs off my shirt. My inability to get excited about anything is beyond rude.

"Don't listen to her Mum—she's in a shitty mood this week," Bridget snaps. I open my eyes wide at her. Implying *Shut up*. "What?" she snaps.

"Don't start," I scowl.

"Well, what's with you this week?"

"You are very preoccupied lately, honey. Is everything all right?" Mum asks.

"Yes," I roll my eyes and blow out a breath.

"Is it work?" she questions, cocking her head to the side and resting her coffee cup on her chest.

7

"Anything juicy?" Bridget asks excitedly.

"You know I can't answer that," I sigh.

"God, you're no fun. Can't you tell me about some hot nymphomaniac sex god you're treating, one who's looking for a blonde travel agent? You know I'm living vicariously through you," she smirks and Mum rolls her eyes.

"I wish I did treat sex gods," I mutter. "I could do with a sex god or two in my life. Besides only women are called nymphomaniacs, men are called satyriasists."

Bridget rolls her eyes, and I can't help but smile. "I don't care what they're called. Just find two and arrange a double date."

"Sure, you're on," I smile. Feeling guilty I look at Mum, "Go and put your outfit on, Mum, let me see what it's like."

"Ok." She jumps from the chair excitedly and disappears down the hall towards her bedroom. Bridget carries on reading the paper. Moments later Mum breezes back into the kitchen in a beautiful, layered plum number. She looks amazing.

"I love it." Bridget claps her hands in excitement.

"You do look beautiful," I nod.

"You don't think it's too tight?" she asks as she turns around and checks out her behind in the oven door, standing on her tiptoes.

I shake my head. "No, it's perfect," I smile at her.

"Oh, Natasha, what color did you say the dress you are wearing is?"

"Not sure yet, I have two to choose from."

"OMG," Bridget holds up both of her hands as if to say stop. "Listen to this," Bridget exclaims as she reads an excerpt from the gossip pages.

"It seems our shores are soon to be graced with the return of the App mogul and millionaire playboy Joshua Stanton. Our spies reveal he is returning to the shores of Australia to be the best man at his brother's wedding and will be staying for three months to reorganize his work visa. Look out for him and his entourage, ladies, he's quite the catch."

Oh shit. My heart sinks.

Bridget is so excited. "Holy crap! He's like famous now, in the gossip pages. Just how rich is he?"

"He's a multimillionaire," Mum answers.

"Entourage— what, so he travels with an entourage?"

"I suppose," she nods and shrugs her shoulders. "I know he employs a lot of people."

"Margaret said he has an executive team working with him now and bodyguards."

I feel sick to my stomach. No one knows about Joshua and me. It happened on a trip when I was seventeen and he was nineteen and he was just a regular sex–charged teenager before he went to America. Our parents would have freaked; they would still freak if they knew. This man is frigging haunting me. What is the hold he has on me? This is what I'm lost about. Is it that he was my first? Or that he is forbidden to me? Even just the memory of him raises my pulse. I have been putting myself through self–inflicted torture for years when I put a Google alert on him. Every goddamn girl he's ever gone out with is splashed all over the internet. Models, actresses, socialites, sluts.

However the hell you put it, he has long forgotten me. My heart sinks.

"Oohh," Bridget gasps, "has he got a girlfriend?"

Mum hunches her shoulders. "I have no idea. No one

special I don't think. His mother would have loved gloating if he had." A cold shiver runs down my back. His mother, piece of work that she is, loves nothing better than to gloat to me how great Joshua is doing. How wealthy Joshua is. How many beautiful models Joshua dates. If I didn't know better, I would say she is rubbing it in my face. Although, I know she has no idea about what happened between us. Nobody does. Maybe that's the problem, I've lived all these years without telling a soul. I need to vent. My feelings swing from lovesick to angry, resentful and hateful, and back to brokenhearted, all within an hour. While he lives this exciting full life I'm still here, the village idiot, pining over a man that doesn't even know I exist. I'm pathetic.

Well, he's going to know I exist after this wedding because I am going to look so unbelievably hot. I'm going to rub his sorry ass in it. I narrow my eyes as I rethink my diabolical plan. Look hot, turn him on, lead him on and then reject him. He's going to be begging for mercy by the time I'm finished with him, if I have to ram it down his puny throat. I've been planning this for six months. Operation payback is going to be a bitch.

I smile. I think the only relief I'm going to get is the satisfaction that I'll have the last word. I had no say in our demise, although it has haunted me for years. Perhaps that was the problem. I lied to him about our breakup. Told him what he needed to hear and not the truth. I've been overanalyzing this for years. In my clinical opinion I am suffering guilt associated trauma. I need to eventually tell him the truth somewhere down the line so I can just move the hell on, and he can release me from this invisible Spiderman hold he has on me. He is the last person I think of every night. I wonder who he's with now and whether he ever thinks of me and misses me like I miss him. I'm sad, sad to my bones, a deep regretful sadness that I can't shake. No matter how hard I try. My seemingly normal existence and happiness is a stage show. Not all the time. I am happy. I just feel an emptiness like something's missing, a hole in my life, maybe similar to someone who grieves a person who has died, a mother who has lost a child. Even when I am happy, there is an emptiness that somehow won't go away. And the memories. God, the memories. They haunt me. My mind wanders constantly, imagining us together in bed, snuggled up, making love for hours and hours. His tenderness, his adoration of me and my body. He did love me when we were together, I know this for certain, it was just so long ago. So why in the hell am I still in love with him after all this time? Am I even in love with him? I don't even know him. I know my emotions are coming to a head because he's due to touch down in Sydney anytime and I will, no doubt, see him. I'm excited and terrified at the same time.

"Does Joshua still play polo?" I ask, feigning nonchalance.

"Ahuh, apparently he has a stables property, and his horses are worth millions."

I nod, disappointed by the answer.

"His mother said he is also into kickboxing now."

"Kickboxing?" I repeat as I frown. "That's random."

"Yes, I know."

"What color did you say your dress is, Bridget?"

"White."

"*White!*" I exclaim. "You can't wear white."

"Who cares," she smiles. "I need to look hot. Josh might be bringing some hot guys to the wedding."

"Haven't we just been hearing all about Jeremy for the last hour?" Mum looks to the ceiling in frustration.

"Yeah, Jeremy Schmeremy," she rolls her eyes. "You know my boyfriend's a dick." We all laugh.

"I'll drink to that."

"Me, too," Mum laughs and we all clink coffee cups. "Hurry up and dump him already."

Joshua

Sydney Airport 5.23 pm, Sunday

Joshua Stanton's private jet comes slowly to a halt on the tarmac. On board are Ben, his large South African body-guard, Adrian, his personal assistant, eight computers with software and a computer technician for each computer. The computer techs are all typical computer geeks.

"I have a large van and driver at your disposal," Joshua tells the lead tech head.

"Ok, that's great," he nods.

"You are all booked in at the Sheraton on Hyde Park for the next three days until you all decide where you are staying. Stay in touch with Adrian with the details. The driver will pick you and the equipment up at 9.00 am in the morning and take you to the office space we have hired."

"Thanks, Mr. Stanton."

"You all have company credit cards, just charge what you need."

"Thank you, sir."

Joshua and Adrian wait as Ben picks up the car keys from the rental company. Ben is flicking through the pages of his iPad double time.

"What the fuck are you doing there?" Josh frowns as he looks over Ben's shoulder.

"Trying to get my bearings. I'm on maps and it isn't

making sense." He turns the screen around to look at it upside down and holds his head to the side.

"Yeah that app is useless; we really should design a decent one." Joshua looks around disinterested, glances at his chunky Rolex watch and puts one hand into the pocket of his navy three-piece suit. He's wearing black Oxfords, a crisp white shirt and a black tie, and his chocolate hair is buzz cut. His piercing blue eyes scan the lobby of the airport. His skin is darkened from his recent surfing trip to the Maldives. "I forgot how hot Aussie girls are," he makes an idle observation while rubbing his chin.

"Yes, I can't wait to check out the Aussie men, apparently they are off the charts as well."

Joshua smiles. "That goes without saying." He widens his eyes at Adrian.

"Hmm, they're conceited too, I found out," Adrian scowls. "Totally," Josh raises one eyebrow and nods his head, still scanning the room.

Ben returns, pushing a trolley of luggage. "This way," he gestures. "This being on the wrong side of the road thing is weird," Ben smirks while driving.

Joshua smiles as he sits in the front passenger seat, Adrian in the back seat. Joshua starts programming the Navigation.

"What are you doing?" Ben asks.

"We are taking a quick detour," Josh answers.

"Really?" Adrian whines. "I need to take a leak."

"Shut up, enough of the back–seat driving, who's fucking this duck?"

Adrian rolls his eyes in the rearview mirror at Ben who smiles at the usual banter. Adrian scowls as he leans his head back into the headrest. "And for the record, I don't fuck ducks."

Josh smiles and nods. "Good to know." Twenty-five minutes later they are driving up a one way street in Rose Bay.

"Where the hell are we going?" Adrian asks. Josh doesn't answer as he cranes his neck and looks up the road.

"It should be just up here on the right. Pull in here." He points to the left. He sits with his elbow on the car door, his thumb under his chin, rubbing the side of his pointer finger back and forward over his lips, deep in thought. They sit in silence for ten minutes.

"Mind telling me why we are here?" Ben asks quietly. "Someone I used to know lives in that dark brick building over there." He points to the large older style apartment block across the road, still deep in thought.

"And we are here, because?"

"I want to find out what apartment 5B is. It looks like there are two apartments on each level. Is the left side A or B?"

"I'll go look," Ben hops out of the car and heads across the road. Josh stays silent, deep in thought. Adrian sits quietly in the back, assessing the situation, trying to work out what the hell is going on. Whatever it is, Josh is acting weird, really weird.

Ben returns. "It's on the right, five levels up."

"Did you get in? Isn't there a security door?"

"No, I went in when someone left."

Joshua nods and looks up. "She's home."

"Looks that way," replies Ben. They all stay silent for another ten minutes, then Josh gets out of the car and walks around to the road side of the car, resting his rear on the door. His hands in his suit pant pockets, his feet crossed in front of him, he continues looking up at the window. Adrian and Ben follow, each standing on either side of him, also leaning on the car.

"What's going on?" Adrian asks quietly. Josh stays silent. Ben blows out a breath, the dark mood Joshua has slipped into is concerning.

"Why don't you just go in and knock, man?" Joshua doesn't move. He's unresponsive and a depressive demeanor hangs over him.

"Do you want me to go in and knock?" Adrian asks, but Joshua shakes his head.

"How long since you've seen this girl?" Ben asks.

"Seven and a half years," Joshua answers flatly.

"Does she know you're back in town?" He shakes his head again.

"So where do your parents live from here?" Adrian opens the back car door and gets out his iPad.

"Toorak, Melbourne. About twelve hours south."

Adrian and Ben frown at each other.

"But I thought we were here for three months so you can see your family?"

"Yes, we are, but they are in another state."

"Please don't tell me we are in Sydney for this girl?" Joshua is still staring up to apartment 5B.

"Maybe," he answers. "To be truthful, I have no idea what we are doing here, I feel unsettled already."

Ben raises his eyebrows. "Joshua Stanton unsettled by a woman; never thought I'd see the day."

"It's... complicated." He blows out a breath.

Adrian's mouth drops open. "But I thought you said."

"Yeah, I lied."

"So, this girl... is her name... Natasha?"

Joshua hangs his head and blows out a breath. "Yes," he answers.

"Hmm, a part of the jigsaw puzzle fits into place,"

Ben smiles. "So you do have a heart?"

Joshua smirks. "I wouldn't go that far."

Adrian lies on his back across the hood and blows out a breath, hands behind his head. "You know, I think Rod Stewart was right on the money." Joshua and Ben frown at each other and then him.

"You know, the first cut is the deepest." All three men smile.

"That is true. You remember every minute in detail. Come on, let's go. Enough of this shit, she fucks with my head."

"Aren't we going in?" Adrian asks.

"No, I just wanted to see where she lives."

"Does she have a boyfriend, married, what's her story?"

"No, no nothing. Nothing I can dig up anyway."

"You've kept tabs on her?"

"Yes, from a distance."

"When did you last speak to her?" After a silence of five minutes, Josh blows out a breath and replies.

"Seven and a half years ago, the day she dumped me." Adrian and Ben look at each other, the shock evident on their faces.

"So, you haven't spoken a word to her since?"

"Nope."

"You haven't called?"

"Nope." They all look back to the window and the lights go off.

Ben urges for a second time. "Just go in, man."

"Even if I wanted to, the law forbids it."

"She had a restraining order put on you?" Adrian gasps.

Joshua shakes his head. "No," he answers quietly.

"Her parents did?"

Josh looks back up to the window. "Something like that. Get in the car, let's go and don't let me come back here. This is pointless."

"Ok. But are we not here because of her? Doesn't that defeat the purpose?"

"Shut up, dick," Josh smiles at Adrian. "Stop making sense." As the car speeds away, Josh puts his head back into the seat and rubs his face. "I need a drink, a strong fucking drink."

———

Bondi, 11.50 pm

Joshua leans over the railing of the balcony looking out to the ocean, sipping his Cointreau and ice out of a thick short crystal tumbler. The place Adrian has rented for him for the three months is swank, on the water. It is a little dated and well below the standard of his LA house. They chose it because it was the only one near a surf beach that had another house next door for Ben and Adrian. Having just run for an hour on the treadmill, he is freshly showered and bare-foot and wearing a loose pair of sweats and a white Bonds tank top. It's March. Here, it's the first month of Fall, a cool briskness hangs in the air. Desperately trying to rein himself in from googling her and finding out her phone number he takes another sip of his liquor and enjoys the warmth as he swallows, temporarily closing his eyes.

"This is a fucking disaster. I should have stayed in Melbourne," he mutters to himself. The doorbell rings and assuming it's Adrian, he saunters to the front door and opens it. A beautiful caramel blonde in a trench coat and white high-heels stands before him, a sexy smile playing on her lips.

"Can I help you?"

"I'm looking for Joshua Stanton," she breathes in a husky voice. He raises an eyebrow. "You've found him."

"I'm a friend of Carson's. He asked me to deliver your housewarming present."

Joshua smiles and raises both his eyebrows. "Did he now, and what would that be?" She opens her coat and there she stands. White silk stockings, suspender belt, a lace white thong and short-cut white satin corset. Her body is tanned, toned and amazing. His jaw ticks, he bends his head to the left as if trying to crack his neck. His eyes scan up and down her body and he stands back, raising his hand, gesturing for her to enter.

"I do love housewarming presents." He smiles a long sexy smile which she returns.

"You know, I think tonight for once, I will too." She takes his hand. "I heard a little secret."

"Oh yes, and what was that?"

"You like having your cock sucked."

"You did, did you?" He smiles. "Show me a man who doesn't." He opens his eyes wide.

"Yes, it's a coincidence don't you think?"

He looks at her puzzled.

"Because tonight I'm in the mood to suck your cock dry."

"Hmm. That is a mood that I like. Coincidental or not," he smiles. "I do have great friends, don't I?" he adds.

"You do. I'm a very expensive housewarming gift."

He unashamedly looks her up and down. "I can see that," he leads her to the bar where he pours another Cointreau for himself. "Do you want a drink?" He holds up his glass and tips his head to the side, cracking his neck again.

She shakes her head. "No thanks."

He smiles, raises his eyebrows and takes her hand, leading her back to the foyer to go up the stairs to his bedroom, still carrying his drink.

"You know you are just the distraction I needed tonight." She smiles.

"What did you say your name was?" he asks.

"What do you want it to be?"

He continues walking up the stairs and stops mid step to turn and look at her. He narrows his eyes and puts his chin to an angle.

"My bedroom is this way... Natasha."

CHAPTER 2

Natasha

"I'm telling you he's cheating," Bridget whines.

"Oh fuck, not this again," I mutter, running my hands through my hair, my elbows resting on the table.

"Just dump him already."

"No, I need proof."

"Why?" I scoff. "I'm over hearing about this wanker, it's doing my head in." I take my phone from my bag and check my messages, trying to block her out.

"Listen here, you," she points her teaspoon at me to accentuate her point. "You listen to all kinds of crazy shit at work and you're going to damn well listen to mine." I roll my eyes.

"Yeah, but I get paid for that and my patients actually respect my opinion and besides, you're different. I can tell you what I think, and I think you should dump the prick."

"So, you think he's a prick now?"

"No, you think he's a prick."

"When did I say that?"

"When you said he was cheating on you."

"Oh God, don't start your shrink shit with me, you're twisting my words."

I roll my eyes. "Listen, if you don't want my opinion, don't ask for it."

"Fine, I won't."

"Good, suits me."

"What are you two arguing about?" Abbie joins us from the restroom.

"We are not arguing," I moan.

"Yes, we are, Tash thinks Jeremy is a prick"

Abbie laughs and nods, "Who doesn't? Jeremy is a prick." We are at our favorite coffee shop, Oscar's. We meet there a couple of times a week. Oscar's is small and unassuming. Its walls are dark timber paneling with big green glass pendant lights hanging low over oversized chocolate leather lounges that have colored cushions scattered all over them. Big wooden coffee tables adorn the center of each setting. The clientele are eclectic, from normal girls like us to doctors and lawyers, punk rockers to gorgeous gay men. Great coffee music always adds to the ambience and atmosphere, although on the last four or five times it hasn't been as enjoyable as it normally is. Abbie, Bridget's and my best friend, and I have had to endure countless hours of Jeremy crap.

Bridget rummages through her bag. "Abbie, I bought you something," she pulls out a white paper bag.

Abbie frowns, "What is it?"

Bridget smiles. "It's a bumper sticker for your car." She pulls it out and we all burst out laughing. It reads:

If you're going to ride my ass,
can you at least pull my hair?

"That's funny." I can't stop laughing. "And you bought me this because?"

"Because you told me you like it when guys pull your hair."

"When did I tell you that?"

"Oh, fuck off. Are you denying it?"

"No, yes, shut up, stop it," she laughs. "Show me a red-blooded woman who doesn't like having her hair pulled." Bridget and I both look at each other sheepishly and raise our hands in unison. She pulls a disgusted face. "God, you two must be shit in bed." She rolls her eyes while we giggle. "Anyway, I can't put this on my car, my dad will freak." She shakes her head as she stuffs it in her bag.

"Ok, back to the conversation. Once and for all tell me why you think he's cheating. I want ten reasons." I wave my teaspoon at her. "No excuses."

"Ok," she nods. "We used to see each other every night but now he's a partner in his law firm. I don't see him much through the week."

"Ok, maybe he's just working," I answer.

"Maybe," she nods. "The sex has dropped off."

"By how much?"

"Well, it used to be three or four times a week and now it's like once a week and usually I initiate it."

"Maybe he's tired and stressed." Abbie pipes in.

"Bullshit."

"Abbie, you can't comment. Boyfriends are different to one-night stands," I mutter.

"Ok, agreed," she nods.

I love Abbie, she's a self-proclaimed sneaky slut. By sneaky slut I mean when we are out and having a great time dancing and drinking, she just disappears. Twenty minutes later we get a text telling us she's gone home. She has a few boys in her kitty as she calls it. We know them as number one, first reserve, tall guy, hot guy, army guy and she has a tradie as well, although I don't know what he does. Number one always has right of way if he's out. Although, I think army guy is rising through the ranks pretty quickly.

Bridget and I know them all by sight but, in all honesty, we have probably not spoken more than a dozen words to any of them. She likes it like this. We love her honesty and good for her if she can do it without guilt—why not? I could probably take a page out of her book and loosen the hell up.

"And," Bridget continues, "he's started to guard his phone." "Hmm, that's not good," We all silently and sum up the situation. "And get this, last week when I stayed at his house, I was looking in his drawer and he has bought all new underwear."

"Yeah, but maybe he just needed new undies."

"No, they were nice like nice, *nice* not everyday undies." We stay silent and sip our coffee as we listen. I purse my lips as I think. "And then there's the manscaping."

Abbie chokes on her coffee. "Manscaping," she blurts out.

"Yes, please stop laughing. This is not funny." I want to laugh myself but instead I frown at Abbie, symbolizing for her to shut up. My ability to keep a straight face when I hear ridiculousness is an added benefit of my job. "Last time we were together I noticed he's like...," she whispers and leans into the table, and we both lean in instinctively to listen. "You know, done some extreme grooming."

Abbey narrows her eyes, "Did you ask him what that is about?"

"Yes, when I first noticed it, he seemed embarrassed and then said he did it as a surprise for me."

"Do you think it was?"

"No, I don't. And, get this, he's shaved off his chest hair."

"God," I breathe and sit back. "I hate manscaping."

"Why?" Abbie pulls a disgusted face. "There's nothing worse than a hairy guy."

"You're kidding," I snap.

"Don't tell me you like hairy guys?" she pulls a disgusted face.

I smile. "I do actually." I nod to accentuate my point. "I like the difference in their body to ours. We are soft. They are hard. We are smooth. They are rough. You know, the whole Yin and Yang thing. It's the differences that turn me on."

"Ugh, all of the guys I'm with manscape and if they don't I comment that I want them hairless before I see them again." Bridget and I are both shocked, our eyes wide.

"You actually say that?"

"Yes, of course, wouldn't you?"

We both shake our heads. "No, God no."

"Girls, have I taught you nothing. Ask for what you want. Men are stupid. They will do what we ask."

Bridget scrunches her nose up in disgust at Abbie. "The guy I'm going out with is a lot of things. He may be an adulterer and a prick, but stupid isn't one of them and Tash is so damn picky." They both turn their attention to me. "When was the last guy you were actually with?" Bridget glares at me.

"What's with the Spanish inquisition?" I roll my eyes.

Abbie chimes in, "Yes, she's right. Are you on the forty-hour man famine?"

I smile, "No one really gets me hot. All the guys I meet are just so...average." I hunch my shoulders.

"Oh no," Abbie scowls toward the counter.

"What?" I ask as I sip my coffee.

"It's tunnel cunt." I can't help it, I spit my coffee all over Bridget.

"Oh fuck, Tash, watch it." She starts to wipe the coffee from her top, as I am in a fit of giggles.

"Who in the hell is tunnel cunt?" Bridget laughs. "And how in hell did the poor girl get that god–awful name?"

"See that blonde at the counter?" We all lean in, "She's an ex stripper and she has her eyes on James." James is Abbie's flat-mate who she worships.

"How do you know she has a tunnel cunt? Actually, what is its definition?" Bridget and I are in fits of giggles.

"Shut up, you two." Abbie scowls. "This isn't funny."

"How do you know she has the hots for James?"

"He told me."

"Oh," I answer as I nod.

"Does he like her?" Bridget asks as she continues to watch her.

"He said not, but I'm keeping my eyes on her just in case."

We all nod. "Good idea," I mutter. We all watch as TC, the new girl on our radar, passes our table.

"Ok, anyway, where were we?"

"Oh, I know, and I don't like to pick up someone random for the sake of it, you both know I'm not like that."

Abbie shakes her head in disgust. "You're missing out. One day you are going to be forty five, married and bored as hell and you'll look back to these years and think I wish I had slept with all those hunks that were hot for me when I had the chance, and my body was smoking hot. You know the well dries up and turns into cellulite."

I smile at her. "It's ok, Abbs, I'm pretty sure you're fucking enough for the three of us."

She scrunches up her napkin and throws it at me and we all giggle.

"Ok, back to you Bridget. I think we need to set a trap." I smile as I call the waitress over to order more coffees.

"Ohh, I do like your wicked mind," she purrs.

"Now let me think," as I rub my chin.

The movie screen plays a rerun.

"Natasha, make love to me. I need this connection with you." His lips linger over mine tenderly. "It won't hurt as much this time, baby. It's getting easier, isn't it?" His open mouth runs down the length of my neck.

Buzz. "Natasha, your ten o'clock is here."

I rein in my now pounding heart. "Ok, thanks, Marg," I buzz her. What the hell. Christ, how can he still affect me this much after seven years apart? I drop my glasses and put my face into my hands on my desk. With my left hand I rub my face in disgust. I literally still have a physical effect from my memories of this man. Why can't I stop thinking about him? My heart rate, my breathing. I'm wet for fuck's sake. Good God! With disgust I head to the bathroom, shaking my head.

Five minutes later, I stare into the mirror in my office bathroom and blow out a deep breath. I look like crap. I wash my face and pull my shoulder–length chocolate hair back into a ponytail. I am in my green scrubs, a mandatory uniform at SSAC, which stands for Sydney Sexual Awareness Clinic. Our boss feels it desexualizes us. If we are all wearing hospital scrubs, we look more professional, more clinical. I have to agree. I actually look sexless. I could be male or female and you wouldn't be able to tell. I don't wear any makeup to work as a twenty-five-year-old, perhaps semi attractive female. I try to play down my looks.

My patients are damaged, beautiful but damaged. They all

have a problem relating to sex or sexualization. They don't need a psychologist throwing her sexuality and seemingly normal life in their face. What a joke. The irony is I'm just as damaged as them. Some days I feel like I should be the one on the black leather recliner chair telling them my problems, venting my insecurities. Today being a prime example. I take a deep breath and talk out loud to myself, like a total head case. *You're just unsettled because he's coming back.* I take a deep steadying breath. *He's long forgotten you, Natasha, it's time you forget him.* With a resigned shake of my head, I mutter into the mirror. *I wish.*

I read through my clinical notes.

Patient: Bethany Marcus

Symptoms: Anorgasmia/inability to orgasm

Clinical Notes: Bethany has been unsuccessful in climaxing for a period of three years. It began when she went through a traumatic experience, i.e., her husband had a twelve-month affair. The marriage has survived; however, Bethany has been troubled since the ordeal. Bethany also suffers violent sexual dreams which are distressing to her. Bethany blames herself for her husband's infidelity.

Aim: Bethany would like to stay happily married to her husband Anthony. She would like to fulfil her role as a wife and mother to her family. Bethany would like to be able to forgive her husband and resume a satisfying sexual relationship with him.

I blow out a breath. I really like my next patient. Bethany is beautiful and smart, with absolutely no confidence. Her cockroach of a husband has done a total number on her and then lets her blame herself for his inability to keep it in his pants. If I had my way, I would just tell her to leave him, but I can't do that. I have to help her work towards her goal, which unfortunately is a happy life with Anthony. I would like to see Anthony but Bethany won't allow it.

I open my office door.

"Hi, Bethany." She smiles shyly and walks into my office. I gesture for her to take a seat. "How have you been since I last saw you?" I ask.

"Not very well," she quietly answers.

"Oh, why is that?" I ask. She stays silent as I sit and wait for her answer. Sometimes waiting for answers is the hardest part of this role. She shrugs her shoulders.

"I see."

"How have you been?" she asks me, and I smile. This is typical Bethany; she always puts others before herself and she sees me as a person and not just her therapist.

"Me? I'm good," I answer. "A little demotivated this week," I shrug and smile. "You know how it is." She nods, grateful that my life isn't perfect. "Tell me what's happening," I urge.

"Anthony told me I am terrible in bed." Her devastated eyes meet mine. *What the fuck.*

"How did this come about?" I ask, trying to control my anger.

This guy is a total worm.

"We were in bed and you know my problem," I nod and stay silent. "I just can't come, I don't know why. It doesn't matter what I do, what I think about, it just doesn't happen."

"I see," I nod. "And what happened then?" I keep my voice monotone so as to not throw her train of thought.

"As usual, he got frustrated and asked what the fuck was the matter with me."

"Ok," I nod. "What did you say?"

"I told him to just finish off as it wasn't going to happen. And then, well he just finished off and rolled over."

"I see," I stay silent to let her finish, but she remains silent. "What happened then?"

"I told him I was coming to you."

"Had you not told him before?"

"No, I hadn't."

"And what did he say?"

"He told me that no expensive doctor could make me receptive in bed, that I'm a cold fish and that he's never been with a woman who is so unresponsive."

"What do you think of that?" I ask.

"He's right," she sighs.

"I don't believe that," I assert. "You may be unresponsive to him at the moment, but it's not physical, it's totally emotional. Bethany, I treat both men and woman who suffer from Anorgasmia and they are in loving relationships with a person they can trust." She nods as she listens. "Have you thought about what we talked about last visit?"

"Yes," she says. "It's not going to be possible."

"Why?" I ask.

"Because he doesn't know I haven't orgasmed in three years."

I cross my arms. "What do you mean?" I ask, already knowing the answer.

"I've been faking it all along."

I nod. This is common. "Do you think you should come clean?" I give her a small empathetic smile.

"No, he would be devastated."

I nod, "So, it's ok if you're devastated, just not him."

"I know how this looks," she whispers.

"How does this look Beth?" I urge.

29

"That I am a martyr."

I smile. "Is that what you think?" I ask her softly.

"Do you?" she asks.

"No, I don't think you're a martyr. Would it matter to you if I did?"

She nods her head.

"It shouldn't matter what anyone thinks Beth, only you."

"I care what you think," she smiles. "You're the only person who knows about this."

I frown. "You haven't confided in a friend?" I ask, a little shocked.

"No. I don't want my friends to judge Anthony, or me for staying with him."

"I see," I answer. "Beth, do you think that the friends you keep are really on your side?"

She looks at me as she processes what I have just asked her and then she shrugs. We both sit in silence as I wait for her to speak, but she doesn't.

Mmm, we will come back to this. "Did you speak to Anthony about foreplay?" She shakes her head.

"Mmm ok, so can I guess you didn't do as I suggested and ask him to try Viagra?"

"I just can't." She looks so vulnerable; my heart goes out to her.

"I don't want him to think that I think he's not good enough for me in bed."

"But it's ok if he makes you feel lacking," I sigh. She nods. "Bethany, I don't know a woman alive that can come in seven minutes of penetrative sex with no foreplay." She nods. "You know, Beth, and this is off the record but I take at least twenty minutes to get in the frame of mind and then another twenty minutes, at least, of foreplay before I even want to think about sex. He needs to know that it's not happening. Maybe he would try harder if he knew."

She nods. "Maybe"

"Isn't that your grudge with him?" She frowns. "That he was dishonest?" She nods and hangs her head, knowing what I am going to say next. "Are you being totally honest with him, Beth?"

"No," she answers. I stay silent, waiting for her to process the information. "Last time I saw you we talked about trust."

"Yes," she smiles.

"How are the trust levels at home?"

"I try, I really do, but I just can't seem to get there."

"Beth, trust is not something that happens. It is a decision you make. You either decide you will trust him from now on, or you move on. Do you have trust that you will be ok if he leaves you?" She shakes her head. "I see, but if you move on with him and you haven't made that decision to trust—to trust him and to trust yourself to be strong—you are setting yourself up for a lifetime of misery."

"I know," she whispers. "It's not completely his fault. I was so engrossed with the kids. I was just so preoccupied that I didn't realize that he needed more sex and I let myself go and I didn't even try to be sexy for him."

"Beth, don't you dare sit there and defend him to me. For the record, you were busy with *his* kids. His children, not someone else's. And you let yourself go. How ridiculous. I sit here and I see a beautiful, smart English girl who has left her family and her country to move to the other side of the world for a man who has taken her for granted."

"He would never have cheated if I was, I don't know, more attractive."

I sigh. "Beth what do you see when you look at me?"

"What do you mean?" she asks. I stand up and walk around in front of her and do a twirl.

"Now, when you look at me what do you see?"

She smiles, "A really pretty smart girl."

I laugh, "That's funny, Beth, do you know that in my past I have had not one but two," I hold my fingers up to accentuate the point, "two boyfriends cheat on me." Her mouth drops open.

"But why?" she mutters under her breath.

I shrug my shoulders. "Who knows, but it has absolutely nothing to do with me." She frowns at me. "Men play up for a number of reasons, Beth. But the main reason is that they are lacking something within their own self–esteem. They need to feel desired or wanted or need their ego stroked. Whatever the reason, Beth, infidelity is the path of a coward. Staying loyal to one person is hard work, and it's something that both you and I strive for. And you can be proud of that. Many women when faced with an affair go down the payback route and only end up feeling a lot worse for doing so." I stay silent, waiting for her to say something but she doesn't. "There is only one way to receive equality in your marriage, Beth."

"How?" she asks.

"Demand it. People in life treat you how you believe you deserve to be treated. If you think you don't deserve to be satis-fied in bed, then you won't be. If you believe your husband can do better than you, then he will think he can, too. Beth, what you need to realize without me telling you is that you and you only can make changes in your life. Forget about Anthony and his problems. Let's work on you." She smiles a shy smile at me which I return. I sit on top of my desk with my legs crossed. "Now, I have some homework for you."

"Ok," she smiles, as she sits up in her chair, feeling a little empowered.

"I want you to go to the adult warehouse and buy yourself a vibrator."

Her mouth drops open. "What?" she whispers.

I nod and smile. "It's time for you to take your sexuality back into your hands. Literally."

She swallows a large lump in her throat. "I've never, I don't think. Anthony will freak," she adds.

"Anthony is not to know about this." She looks at me wide-eyed. "What I want you to do is everyday fire up the vibrator and give yourself foreplay without the expected orgasm at the end." I wait for her to speak. She doesn't. I smile. God, I love their faces when I start talking sex toys. I walk over to my desk, open my bottom drawer and pull out my large demo vibrator. I turn it on, and her eyes widen.

"Don't worry, it's not like that," I smile.

"Oh God," she laughs and puts her hand on her chest in relief. "See how this feels?" I rub the side of the shaft over the palm of her hand. She smiles and nods. "If you rub the side of the shaft over your outer lips and clitoris, it feels like the best oral sex you've ever had."

"Oh," she whispers, eyes wide.

"Have you ever watched any porn, Beth?"

She shakes her head. "Only in high school," she whispers. "And I didn't really see the appeal."

I smile and nod. "I want you to watch a few things for me." She frowns, not understanding. "I want you to go onto a website called YouPorn. It's the same as YouTube, but it's people posting videos of sex."

"Um, ok." She looks worried.

"On the left-hand side of the page there is a category list."
She nods. "Click on love."

She frowns, "Love?"

"Yes, there are some really tasteful lovely videos of couples in love having sex and trust me it's nothing like the wham bam come in the woman's face porn most woman are exposed to. Watch it with no sound, a lot of women are very audile, and the sound of porn is what turns them off."

"Oh," she nods.

"And also click on the massage tab."

"Massage tab?" she repeats.

"Yes, a lot of my patients find it really erotic watching someone get a slow massage finished by an orgasm." I smile. "It's very tasteful and kind of hot." We both laugh. "And I want you to try something else."

"Um, ok," she nods.

"I want you to go and buy yourself some lube and begin to explore your body with your fingers again."

"Oh, God." She looks down and twirls her hair between her fingers.

I smile. "Beth, don't be embarrassed, I talk sex all day. It's my job."

"Ok," she mutters and smiles.

"Most woman have not brought themselves to orgasm with their fingers since they became sexually active and it really is a good way to reconnect with what you like and what you don't like. Women's bodies change when we have children and what used to arouse us doesn't necessarily do it for us anymore. Remember, Beth, you need to take responsibility for your own sexual health. Trust me, your husband will thank you later." She smiles as she stands up to leave my office and shakes my hand.

"Those two boyfriends were idiots," she winks.

"I know, "I smile, and I wink back, "their loss." I laugh and scrunch up my nose. "Remember I want thirty minutes a day private time."

She smiles. "Ok, ok, I will. I'll tell you how it goes next week."

"Good, I look forward to it." As she exits my office, I smile to myself. I should open a sex shop—I would be a fucking millionaire.

———

Monday mornings, is definitely my hump day. Hard to get out of bed, harder to go to the gym before work, a healthy breakfast tastes more like cat food than All Bran and it's damn near impossible to get motivated for the week at work. It's freezing cold, too, to add salt to my wounds. It's windy as hell. God, I'm whining today. Normally I have the excuse of too big a weekend, still silently suffering a hangover, carb overload, no exercise. Not today. I know the reason. It's like the frigging day before Armageddon, like I'm walking to my execution, I'm so nervous I feel sick to my stomach. I thought I would be excited.

Though I'm looking forward to seeing him this weekend, I know that after Saturday night, the beautiful man in my memories will be dead to me. He has long been dead. It's just that damn movie screen inside my head keeping him alive, hero-worshipping him. I know this is probably going to be the last week I can dream about him from afar, but reality is a bitch. A bitch that's going to bite me hard in the ass on Sunday morning. I'm dreading it. It's like I've already started to mourn the loss of him, even though he's not even mine to lose.

I am on the train, it's a one hour trip to work as I purposely looked for a job well out of my zip code. Don't want to bump into any of my sexual psychotics at the coffee shop or grocery store. It's a hassle getting to and from work, but I feel safer having that bit of anonymity away from my patients. In the line of work I do, my patients don't want to bump into me either so it's a win-win both ways. I shuffle up the aisle and take a window seat. I lean my head on the window, close my eyes and start to doze. I just need to get through the week. My mind wanders back to the man who haunts me, even in my sleep.

————

Finally, this week is over; it's been a marathon just getting through it. I am sitting on the plane waiting to exit at Melbourne airport.

"Why do they take so long to open the doors?" Bridget yawns as she stretches in her seat.

"Hmm, I know," I answer as I stretch my legs. Brock, our brother, is sitting across the aisle with our parents and gives me a wink. I love Brock, he is in the navy, a seal. He is home in Sydney for three months which is unusual for him. He's hardly ever home. You know, off saving the world and all that. He is six two and pure hard-ass, he dotes on Bridge and me. Way over the top protective but I kind of like it. Bridge hates it. Brock punched her last boyfriend in the nose at Christmas lunch a couple of years ago. It was hilarious, although Bridge didn't see the humor. What I didn't tell her was that if Brock hadn't done it, I might have. Mark was his name, of course a total wanker. Boy, she sure does attract losers. I smile at the memory.

"What's so funny?" Bridge asks me. I shake my head. If she only knew what I was thinking about. I finally enter the aisle and Brock grabs me from behind in a headlock and gives me a rough hug.

"Your snoring kept me awake," he whispers.

I nudge him with my elbow. "Shut up, I don't snore."

"Yeah, you do," he laughs, and he pushes me forward, so I bump into the guy in front of me who turns around and glares at me.

"Sorry, I tripped," I whisper. He glares at me and continues up the aisle.

I turn around and punch Brock. "Cut it out, how old are you?"

"Let's go out for dinner on the way to the hotel." He gestures to Dad to go into the aisle.

"Good idea," Mum answers. I roll my eyes at Bridge. I want to go straight to bed. I'm exhausted. I've had a shit of a day. My most hated patient, Roger, the sex addict, had a two-hour block appointment. Why does the receptionist make those appointments anyway? I will have to put a stop to it. I had to listen to every last detail of his latest orgy. Seriously gross. Why he feels I have to know everything is beyond me. Imagine a 1980s bad porn movie and that is the exact vision of Roger: bad moustache, comb–over, dyed hair, rates himself big time, overdose on the aftershave that smells more like fly repellent. Seriously, he is beyond help. Gives me a cold shiver just thinking of him. God, I feel sorry for his wife. Imagine having him for a husband and he's a sex addict who wants it all the time. Shit, it doesn't get much worse, poor bitch. I wince.

"What's wrong? Why are you pulling that face?"

I smile and shake my head. "Nothing, I'm tired. Can't we just get room service?"

"Tash, just lighten the fuck up," Brock chimes in. "We are on vacation. Chillax will you."

. . .

Five hours later, I lay in bed in my hotel room. It's the night before the wedding, and my mind wanders. Tomorrow is the day. I'm going to see him. Thank God, Bridget and I have a room each or else she would be onto me. I have been tossing and turning for two hours now. I am punching the pillow and changing positions, trying to get comfortable. Trying to calm myself into a slumber. How am I supposed to look tempting with no sleep?

The movie screen plays a particularly painful memory, one that I hate and desperately wish to remove from the memory bank. It has the same effect every time, bringing me to my knees. Reactivating my guilt that usually ends up with me on my knees in the bottom of the shower, throwing up and in tears.

Two weeks after Josh and my beautiful lovemaking holiday, I was missing him like crazy, crying by night, depressed by day. I lost five kilos in two weeks and had bags under my eyes. I didn't leave my room except to go to school. This pain was self-inflicted. Both Josh and I knew he was going to America for four years shortly after our holiday. We knew we had no future together. That didn't make it any easier, and we had had no contact. My tender teenage heart was utterly devastated.

I came home from school one afternoon to find the house in uproar. It was one of the few times I heard my father swear. As I opened the door my father yelled at my mother.

"What the fuck does that boy think he's doing?" I stopped mid step as I was slowly heading down the hall. I heard my mother talking way too fast while pacing. I slowly walked into the kitchen and looked at the two of them, raising my eyebrows.

"What's going on?" I whispered to my mum.

38

Dad was on the phone. "Good God, he's gone fucking mad," he yelled.

I frowned. "Who?" I mouthed at Mum.

"Joshua," she replied.

Oh shit, this can't be good, what happened? Do they know? Am I next? I quietly made myself a cup of tea as I listened to the conversation.

"He said what? And then what did you say?" he listened. "And did you tell him that's ridiculous? Surely he can't be serious?"

"What?" I mouthed to Mum again.

"Joshua seems to think he's fallen in love with a girl from Sydney and he's not going to America."

My eyes widened. Holy shit. "How do you know this?"

"I've been on the phone to Margaret all day on and off. He seems to think he's transferring to Sydney Uni, apparently to be near this girl."

My father hangs up the phone. My eyes are the size of saucers.

"Who is she?" I whispered.

"Some fucking idiot, no doubt," my father snapped. Shit, he's really mad. "He's known her for two frigging weeks, and he's throwing away an internship at Apple. This is the opportunity of a lifetime; he will never get this chance again."

I sipped my tea in silence while my parents continued their outrage.

I asked my mum, "Why is America so important?" I was genuinely interested.

"Josh developed an app as a hobby; it was a carb counter for diabetics."

"What does that mean?" I asked.

"It has ended up being used all over the world. It had to be tweaked a bit, but doctors and hospitals are using it to educate diabetics."

"What's an app?" I asked.

"It's the way computers are heading, something to do with Apple computers, new technology stuff."

"Oh," I murmured. "I had no idea."

"No, and Joshua doesn't get it. He gave this technology away but if it were designed on the market it would be worth millions."

My mouth dropped open. "Millions," I repeated.

"Yes," said my mother. "Steve Jobs, the founder of this organization, has personally invited Joshua to come and work with him."

"Who's Steve Jobs?" I asked.

"He owns Apple, he's one of the smartest, richest men in the world."

"And he wants to work with Josh," I replied. Suddenly, the very serious ramifications if he didn't go became all too obvious. My dad nodded and I raised my eyebrows. "Shit," I whispered.

"Exactly," my father nodded. "Joshua is going to throw his whole future away for a girl he hardly knows and in twelve months down the roadwill leave anyway."

"You don't know that," I snapped.

"True," my mother nodded, "but if she did love him, surely she wouldn't let him give up this chance. He can't be that stupid, can he?" she muttered to herself as she rubbed her forehead. I wandered out into the backyard and sat on the back step idly patting Sadie, our cocker spaniel. Shit, this was heavy. I knew I was the girl and part of me wanted to jump off the step and punch the air. He'd missed me, he did love me. I was thoroughly thrilled with myself and trying to stifle the huge grin threatening to cover my face when the phone rang again. I walked to the door to listen to the conversation.

"Well, where is he now? Well, find him, go out and find him and then what did you say? What? He's going to marry this bimbo...for heaven's sake...he said what?...Good God, he's lost his fucking mind...yes, I know...hang on I will see. Natasha, have you heard from Josh?" I shook my head. "Yes you're probably right, they are close. If he rings you, tell him to ring home, everyone is frantic." I nodded in agreement. "Seriously Robert, if you have to get on a plane and kick his ass all the way to America, you do it; he can't screw this up. He will thank you in years to come."

My elation was very quickly turning to shit. I went into my room, shut the door and threw myself on the bed. *Shit Josh, this is extreme.* I jumped up suddenly to check my phone to see if he had rung me. No, nothing. Poor Josh. All that pressure and now he'd taken off. Maybe I should ring him? I checked my phone again, still nothing. I hoped he was ok. This was a total fuck up, shit what was I going to do? I started to pace in my room, shaking my hands as if they were cold. Should I ring him? Maybe, no he doesn't need my interference.

Three hours later I was so worried I had started dry retching. I was really starting to freak out. Still pacing in my room, my parents were waiting up to hear if he had been found. It was 12.50 am when I heard my mum's phone receive a text message. I bounded down the hall.

"Thank God," my mum smiled. "He's home. We can all go to bed now." She put her arm around me and led me to the hall. "He's safe," she smiled. I hauled my sorry ass to bed. That night I didn't sleep. I knew deep in my gut what I had to do if I truly loved Josh. I needed to set him free so he could carry on with his life's work, but should I tell him the truth? No, then he would make the decision for me. I knew if I was in his position, I could never leave him. I wouldn't have the strength. What if he did stay? Would we last? This I didn't know. I needed a crystal ball. My dad was right. He would fuck up the rest of his life. The cold hard reality was we couldn't have a future together, not in our family's eyes. Oh, what to do, what to do.

At 5.00 am I came to a heartbreaking decision. I knew what to do and it turned my stomach just thinking about it.

The next day I faked sickness to get the day off school. My parents went to work, and I started to pace again, waiting for his call. At one o'clock my phone rang. It was Josh— he thought I was on lunch break. I braced myself.

"Hi," I answered.

"Hi baby," he said happily down the phone. Oh shit. "Have you missed me?" he asked.

"Where are you?" I asked.

"At home. I have news" he announced, and my heart sank. "I'm coming to Sydney tonight."

"Why?" I whispered quietly.

"To see you. You didn't answer my question, have you missed me?"

"Have you?" I whispered again, my voice too hoarse to speak.

"So fucking much I can't stand it. I think I've come up with a solution though. We will talk about it tonight. Pick me up. What time should I book the flight for?"

I stayed silent and closed my eyes...silence again.

"Natasha, what's wrong?" His voice betrayed his worry. I stayed silent. "Baby, are you ok?" he asked quietly.

"Not really," I whispered past the golf–ball sized lump in my throat. He didn't know that I knew about his so called solution... again silence...

"Why aren't you ok?"

"It's complicated," I whispered.

"Tell me tonight. We will work it out. I'll book the flight and text you the details. I'll be there soon." This was it. I knew to save his future I had to hurt him and rip my heart out in the process, but again I stayed silent, unable to talk without breaking into full–blown sobs.

"Josh, you can't come to Sydney."

"Why?" he whispered, "why not?"

"It's not a good idea."

He stayed silent. This time I could almost hear his brain ticking. "I need to see you," he snapped.

"No, Josh, you can't."

"Why not?" he was getting annoyed.

"I don't want to see you," I covered my mouth with my hand so he couldn't hear my chest quivering with unshed tears.

"You don't want to see me?" he whispered.

"No, Josh, I don't," I lied again. While I closed my eyes, he stayed silent for a minute.

"I don't believe you," he yelled. "Have my fucking parents been in your ear?"

"No," I lied again.

"You know, don't you?" he snapped.

"Know what?" I acted innocent.

"I'm coming to get you, whether you like it or not," he yelled. I started to cry, holding my stomach because the pain was unbearable. I dropped to my knees on the lounge room floor and closed my eyes, trying to catch my breath as I stabbed the final knife into my already broken heart.

"I've met somebody else."

"What?" he yelled, making me jump. "Are you fucking kidding me?" he screamed down the phone. "Two weeks, it's been two fucking weeks!" he yelled, "and you've met someone else?"

"Yes," I sobbed. He stayed silent. I knew I'd broken his heart as well as mine and I was now on my hands and knees on the floor. Again, silence.

In a deathly voice he asked, "Have you slept with him?"

I could hardly answer. How could he even think that? My chest was breaking. "Yes," I sobbed.

He made a guttural noise, and the phone went dead. He had hung up. I collapsed into the fetal position on the floor, knowing he was probably on the floor like me. I was a cold heartless bitch; how could I say that? My heart was broken, my chest hurt. I was crying so loudly I was sure the neighbors could hear me.

I stayed in bed for a week, unable to eat and hardly able to keep anything down, while my mother doted on me, thinking I had a stomach bug. I lay motionless, staring at the ceiling. I had no tears left.

Even to this day, seven years later, that memory brings nausea to my stomach every time I think of it. It is as if it happened yesterday. I am brought back to a young seventeen-year-old girl lying alone on the lounge room floor clutching the phone. The pain is so vivid it's unbearable. I do what I always do when this memory haunts me. I get straight up, put the television on and get into the shower. Sometimes I stay in the shower for over an hour—it is as if I am trying to wash the lies away. Although it's not possible, if only I could. I've never forgiven myself. I should have told him the truth. He deserved the truth. Something's got to give as this is unbearable. Why do the memories of this man haunt me...how do I escape him?

"You know what shits me?" I moan as I look into my compact mirror at my face, turning my head. "When I pay good money and say I have a wedding and I want to look hot, that does not mean code for I want to look like the tooth fairy on crack."

"I know, right," Bridget tuts. We are in the back of a cab surveying the damage from our hair and makeup appointment. "At least your hair looks good. The silly bitch put so much hairspray in my hair, I'm like a Venus Fly Trap. I hope there are no flies at the reception as they will all get stuck in my hair." I giggle as I pull a disgusted face. At least the makeup disaster has taken the edge off my nerves, only three hours until I see him. I smile out the window as I hunch my shoulders. I feel like a little kid at Christmas.

"Do you think I should have spray tanned?" I ask.

"No, too much skin. You would have looked like a Penthouse bunny."

"Maybe that's the look I'm going for," I smirk.

Bridget narrows her eyes and laughs, "Well, you do have the makeup for it."

"Very funny. Ha, ha."

I look into the mirror at the young woman staring back at me, my long dark brown hair is set very Raquel Welch. I've successfully removed my Steve Tyler makeup and reapplied. My bronze sky high, strappy shoes are on, and I am waxed to within an inch of my life. I stare at my reflection. My charcoal Grecian–style dress is fitted but drapes in all the right places. It is backless with a thigh high split down one leg. The dress is understated elegance, I think; a little sexy without trying too hard. I look good, if I do say so myself. I like this dress better than the other option. Josh has never seen me like this. I was a girl when he left. I'm now a clinical psychologist, fit and in every part of my life confident and assured. Too bad I'm being eaten alive by guilt, suffocated by a love I don't even have. I pull my shoulders back and take a deep breath. *Perk up, old girl*, I say out loud to myself, *today you start to heal*. Time to rip off the band-aid.

We arrive at the church which has a lovely old-world feel, sandstone with a large circular driveway, sweeping oak trees and lots of lead light windows. There are roses everywhere and the crowd is congregated out the front. Eventually we are led in and my grandmother catches my hand as we walk into the church.

"It'll be your wedding next," she winks. I smile and roll my eyes.

We are ushered to our place in the second row. Gran looks down and exclaims, "My God, darling, how on earth do you walk in those shoes?" I smile and lift my hem a little to give her a full view of my beautiful expensive shoes that I may marry because I love them so much.

I step aside to let Gran into the row of seats before me and glance up straight into the ice–cold stare of Joshua Stanton. The sight hits me like a physical blow and I involuntarily step back and grab the church pew for support...Dear Mother of God...he is breathtaking...so different yet so familiar. He is glaring at me... Holy shit, is he angry? Surely not. I swallow and shuffle up the church pew. He follows me with his eyes, and I can't look away. My heart has stopped beating. He is mad, or maybe he's just shocked to see me. My mouth is so dry I can hardly swallow. I look down, suddenly super self-conscious. I think I'm having a hot flush. Oh shit, did I bring deodorant? I'm going to need it. I pat my forehead.

Bridget frowns at me, "Are you ok?" I nod, unable to speak. I look to the floor to try to calm myself and my heart that is having an epileptic fit. I can't help it; I look back up. He is still glaring at me. Holy fuck, is anyone else seeing this? I pat my forehead again and downcast my eyes. *Crap, crap, crap, crap.* What did you expect, you idiot? Of course he hates you. I'm getting seriously claustrophobic. I need fresh air. I want to run from this church and do some serious binge drinking. I blow out a large breath.

"What's up?" Bridget whispers. "Hot flush," I murmur.

She screws her face up in question. "What?" she mouths as she frowns at me. I shake my head to try and signal for her to shut the fuck up, he's watching. I look up again and see a trace of a smile on his face. Bastard, he's doing this on purpose. He knows he's affecting me. Christ, why am I such a loser? Gran distracts me and takes my hand, thank heavens for Gran. I give her a weak smile as she pats the back of my hand. The service begins and I am of course totally distracted. I am not even looking at the bride and groom.

My eyes are fixed on one person only. Every now and then he looks at me and our eyes meet, but he pulls away every time. He's absolutely beautiful, it hurts just to look at him. The priest signals it's time for me to do a reading. Shit, what if I can't talk? I shimmy out and head towards the steps when Joshua comes over and offers me his hand, and as I grab it, he squeezes it hard. Once again, I am reminded by a strong jolt of sexual energy that he zaps me with. I gasp and look up to see him smile a small, satisfied smile. Shit, ok, he's affecting me. Its official, I don't have one cool bone in my body. I may as well be an open book. Please ground, swallow me up now. Why in the hell am I so physically affected by this man? It's abnormal. I blow out a breath and start my psalm reading with goosebumps scattering all over my body.

I hope my nipples aren't on high beam in the house of God.

I am achingly aware of his carnal searing gaze fixed upon me. As I read, I see through my peripheral vision that he looks me up and down three times that I count. He clenches his jaw and moves his head to the left side as if trying to crack his neck whilst not taking his eyes off me. I can't help but let a small smile slip. I know this move, he's always done it, and it appears he hasn't broken the habit. He does this when he is aroused. When we were together, he would do this when he saw me naked or in a swimming costume. My insides do a little jump for joy as it becomes clear to me, I still do it for him. Thank God, operation slim down has paid off, and all those gym visits are having the desired effect. I feel a little of my confidence return. I finish my reading and go to return to my seat, and he holds out his hand to help me down the stairs, he squeezes it again and I feel the heat emanate from his body. I smile at him, but he doesn't smile back. What in the world is going on here?

As I make it back to my seat, the bride and groom and party move over to the side to sign the marriage certificate, Bridget frowns at me. "What?" I whisper.

She leans in and looks around to make sure no one else is listening. "Why was he looking at you like that?"

"Like what?" I whisper.

"Like he was going to bend you over the church pew." I open my eyes wide at her to signify shut the hell up.

"Well?" she asks again.

"Don't be stupid," I snap as I rearrange my dress.

"I mean it," she says. "And you, you were all flustered."

"I was nervous, that's all."

"Bullshit," she whispers. "I can smell his pheromones from here."

I can't help it, I smile.

"What's funny?" she whispers. For some strange reason I

want to laugh. It feels good talking about this to Bridge, even though I have to deny it.

"So how did they smell?" I whisper.

She frowns at me and I raise my eyebrows. "The pheromones, how did they smell?"

"Fucking awesome." We both giggle and then she winks. "Too bad he's off limits."

Oh yes, I forgot to mention a small detail, a detail I try and

not give too much thought to because it does my head in every time. Joshua and I share more than a history, we share blood. We are first cousins. His father and my mother are brother and sister, so when I tell you I can't have this man, I truly mean it.

CHAPTER 3

Natasha

THE FAMILY PHOTOS outside the church are a painful reminder of just how closely Joshua and I are related. His younger brother Cameron comes up behind me and grabs me in an embrace and spins me around.

"Tassshhh," he laughs as he pulls me under his arm and kisses my hair. I smile and put my arm around his waist. This is a normal cousin relationship. A distasteful thought flashes through my mind as the word incest rolls my stomach. My God, how can I be so physically attracted to a relative, and I'm not imagining it. It's overbearing. I have never experienced it before. It's as if my body has a spiritual connection with his and my mind is being totally left out of the equation, making no sense or reason. I frown as I sum up the events so far and I'm shocked to my core. I knew I found him attractive before. But now, now the attraction is unbearable.

Josh comes over and kisses Bridget. "Didge," he smiles. This is the pet name the Stanton boys call her.

She grabs him in an embrace. "Josh," she laughs. "I've missed you."

He smiles, "Of course, who wouldn't," he winks.

She rolls her eyes. "You still have tickets on yourself." They both laugh as she slaps him. My mother comes over and grabs him in an embrace. I can't hear what they are saying but she has her hands on his cheeks as she speaks. My eyes are transfixed as I watch the comfortable interaction. This is the first time as an adult it is actually sinking in, *fuck we are related.* My family love him too. I'm such an idiot. After a minute of speaking to my mum he turns to me and dips his head.

"Natasha," he smiles and gives me a kiss on the cheek. He rests his hands on my waist as he pulls me into him. I lean into him and put my hands around his neck. His lips linger a little too long on my cheek and my heart stops. I close my eyes as I try to control my breathing before I gather my senses and pull away. We have a familiarity with each other that is still present. I know he feels it too, as he rubs his forehead with obvious discomfort. Discomfort at what our body language has just revealed to each other without a word spoken.

Two men are with Joshua who I've not met before. He introduces them to Bridget and my mum and dad and then heads over to me.

"This is Ben and Adrian," he smiles to me, "they are friends of mine who work with me in America." I smile and shake their hands. "And this is Natasha," he smiles. He seems nervous and I see them glance at each other. Adrian comes forward. He's athletic, tall and blond, immaculately groomed and dressed.

He holds his hand out. "Hello," he smiles. I smile back as we shake hands. I feel comfortable instantly—he's got a sort of honest quality about him. He looks at the other guy, Ben, as if to prompt him to shake my hand, but Ben is just staring at me. My eyes flick back to Adrian. Josh has turned around to talk to his brother. Adrian smiles and shakes his head, "He's not used to seeing such a gorgeous woman."

Ben snaps out of it, "Oh sorry, I was miles away." He shakes my hand. "Nice to meet you" he says in a heavy accent.

I raise my eyebrows. "English?" I ask.

"No, South African."

"Ahh," I smile. "So, you guys work with Josh?" I ask.

"Um," Adrian laughs. "Ben is his bodyguard, and I am his Operations Manager."

"Ohh," I smile. Slightly shocked. "Why does Josh need a bodyguard?" I ask.

They shoot each other a look. "Oh, you know," Adrian smiles. "Paparazzi and whatnot."

"Ohh," I answer as I nod, feeling stupid.

"So, Natasha," Adrian asks, "what do you do?"

"I'm a clinical psychologist."

They both look at each other again. "Oh God," Adrian laughs. "Don't psychoanalyze me, you'll find out I'm crazy."

I clink my glass to his. "You and me both. Don't worry, I won't tell if you don't." He giggles and hunches up his shoulders. I do like him. Joshua rejoins us. He has both hands in his suit pants and he still looks nervous. I can't help it, I'm watching Ben and Adrian who are trying to communicate something to each other without speaking, something about Josh. My eyes turn back to Josh who's watching me silently. Adrian smiles again and hunches his shoulders as if he's excited about something. What's going on here?

"Can I get you a drink?" Ben asks Josh.

"No thanks, I will wait till after the speeches."

"Yeah right, good idea," he smiles. Cameron, Josh's little brother, comes over and grabs me from behind and kisses the back of my head. He's over six foot so he's not really so little. He has his hand around my waist as he addresses the boys. I see Josh's gaze drop to where his hand is on my waist. He raises his eyebrows at Cameron who instantly removes his hand... *what*.

"So, you boys have both met our beautiful cousin Natasha?" he smiles at Josh and winks. Josh narrows his eyes at him, huh, does he know? Holy crap, what the hell is going on? The look of total shock on Adrian's and Ben's faces is evident. They look at each other and then at Josh who bites his bottom lip and looks at me. Ok, now it's obvious, Ben and Adrian know. Holy shit. What the hell has he said?

Cameron smiles and winks. "Just keeping it real, boys," and he walks off. I want the ground to swallow me up. I am a total disaster. Josh has told his friends. I must look like a total slut. Holy fuck. *I need a drink.* Adrian and Ben stay silent, still wide eyed. I go to walk off.

"Natasha," Josh goes to grab my arm, but Adrian stops him. "Just leave it," he whispers.

"Can I talk to you, Tash?" Joshua asks me. Embarrassment hits, oh fuck. I scurry to the bar to find a drink. I scull my first glass of champers without even tasting it.

Bridget comes over and does a low whistle. "There is some talent in the house toniiiiight. The Stanton boys do associate with good–looking men."

"Hmm, do they? I haven't noticed." This night could be the very death of me.

Dinner is finished and out of the way, a beautiful five course banquet with no expense spared. Fairy lights are strewn all through the ceiling and the trees outside in the garden. Large candelabras with twelve candles adorn every table. The venue looks like a romantic fairy tale. Bridge and I are giggling at each other at the table. The tinkling of a teaspoon on a champagne glass brings the attention of everyone in the room. Ah, the speeches. I smile at Bridge and take a sip of my champagne. Joshua is standing next to his brother at the bridal table, champagne glass in hand. Scott is sitting back in his seat smiling, maybe a little unsure of what his brother is going to reveal. Josh dips his head, as the crowd grows silent. He smiles a breathtaking smile. I'm weak from want of him.

"Hello everyone, on behalf of my family I would like to thank you all for coming to celebrate with us the marriage of Scott and Alyssa." He turns and holds his glass up to the two of them. "Firstly, I would like to thank Scott for giving me the honor of standing up for him today. It means a lot to me, Scott. Know that I love you." The crowd gushes. Bridget looks at me with puppy dog eyes. I smile as I listen. His voice has changed. He sounds slightly different, he has an American accent. Not strong, but definitely there. My eyes are transfixed by the beautiful man standing up before us all. A man who is as dear to me as breath, a breath I hold as I listen closely. "Alyssa, firstly, to you. You are an incredible person. One, for putting up with him." He raises his glass at Scott who shakes his head and the crowd laughs. "When Scott told me, he was going to ask you to marry him, I asked the obvious question. Why? What in the hell do you want to do that for?" The crowd laughs again, and he raises his eyebrows. "The answer he gave me however silenced me, forever. He told me he had found someone who loved him for no reason, and that gave him a reason to want to love her back"

The crowd gushes again, and he smiles as he raises his glass to Alyssa. "So, to Alyssa, thank you for loving my brother for no reason." The crowd giggles. "I only hope that my other brothers find the happiness that you both have found today. I believe in a prophecy I heard a long time ago. Soul mates don't finally meet somewhere at a certain place at a certain time, they're in each other, all along." I smile a sad smile. I know what he means. "So, on that note," he smiles. "Tonight, I would like to make a toast to three people." Everyone giggles. "To Alyssa and Scott."

Everyone repeats "To Alyssa and Scott."

"And to my soul mate," he raises his glass, "who has been with me all along, but is absent from my side." He raises his glass to the crowd, and everyone claps and cheers. I can't help it, I try, I really do. But hot tears are bursting the dam. I blink repeatedly to try and stop them while looking down at the table. I grab a napkin from the table and wipe my eyes quickly before anyone sees. On raising my head, I look straight into the longing stare of Joshua who is now back sitting in his seat. We sit silently staring at each other as the party continues around us, both oblivious to the chatter. I give him a sad smile as I wipe my eyes again. That is exactly how I feel about him. He is my soulmate, but he is absent from my side. I know it's just a coincidence that he put that in his speech, but hearing it come from his lips has broken the dam. I stand and make my way to the bathroom.

"Are you ok?" I am stopped on the way by Adrian. I smile and nod, unable to speak past the tears in my throat. "I loved that speech too," he smiles as he rubs my arm. I smile again and continue on my way. Embarrassment is heating my cheeks and I am still unable to articulate anything. Ten minutes later, I stare at the reflection looking back at me in the mirror and the memory bank starts to replay. I can literally feel him, taste him,time has erased nothing. It was as if it happened yesterday.

I love you, Natasha. I never thought it was possible to feel like this about anyone. I can't stand the thought of being on the other side of the world and separated from you. Come with me.

Stop it!

With the formalities over, I am on my seventh champagne and Joshua has started to drink and relax. I wish I could relax—all the alcohol is doing is making me unashamedly check Josh out. My eyes constantly flick back to him every five minutes and like clockwork every five minutes my eyes lock with his. He doesn't even pretend not to look at me. He is drinking his Corona with one hand in his pocket, his eyes not leaving me as he tips his head back. He stands at over six foot four tall, totally ripped with muscle. His dark skin and chocolate hair all add to the alluring appeal. And his posture, the way he stands, legs wide. He's just so...Alpha. So freaking hot. His piercing blue eyes bore into me, even the way he is drinking his beer is seducing me, the way he's watching me, *God*. I'm not the only girl in this place under his hypnosis, every woman here is affected by his physical presence. He stands out. So tall and so athletic, and Bridget is right, his pheromones do smell fucking awesome. He can give a great come fuck me look too. Because any moment, I might do just that.

Bridget walks over. "Ok, spit it out."

"What?" I ask.

"What's with Joshua?"

"What do you mean?" I look anywhere but at her.

"Don't shit me, the LUST between you two is ridiculous. I've been watching him." Shit this can't be good.

"*And?*" I repeat.

"He's looking at you like he wants to kill you."

"Kill me?" I shriek.

"Yes, either that or eat you."

I giggle into my champagne glass. "What's so funny?" she asks mortified.

I shrug, "I can think of worse ways to go."

She frowns at me. "Death by oral by Joshua Stanton."

I shrug again, "Could be fun." Her mouth drops open.

"I fucking knew it. What's going on?"

Shit, this champagne is giving me loose lips, and loose lips sink ships.

"I don't know what you are talking about. Come on, let's dance."

The dance floor is tucked into the corner of the building, and the lights are dim with the customary disco lights in full swing. A DJ is in the middle of the front center and a bar that hugs the wall just off the dance floor. Joshua is still staring at me as I grab Bridget's hand and lead her over to the dance floor.

"I wanted another drink," she scowls. At the back of the dance floor I notice there are mirrors all the way around the walls. It's sort of off putting watching yourself dance so I put my back to the mirrors and face the bar. To my relief Joshua, Ben and Adrian saunter down to the bar. Is he following me? I tally up a small victory and smile to myself, my plan is working.

I continue to dance, occasionally looking in the mirror to see if he is still there. He's more than still there, he's staring at me from behind. I can feel the heat from his penetrating gaze. Even as he drinks, his eyes don't leave me. I feel like the prey being hunted. Boy, I wish he was hunting me. Not in the plan, Natasha, remember, just prick teasing. Nothing more.

Adrian and Ben are talking to him but he's not answering, he just keeps staring at me, occasionally nodding. My God, he's beautiful. He's undressing me with his eyes, and I love it, I wish it were for real. Ben turns to look at me and says something to Adrian and Adrian turns to look at me too. Shit, they *are* talking about me. Joshua says something and Ben smiles and rubs his arm. Huh, what did Josh say that would earn him a sympathy rub? Suddenly, I'm bumped from behind. I stumble forward into Bridget and grab her arms for support.

"Ooh sorry," a short bald guy smiles.

"It's ok," Bridget answers, nodding and smiling. He seems harmless enough. For some reason though, he sees that as an open invitation to dance with us. His dancing style is Saturday night fever gone wrong. His arms are flying all over the place and he's sweating up like a treat. His buttons on his shirt are so stretched they might pop any minute. He's a close dancer. Oh jeez, I hate those. The song changes to 'Sexy Back' by Justin Timberlake and he really turns up the heat, getting closer and closer. I look to Bridge to find the bitch giggling and shaking her head. I pull wide eyes at her and she shakes her head. Oh no, what's he doing now? Shit. He's circling me doing maraca hands—this is beyond the pale. Oh God, he's standing behind me doing peekaboo over each of my shoulders. Bridget is full laughing now and so am I. This guy is a freak.

Some idiot has moved into my mirror image of Mr. Stanton, so he is temporarily out of my line of vision. I hope he is not watching this. The guy dances around to the front of me again and leans in, and I instinctively lean back. He stinks of body odor and I pull a disgusted face to Bridget who just keeps giggling with her head down. Even she's embarrassed by this spectacle of a man.

"What's your name, pretty lady?" he says while he rolls his hips, obviously trying to be sexy.

Huh, what the? Oh, buzz off, baldy. I'm trying to prick tease here and you're cramping my style. I smile, shake my head and hold my hand up to Bridge to signify getting a drink, and she nods in relief. We make it to the bar in a fit of giggles. Joshua is talking to Ben and another man I don't know, and Adrian is standing alone. We get our drinks and amble over to him.

"What's so funny?" he asks over his wine glass.

I shake my head and Bridget smiles. "Natasha is the ultimate dance floor idiot magnet."

I shake my head and throw a piece of ice at her. "Shut up," I giggle.

"No, seriously, Adrian, you have no idea," she puts her hand on his forearm. "Every time we are out Natasha gets some crazy disaster stalking her on the dance floor."

Adrian rolls his eyes at her. "I'm sure she gets some pretty hot ones as well."

I smile at him. Adrian's gay.

"Yeah, she does, she's a guy magnet."

"Shut up, I am not," I stammer.

"Are too," she giggles into her glass.

"No one that matters," I smile.

"Oh really?" Adrian smiles at me and raises his eyebrows. "So, who matters?"

My eyes fly to him and I take a gulp of my champagne, and he gives me a cheeky smile and a wink. He knows exactly what he's doing, he is trying to find out info. He very slowly looks at Josh, so my eyes follow his line of vision. I look up and see Joshua staring at me. Bridget is right, he is looking at me like he wants to eat me. I glance back to Adrian who winks at me and raises his champagne glass. I look to the ground and smile self-consciously. I think he knows everything. Oh crap, I hope he doesn't know everything. But why would Josh tell him? It was so long ago, unless he's affected like me? Maybe he's embarrassed. I can't help but like Adrian. He's a cheeky son of a bitch though, fancy milking me for info. I don't know what to say next without revealing anything and a dance track comes on that I love, so I grab both, Adrian and Bridge, by the hands. "Come on, we're dancing."

Oh boy, I'm feeling very tipsy. The champagne is going to my head big time. Stop drinking, Tash, I chastise myself. Adrian is a great dancer—I don't know why I didn't see it before. He is so obviously gay. Way too beautiful to be hetero. Josh is still watching me like a predator. I feel like I'm on the discovery channel. Every now and then I watch his tongue lick his bottom lip and I'm finding it very difficult not to dance slutty, when all I really want to do is walk over and dry hump his leg. Getting lost in the alcohol fog.

I start to lose my inhibitions and dance freely. I run both of my hands from my breasts, down my sides to my behind and circle it slowly, while I watch him in the mirror. Direct hit. Josh tenses his jaw and cracks his neck to the left—he's aroused. It seems I'm not the only one who is quickly losing my inhibitions. The song finishes and Rhianna's voice rings out.

Shine bright like a diamond.

Oohh, I love this song. Suddenly, Joshua cuts through the circle, grabs my hand and pulls me into the back corner.

"We're dancing," he snaps, and he turns around while still pulling me by the hand and my body slams into his, *oh shit.*

Shine bright like a diamond

He turns me quickly so that his back is to the crowd. He's a lot taller than me so I am totally shielded from everybody.

Fine lights in the beautiful sea, I choose to be happy.
You and I, you and I, we're like diamonds in the sky.

He places his two hands on my behind and pulls me close to him, his eyes not leaving mine. I'm like putty in his dominant hands. I tentatively put my hands around his neck, unable to breath, unable to look away from his searing stare. We move our hips slowly in sync to the rhythmic beat, and my heart is about to jump from my chest. He pulls his hands tighter into me, pulling me against his large erection. His gaze drops down to my breasts that are pushed up against his chest and he looks back up into my eyes, giving me the best come fuck me look I have ever seen. Instinctively my eyes close, as his breathing too has come to a halt.

Dear God. He smells divine.

So, shine bright tonight
You and I, we're beautiful like diamonds in the sky.

I can't help it, I gently stroke my fingers down the back of his neck and he gives me a slow seductive smile. He lip-syncs the next few lines of the song. He must like it too as he knows the words.

You're a shooting star I see, a vision of ecstasy
When you hold me I'm alive.
We're like diamonds in the sky

My heartbeat reaches a peak as our slow seductive rhythm follows the beat of the music, and his hands move lower and follow the curve of my bottom. He clenches his jaw and pulls me up for a deeper connection to his engorged manhood. I can feel his pulse through his pants. Second by second, I am losing all coherent thought. He's taking me over, the power he has over my body is now more evident than ever. I bring my hand and place it tenderly on Joshua's cheek. He closes his eyes in reverence and brings his mouth down to my neck, instinctively rubbing his lips down its length. Once again, I am blessed with him grabbing my behind, and this time he doesn't hold back, and he grinds himself into me.

My core starts to throb as I feel a rush of moisture to my most sensitive area. He feels so good. Slowly he raises his face and runs his teeth along my jaw, breathing heavily into my neck, and my mouth opens as my head throws back. I think I'm going to come right here, right now, *shit*. Our breathing is heavy, and we are completely lost in the moment. A moment I've waited so long for, and he's here, he's here with me. He feels it too. Very slowly I raise my face and look into Josh's dilated eyes, willing him to kiss me, his eyes drop to my mouth, his chest rising as he struggles to control his breathing. Very slowly he bows his head.

Margaret Stanton is standing in the corner near the bar, her eyes fixed firmly on her son and her niece in the far corner of the dance floor. She's radiating with anger as if a red glow could be seen around her. Her unmatched beauty and social standing can't help her with this. She's warned him, time and again, she even warned him just this very morning to keep away from this girl. She is way past angry, she is furious. She swirls her red around in her wine glass as she glares at the dance floor. James Brennan, her husband's best friend and business partner, is standing next to her. He gestures to the dance floor with his hand as he takes a sip of his scotch, and he glares at her as he talks into his short tumbler.

"I told you to handle this."

"Do you think I haven't tried?" she snaps, her eyes shooting back to the dance floor as Joshua once again pulls Natasha against his hips.

"I'm warning you, Margaret, I won't play your stupid little games." He rolls his shoulders. "Put a stop to it or I will."

She takes a sip of her red as hatred drips from her lips and she raises one eyebrow. "Don't threaten me, James, I'm not the one who will lose everything."

He plasters a fake smile as someone walks past them, nodding his head as a greeting. "Keep telling yourself that, Margaret," he sneers. "You have more to lose than me, Joshua for one. Do you think he will respect you once he knows?" he whispers.

She narrows her eyes. "Keep your voice down!" she snaps. "He will never know; over my dead body will he ever find out."

"The only way this will be revealed is if this pathetic little lust story on the dance floor continues. Stop it, now." His voice drips with contempt, and she swallows the large lump in her throat and glances back to the dance floor to catch Joshua run his lips down Natasha's throat.

"Good God," she snaps. "This is worse than I imagined." She rubs her forehead. She gestures to Cameron who comes over with Scott immediately. "Go out on that dance floor and ask Joshua what the hell he thinks he's doing." Cameron looks around the dance floor to see Josh running his teeth along Natasha's jaw, while grinding his hips into hers.

"Shit," Cam mutters. Margaret goes to walk off, but James grabs her by the arm.

"I'm warning you, Margaret, take care of this or I will."

She throws him a fake smile worthy of an Oscar nomination and lifts her chin.

"Don't threaten me, James, you won't like me when I'm angry. Stay away from my family, especially Joshua. This is your first and final warning."

Our lips touch. Immediately the electricity between us jolts me and awakens my senses. Senses that have laid dormant for seven long years. I'm lost, I'll do anything he wants.

"Josh, fucking cool it." We are snapped back to reality by Cameron, Joshua's little brother, on the dance floor. Fuck, *fuck*, what are we doing. *Shit*. We immediately step back from each other. Josh looks at Cam who gestures to the side of the dance floor where Scott the groom is glaring at both Joshua and me. Immediately I want to die. We both quickly scan the room to see who has witnessed our loss of control. I look at Joshua and the horrified look on his face mirrors mine. I practically run to the ladies' room, oh my God, who saw that? What the hell am I doing?

I make it to the ladies' room but as soon as I get there I burst into tears, unable to control my stress at being so stupid. My heart is still racing, and my body is aching from the loss of his. I start to pace while shaking my hands. Shit, shit, shit, holy fuck, what was that? I burst into a cubicle and sit on the toilet with my face in my hands. I'm a disgrace. Perspiration seeps from my pores. *Oh my God.* All alone in the cubicle I start to sob, so close but so far.

Joshua

Joshua storms off the dance floor and barges into the first door he sees to the right, the kitchen. Luckily the kitchen staff have already gone for the night. He needs to get away from the other guests, he's too worked up, too angry with himself. "Fucking hell," he yells as he punches the stainless-steel bench. He starts to pace, rubbing his hands through his hair. Adrian and Ben gingerly walk in after him, unsure what to say. This is a shock to their system; they have both been with Joshua a long time and this is uncharted waters to them.

"Joshua, calm down," Adrian quietly comforts.

"Calm down?" he yells. "Calm down, it's a bit fucking late for that. I shouldn't have fucking come; I knew this would happen." Adrian and Ben frown at each other.

"Why do you say that?"

"How bad was it?" he looks to his two friends.

"What do you mean?" frowns Adrian.

"How bad did it look?"

Ben smiles and nods, "Pretty fucking bad."

Adrian pipes up, "If it makes you feel any better, she lost control too."

Joshua looks at his friend, "Where is she, I need to see her."

Adrian widens his eyes, "I think you've done enough damage for one night."

"Just go and fucking find her," he yells. "If I want your opinion, I will fucking ask for it."

The door bangs open and Scott storms in. "I fucking warned you," he yells.

Joshua hangs his head. "I know," he answers in a defeated voice.

"What the hell do you think you're doing?" he screams at Joshua. "What if Dad saw that?"

"I know. Fuck," Joshua whispers and rubs both hands through his hair. He links his fingers of both hands together on top of his head and blows out a breath. "I... I lost my head."

"I know!" Scott yells. "Find it or leave. Seriously, my fucking wedding. Are you kidding? Do you have any idea of the carnage if someone had seen that?"

"I know, I'm sorry." Scott scowls and looks down at Joshua's obvious erection. He shakes his head in disgust and storms out. Josh blows out a breath with his hands linked on top of his head. He looks to Ben and Adrian and shakes his head. They both stare at him, shocked to the core. They have never seen him like this before. He never touches anyone in public. He rearranges his groin.

Suddenly the kitchen door bursts open. Oh shit, it's Brock. He's radiating atomic anger and he points at Joshua and yells, "You fucking prick!" He grabs Joshua by the suit lapels and slams him up against the fridge. With his forearm across his throat, he pulls him out and slams him back into the fridge. "What the fuck was that Stanton?" he yells. Joshua doesn't answer and he doesn't fight back, although he's bigger than Brock. If he wanted to, he could end this now. Ben goes to move in, but Joshua shakes his head at him. "Mind telling me why the fuck you're dry fucking my sister on the dance floor?" Joshua bites his bottom lip and glares at Brock, "Answer me, fucker!" he yells. "She's not a slut, Stanton" he yells.

Joshua narrows his eyes. "I fucking know that," he snaps.

"No, you don't, you just treated her like one." Joshua closes his eyes and drops his head. Brock slams his head again. "I know the dirty sluts you're used to, Stanton, and, believe me, she is so far out of your league it's not even funny."

Joshua narrows his eyes and glares at Brock as his anger escalates. "Back the fuck off, Brock!" he yells. He twists his arms to get out of his hold and then pushes Brock who comes back with another push.

Ben steps in. "Stop it, you two, enough already." Both men stare at each other, breathing heavily, their fists clenched at their sides.

Brock points his finger in Joshua's face. "The sooner you fuck off back to America the better. I'm warning you. If you go near her again, you're a dead man."

"Go fuck yourself!" Joshua sneers. "I'll do what I want." Brock storms out of the kitchen. All three men stay silent, and Josh kicks the bin in frustration. Adrian's eyes are the size of saucers.

"So, I'm guessing he's the restraining order," Ben whispers. Joshua shakes his head, "No, he's just a parking cop."

"If he's a parking cop who in the hell is the restraining order?" Joshua turns to face his friends.

"My mother."

CHAPTER 4

Natasha

THERE IS ONLY one thing worse than waking with a hangover. Hazy images of yourself from the night before. I look around the room to try and get my bearings. That's right, I'm in my hotel room, alone. I trudge to the bathroom and stare in the mirror at the ugly raccoon looking back at me. The ugly raccoon who does a great impersonation of a dog on heat, on dance floors at weddings. I cringe as the memory of last night comes forth to my foggy brain. I pinch the bridge of my nose. Shit. What came over me? I put my head in my hands. Why in the hell did I drink last night? He must think I'm a total hooker I couldn't have appeared any easier if I tried. I feel like shit this morning. Hopefully he was drunk. Then he won't remember me making a total fool of myself. One minute we were dancing, the next thing kissing. I tap my forehead as I remember and smile. *What am I smiling about?* A knock bangs on the door. Unfortunately ,I know exactly who it is. I frown again as my brain hits my skull. Knock, knock, knock. "Alright, I'm coming, I'm coming."

I open the door to a cranky looking Bridget. She smiles a plastered-on smile.

"What happened to you last night?" I turn, walk over to the coffee maker and flick it on. Coffee will help me with this conversation. I'm not in the mood for this shit. I stand with my back to her trying to look busy. If I look her in the eye, she will know without a doubt that I'm lying.

"I must have eaten something, and I couldn't stop vomiting. I didn't want to interrupt your night, so I just got a cab." She stays silent as she listens to my explanation. "Do you want coffee?" I ask, hoping she bought the blurb of lies I have just sent her way. "It was a nice wedding, wasn't it? The bride looked gorgeous, didn't she?" I'm babbling and talking way too fast. "What time did you get home?" I ask as I turn to face her armed with my caffeine.

"I went out with the Stanton boys. We went clubbing." I nod, staying silent.

"Do you have something to tell me?" she asks with a raised brow.

"No, why do you say that?"

"I don't know if you noticed, but I was at the wedding yesterday." She rips her hair down from its bun with such force it's a wonder she doesn't scalp herself.

"Yes, I know," I mutter.

"And I was on the dance floor last night." Dread fills my stomach. "I'm waiting," she continues to scowl at me.

"Why do you think I have something to tell you?"

"Because the Stanton boys all know what's going on."

"What?" I snap. "How do you know?"

"When I was with them last night, I came back from the bar and they were talking about you and Joshua."

Holy crap, my eyes are the size of saucers. "What did they say?" My heart rate doubles as I hold my breath.

She holds up her hand. "Tell me what's going on."

"Was Joshua with you?" I ask, secretly hoping she has some info for me, something I can cling onto, anything?

"No, he left after the dirty dancing affair as well." I put my face into my hands. "Cameron said I should ask you about it. He seemed shocked that I didn't know."

"Know what?" I whisper, my eyes wide.

"You tell me!" she yells.

"Oh God, this is terrible," I wail.

"Tell me," she urges. Again, another knock, thank heavens for Mum's impeccable timing.

"Come in," I yell a little too fast. Bridget scowls at me. I smile as I open the door.

"Hi honey, are you feeling better? I wish you would have come and gotten me last night. You didn't need to catch a cab on your own. Why didn't you just find me instead of texting me?"

"Yes, why is that Natasha? It's very unlike you." Bridget scowls at me as she folds her arms in front of her.

"Come on, we have breakfast at the Stanton's." I am so not going there. How do I get out of this?

"I still don't feel well. I can't come, Mum, sorry. I don't want to risk throwing up in public or on Margaret for that matter." The thought tickles my fancy and I stifle a smile.

Bridget narrows her eyes at me. "I bet," she snaps. Mum gives me a reassuring smile that only a mother can give.

"No worries. It's a shame though. We never catch up with them, never mind, next time." She rubs my arm and heads over

70

to the lift entrance calling from the hall for Bridget to hurry up. "When we get home, we are meeting Abbie at Oscar's and I want the fucking truth," she pokes me hard in the chest.

"Ow, ok," I whisper, trying desperately to get rid of her. I do wide eyes to her to signify my distaste for this conversation. I dread the impending conversation—my stomach dry-retches just thinking about it. I'm not stretching the truth too far actually; vomiting could be in the very soon foreseeable future. This is a total nightmare. I want desperately to go to breakfast to see him. I need to see him. It's a need, not a want. I want to see his face after last night, but I can't risk seeing Scott, his brother. I am so embarrassed. I wish I had a vision of what last night looked like. Did I look like the instigator? Was I the instigator? Did he reciprocate my desire? Or did I imagine it?

For the next three hours I act like the total loser I am. I download Rihanna's 'Diamonds' track and listen to it on repeat while lying on my bed staring at the ceiling, only leaving the bed to dry-retch into the toilet every now and then. I reminisce about dancing with him last night, the feel of his unrestrained strength under my hands and the divine smell of him. Hmm, the way he bit my neck. I get goose bumps just thinking about it. His want for me, his pure maleness...is that even a word? I can't help but smile—my God, he sure does shine bright, like a diamond that is. He's still got it and, worse than that, I still want it. Joshua Stanton is too beautiful for words.

Oscar's, 6.00 pm

Bridget hasn't talked to me all day other than to tell me Joshua didn't show for breakfast with his family. We are waiting for Abbie to arrive, sipping our coffee in silence. I don't know why she's pissed off as I'm the one everyone is talking about. I just wish I knew what they were saying.

Abbie finally turns up in a rush and is obviously flustered. "Hi, what in the hell is the crisis meeting about?" She unloads all the crap from her bag, looking for her wallet. "Is it TC? Have you heard anything?" Her eyes search mine. "Has she made a move on him?"

"No, nothing like that," I answer. "How would we know anyway?"

"What's so bloody urgent then? I am going on a date tonight."

"Who with?" we both say in tandem.

"Tristan, army guy."

We all smile. I think she likes him.

Bridget sits back. "Natasha has something to tell us." She folds her arms in front of her. God, she plays the bitch well.

"You do?" Abbie smiles, her face questioning and eyebrows raised.

"Um," I don't look either of them in the eye.

Bridget points her spoon at me. "Enough of this shit. Out with it."

Abbie looks between both of us. "What the hell is going on?"

Obviously, she is shocked at bitch Bridget's venom. My moment of truth has arrived, and I am about to be judged by the two people who mean the most to me. They are important. Their opinion matters, it really matters. I blow out a long and steadying breath as I try to calm my nerves.

"I...I...had a steamy month–long sexual affair with Joshua when I was seventeen." I say it in a rush to get the words out.

"What the fuck!" Abbie spits out. I stay silent as I see the color drip from their faces, my eyes flicking between them.

"Hang on, back up." Abbie is confused and holds up her hand in a stop signal. "Your cousin?" she asks, mortified.

"Yes," I nod.

"The gorgeous one?" I nod again.

"What? You slept with him?" I nod. "Your cousin," she repeats as she frowns. "More than once?" I nod. "How many times?" Abbie is in total shock. I shrug my shoulders. "How many times?" she repeats.

"Four or five times," I answer.

She puts her hand on her chest. "Oh, thank God."

"Every day for a month," I finish my sentence.

"Fuck off," Bridget snaps. We both look at her. She has been blissfully silent up until this point. "You slept with Joshua four or five times a day for a month? When was this?"

"On holiday before he went away."

"Where was I?"

"You were in England with Jenna." She nods as she processes the information. I can almost see her brain ticking.

"And last night was the first time you've seen each other since." Once again, I nod. "How do we not know this?" Bridget asks, the hurt in her voice cutting me. I'm a bad friend who keeps secrets.

"Bridget, I'm sorry. I couldn't tell anyone because I'm ashamed." Abbie has her hands in front of her mouth like she's praying.

"Hang on," Bridge whispers. "How old were you?"

"Seventeen," I answer, knowing for certain what the next question is going to be.

"Don't tell me," Abbie whispers, eyes wide.

I nod, "Yes, I lost my virginity to him."

"Fuck off," Bridget snaps again.

"Were you his first?" Bridget's hands are running through her hair.

"No, he had slept with lots of girls before me."

"Shit. This is fucked up Tash," Bridget whispers.

"I know," I give a weak smile and nod. "I think..." I stay silent. "I think..."

"What?" Bridget snaps as she sips her coffee. Her patience is running thin.

"I think I'm in love with him."

"Fuck off," Bridget snaps as she chokes on her coffee.

"Will you stop saying that?"

"Well then, stop shocking me."

"Why do you think that?" Abbie looks like she is going to vomit, her face screwed up. She's holding her stomach.

"Because... because," they are both leaning in towards me, on the edge of their seats. Bridget is biting her thumbnail. "I think I'm in love with him because I haven't...I haven't..."

"You haven't what?" Abbie snaps.

"I haven't slept with anyone since." They both stare at me like I have just grown two heads and their eyes bulge from their sockets. I sit back and, God ,what a relief, that was cathartic.

"You haven't had sex in seven years?" I nod and give a sheepish smile. I wish I had a camera. They are speechless, and the look of total horror on their faces makes me giggle.

"How is that possible? You've had heaps of boyfriends. You've even had two marriage proposals."

I shrug. "I told them I was waiting for marriage. Obviously, I kept them sexually satisfied in other ways, but you know what? The only reason they proposed to me was they thought I would be good marriage material since I wasn't easy."

"They believed you?" They are both mortified. Abbie looks up at me and starts to giggle.

"What's funny?" Bridget smiles.

"Her," she points to me, "she is."

Bridget looks at me and starts to giggle as well.

"What's funny?" I laugh.

"You're a fucking psychologist who treats messed–up people all day and you're more fucked up than the rest of us. You're the world's biggest prick teaser." I laugh and nod.

"Yes, I suppose."

"Oh my God!" Bridget holds her hands up to her face. "Tash, this is like frigging Bold and the Beautiful. You do know that, right?" I nod.

"So what, you've been in contact with him all along?"

"No. Not a word. Remember Josh nearly didn't go to America because he met a girl in Sydney?" Bridget nods.

"That was me." She gasps, eyes wide, and puts her hands up to her mouth.

"No way." I nod again.

"If you haven't been in contact, what's with the celibacy?" I shrug as I chew over her question.

"It hasn't been on purpose. Every time I'm with a man I think I'm going to go through with it but when it comes close, I can't do it. I feel like I'm cheating on him and, to be fair, the guys don't really get me hot for it."

"Shit," Abbie whispers. "This is a fucking crisis meeting if I ever saw one."

I smile. "I know."

"Ok, let's rehash," Abbie takes charge of the crisis meeting with her spoon pointing. "So, you were in love with Joshua."

I nod, "Correct."

"And last night was the first time you have seen each other since."

I nod again, "Correct."

"And what happened?" she looks to Bridget who is still biting her thumbnail as she hunches her shoulders.

"I think he still is attracted to her. No actually, I know he is still attracted to her. He was watching her like a serial killer stalking his next victim." I can't help the broad smile from appearing on my face.

Abbie looks back to me. "And this is good, is it?" I hunch my shoulders and nod. "So, are you still attracted to him?"

I nod again. "Yes, seriously."

"What happened at the wedding?" She looks between Bridget and me.

"We danced."

"Dirty danced," Bridget adds.

"And then we kissed."

"Kissed," Abbie repeats. "In front of your family?"

"Yes, it wasn't planned, I was just so turned on. He makes me so crazy I forgot where I was." She pinches her lips while assessing the situation, deep in thought.

"So, it's physical then?"

I nod, "I think so. I lose all coherent thought when he is anywhere near me. He just has this way. I don't know, I can't explain it. His body talks to mine."

"What so, he's like, dominant?"

I nod. "Totally and he's seriously fucking hot, so it's a lethal combo. The way he touches me, it's like he will die if he doesn't have me. He consumes me, I feel like I can't breathe. Like I was meant to please him, to hold him."

Her eyes widen. "Hmm," she's thinking, "has he called you today?" I pull my phone out of my bag and check it for the hundredth time today.

"No," I answer flatly while looking at the screen. "Does he have your number?"

"I don't know," I answer.

"What are you going to do?"

"I don't know. I have to get some closure. I know that for sure. I can't move on until I can get him out of my head."

"Is that what you want? To move on."

"Yes. We can't have a future together. I know that. We both know that, but there was something still there. I felt it and I know he did, too. He forgot where he was as well, but I need to finish this for once and for all. I'm sick of this longing from a distance shit." We sit in silence.

"This is heavy shit, Natasha," Bridget whispers.

"I know, I need to sort my shit out and I will. I feel like maybe it's coming to a head now he is back, and I will be able to finish it up."

"Good," Bridget smiles. "Can you imagine the shit that would go down if the family found out?"

I roll my eyes, "Don't even go there."

Sunday morning I was positive I was going to hear from him. Sunday night I was pacing, staring at my phone, willing the bastard to ring. Monday morning I had decided to ring him, Monday afternoon decided against it. I already looked desperate. Looked desperate, God, I was desperate. Monday night at the gym I ran 12 km, a feat I hadn't done before. Ok, I train better when stressed, a no brainer here. Then I went home and ate a whole block of chocolate. Tuesday morning I had all but given up—he probably hadn't even thought about it again. I'm overreacting as usual where he is concerned. He really is pissing me off though. Ring, damn you. At lunchtime my work friend Simon walks into our staff room.

"Do you want to go grab some sushi?"

"Sure, why not?" I grab my bag. I love Simon. He's tall with blond curly hair, sort of surfie looking, not my type though. He's hard to explain, but you know those guys that are just too nice. Anyway, he's a great friend and he always says the right things. There has got to be some perks to hanging out with psychologists. We drive and then walk to our favorite Sushi Train in the city, a place we usually frequent about once a week when we have a long lunch. We plan them on the same days for this purpose especially. Simon is telling me in great detail about the date he had on the weekend. He thinks the girl is a stage one clinger. Apparently, she was talking babies. I smile, although my thoughts are anywhere but on Simon's date and proposed children. He opens the door to the restaurant in an exaggerated bow and holds his arm out to me and I link mine with his.

"Our sushi awaits milady," he says and gives me a wink. He always calls me milady in reference to the historical romance novels I love. I smile at our ease with each other. He is so uncomplicated. Why can't I love a guy like Simon? Why do I have to have bastard player lover syndrome? We watch the train come around the table, while the group in front of us pay their account. They finish with the cashier and turn, and I bump head-first straight into Joshua. Ben and Adrian are behind him. Oh shit, I step back in shock. What are they doing here? My arm is still linked with Simon's and I just stare at Joshua dumb-founded. I did not expect this. Adrian comes forward and gives me a kiss on the cheek.

"Hi Natasha," he smiles at me.

"Oh hi, Adrian," I push out. "Ben," I nod to him and he nods back. I smile at Joshua and he just glares at me. *Shit.* This is uncomfortable. Unable to control myself I take a quick peek at him, why does he have to be so damn attractive in his grey pinstripe suit? Looking all flawless. His dark olive skin and square jaw only accentuate his piercing blue eyes. His body radiates power and at the moment... anger. I can feel the contempt dripping from his every pore. Of course, I look like total shit in my scrubs and no makeup. This is a total disaster. I drop Simon's arm like a hot potato.

"Um, this is Simon." I introduce him to the three men.

Adrian shakes his hand first. "Nice to meet you, Adrian."

Simon smiles, "Pleasure." Then Ben holds out his hand, Simon shakes it and then Simon holds out his hand to shake Joshua's hand. Joshua stares at him blank–faced and keeps his hands in his pockets, unwilling to shake his hand. I frown uncomfortably.

Simon raises his eyebrows. "Problem?" he says to Joshua.

Joshua glares at him. "You tell me," he snaps. Oh shit, what is he playing at?

Adrian cuts in, "We had better be going." He seems embarrassed. "Lovely to see you, Tash," he smiles and gives me a quick peck on the cheek. Ben smiles and Joshua storms off. Simon and I look at each other. I am unable to hide my horror.

"Who was that?" Simon frowns.

"Ex–boyfriend," I mutter.

"I know why he's an ex. He's a prick." I smile and nod nervously. I hardly taste my damn sushi. I just stare into space. Simon is oblivious, rambling on and on about crap, who cares whatever. For ten minutes I listen to his constant jabbering. He is really starting to annoy me now. Just shut the fuck up, I'm trying to think here, I'm holding my temples. What an absolute bastard, I am boiling mad. How dare he be so rude to my verbal diarrhea friend? I take out my phone and text the number I have for him, not even knowing if that is in fact still his number.

You're an asshole.

I wait and scowl. It probably isn't even his number. I stole it off Mum's phone about two years ago. Bloody Mum can't even save a number right. My phone beeps a message.

No, you're the asshole.

What! Is he kidding? How am I an asshole? How dare he? Who the hell does he think he is? I text back.

You have got to be kidding.

I smile. There, that showed him, how dare he say I'm an asshole? I am definitely not an asshole. He is un-fucking-believable. My phone beeps with a message.

FUCK OFF

What the fuck? Red steam is shooting out of my ears. No guy, or anyone actually, has ever told me to fuck off, and especially not in capital letters in print. I am infuriated. I want to throw my new iPhone across the restaurant. I start to drum my fingers on the table, double time. Simon is still oblivious to my rage, God, he really is docile.

"Come on, let's go," he smiles.

What shall I text back? I need the upper hand. I am tapping my front tooth with my fingernail while I think. Simon is right, he really is a prick. I sit in Simon's car, silently looking out the window as I troll my brain for a good comeback. I've got nothing. Use your brain Natasha, I'm sure there's one in there somewhere. I just know at 2 am tomorrow morning an awesome comeback is going to pop into my head, and it will haunt me for the rest of my life. I have to text now, or it will look like I am thinking about my reply, even though I am. This is a total disaster. In the end I text the lamest reply in human history.

Gladly.

That night at Oscar's, Bridget and Abbie laugh as they read the texts.

"How did it go from you're an asshole to fuck off?"

"I don't know." I shake my head as they continue to pass my phone to each other.

"And why does he think you're an asshole?" I slump on the table and put my face into my hands. "Probably because I am an asshole, a stupid beyond belief asshole."

They laugh again. "He knows you better than you think."

"Thanks a lot," I sigh. "This isn't funny, bitches."

"Yes, it is." They both huddle together and giggle.

It's frigging hilarious."

Wednesday at work drags. I'm still fuming. I have thought of nothing else since I saw him yesterday. Fuming is a lot more satisfying than pining. I'm just so off him. After lunch I get a text from Bridget.

We are going out tonight.
Spying on Jeremy, time to bust a move.

Great. I smile as I read the text. I need some NCIS action and it will take my mind off prick-face. I text back.

Sounds good. Is Abbie coming?

She replies.

Of course, meet me at mine at seven.

We are standing together in a line in Bridget's bedroom, looking at our reflection in the mirror. "We look like hookers," I grimace.

"That's the point," she replies.

"Are you sure you read the email right?"

She nods. "Yes, what do you think? I just thought this shit up?" Jeremy accidentally left his email open last night and Bridget snooped. Apparently, he is going to an upmarket strip club tonight with his work friends and we are going to sneak into the joint to bust him in the act.

"What time does it open?"

"Half an hour," she replies. "We had better get going."

An hour later we are sitting at a table in the back corner of what is probably the classiest night club I have been in. The walls are a deep smoky grey and the lounges and pendant lights are all in black velvet. Huge silver gilded mirrors hang on the walls and giant palm trees are in massive ceramic pots surrounding the perimeter. Whoever the interior designer was hit the target. It can only be described as sensual. I have never been in a space like this before, it screams opulence and fantasy. The sound system is amazing, and the music seems to be surrounding us.

"This wig is itchy," I scratch my scalp.

"Why did you wear it then?"

"Because I don't want to run into one of my patients. I'm in disguise."

"Oh phooey, you look like Natasha with a long blonde wig on."

I nod as I sip my margarita, "Yeah I know. Mmm, this is good, it's super icy. Do you see him?" We all look around.

"No, it's pretty empty actually." We all relax.

A cute blond bartender comes over. "Can I get you beautiful ladies anything to drink?"

"Sure, three more margaritas. Thanks." He smiles and nods. "What's upstairs?" I ask as if interested.

"Just more booths with views to the stage." We all nod, trying our best to look cool and uncaring. "Is anyone up there?" I ask.

He smiles and shakes his head—he is so onto us. "No one yet," he gives me a wink. We all nod, a little more than relieved. At the end of the bar there is a second set of stairs and there is a large red velvet rope across the bottom of the stairwell.

"What's up there?" I ask.

"That's the VIP room for private parties." Abbie frowns, "Private parties?"

He nods and smiles. "Yes, only one group at a time."

"What goes on up there?" Bridget asks.

He shakes his head and smiles. "You don't want to know." We are all shocked to silence.

"Is anyone up there now?" Abbie asks.

"No, it costs $5000.00 just to get up there." We all look at each other.

"Do people really pay that?" I question.

"You would be surprised. It's used every night."

"What do you get for five grand?" Bridget asks.

He smiles as he walks off. "Anything you want, pretty much. But mostly sex and cocaine."

"Wow," I mouth to the girls, and they nod in agreement.

"Shit, anything you want." I chew my ice. "This place is a high– class brothel." Oh shit, a disturbing thought enters my brain. Panic sets in.

"Bridget, what are you going to do if we do see him here? Please don't cause a scene." I'm beginning to regret this decision to come here. It could get embarrassing.

"I'm not giving him the satisfaction," she sneers. "I am just going to watch him and then dump him tomorrow and tell him I'm sleeping with someone with a massive dick who rocks in the sack." We all laugh. Good plan, I like it. The music starts, and the song 'Bad to the Bone' blares through the sound system and we all smile. Of course, this song is playing, so typical strip joint.

A beautiful blonde saunters down the catwalk. She looks like she just stepped off a Sports Illustrated cover shoot, all muscly and oiled up, although the fake tan is too the extreme. She oozes confidence. She intimidates the three of us as we all sit in silence, entranced like she is dancing just for us. As she gets to the end of the runway, she slams into the side splits. Shit, she's flexible too. She comes straight up into a bend back to handstand up. Yep, she's good alright. She slowly but surely commands everyone's attention in the room, including ours. We watch, riveted, as she slowly peels every piece of clothing from her hot body. She's a dancer obviously, and I have to say she is blowing the preconceived idea of what a stripper looks like out the window.

"Fuck, she's hot," Abbie whispers. I nod, unable to take my eyes off her and Bridge answers, "I know, right?" She doesn't look easy— she looks alluring, sexy. She takes off her bra to expose the best set of fake tits I have ever seen. We all sit mesmerized, mouths open.

"That's it," Bridget whispers. "Decision made; I'm getting my boobs done."

We all nod. "Good idea," notes Abbie. She slowly turns around to turn her back to the audience and bends over without bending her knees and slides her G–String down her legs to reveal her beautifully pink vagina and anus, not a hair in sight.

"Holy crap," Abbie whispers. "I think I'm in love." The whole club including us are collectively holding their breath, and as she slowly starts to touch her breasts with both her hands we all lean in towards the stage.

"Fuck, this is hot," Bridget whispers. I nod, still too entranced to speak. She lays on her back with her legs spread to the audience and starts to finger–fuck herself in time with the music, groaning and writhing on the floor. We all look at each other wide-eyed, and a little shocked to be honest. I don't know what we were expecting but it wasn't intimately watching an attractive woman bring herself to orgasm. She slowly brings her fingers to her lips and starts to suck them in her mouth. The audience makes a collective groan, *shit*. We are so out of our depth here. She rolls to her knees and puts her rear to the audience still going hell for leather with her fingers. We all sit shocked, silent and wide-eyed as she brings herself to a screaming orgasm. Moments pass and she sits up onto her knees and sucks her fingers dry. The crowd goes wild with everyone rising to a standing ovation, including us. She stands and bows, the room is a buzz. The atmosphere is suddenly pumped full of testosterone and pheromones. We clink our glasses together and giggle.

"Holy shit," I whisper. "Why am I turned on?"

"I know, right?" Bridge nods.

Abbie laughs while draining her glass, "I have a good mind to give her my number."

After about our sixth cocktail and having lost any inhibitions we ever had, we realize we are actually having a really good time. "Girls, I don't want to sound pervy, but I actually love this place. The girls are all gorgeous, classy and entertaining. The cocktails are amazing. And look at the crowd," Abbie gestures around the room with her hands. "The crowd is all well behaved, all staying silently in their seats. If this was a male strip show the women would be screaming like lunatics and jumping on stage, trying to rip clothes off." We all pulled a disgusted face.

"I know, I always assumed strip joints would be the same, but they are definitely not on the same page. This is top shelf though remember." We all nod. A few acts of more beautiful girls and I make a surprising discovery.

"Did you notice something?" I lean in to whisper to my friends. They both quickly scan the room with their eyes, thinking I've seen Jeremy. "No, not that," I shake my head. "There is not a welcome mat in this place."

The girls both frown and look around, "You're right, this place is pubeless. Not a pubic hair in the joint."

"Why is that?" Bridge frowns.

"I don't know—do men really like this?" I hunch my shoulders.

Abbie smirks, "Really, if I had to choose between a waxed one and a hairy one, I would go waxed every time."

"I suppose." We all nod.

"Anyway," Abbie puts both of her hands onto the table. "I am booking us in tomorrow afternoon to Beautiful Behinds."

"What for?"

"We are going to get Brazilians and anal bleaching." I choke on my drink. "Anal bleaching, are you mad?"

"No, did you look at these girls?" I nod. "Their bits are all porn star pink."

"What, so it isn't natural?" Bridget frowns.

"No, it isn't natural. They get everything bleached so it's a pretty pink color. Guys love it."

"Fuck off, do you get it done?"

"Of course," she smirks. Oh, I'm shocked, how do I not know this? "If you want to look pretty for Mr. Stanton you had better get it done too." She grabs my arm on the table, "I'm pretty sure he is used to pink bits." I frown as I drain my glass. Mr. Stanton looking at other girls' bits is not something I want in my head.

"Knowing my luck, the bleach will give me a third–degree burn, and I will end up in hospital with a ring of fire." The girls laugh.

"Bags not changing the dressing." They clink their glasses together.

Every time a new group of men filter in, we all put our drink menus up in front of our faces as they walk past.

"They should rename this place," I scoff. The girls frown. "The Drycleaners." They frown again. "You know where you would go to pick up a suit." They both laugh. "Seriously, look at the demographics of this place. All men, rich, over thirty, in very expensive suits. Where do their wives think they are?" We all narrow our eyes as we take in our surroundings.

"Shit," Abbie whispers. "They are all on frigging work conferences." We nod.

"You're right, these are all men who work together.

Fuckwits," Bridget snaps. Blondie bartender comes over, "Last drinks at half price, ladies."

"Half price, these cocktails are $20.00 a pop," I answer.

He smiles. "I know, at 1.30 am they double in price."

"Why?" we all ask, mortified.

"That's when the shows start."

We all frown, "Haven't we been watching shows all night?" He smiles and shakes his head. "No, I mean the real fun."

Sure enough, over the next 15 minutes we watch as group after group of men in expensive suits fill the place. So many, in fact, we are flat out trying to keep up our spying duties and some are slipping through the cracks.

"Shit, is he here?" Bridget whispers.

"I have no idea," I answer. "I've lost track. I think the place is full," as I crane my neck to look around the crowd.

"I know, this is crazy. The drinks are hell expensive. Rich men are seriously stupid."

We are all feeling quite tipsy and at 1.30 exactly the lights all go out except the stage spotlights and silence falls over the audience. We are all experiencing a serious case of the fuzzies and very loudly shh, shh each other. We're holding hands under the table and giggling, feeling quite apprehensive about what is about to unfold. Thankfully, it looks like Jeremy is a no show. The track 'My Pony' rings out on the high-powered sound system, a remixed version. Two girls walk out onto the stage and the crowd goes wild. Some of the men chant their names— it seems they have a following. The three of us sit still in silent amazement as our eyes are transfixed by the stage. A stunning brunette dressed as a hot policewoman complete with hat and baton leads a beautiful redhead dressed in prisoner get-up onto the stage by the handcuffs. "Oh, fuck," Bridget whispers as she squeezes my hand. The redhead is led out and sat in a chair at the end of the runway. The policewoman walks around her a few times, sizing her up. She bends down and grabs her by the hair. Pulling her head back, she bends and gives her a slow passionate tongue kiss and the crowd goes wild. Bridget hits me on the leg and when I glance at her she nods at Abbie. I look over and Abbie is so into it her mouth is open. Bridget and I get the giggles.

"Wow," I mouth to Bridget, and she nods. The policewoman stands and walks around her again in a slow torture kind of build–up, and the crowd goes silent again. She very slowly starts to undress the prisoner, and my heart is in my throat. After what seems like an eternity, she slowly slides her G–String down her legs as she sucks her breasts—this shit is hot. My God, I'm getting turned on, *what the hell?* She slowly starts to finger-fuck the prisoner who lies back in the chair. The audience are collectively holding their breath and we are sitting forward in our seats. The brunette drops to her knees and the crowd goes crazy—oh no, don't tell me. *Oh my God.* She starts to go down on the prisoner. The audience falls silent again, listening for the sound effects. I am interrupted from my lesbian fantasy as Bridget taps my leg again. I look at her and she nods towards the door and pulls up her drink menu. I grab mine quickly and peer out to see him, but to my horror the face I'm looking at isn't Jeremy's. My stomach drops as I watch Joshua Stanton, my Joshua Stanton, walk in with a group of men. They are laughing with the girls on the door and I sit still, too stunned to react. He puts his arm around one of the girls and whispers something into her ear. She giggles and slaps him. What in the hell did he say? This night just went from hero to zero in a millisecond. Abbie has just noticed what we are looking at. "Oh fuck," she whispers, the shock on her face evident, and she pulls up her drink menu.

This is something I don't want to see, the room is suddenly suffocating and I need to get out of here, like now. I watch as they enter and walk over to the stairs with the red rope. They have been here before; they know the drill. He is with six other men, all in suits. I don't know any of them, but one looks like his bodyguard, actually yes, it is, it's Ben. A bleached blonde walks over and talks to them, and I watch in slow motion as Joshua gets out his wallet and hands over his credit card. Oh dear God, no. They are going upstairs to the VIP room. I feel sick.

I want to run over and stop him. To beg him to come home with me because I know if he goes up there, I can never touch him again. It will have gone too far to go back. Silently in my head I start to pray, don't do it, baby. Please don't do it. I start wringing my hands together under the table and I have broken out into a cold sweat. The group of men all bundle up the stairs as soon as she unhooks the rope. Just as Joshua is about to take the stairs he stops as he notices something and looks towards the stage.

My eyes flick to the stage to see what he is looking at. The policewoman is now on her knees fucking the prisoner with the baton. My eyes go back to him. *No.* I watch in horror as he clenches his jaw and cracks his neck—he's aroused. The pain of watching the man I love become aroused by another woman, or two in this case, is crippling and I put my head down onto the table unable to speak. Bridget rubs the back of my head, unsure of what to say. No, I need to see this. I look back up as he calls the blonde back over and lights a cigarette. Huh, he smokes now? I watch as he says something and gestures to the stage. She nods and smiles. Just when I thought this nightmare could not get any worse, I watch as he runs the backs of his fingers from her throat down between her bare breasts and down to her G–String. He rims his fingers around the inside of the waistband and gives them a jerk before he lets her go. With his cigarette between his teeth he says something, and she gives him a filthy smile before he turns and heads up the stairs. I'm in shock, did that just happen? I look to my dear friends, and their faces say more than words. Bridget grabs my hand and Abbie rubs my leg. There are no words for this situation, no words at all. I put my hand over my mouth—I think I'm going to be sick.

"Tash, let's go baby," Bridget whispers. "We have seen enough." I shake my head, still unable to speak. I shake again. I don't want to leave him here. I don't want him to wreck it. "Tash, come on, we have to go."

I look at the girls again. "I don't want to leave him here, please don't make me," I whisper. The act on stage finishes. The crowd goes wild and the girls both bound up to the bar to get a drink. Blonde bimbo says something to them and they both smile and head up to the VIP room, obviously at Joshua's request. My heart drops lower than I ever felt possible. Bridget has had enough; she is getting mad.

"He's a fucking prick, Natasha, just leave it. You can do a lot better." I know they are right. If I cause a scene, I will never forgive myself. It is with deep regret I allow my friends to scrape me up out of my seat and lead me out of a place that will haunt me forever, a place that has my heart splattered all over the table. A place where I saw his other side.

We sit in silence in the back of the cab, everybody too afraid to speak, determined not to say the wrong thing.

"Where to ladies?" the cabbie asks.

Before anyone can speak, "The nearest McDonalds," I say flatly.

The cashier is cheerful and happy, "What will it be?"

"A super–sized Big Mac meal with Coke. An apple pie and a chocolate sundae, extra salt on the fries." I look back at my friends who are both wisely staying silent, pretending to look at the menu board. Operation slim down is officially over.

CHAPTER 5

Natasha

IT'S BEEN FOUR DAYS. Four days of nothing since I saw him go up the stairway to hell. My mind is torturing me with visions of him with those two girls and what went on upstairs. The way he touched the blonde one with the backs of his fingers. Every time I close my eyes, I see it and it kills me. The way he smiled at her with the cigarette between his teeth, the way he cracked his neck. That's the worst one, it rolls my stomach. I feel sick at the thought.

A broken heart is lonely business, and no one can take away the hurt. I feel so alone. I haven't left the house other than to work, haven't slept. I have however eaten everything on the southern side of the planet; there's a lot to be said for comfort eating. I am full stomached and empty hearted. The emptiness is overwhelming.

As I wait for the bartender to serve me my drink, I notice Bridge and Abbs discussing a man standing next to me at the bar. I roll my eyes and shake my head at them. Determination doesn't come close to the scheming these two are doing tonight. We are at the Ivy, our favorite nightclub, and I am pimped up to the nines. I'm in a tight charcoal strapless dress and black stiletto ankle boots, their choice of course. I feel like Prostitute Barbie with my hair all out and full, not to mention the hooker makeup they have applied. They both want me to pick up a random guy and have a one-night stand. I have been forced to listen to the benefits of this for two frigging days.

They think I am only under the influence of Joshua because he has been my only one, which is probably true. I told them if they find a guy who can get me hot then I will do it. However, I know this is not an easy feat. If it was, I would have done it years ago. Apparently, it should be someone I don't know, but the thought of that scares me a bit. What if I get back to his house and he's a serial killer? There are a few guys who I do know and sort of like and I know like me, maybe I should do it with one of them. I can't believe I am even considering this. I sound like Abbie. She knows she will have sex later that night, by lunchtime that day, it's totally preconceived. The poor bastard she picks is in for it, whether he likes it or not. Though I'm sure he's not complaining.

Can I really do this? I shuffle forward in the line at the bar while I think. Let's recap, I haven't had sex in seven years. I think I'm in love with a total asshole who fucks multiple strippers at the same time. I close my eyes as I imagine the orgy. The human imagination can be so cruel. I shiver in contempt. I need to move on, and I think the girls might be right. I do need to take control of my life and I intend on doing it tonight. How in the hell am I going to get through it? I look around the room for divine intervention as I take a deep breath. Alcohol, that's the ticket. If I get drunk enough maybe it will take the edge off, calm my nerves so to speak. My turn comes around and I shuffle up to place my order.

"What will it be?" asks a pretty girl with massive boobs. Um, am I really going to do this? Oh shit, fuck it.

"I'll have six Tequilas please."

Joshua

I look around at the women seated around Ben and me at the Ivy on the deep leather lounges in a half circle. We have been here a few times—it seems Adrian's club of choice. I'm not a fan really, the women are all desperate and money–hungry. They can smell my wallet from a mile off, attractive enough though. I smile at Ben as I listen to the two girls either side of him compliment his accent. "Ben, you sound so gorgeous when you say that, can you say it again?" My eyes roll. God, why does he tell them his real name? I rub the side of my pointer backwards and forwards over my lips, my elbow resting on the armrest as I listen to the small talk. I take a sip of my Cointreau and ice. I really would rather go, this redhead next to me is annoying as fuck.

"So, do you have an accent?" she gushes.

"No, I don't."

"Do you live near here?"

"No," I answer again, deadpan. I can't even pretend to be interested; in fact I'm being quite rude. Ben flashes me a dirty look; he's obviously interested here. I frown as I rub my eyes— where the fuck is Adrian? He drags me here then pisses off, fucking typical.

"So, you live in America?" she asks. I nod as I take a sip. This is unbearable. I'm going to the bar, as anything is better than sitting here with this idiot. I stand and walk to the bar without an explanation. I'm not going there. Ben is on his own with this one. Adrian finally appears through the crowd and walks over to me. He takes my drink from me and sips my Cointreau. I scowl at him, and he gives me a devious smile over the rim of the glass.

"Natasha's here."

My eyes go wide. "What," I snap. "Where?"

"Downstairs dancing." Before I can stop myself, I am striding towards the stairs. Adrian is running beside me like the personal assistant that he is.

"Did she see you?"

"No," he shakes his head. My heart has started racing at just the mention of the fucking bitch's name. I stop on the stairs and Adrian runs into the back of me.

"Ow, what are you doing?" he snaps.

I turn to him, "Did you know she would be here?"

"No, I hoped," he smiles. "Bridget told me they often come here."

"When?"

"At the wedding."

I tilt my head. "Why?"

"Because you haven't slept or eaten since we saw her in the restaurant on Tuesday. And you're a total nightmare to be around."

"Fuck off. Excuse me if I don't want to play happy family with her new boyfriend."

"He's not her boyfriend, I already told you this. Who do you think you're speaking to? I know you better than anyone," he snaps back.

"Fuck off," I mutter as I continue down the stairs, two at a time. We arrive at the lounge next to the dance floor and I go straight to the bar. I'm not up for this shit tonight. I need another drink to temper my sexual attraction for her before it becomes an addiction. Whatever you call it, it's a fucking nightmare. Adrian comes up beside me. I can't even look at her—my nerves are shot.

"Do you see her?" I ask softly, as I keep my eyes face forward. "Yes," he smiles. As I hand him his drink he points with his chin. "She's over there with Bridget and another blonde girl." He cranes his neck and does a low whistle, "Fuck, she looks hot, Josh."

With that comment I can't help myself, I have to look. I turn to see her laugh out loud with a carefree flick of her hair and my insides melt. I love the way she laughs. I miss the way she laughs. Those dimples do me in, every time. She's perfect, my eyes swipe down her from head to toes. Looks hot is the understatement of the year—she looks fucking edible. My cock immediately twitches to attention. Why in the hell does she affect me like this? She's wearing a tight dress that shows every curve on that beautiful body, and those tits. I haven't seen her dressed like this before—she's asking for it. Actually, she may be begging for it by the end of the night, either that or begging me to stop. I smile as that thought crosses my mind. My eyes drop as her long muscular legs demand my attention in those sky-high boots. Boots that belong around my ears while I bury myself deep inside that beautiful tight... This isn't good.

I rub my face and turn back to the bar. Seriously fucked–up shit going on here. This is unbearable. I need to get the hell out of here before I do something that I will regret. Something that will entail her being bent over the bar while I take her from behind. Hard. Where did that come from? I rub my forehead as cold sweat breaks my brow. I can feel my willpower slipping inch by inch, moment by moment. The brain in my cock overtakes the gears of my brain, too much blood in one part, not enough in the other. Shit.

"Go and talk to her," Adrian urges.

"Are you kidding? No." I glance back as she turns her back to me and starts to dance. God that ass, fuck me. What I could do to it. My cock gets harder. This happened at the wedding, and the last time I saw the bitch. Just the sight of her and I could orgasm. My heart starts racing again at the thought of what sex would be like with her. Fuck, it's almost primal. My eyes flick back again, the urge of ownership over her that fills me is disturbing. I need to go home before I drag her kicking and screaming out of here.

Natasha

I'm well on my way to drunken heaven by my fifth drink and fourth shot. I think I will be unconscious before I'm able to come through with the goods though. I'm finding it hard to even dance with men, knowing what the night might hold. How do people do this regularly? At this point in my life, celibacy in a monastery is alluring. And the men. Seriously, is this the best we've got? Not a single person here interests me.

Todd, a guy we know, is paying me extra attention. I think he is scenting action, either that or my suspicions tell me Abbie has told him I like him. Liar. Why is he so short? Actually, he isn't that short—it's just that I'm attracted to Amazonian men, six foot two being my cut off, or maybe six foot four like Joshua. *Stop it, you idiot.* Todd has started following me around and dancing a little too close. He keeps talking to me and because it's so loud he has to talk into my ear. He keeps lingering a little too long after he speaks, waiting for a reaction. How in the hell do I get out of this? I'm starting to feel uncomfortable. I head to the bathroom to try and gain some distance and give myself time to think. As I sit on the toilet with the lid closed, I give myself a pep talk. Come on, Natasha, snap out of it. It's now or never. I do suppose Todd is as good as anybody, at least there is absolutely no chance of falling in love with the dick. And, anyway, even if Josh did want me, do I really want to live my life having slept with one person? That's just stupid, really stupid. I finish up and wash my hands and it's with the last thought in my mind that I look at myself in the mirror. He doesn't want you, Natasha, move the hell on.

Thirty minutes later and with a serious pep talk from Abbs under my belt I find myself dancing with Todd. We have moved across the whole dance floor towards the back wall, as he keeps moving forward and I keep moving back. I can't help it. I'm really trying, but I'm just not into him at all. Just when I think it can't get any worse, he slides his hand down the length of my arm and grabs my hand. I look down at our entwined fingers and I know I have to make a decision. Sink or swim Natasha, what's it going to be? He moves in for a kiss, but I duck my head and he rests his lips on my forehead.

"Natasha, look at me," he puts his finger under my chin to bring my face up to his.

"Fuck off!" I jump back in shock. My eyes widen as they fly up to Joshua who is breathing heavily and glaring at Todd. "I said Fuck off!" he repeats. Oh shit, impeccable timing, where did he come from?

"Joshua, stop it," I stammer. Immediately my heart races at the sight of him. Todd goes to grab my hand, but I pull it away.

"Don't, Todd," I shake my head. Abbie is aware of the impending situation and quickly comes to my rescue, grabbing Todd's hand and leading him away.

And there he stands, all 6 foot 4 inches of male perfection. Testosterone is obviously coursing through his veins as he sucks in precious air to try and calm himself. And here I stand, absolutely off the charts thrilled that my knight in shining armor has come for me. The smile on my face is nearly beaming off my face. He grabs me around the waist and jerks me to him.

"You find this funny?" he snaps.

"Yes," I smirk. That sounds ridiculous. I should be mad, I should be fuming. What I am is thoroughly thrilled. Just the sight of him, no wonder I'm not attracted to anyone else. He's beyond beautiful, even when he is acting like a psychopathic maniac. He pulls me close and wraps his large arms around me, then he puts his lips to my temple.

"Stop making me act crazy," he whispers as his hands clasp the back of my waist.

"Act crazy, you are crazy." I do wide eyes at him to accentuate my point as I smile.

"And that is funny because?" He looks puzzled.

"I attract crazy people, Josh." The alcohol is finally starting to kick in and I find myself woozy on my legs.

"Were you going to fuck him?" he snarls in my ear. I step back, shocked and hurt that he would think that, although it could have been true. I shake my head.

"Liar," he snaps. His voice has dropped several degrees. He snarls again. "Tell me," as he gives me a jerk.

"Josh, stop it, let me go." He's beginning to frighten me. I try to pry his hands from around my waist. "Stop it," I repeat.

"So, you want to be fucked tonight, do you?" he whispers in my ear as he grabs a fistful of my hair and pulls my head back. Goosebumps scatter over my body as his breath blows onto my neck. He jerks me again. "Answer me." My eyes dilate as I look at his lips. I can't help it, I slowly lick my lips and look back up into his eyes. Yep, alcohol's taken the inhibitions alright, too bad it's with the wrong man.

"Kiss me," I whisper. He stills.

"What?"

"Kiss me," I repeat.

"That's not a good idea," he whispers.

"Why not?" I ask.

"Because if I kiss you, I won't be able to stop."

"Then don't," I whisper again. Oh no, dog on heat act 2 happening here.

"If I kiss you, in about two minutes you will be flat on your back on the bar with those sexy little boots around my ears, while I fuck you so damn hard you won't remember your name." Mmm, that sounds good. I look to the bar as the visual picture rolls in my head. My breath catches and I slowly look back at him. He narrows his eyes at me.

"You like the sound of that?" he frowns. I slowly nod and smile as I bite my bottom lip, and my blood heats further. The next thing he is on me. I'm pushed up against the back wall as his tongue dives into my mouth. His grip on my hair is painful, as he moves my head to bite my neck. His magnificent strength takes me over and his hand runs down the length of my body and moves up my skirt hitching my leg around his waist. I am losing all coherent thought and the word hoe rolls around in my head as I imagine what we must look like. People talk about girls who do this in public. The backs of his fingers skim my G-string, and he breathes heavily into my ear. Once again, he takes my lips in a seductive slow pattern as he slowly slips his fingers under my G-string and rubs the backs of his fingers through my dripping wet sex.

His eyes close. "Fuck," he whispers. Oh yes, what this man

does to me. He moves his hand and grabs my behind as he pulls me forward into his waiting hard cock. God, I want it. I want it now. We are suddenly bumped from the side. I look up to see Josh looking at someone over my shoulder. He looks down at me and gives me a quick kiss on the lips.

"Go home, naughty girl." I frown and then he pushes me to the side as Todd comes in with a punch. *What the hell?* I feel like I am in a scene from fight club. Joshua and Todd are in a full-on fist fight in the middle of the dance floor. I am getting bustled around by the crowd when I feel a hand grab my arm and pull me free. I turn and see Adrian looking very concerned. "Natasha, come with me." I nod and follow him off the dance floor just as I see Ben run onto it. He separates the fight, but the bouncers have a hold of the two of them and drag them off somewhere. Ben follows.

Holy shit, what the fuck just happened?

CHAPTER 6

Natasha

WHAT ON EARTH does it mean when you see a man at a wedding, and he kisses you...passionately? Then the next time you see him he tells you to fuck off...Unnecessarily, and then you are forced to watch him fondle a stripper... Painfully. The next time you see him he tells you he wants to fuck you so hard on the bar you won't remember your name...most orgasmically, only to not call you for four days? I sit at my desk tapping the end of my pencil, as I go over the case notes of the nut job I can't stop fantasizing about. It's been four days and I have to say it's exactly as I expected— doesn't he know how to use a fucking phone? What's with the hardcore act? I'm so over it. I know he's attracted to me—does he really think I can't feel it? I could cut the air with a knife when we are together, the sexual chemistry is blanket thick. Like nothing I've ever felt. When he's away from me, however, it is totally another story. I can't read him at all.

How come he doesn't call me? I put my head into my hands. Ring, damn you! I glare at my phone trying to send a telepathic message through it to him. My google alert on Monday morning did its job and alerted me at 8.00 am that Joshua had in fact spent the night in jail after being arrested on Saturday night. Obviously, something else must have happened with Todd after the bouncers stepped in. I hope he's not hurt. What if he gets charged? He's probably pissed at me... again. Well good, 'cause I'm getting pretty pissed off myself here. Who the hell does he think he is? If he wants to start a fight, he's going the right way about it, the asshole. How dare he interrupt my night with promises of passion and legs over shoulders only to tell me to go home? Which I did of course, like a lap dog secretly hoping he would turn up there. I wonder how long he was watching me, as he seemed to step in just in the nick of time. I can't help but imagine what would have gone down if Todd the idiot hadn't stepped in.

Perfect bloody timing, Todd, good one.

By Friday I am sick of the sight of myself and have just about slipped into a carbohydrate coma so after work I head to the gym. I've put on three stress kilos since a certain Mr. Stanton reentered my life and the joke of it is, I actually reprimand people all day about the repercussions of comfort-eating. When in fact I should be teaching them how to do it right. I hammer myself on the treadmill for forty minutes only to get off and feel faint. I drain my water bottle and head to my locker to retrieve my belongings and check my phone. Nope, still hasn't called. *Asshole.* I have three missed calls from Bridget though. I head down the stairs as I dial her number.

She answers at the first ring.

"Hi Tash."

"Hi, what's up?"

"Nothing, just checking in."

I lean on the side of my car as I take her call. "Where are you?" I ask.

"Um," she sounds evasive.

"So, where are you?" I repeat.

"I'm at Josh's."

"What?" I snap.

"He's not here," she quickly adds.

"Where is he?" I immediately ask.

"I'm not sure, I'm with Cameron and Will."

"Oh, that's right," I reply, disappointed. Josh's two younger brothers are staying with him for the week. Mum had told me this, although I had forgotten. "Say hi for me," I whisper.

"I will," she smiles down the phone. I pull my jacket around my shoulders as the cold air chills me.

"Do you want to come out tonight?" she asks.

"Where to?" I ask.

"The boys have tickets for some show, and they bought some extra tickets in case we want to come."

I smile at the two muscle men leaving the gym. "Oh, I don't know, I told Abbs I would catch a movie."

"No, I've spoken to her. She's keen to come to this show."

"Oh," I answer flatly. "Is Josh coming?" I scrunch my eyes shut as I say it, knowing how desperate I sound.

"No, the boys said he's going to some kickboxing thing." She lowers her voice so they can't hear her. "If you come, we might be able to get some info on him," she whispers. I nod as her plan rolls around in my head. This is true—they are staying with him so maybe I can find out if he is seeing someone else.

"Do you think they know anything?"

"Of course, they must. Brothers talk, don't they?"

Three hours later, I find myself at the Luna Park Convention Centre with Abbie, Bridget, Cameron and Will. We grab some drinks from the bar and head to our seats. As we are walking to our seats, I notice the crowd is all mostly male and a bit rough around the edges.

"Why did we come here again?" I frown at Bridget as we walk through the rows of numbered seating. "What are we seeing?" Bridget hunches her shoulders.

"Beats me. Cam, what are we seeing?" she asks.

"Josh is fighting tonight." I stop dead in my tracks. Cameron and Will turn to face me.

"Fighting," I repeat. "What, what do you mean?" I am shocked, this was not in the brochure.

"He is in a cage fight tonight." Will starts to laugh at the distress on my face.

"Cage fight," I repeat.

"Yeah," Cameron nods.

"That's crazy talk, you can't be serious?" My eyes are bulging out of their sockets. Will laughs again.

"He's done it before, Natasha. Chill."

"Josh," I repeat. They nod. "Josh, Josh. Like our Josh."

"Apparently, he is pretty good. I haven't seen him, but Will has in America. He kicks ass."

I put my hands up to my face and push on my cheeks. Oh my God, this isn't happening.

"Are you mad?" I whisper.

"I can't watch Josh in a cage fight. What if he gets hurt?" Bridget looks from me to Abbie and starts to giggle.

"Since when has Josh been cage-fighting?" she asks Will. "This is ridiculous."

He shrugs. "I don't know, maybe six months."

"Why?" I ask.

"I don't know. He likes it I suppose." He smiles.

"What, he likes bashing the shit out of people?" I frown.

Cameron and Will laugh. "Yes, exactly." They keep shuffling up the row to our seats while checking the numbers on the tickets.

I stand still. "I don't think I can stay," I whisper to Abbie. I feel like I am going to be sick.

She shakes her head. "Just stay for a bit and then I will come with you."

"Ok, deal." In quick succession I scull my drink and head to the bar for something stronger. I stand in line at the bar and take in my surroundings. There are massive screens around the perimeter and two bars fully stocked with all the trimmings.

The crowd is eclectic from age eighteen and up. I notice more women seem to be lingering at the bar, probably escaping the brutality of this horrible place. I hear the crowd roar and my eyes are drawn to the big screen to see two men in capes walk into the fighting arena. They remove their capes, looking like body builders or something. *Jeez.* I look away from the screen suddenly panicked at what I am about to witness, and the crowd goes wild again.

My eyes are once again drawn back to the screen, my heart racing. The two men touch fists and then start to push each other around, inciting the other to make the first move. One man is of European descent, maybe Italian or something, and the other is bald but very Anglo Saxon, maybe English, but it's hard to tell. Shit, this is hard to watch, but I find I can't look away. These men are huge and aggressive, and they are fighting in a frigging cage in front of about 10,000 people. Every now and then they get too rough and the umpire steps in. They do seem pretty evenly skilled. I see what Cam means; it is sort of kickboxing. Although every now and then they connect and wrestle to the ground. I find I'm holding my breath. They would have to be hurting each other. I can almost feel the hits myself. I wince as a punch connects. I can't work it out, from what place deep inside does a person get the anger to get off on this shit? The adrenaline in their systems must be through the roof. How in the hell has Josh strayed so far from the man I knew? He does this, he does this for fun.

I run my hands through my hair as this information sinks in. I honestly don't know him anymore. I haven't a frigging clue who in the hell he is. He isn't the smart, witty, surfie guy I fell in love with. He's morphed into a smoking, stripper–loving, cage–fighting bad boy. Who, unfortunately, I find totally fascinating and not to mention utterly gorgeous. There is definitely nothing left of my Josh though, my beautiful gentle Josh. The thought saddens me deep to my bones. I'm grieving for a man that no longer exists. A man who for reasons beyond my control I can no longer reach.

It is with a heavy heart and a clear mind that I buy the drinks and head back to our seats. Perhaps this is a good thing, the realization of the current events. I suppose that in all honesty it is definitely better for both of us that we never hook up again. We are related after all. I just wish I didn't have this visceral attraction to him, it's becoming embarrassing, and damn hard to control. On my return I am surprised to see Abbie and Bridget standing and cheering with the boys. Oh no, they are getting into it, and Abbie is wolf-whistling. They are going for

Mr. Italy and he seems to be coming out on top. A few more rounds and finally the ref steps in and announces Mr. Italy the victor. The crowd goes wild. Abbie and Bridget are jumping up and down on their seats. They are so annoying. I am sitting, head down, playing on my phone. I could not be more distracted if I tried. After the fight is over there is a ten–minute break until the next one. Cam sits back with his arm over the backs of the chairs. The others are all standing.

"Tash, are you ok?" he smiles behind everyone's legs. I nod. Though at the moment I really don't think I am. The dam in my throat is threatening to burst. It's all too much—how much more can I take? He holds out his hand to me and I grab it. He squeezes it in a reassuring gesture.

"He will be ok," he whispers, and my eyes widen at him. Does he know? As if he can read my thoughts, he nods his head.

"Yes, I know," he answers.

My eyes widen. "How long?" I whisper. He stays silent and looks at me, slowly stands and moves over past the others to sit beside me. He sits down and puts his arm around me but doesn't answer, then pulls me in and kisses my forehead.

"How long Cam?" I repeat. He blows out a breath and shrugs his shoulders. "Please," I beg.

"All along," he sighs. "I've known all along." I put my hand over my mouth. Tears fill my eyes, I'm so ashamed.

"Hey, stop it." He squeezes my shoulder, "It's ok."

"No Cam, it's not ok." I hang my head. "How do you know?" I ask, my quivering voice revealing my oncoming tears.

"We all know," he shrugs his shoulders.

What. "Who's we?" I ask, horrified.

"My brothers." Oh God. "And my mother."

What the fuck! "Your mother," I stammer once again, putting my hand over my mouth. "How, but why, but how?"

He smiles at my babbling. "Let's just say, Josh didn't handle it very well when you broke up with him." My heart drops for the ten thousandth time this week.

"What do you mean?" I ask, as the tears once again burn the backs of my eyes.

He shakes his head. "I've said enough already, speak to Josh." He gives me a sympathetic smile as if he knows what torture I am going through at the moment.

"Josh is acting weird, Cam," I whisper.

He nods. "I know, you make him crazy." He takes a gulp of his beer as he looks straight ahead. The next fight starts and once again the deafening music begins, and the crowd jumps to their feet. I stay seated. My mind is in a total jumble. He didn't handle it well, what does that mean? I pinch my bottom lip as I think. Abbie climbs over the seats to get back next to me. She's having the time of her life.

"Check this out." She hands me the binoculars and I shake my head.

"No thanks." I hold up my hands. "I'm good."

"Ok, you're missing out, these guys are hot." I roll my eyes, whatever. She really is acting like a little kid.

"Smell that testosterone!" Abbie inhales deeply while holding her stomach and Cameron and Wilson burst out laughing.

"See, I told you girls you would love this shit." I am totally distracted. I am not even watching what's going on. His mother knows, *bitch*. I was right—she has been rubbing my face in it all these years. Bridget returns from the bar with more drinks, two for me. I look up and she gives me a sympathetic smile and a wink. She must have overheard the conversation between Cam and me. I nod as I take my drinks.

"Thanks, babe," I whisper. She bends and gives me a kiss on the top of my head and then wrecks it by running her hand through my hair and messing it up. I swat her away as I giggle. I am distracted from my disturbing thoughts of not handling things well by Will yelling.

"Here he comes." I stand up instinctively. Oh shit, my hand flies up to my mouth. I go to walk out but Cameron grabs my jacket.

"Stay," he yells over the crowd. I swallow and nod, what a total nightmare. Joshua is wearing a black robe sort of thing and he is followed by a man who is talking to him.

"Who's that?" I yell across to Will.

"That's his trainer," he yells back.

"How do you know?" I ask.

"I met him in LA."

"Oh what, he travels with Josh?" Cam nods.

"Yeah, he goes where Josh goes." I frown. Cam shakes his head and smiles. "You know, life of the rich and famous, entourage and all that."

I nod, I really have no clue what's going on, do I? I am still trying to digest the whole entourage thing when he takes off his cape. *Sweet mother of God.* Every single muscle on his body is visible to my eyes, he's so cut.

"Holy shit!" Abbie yells so close to my ear that she nearly bursts my ear drum. I pull away and frown as I clap my hand over my ear. "You could grate cheese on that stomach." I nod, shocked at the fine specimen before me. He turns and I see a massive tattoo running from his hip bone up the length of his torso on his side.

"He's inked," Abbie whispers. She grabs the binoculars

from Will and looks at the stage. I am still staring dumbstruck at him. Fuck, he's hot. Seriously, how can anyone be so goddamn attractive? I look over at Abbie and she has handed the binoculars to Bridget who is now looking at the stage. She pulls the binoculars down, her face filled with horror.

"Fuck off," Bridget whispers, her eyes bulging.

Cameron bursts out laughing. "I've been waiting for you to see that."

"What?" I snap. She hands me the binoculars. I look at the stage and see him deep in conversation with his trainer. What are they going on about? He turns and all of the blood drains from my face. The ink isn't a picture as I first thought. Joshua has the word Natasha in running writing down the whole length of his body.

Holy Fuck.

CHAPTER 7

Natasha

My eyes are seeing it, but I don't believe it. Why in the hell would he do that? Before I can apply my brain to mouth filter, I call Will over to me. "When did he get that?"

He shrugs. "A couple of years ago."

"How many?"

"How many what?"

"Years?"

"Um, I don't know, three or four."

"Is it me?" I frown.

"Of course, it's you." I sit back down, my mind now officially in overdrive. We haven't been together for seven years, so why three or four years ago? Abbie comes over, cuddles me and whispers in my ear.

"Looks like you're not the only fucked up one, Tash." The crowd goes wild and I immediately stand to see what's going on. Joshua is going ballistic, kicking and punching this guy. I think he's trying to kill him. Good grief, he's so aggressive. I sit back down and put my hands over my eyes. This is unbearable. He's going to jail again tonight, probably for life. After what seems like an eternity, the fight finishes, and Joshua is announced the victor to the once again screaming crowd. I, however, am furious. What in God's name does he think he's doing here? This is definitely not a sport; this is barbaric. The kind of shit you see on cable.

"Can we go?" I ask Cameron.

He smiles and nods. "I'm just going to go to the bathroom, then we will head out." He disappears up the steps two at a time. Abbie and Bridge flop down onto the chairs either side of me.

"OMG," Bridget whispers. "Let's talk about Josh's tatt."

"Let's not," I reply.

"Why are you so pissy?" she asks.

"Are you serious?" I snap. "This is bullshit."

"What's bullshit?"

"This," I gesture at the arena around us. "This isn't fucking kickboxing. This is how to kill a person in fifteen minutes."

She nods, "But it's totally hot, right?" I shake my head in disgust at her.

"You're an imbecile," I snap. Will's phone rings and he smiles and talks to someone on the other end and hangs up.

"Cam's too lazy to walk back so we have to meet him at the door." We nod and join the queue to get out. Ten minutes later, I have a tipsy friend on either side of me linking my arms as we head towards the exit. Abbie is still going on about banging Mr. Italy and asking Will to go and find him to tell him the mother of his children is waiting for him, presuming that's her. Will is very wisely declining to do it, although he is finding it quite funny.

"I thought you were the mother of my children," he says as he elbows her in the stomach.

"Hell no," she replies. "I'm way, way, way, way," she moves her hand around in the air "too hot for you," and she pokes him in the chest. Abbie and I are in fits of giggles. She really does know how to take my mind off things. Cameron joins us from the left and Bridget grabs his arm to link with hers, then we walk a little bit further before Cam stops and turns around.

"What are you doing?" he yells out. We all turn at once to see who he is talking to. Joshua is standing still in the middle of the crowd, glaring at us. He is in faded blue jeans and a white

T–shirt and has an gym bag with the strap across his body on one shoulder. Perspiration is still beading on his forehead, a side effect from the exertion of the fight. He takes a sip from the bottle of water in his hand. The veins in his forearms are pumping, no doubt from the adrenaline in his system. My mouth goes dry. Why does he have to be so damn attractive? His piercing blue eyes bore into me and he has a slight sheen of perspiration all over his skin, adding to the whole alluring effect. *Damn it.* He is radiating anger and glares at Cam as he storms past us.

"What's wrong with you?" Cam asks. He turns to talk to Cam but speaks directly to me.

"What in the fuck is she doing here?"

Will steps in front of me. "Stop being a prick, Josh. She's here with us." My cheeks heat with embarrassment. I turn and start storming to the cab rank. I have never been so humiliated. Abbie and Bridget scuttle after me, both of the boys staying with Josh.

"You're not to hang out with her, I told you that." I stop and turn. That's it. My blood has boiled. Who in the hell does this guy think he is? Master of the universe? I will not take one more fucking minute of his shit. I storm back to where he is standing and push him hard in the chest. "What is your problem?" I yell, and he staggers back.

"You are, actually!" he yells back.

I scowl. "Who in the fuck are you, and what have you done with my Josh?" I scream.

He comes up really close to my face and yells. "He isn't your Josh."

"No, I know he isn't. This version is a giant, aggressive, stripper-groping prick who I can't stand the sight of." Everyone falls silent.

"Burned," Will giggles.

Josh and I both look at him and yell "Shut up," in perfect timing.

"Stripper-groping," he repeats.

"What's that supposed to mean?"

"Natasha, leave it," Bridget steps in. "Let's go." She can see this is about to get ugly, really ugly.

"I mean, asshole," I scream in his face, "I was at the strip club last week, and I saw your little display with the blonde whore. How was the threesome?" He narrows his eyes and steps back as he weighs up my words.

"What, are you spying on me now?" he sneers.

"Don't flatter yourself," I scream. "It seems to me you are spying on me. What's with the nightclub caveman act, Josh? Why in the hell did you hit Todd like that?"

He stops still and stays deathly silent.

"Todd, is it?" he sneers. I don't answer. Ok, that was the wrong thing to say.

"So, Todd is the poor bastard you're currently fucking, is he? I thought as much."

Cameron steps in, "Josh, just go home. You're being a dick."

"Fuck off, Cameron. I'm talking to Natasha—this is a private conversation," his voice dripping with sarcasm.

He leans into my face. "You can go and tell your little friend Todd that if I see him again, I'm going to beat the living shit out of him. I hope you were worth it."

"Fuck off, Josh, I'm not seeing him. You're acting crazy. I've a good mind to get you admitted."

He fumes. "Oh yes, I bet your little fuck buddy from work would love that too."

"What so, I'm fucking everybody in Sydney now am I? You idiot," I yell.

"It wouldn't surprise me," he yells and, that's it, I snap. That is the last straw—I no longer have any control. I slap him hard across the face, the sound echoing back as it hits the buildings on either side of us. He grabs me by the shoulders and shakes me, his fury erupting as mine has. The others quickly step in and break us up, pushing us apart. I glare at him and he glares at me.

"Stay the fuck away from me!" I yell.

He folds his arms. "Now, who's flattering themselves, you couldn't pay me enough to touch you." I don't know why I'm shocked he just said that, but I am.

I shake my head at him. "Nice, Josh, nice. You must be so proud of the person you've turned into. You were a lot nicer when you were poor. What a mean, pretentious prick you've turned into." I turn and storm off. In the distance I can hear Cam and Will giving Josh a hard time about what he has said to me. The girls quickly catch up and we join the cab line. We hear Cam yell out, "Sorry, girls," as they get into the back of a limo waiting outside the arena for them. It drives off. We all stay silent for a few minutes.

"That went well," Abbie smiles. "Isn't it a shame he can talk

— he's so pretty with his mouth closed." We all burst out laughing.

"Seriously, Abbs, I love you".

I smile. I'm warm and crumpled and sleepy, my eyes refusing to open. Why is she so frigging early? My doorbell buzzes again. "Go away, I'm too tired," I mumble into my pillow. BUZZZ BUUUU-UUZZZZZZZZZZZ BZ, BZ, BZ, BZ, BZ. It's still pitch-black in my bedroom—those expensive drapes were worth every cent. It buzzes again. For Pete's sake. Alright. I pull my weary ass out of bed and stagger to the foyer. I hit the door button to unlock my front door as I head to the bathroom for my morning wee. I hear Bridget come in and I instantly yell to her

"Why are you up so early? Did you wet the bed? Make me some coffee, bitch, and you can forget it. I'm not going to Mum and Dad's this morning." I look at my watch on the bathroom vanity. "Bridget, it's only 7.30 am. Have you gone frigging mad?" I know why she's here so early. She thinks I'm a donkey on the edge and, to be honest, she could be onto something. I feel scattered. She doesn't reply. I hear the teaspoon hit three times on the side of the coffee cup. I waltz out of my bathroom while stretching and yawning. I feel like shit. I open my eyes from my stretch to see Joshua standing in my lounge room with two cups of coffee. *What the.*

"Joshua...what are you doing here?" He looks me up and down and smirks.

"Nice pjs." Oh my fuck. I look down to realize I am wearing odd flannel pajamas. Checkered bottoms and bunny top and to cap off the whole alluring look the buttons are done up in the wrong button holes. I scratch my head in embarrassment, only to feel my hair standing up on end like the Paddle–pop Lion. I bet I have raccoon mascara eyes too. I must look like a treat. I'm too busy being mortified and self–conscious to remember how mad I am at him. I stay silent, waiting for him to say something, while praying for the earth to swallow me up.

"Um," he shuffles on his feet and passes me my coffee.

"Thanks," I whisper as I take it. He takes a sip while carefully choosing his words.

"I...I just came to apologize for last night." I stay silent.

"What exactly are you apologizing for?" I ask as I raise my eyebrows.

He thinks about his answer as he rubs his chin. "The insinuations," he drops his head in shame.

"The insinuation I'm a whore," I whisper.

He hangs his head. "Yes."

I sit down and gesture for him to sit down, but he stays standing. "Josh, why are you so angry with me?"

"I'm not."

I raise my eyebrows. "Are you going to continue to lie to me?"

He narrows his eyes. "Stay the hell out of my head, Natasha. I didn't come here to be psychoanalyzed."

"What did you come here for?"

"I told you, to apologize."

"Is that for my benefit or your conscience?"

"Stop it, you're doing it again."

"Doing what?" I snap.

"The psychology shit," he frowns. "Just forget it." He puts his coffee down on my table so fast it spills. "I knew there was no point."

Oh shit, he's going. I have to stop him.

"Josh, wait, I'm sorry. I'm just really mad at you." He stops and turns.

"For what?" He puts his head on an angle.

"I saw you last week at the strip joint." He rubs his chin again. Ah, my first sign he's uncomfortable. I'm really not playing fair— I'm totally psychoanalyzing him.

"Tash, what were you doing there?" His voice has gone soft, cajoling.

I look at the ground in embarrassment. "We were there to spy on Bridget's boyfriend, never in a million years did I think I would see you." He nods as he listens. I stay silent, trying to gather in my head what to say next.

"Natasha, I'm single," he murmurs.

"I know." I'm starting to feel emotional. Cut it out, crybaby. "Would you have gone up the stairs if you had known I was there?"

"You know I wouldn't have," he says gently.

"Josh, I can't handle you being so aggressive towards me."

He nods. "Me neither. I'm sorry. I've been acting like a prick." I smile and he smirks back in return.

"You have. You can take me out to breakfast to apologize if you want."

He frowns as he looks me up and down. "I might just take you pajama shopping too."

"What's wrong with my pajamas?" I smirk.

"Nothing if you live in a nursing home." He does wide eyes to accentuate his point.

"Give me ten minutes," I smile. He nods and flops onto the couch.

Ten minutes later, I am showered and in my room hyperventilating about what I am going to wear. Alluring and sexy without trying hard is a fine line, one that I have to execute to perfection. Shit, where are my favorite jeans? Damn it, in the dirty washing basket. It doesn't pay to be lazy.

I settle on a pair of faded worn blue jeans, a slouchy white T-shirt that hangs off one shoulder, white flip flops and a wad of chunky gold bangles. My chocolate-brown layered hair that is midway between my shoulders and elbows is loose and my makeup is natural.

"Ready?" I ask as I head into the lounge room where he is waiting. He smiles and nods. His eyes scan me up and down, his jaw ticks and he gently cracks his neck. Hmm. As he stands my heart jumps a beat. Dear God, he really is divine. He is wearing dark green army-style cargo pants and a black slimfit plain T-shirt with a V-neck. I can see every damn muscle in his arms. His big blue eyes lock onto mine and I feel it impossible to look away. The sexual energy beaming from his body is demanding attention from mine. His dark tanned skin and square jaw only highlight his big bee-stung lips. Everything about him is silently screaming sex to my body. My stomach flutters with nerves. How in the hell am I going to get through breakfast without jumping him? Bridget is right—he does smell fucking awesome. I made myself a promise years ago, that if I ever had a chance to spend time with Joshua again, I would be nothing but totally honest. Can I really do this? Never again in my life am I going through the disappointment in myself for lying to him. I couldn't bear it. He smiles.

"Let's go then."

"I'm nervous, Josh."

He stops and turns to me. "Nervous," he repeats on a frown.

I nod again. "What about?" he gently asks.

"Do you think we still have anything in common?"

He shrugs. "I don't know. I think it's pretty obvious we both have hot tempers."

I smile. "Yes."

"And I'm hungry and tired because I didn't sleep much last night," he smiles.

"Me too," I whisper.

He holds up his arm for me to take. "I think that's a good start, don't you?" I nod and link my arm with his.

"Let's go." I smile. I feel better already. His eyes twinkle as he gives me a warm smile, one that could melt the whole of Antarctica, and I instantly feel at ease. The unseen tension has immediately disappeared, and we have both noticeably relaxed. Honesty. He wants honesty. As soon as I told him I was nervous the tension disappeared. I need to remember this for future reference. We head down the stairs.

"How long have you owned the apartment?"

"Um, about six months I guess," I answer.

"It's a nice place." His eyes wander around the cream room with high ceilings. The large taupe lounge wraps around in a horse-shoe shape. A huge cane pendant light hangs low over the industrial coffee table and thick pile rug. "You have good taste."

"Thanks," I smile nervously at him.

Half an hour later, we are arriving at my favorite café, waiting to be seated by one of the waitresses. I can't help but notice the amount of attention Joshua gets from the female population. Every woman is taking a double look at him, but he doesn't even seem to notice. I'm sure he is used to this. I, however, am finding it a little annoying. I suppose it's not every day you see a six foot four muscled–up man whose chiseled jaw, olive skin and chocolate buzz–cut hair screams 'Do Me'. A pretty redhead shows us to our seat.

"Would you like to order some drinks?" She looks from me to him and back again.

"Yes, I'll have a tall latte, double shot," he smiles.

"I'll have a skim cap, please." She scribbles on her pad and leaves us alone.

He rests his elbows on the table and links his hands together under his chin, waiting for me to speak first. His eyes have a mischievous glow to them.

"So, Josh, tell me about your life."

He shrugs his shoulders. "What do you want to know?"

"I hear you're wealthy."

He smiles, "In some things."

I tilt my head on the side, "What do you mean?"

"Well, I have money. It depends on your definition of wealthy."

"Oh, I suppose. What's your definition?" I ask, surprised.

He shrugs again. "Happily married, healthy kids."

Smiling, I rest my chin on one hand while I find myself swooning at his feet. "Are you dating?" I ask.

He scrunches up his nose, "Hell no." Our drinks arrive and the waitress's eyes linger a little too long on Mr. Orgasmic here. I narrow my eyes at her. Ok, enough, buzz off.

"You?" I frown.

"Huh?"

"Are you dating?" I ask .

"No, nothing like that. Mum told me you had a boyfriend." I nod a little embarrassed.

"Um ex–boyfriend," I murmur.

"What happened? Why did you break up?"

I shrug. He smiles, "I see you're still a shit liar."

"I hoped you hadn't heard about that," I wince.

"What? Heard that some poor bastard asked you to marry

123

him and you knocked him back and then dumped his sorry ass?"

I put my hands over my face in embarrassment. "It sounds cold when you put it like that." I peek out from my hands to see him smirking at me.

"What happened?"

"We were never going to work out. I have never been so shocked in my life as the day he proposed. It was awful." His thumb is under his chin and he is wiping the side of his pointer across his lips as he listens while leaning back in his chair, his gaze locked onto mine.

"Why wouldn't you have worked out?"

"We weren't...compatible."

He raises his eyebrows. "Compatible," he repeats. *Why did I say that?* "You mean sexually?" His eyes darken with an emotion I'm familiar with. Arousal.

"Among other things," I quickly add. I suddenly feel very uncomfortable. "Why aren't you married?" I blurt out.

He smiles a slow sexy smile. "I haven't found anyone who fits the job description."

"What's the job description?" I breathe. His eyes bore into mine with an intensity that heats my blood.

"Someone who fucks like a slut, with the morals of a nun." I choke on my tea. Of all the things I thought he would say, that was definitely not it. I feel a familiar frisson of uneasiness creeping up on me.

"You can't be serious?" I gasp.

"Absolutely," he nods as he takes a sip of his latte, his eyes not leaving mine.

"You want to marry a slut?"

He nods again. "It depends what your definition of a slut is. What do you think a slut is?" he asks.

"Someone who will sleep with anyone," I reply.

He nods and takes another sip of his latte. "You see, I think a slut is a woman who loves to fuck." I swallow the large lump in my throat. His voice has dropped to a low husky sound, one that is screaming to my subconscious. He continues, "I couldn't be with a mousy woman who doesn't love to fuck as much as I do. I have an insatiable appetite for sex," he licks his lips. "High maintenance so to speak." His eyes burn into me once again, silently daring me to say something. His eyes drop to my lips. Want pools in my stomach. "The woman I marry will have to endure hours and hours of being tied up to our bed, legs spread wide while I pleasure her with my tongue and fuck her with my hands and then put up with me continually driving into her tight cunt with my cock so hard she won't know where I end and she begins. Only to be rolled over and taken again from behind. Constantly. She would have to love taking me orally and vaginally and anally... Repeatedly." He gazes at me again and steeples his hands under his chin.

For the love of God, my mouth has gone dry.

"Can I take your order, love?" I jump. Oh shit, did she just hear that?

"Um, bacon and eggs please, and an orange juice." I am embarrassed and put my head down to hide my blush.

"I'll have the same." He smirks a sexy smile at me. *Bloody hell.* Ok, my brain is fried. I can't even speak as I visualize exactly what he has explained to me. Orally, vaginally and anally, *shit.* To me that sounds like the exact thing I might like to do today. Is he trying to drive me out of my frigging head? He's not playing fair.

"So, precious." My eyes snap up at the nickname he used to call me. "Do you know anyone that you could put up for an interview?" I scowl at him. He's playing with me, the bastard. He knows exactly what he's doing.

"Yes, I do, actually," I reply. Actually, no I don't. Only me. I would rather cut off my left arm than put someone else up for that position. I scan my empty head for a witty comeback. Nope nothing, another 2 am regret coming up.

"Are you purposely trying to turn me on?" I whisper.

"Is that what I'm doing?" His gaze bores into me, burning holes with its heat.

"Yes," I whisper. "You know you are." He inhales a deep breath through his nose as he leans back in his chair and rearranges his penis unashamedly in his pants. My eyes drop down to between his legs and I swallow a golf ball again. Ok, if he gets away from me today without giving me what I need, I am going to need admitting myself tonight. "Why are you hard?" I can't help myself. I have to ask.

"I'm always hard when I talk about what I need in a wife."

"You have this conversation often?" I'm offended.

"No, first time," he smiles.

I narrow my eyes. "Bastard," I whisper. "Stop playing with me." He smiles as he takes another sip of his latte. Breakfast arrives and we eat in silence. He's seemingly relaxed, I'm practically panting at the visuals in my pea brain. Tied to a bed. *Damn,* yes please. "So, have you had any serious girl-friends?" He shakes his head as he takes another bite. "Why not?"

"I can't be monogamous so," he shrugs, "I guess it's not fair."

"Huh, what do you mean you can't be monogamous?"

"I've never been with just one person."

I frown. "What, never?" he shakes his head again. "How do you? I mean what, so these girls you...mess around with know they are one of many?"

"Pretty much." I stop eating and put my knife and fork down as I frown.

He smiles, "What's wrong with that?"

"You're a frigging pig." I answer.

He shrugs. "I like to think I'm honest."

"Seriously, so girls are happy to have you for half an hour and give you back?"

He puts his knife and fork down. "No, they get me for about four hours and when it's over I have nothing in common with them and I don't particularly want to spend time with them, so I leave."

I shake my head in disgust. "You know the way you just spoke about women makes me think I have absolutely nothing in common with you anymore."

He looks offended, "Are you kidding?"

"What?"

"You think what I do is any worse than what you do?"

"What do I do?"

He rolls his eyes at me. "Make men fall in love with you so much that they want to marry you and then you dump them when you get bored. No thanks, I would rather do it my way. Like I said, at least I don't hurt anyone." He raises an eyebrow.

"I'm sure these girls get hurt," I snap. Who in the hell does he think he is, anyway, frigging Dirk Diggler?

"Trust me, the kind of girls I go out with don't expect more."

I roll my eyes at him. "Can we just drop the subject because your mouth is seriously pissing me off?"

He smirks. "I thought you liked my mouth."

"No, actually, not anymore. It's a turn off to think how many women you've slept with." He looks down and he butters his toast while he processes my words but doesn't say anything.

He stays silent as I finish my breakfast. I know the last line I have just thrown him has hurt his feelings but I couldn't give a rat's ass. There is no way in hell I'm going back there if that's how much respect he has for girls he's intimate with. That's right, he doesn't even know what intimacy is. Yuk!

"Let's go," I say as I finish the last of my coffee. I stand and head to the cashier. He follows and puts his hand on my lower back. I squirm away. He pays and I head to the car.

"Where are you going?" he calls after me.

I turn to look at him. "You can take me home now, thanks." I turn back towards the car. I lean on the side of his Audi, my rear up against the door.

He leans on the car next to me. "Why are you mad?" he asks as he stares straight ahead.

"You have to ask?" I frown.

"Natasha, I'm not monogamous because I haven't found a girl I connected with."

"Why not?" I ask.

He shrugs, "I don't know. Maybe I never will." He gives me a weak smile. That does sound a little better than what he told me ten minutes ago.

"Why didn't you just say that instead of being so seedy?"

He bumps his shoulder into mine. "You don't like seedy?" he smirks.

"I hate seedy." I bite my bottom lip to stifle my smile. "Anyway, I thought I was taking you pajama shopping."

"What's wrong with my pajamas?" I gasp.

"You have to ask?" he smiles as he throws my line back at me. I narrow my eyes.

"Ok, but I'm picking, I want another flannel pair."

He feigns a disgusted face. "Flannel," he repeats. "I hate flannel."

"Well nobody sees my pajamas and I like them," I smile. His face drops.

"Why does nobody see your pajamas?"

I shrug and peek up at him, hating myself for revealing so much information. "It seems I have the opposite problem to you Josh." I quickly start to walk up the road. I am not having this conversation with him—how embarrassing. He doesn't follow. He stands still, and I know I've shocked him. I turn. "Are you coming?" I yell out.

He nods and starts toward me. He reaches me and links his arm with mine as we turn the corner. "How long?" he blurts out.

"What?" I ask.

"How long?" he asks again.

I shake my head. "I'm not having this conversation with you, Josh, forget it."

"Natasha, I need to know." He stops still.

"Why?" I frown.

"I just do," he repeats.

"Years, Josh, it's been years."

"Years," he repeats. "Why has, I mean that's not possible, I mean." He stops again still. He looks at me and all traces of amusement have left his face.

I can't help it, I giggle. "What?"

He looks shocked. "What's funny?"

"You are," I answer.

"How am I funny?"

"Why are you so shocked I haven't been with anyone for a long time?"

"You had a boyfriend for years. Do you expect me to believe you didn't sleep with him?"

"Believe what you want, you asked me."

"Why?" he whispers. I shrug. "Tell me" he demands. I stay silent, my eyes searching his. I want him to work this out for himself. He must know how I feel about him. Surely, he can't be that stupid.

"Listen, are you taking me shopping or not?" He nods. "Just drop the twenty questions ok."

He seems to regain his composure. "Ok," he nods. "Where to?"

"I have to buy a dress for a wedding in three weeks."

"Whose wedding?"

"A girl I went to uni with. Actually, will you come with me?"

"What, to the wedding?" he frowns.

I smile. "No, I don't think that's a good idea," he answers.

"Why not?"

"Because you know it's not like that between us anymore, Tash."

Did he just really say that? I fake a smile and rearrange my shirt to hide my hurt.

"I know but we are friends, aren't we?"

He nods. "Yes, but that's not what I meant."

"I know what you meant. If you don't want to come, I can ask Simon."

His face drops. "You want to ask Syral?"

I roll my eyes. "It's Simon. I'm sure he would love to pick up the slack," I whisper. I'm wicked. I'm so playing him right now. Come on, baby. Take the bait. "Well, if you won't come with me as a friend then I'm sure he would come as a friend. You know what I mean. Pick up the slack, so to speak." I smile sweetly at him.

His voice drops several degrees. "Are you threatening me?"

"What do you mean?" I quickly duck into a boutique to change the subject.

Ok, I've planted the seed. Let's watch it grow. He follows me and stands just to my left as I start to flick through the clothes on the rack. I can feel the heat radiating from his body. I inhale deeply, he sure does smell good. The idiotic shopgirl's jaw is on the ground as she stares, yes, stares at my shopping companion. I turn back to see what she is looking at. Joshua is leaning up against a pole with his hands behind his posterior and his eyes closed. He's obviously tired. I smile. Yes, if I saw a God like him in a store I would stare, too. He looks perfect and a disturbing thought enters my brain. I am totally punching above my weight here with him. Utterly gorgeous, crazy rich and so intense in the bedroom that he'd bring any woman with a pulse to her knees. Basically, he could pick out any woman he wants. And here I am thinking I can make him jealous with Simon, frigging Simon, the motormouth. What am I thinking? He opens his eyes on a start and quickly looks around. I give him a broad smile. He shuffles his feet and returns his own beaming smile and mouths the words, "Sorry, tired."

I nod. "Me too," I mouth back.

"Come, on," I grab his hand and lead him to the change rooms. The familiar heat rises from where we touch. He's on fire. I am armed with ten dresses, surely something will fit. I sit him on the large velvet chair just outside the change room. He doesn't seem to know the drill.

"You want me to sit here?" he asks.

I nod and smile. "Yes, haven't you been shopping for girl's clothes before?"

He does wide eyes at me. "No, why would I?"

"What about other girlfriends?" I look puzzled.

He smiles a broad smile as he runs his hand through his hair. "So, you're my other girlfriend now?"

I smirk, embarrassed at my slip–up. "You know what I mean."

He nods. "No, I avoid shopping at all costs. The only person who drags me shopping is Adrian and that's a painful experience. I would rather have my teeth pulled out." I head into the changing room.

Thirty minutes later I have tried all of my dresses on. Josh has been the perfect gentleman and waited for me, without as much as a whine. He hasn't even asked to see what I'm trying on which is basically a prerequisite when shopping with someone. The last dress I try on is definitely something I would not normally wear. A very cute Sass and Bide number. It's black and skin-tight with leather panels down the side, a high back and low front. Frankly, I'm loving myself sick in it and I decide to set a trap. The back zipper is hard to reach so I decide to put to use my shopping buddy rights.

"Josh, can you come in here for a minute"

"Huh, in there?"

"Yes, that's what I said, didn't I?"

"Um, ok." He pulls the curtain over and steps inside, looking uncomfortable. His gaze travels down the length of my body.

"Pull the curtain closed," I whisper. He turns and closes it behind him. His eyes drop once more.

"What the fuck are you wearing?" The atmosphere in the change room suddenly becomes thick with want. My pulse quickens. His eyes come back up to my face, his jaw ticks and he cracks his neck. Jackpot. I love it when he does that. I don't know if it's what I'm wearing or the fact we are alone. But I want him—I want him now. His eyes drop to my hardened nipples and his mouth drops open with arousal as he takes a deep breath.

"Fuck Tash," he whispers as he closes his eyes, trying to block me out. "You need to get that dress off now if you want to walk out of here untouched."

I smile and bite my lip. "I'd better leave it on then."

He closes his eyes. "Stop it."

"No," I whisper. The next second, he grabs me and spins me around, so my back is to his front. We stare silently at our reflection in the mirror, each breath deeper than the last. His hands splay across my lower stomach and he pulls me back into his hard length. My head goes back to lean on his chest and my eyes close.

"Precious girl, you fucking turn me on, do you know that?" he whispers.

I can't stop myself. I have to play. "What turns you on about me?"

His eyes drop once more. "The curve of your waist. I love how you're cinched in here." He runs his finger from my breast down to the curve of my waist. "And those beautiful tits." He brings his lips down to the base of my neck and runs his open mouth back up to the top as he tightens his grip on my stomach. "Your smile." Goose bumps have scattered all over my body.

"My smile?" I whisper.

"Yes, your smile, it melts me. Those dimples," he bites my neck hard. "I fucking love them." Of all the things I thought he would say, that was the last, but for some reason it means the most.

"Josh," I whisper as I bring my hand up around the back of his neck. My head drops back again. No longer able to resist, I turn to face him, and we stand in silence. Our eyes lock.

"Can I help you in there? How are you going for sizes?" The idiot salesclerk is back. For fuck's sake, will everybody stop interrupting us? I'm about to lose it. He jumps back and runs his both hands through his hair. Obviously as frustrated as I am.

"No thanks, I am taking the one I've got."

Josh comes close to my ear and whispers. "You are not wearing that dress to the wedding."

I frown at him. "Watch me."

"I mean it, don't fuck with me."

I scowl at him. "You can't tell me what to wear, Joshua."

"Yes, I can, and since when have you called me Joshua?" he mutters as he leaves the change room. I narrow my eyes at myself in the mirror as I redress. I call you Joshua when you piss me off, asshole, and recently that's all the bloody time.

I exit to see him at the cashier with his credit card out. He looks at me deadpan. I walk over and place the last two dresses on the counter and get my wallet out.

"I've got it," he snaps. I roll my eyes and wish the annoying salesclerk would leave so I can tell him to fuck right off. Who does he think he is?

We walk to the car in silence. I'm not playing his stupid game. If he's got the shits, then he can come clean about what. I'm not asking. He stalks into a coffee shop just where the car is parked. After ordering us two coffees he returns to where I have sat. He sits and starts to read the paper that has been left on the table. Am I in the twilight zone? What the hell just happened? One minute he is telling me my smile turns him on and biting my neck. The next minute he's snapping orders. I'm too tired to deal with this shit today. I've hardly slept all week. I wait for my coffee in silence. His name is called, and he goes and retrieves our order. I take it without a thank you. If he wants rude, two can play at that game. He sips his coffee while watching me. I ignore him.

"You are not wearing that dress with Syral"

"It's Simon," I roll my eyes. "And yes, I am. I gave you the chance to be my date and you turned it down, remember?"

He shakes his head as he drinks his coffee. "I told you, don't threaten me."

"And I told you, don't tell me what to do."

"When did I tell you what to do?"

"When you told me not to wear the dress."

"I mean to the wedding for Christ sake. Someone will fuck you on the bridal table."

I break into a smile—surely, he can't be serious. "You had better come then, to protect me."

His eyes twinkle and he shakes his head. "Who will protect you from me?" He gives me a wink as he sips his coffee.

I smile. Bastard, he's got me. "Are you coming or not?"

"Yes," he snaps.

Hah! I won. I chalk up a silent victory. "Can you take me home now?" I say sweetly as I bat my eyelids. "You've dragged me around the shops enough for today." He smirks as he shakes his head.

The drive home is awkward. I am deep in thought about how I can prolong our visit and I have no idea what's running through his mind. Twice though, he cracks his neck. So that's a good sign. He pulls up at my house and turns off his car, but he seems nervous. I'm nervous—can I do this?

"Do you want to come up for coffee?" I grab his hand. I internally kick myself. Coffee, we just had frigging coffee. What a lame thing to say. He looks down at our entwined fingers as he swallows, and I can almost hear his brain ticking.

"It's not a good idea, Presh." The sound of him calling me Presh which is short for precious, his pet name for me, opens a wound in my chest that I can't deny. I nod, unable to speak. I can feel the tears forming. I don't want to say goodbye. What's going on with me? I'm acting like a lovesick fifteen–year–old. My eyes cloud over and I go to quickly get out of the car before he sees. Too late, he grabs me by the arm.

"What's wrong?" he whispers. I shake my head, the lump in my throat blocking my vocals.

"Tash, talk to me."

"I don't want to say goodbye, Josh." His eyes drop. "We can't even be friends, can we?" I ask.

"We can be friends, Tash. It just can't be like it was with us."

"I know," I whisper. I get out of the car and turn and give him a wave. "Thanks for taking me shopping," I smile. He nods but doesn't say anything. I head into the building and take the stairs. I need to clear my brain. I feel so needy. This is unlike me. I walk into my apartment, head for my bedroom and flop onto the bed. Hot tears are wetting my cheeks and I don't even know why. That's a lie. I do. I want him to want me as much as I want him. I head to my therapy of choice and have a steaming hot shower. I sit on the bottom of the shower feeling sorry for myself, like I have done thousands of times before. The tears have stopped finally. I'm in there so long the room is full of steam. I stand up and open the door so I can turn the fan on. I'm hit with the visual of Joshua leaning up against the wall in the bathroom. How long has he been there watching me? Did he hear me cry? His eyes search mine for the second time today and my breath catches.

CHAPTER 8

Natasha

I STAGGER BACK at the sight of him. Shit. He's standing with his hands linked on top of his head. His eyes are cast down, and he is leaning against the wall.

"Josh," I whisper. "What are you doing here?" He looks at me and shakes his head, unable to answer. "Baby, answer me."

"Stop calling me that," he snaps.

"No, I told you I won't."

He swallows and looks down again. It is then I notice I am totally naked. I quickly grab a towel from the rail and wrap it around me. He still looks down and his hands are still on top of his head, as if he is trying not to touch me, trying to restrain himself. The room is filled with steam, I am dripping wet in a towel and the man I am beyond physically attracted to is looking at the floor rather than at me. What's wrong with this picture?

"Josh, answer me," I repeat.

His eyes meet mine with a sadness in them that nearly breaks my heart. His hands are still linked on top of his head. "I'm not strong enough, I can't do it," he whispers.

"Strong enough for what?" I frown.

"To not want you." He closes his eyes as if in pain.

"Baby," I whisper as I wrap my arms around him. "I want you to want me."

"No, Natasha," he pushes me away. "I can't do this."

"Josh, talk to me. What's going on?"

He shakes his head. 'Why did you do it?"

"What do you mean, Josh?"

"Why did you leave me before you even gave me a chance?" That's what all this anger is about? I smile.

"You find this funny?" he snaps. "I knew this was a waste of time." He turns to walk out of the room.

"Josh, no." I am suddenly panicked. "I didn't do anything but save you from yourself."

He frowns at me. "What do you mean?"

"Josh, you weren't thinking straight. You were going to fess up to our parents." He frowns again. "I was young, and you were my older cousin." He shakes his head as he listens. "Josh, if my father found out he would have killed you—he would have thought that you forced me."

He steps back, shocked at my insinuations. "It wasn't like that," he whispers as his face drops.

"I know, but that's how it would have looked. I had to do it." His anger reignites. "You had to conveniently sleep with someone else to save me? Do you think I'm that stupid?" he yells.

I step back. "No, Josh, I lied to save you." He frowns again. "I lied. I would never sleep with anyone else, Josh."

He narrows his eyes at me. "What's that supposed to mean?"

I can feel those uncontrollable, frigging tears appearing once again.

"How could you, Josh?" I choke out past the lump in my throat.

"Do what?"

"How could you think I actually slept with someone else? I was totally in love with you. It broke my fucking heart, Josh, and you believed it. Just like that you believed it."

"It came from your mouth," he points at me. "You are the one who said it. Let me see, it went like this. Have you slept with him? And you replied yes!" he yells.

I step back and cross my arms. "So, you don't believe me?" I whisper.

He drops his head again, his hands still linked on top of his head. "Let's just leave it." He drops his hands. "This is stupid."

"No, Josh, you're stupid." His eyes ignite with rage.

"Do you really expect me to believe you didn't sleep with him?" His eyes are questioning and hurt.

"I didn't, I promise. I would never have done that to you. I kept waiting for you to work it out. Why didn't you work it out, Josh?" Hot tears stream down onto my cheeks, tears of guilt. Through the lump in my throat I whisper. "Have you ever thought of me, Josh?" He nods, his eyes sallow. The sight of the emotion in his eyes opens a wound in my chest, and a sob escapes.

"Josh, I've missed you, so damn much it hurts," I whisper. He stays silent as he inhales precious air deeply into his lungs. He lifts his hand and runs it over my hair.

"Show me." He continues stroking my hair and wraps his fingers around the back of my neck. I look up at his lips as he lowers them to mine. He kisses me gently, swiping his tongue through my open mouth. A shiver runs through my body and a groan escapes me, one I can't control. The kiss deepens and his tongue takes over every sense I own, taking what he wants. He brings his hands to my face and holds my cheeks as he kisses me again, deeper this time. His tongue demanding arousal. My body happy to oblige. A shiver runs through me as I feel a very familiar pulse start to throb between my legs. I can't believe it; we are alone and he knows the truth. The last thought scatters goose bumps over my body.

"Show me," he whispers in my ear as he bites it. "Show me how much you have missed me." He runs his open mouth down the length of my neck. I pull back to look at him and his eyes have changed. They are now dark with desire. They call to a part of me that only he knows. Without breaking eye contact he grabs the bottom of his T-shirt and pulls it off over his head. Each breath I take is deeper than the last, my heart racing out of control. My eyes drop to his chest, holy fuck this body is ridiculous. It takes my breath away. He is tanned and muscular and his chest has a scattering of dark hair that picks up again below his navel in a thin line that disappears into his cargo pants. I look back up to see the anxiety etched on his face. I run my fingertips down the length of his body until I reach the tattoo. Ahh, that's why he looks nervous, he doesn't know how I will react. I turn him and lift his arm. He lets me and raises his arm for me to see. I follow my name with my fingertip slowly. My God, I adore this man.

"When did you get this, baby?" I whisper... silence, he doesn't answer. "Josh, answer me and I want the truth."

"On your twenty-first birthday—it's your birthday present." He closes his eyes as if pained. I can't help it, tears instantly overfill my eyes. I bend and slowly kiss the tattoo. Overcome with emotion I can't hold the tears back as they run freely down my face. I hold him in an embrace around the stomach as I sob against his body. He runs his fingers through my hair.

"Happy birthday, precious girl." I stand up and that's it. I know it's over. I will do anything he wants. With dark eyes he ticks his jaw and cracks his neck. I love that. "Now stop with the blubbering and show me how much you've fucking missed me." He smiles and bites his lip as he grabs my shoulders and pushes me down onto my knees. I drop, eager to taste him. Desperation hits as I rip his pants down. His engorged length falls into my hands and I lick my lips as I size up the perfect manhood in front of me. Holy mother fuck, he's frigging huge. Has he always been this big? He gently runs his fingers through my hair and lifts himself into my waiting mouth. I close my eyes as I swirl my tongue around the tip and gently suck.

"Fuck," he hisses and leans back against the wall, unable to hold his weight on his legs any longer. His response urges me on, and I take the full length of him. I suck harder and hold onto his hips for balance. Slowly but surely, I build a rhythm, each stroke deeper than the last, each suck more powerful. The contrast between the hard, powerful lurches of his hips into my mouth and the gentle stroking of his hands on my hair bring me to an involuntary groan. I am rewarded with a gush of pre ejaculate. God, he tastes good. His breathing is labored and he leans his head back against the wall.

"Fuck, Tash, you suck me so good," he breathes. He pushes the hair from my forehead and runs his fingers down my cheeks, feeling them dip in as I suck. His mouth drops open as he watches me, and the look in his eyes is pure predatory. Our eyes lock and something shifts between us— memories reawaken. An unspoken language that only we can understand. I close my eyes to block out the intimacy. It's too much. Too fast.

He pulls himself free of my mouth and bends to kiss me, a slow gentle tongue kiss.

"Stand," he whispers. "I need to be inside you, precious girl." I stand and he kisses me again as he pushes me back to the vanity and lifts me to sit on top of it. He slowly undoes my towel from my body and stands back to look at me. I feel self-conscious. It's the middle of the frigging day and I'm spread eagled in front of the most beautiful man on the planet. His eyes drop to between my legs.

"Perfect," he whispers. I smile as I internally thank Abbie for the appointment at the Beautiful Behinds waxing salon yesterday. I owe her...big time. He runs his hand down the front of my neck to my breasts which he cups with his hands, my nipples hardening under his attention. He lets out a low groan and closes his eyes. Seriously, this man is hot. I think the phrase god's gift to women is definitely appropriate in this situation. His mouth drops open again as he watches with dark eyes his fingers run down the length of my body and he swipes them through the wet flesh between my legs. I whimper and throw my head back to lean on the mirror.

He starts to kiss my neck with an open mouth and gently starts to spread my knees with his hands, running slowly both hands backwards and forwards from my knees to my hips. I know he's trying to calm himself. His breath is quivering as he sucks in air. Just the thought that he could be this aroused from my body starts to liquefy my insides and I find myself panting, anticipating his next move. His fingertips circle through my swollen flesh and his thumb rubs over my clitoris. I shudder with arousal. "Fuck, you are dripping wet," he smiles into my neck. I grab the back of his head and bury it into my neck. I can't even speak, let alone answer. A low moan escapes me. Even if I wanted to stop and I don't, it would not be physically possible at this point. My body has gone into overdrive and is on a one-way race track to orgasm. He steps back and once again stares down at my open weeping flesh, he cracks his neck hard and I know he's gone past his physical limits of restraint. His mouth slackens and he slowly pushes one of his fingers into me, twisting his hand as he does. He closes his eyes as he moans. "Fuck!" I smile and bite my lip. I like that response. I like it a lot. Standing back with eyes still focused on my sex he slowly fucks me with his finger and then adds a second as he twists his hand again. I groan and lean my head back. Shit, I think I'm going to come from just this, how embarrassing. He seems to lose control and bites my neck hard as his strong fingers pick up the pace.

"You're so tight, precious. I wanted to come with you the first time, but it's not going to work." He bites me, taking possession, and it's almost painful. Goosebumps scatter again.

"Huh," I whisper. "What do you mean?"

"If I don't make you come first, I won't be able to get in— you're too tight, baby," he whispers into my ear as he bites it. On hearing those words my legs open wider by themselves, and he starts to scissor his fingers. Oh dear God. This is too good.

Once again, he takes my mouth hard, a take no prisoner's kind of kiss, biting my bottom lip as he pulls away. He bends and picks me up over his shoulder and walks down the hall, bangs open my bedroom door and throws me onto the bed. Oh fuck, this is going to hurt. I just know it. I think I said once before who does he think he is? I can tell you one thing, he puts Dirk Diggler to shame. Shit, and he said I'm tight. Before I can think anymore, he crawls over me and settles his hips to cradle between my legs. He gently starts to rub the side of his shaft through my swollen flesh, while holding his weight up on straightened arms as he kisses me passionately again. A gentle hard rub, one that has my body involuntarily lifting off the bed to meet him. Damn, he's good at this. His hand runs from my jaw down to my breast to my hipbone, then underneath my knee as he brings my leg around his hip. All the while he is kissing me passionately. I don't have a fucking chance against this god. Slowly he kisses down my throat to my breasts which he immediately brings to attention as he sucks both of my nipples hard between his teeth. My back arches off the bed, a sheen of perspiration now covering both of our bodies. I run my fingers through his hair. He pushes my legs apart until they are touching the bed and he gives me a carnal smile as he disappears down my body. Shit, it's daylight. Surely, we can ease into this in the dark for Pete's sake. But my thoughts are instantly erased as his hot tongue swipes through my flesh. I jump off the bed, the sensation burning through me.

"Sshh, precious girl, I've got you. Relax, baby, I won't hurt you." He reaches his hand up and links his fingers in mine, and our eyes lock. The intimacy of the act once again undoes my emotions and I put my head back onto the mattress to hide my glassy eyes. Fuck, what am I doing? I'm going to get hurt, I just know it. This can only end badly.

His tongue goes to work stroking deep long licks through the length of my sex. I start to quiver. "Sshh, baby," he stops and stills to calm me. "Take your time, relax. Let me enjoy you." I nod and squeeze his hand, unable to articulate words. This is too much. He squeezes my hand back and then brings his fingers down to part me open to his gaze. I'm holding my breath. Actually, no, I'm not holding it, I can't breathe, my lungs have no air. I'm waiting for his reaction, for him to say something.

He closes his eyes and whispers. "Do you know how long

I've waited to have you like this?" My glassy eyes meet his and I nod. I ,too, have waited long and hard for this.

"Let me come inside you."

I frown at him. "Josh, I don't think."

"I'm clean, I promise. I don't want anything between us. I want it to be just you and me. I've waited for this. I've never had sex without a condom on before and I want that with you. Don't take it away from me," he whispers. *Oh shit.* Goose bumps scatter and his words ramp up my libido to fever pitch. As if he can sense my desperation, he starts his oral assault again, his tongue taking what it wants from my body, his eyes closed in reverence. I start to whimper as my hips start to sway on their own to the rhythm of his tongue. I'm close. He brings my legs up over his shoulders and he, too, is losing control. He can sense my oncoming orgasm approaching like a freight train. I'm panting, covered in sweat, as I watch his head move between my legs, feel his strong shoulders under my legs. He closes his eyes and groans into me. That's it, I can't hold it any longer and I scream out as I am racked with violent shudders.

"Fuck," he whispers as he lets me gently come down with gentle laps. I look up into the face of a triumphant male as he whispers, "Again."

"Josh, no." I try to move up the bed to escape. It's too much, I'm way too sensitive. He grabs my legs and pulls me back down the bed. He parts my legs with force and once again his tongue is on me. I shudder. *Holy fuck.* Any chance I had of escaping is out the window and I know he has crossed the line and is running on pure instinct, race to orgasm. I lie back and try to calm myself. He runs his teeth over my clitoris and I jump again.

"Sshh, Presh, let me have my way. I don't want to hurt you later, and I need you soft and open from orgasm. I'm, well, not small and you're too tight and I'm way too turned on to be gentle." He reaches up and grabs my hand again, my other hand rubs over his head and shoulders. He's right. I need to lie back and relax. I try to calm my breathing. Within seconds my hips are swaying again, and he adds a finger, then another, as he twists his hand on entry, his dilated eyes boring into me. He slowly fucks me with his strong fingers, and I fall apart just watching him, he's so turned on, so frigging hot. He adds a third finger and I wince. "Baby," I whisper as my spine involuntarily lurches me off the bed. "Josh, I need to..." I whimper again. "Oh God...Josh, please," I beg, as I run my both hands over his head.

"Natasha, I have you for one night, don't fucking rush me." I nod once again, unable to speak, his fingers now working me with such force the bed is rocking. It feels so good. I've needed this for so long, needed him to do this to me. I can't wait to take him inside me. He bites my clitoris and I moan, and he sits up to watch me. I can see the muscles in his arm and shoulder flex as he rides me hard with his hand, the veins in his forearm pumping with blood. A thick sheen of perspiration covers his body. He smiles a sly smile at me as his thumb swipes over my clitoris and with three more pumps of his finger he mouths the words, "Come for me." I explode into a violent shudder as I scream and spiral into the most intense orgasm I've ever had. Before I can even move, he's on me and with one hard lunge he's in to the hilt. Oh fuck, he's big.

"I had to go fast, baby, so I didn't hurt you," he whispers. I nod, trying to catch my breath. He stays deep and still, allowing me to adjust to the overwhelming sensation that has my heartbeat sounding in my ears. His breathing is heavy, his eyes closed, as he rests his forehead onto mine, trying to calm himself. Holy fuck, I am so out of my depth here. This isn't sex. This is a life changing event. He opens his eyes and I see a depth of arousal I have never seen before in any man, in life or porn, and it's somewhat unsettling. This is going to hurt.

"I'm going to move now, Presh. Are you ok?" I nod and he circles his hips as if trying to stretch me. God I can't stretch anymore. I've reached my physical limits. He slowly pulls out, his eyes shutting as he does and gently pushes back in. Ok that felt good, no pain. I will myself to relax. He pushes forward again and circles his hips, repeating the addictive movement of before. I grab his behind, my lust taking over, and the next time he pulls out I pull him back into me.

"Again," I whisper. "Faster." He bites my neck painfully and slams back into me, his physical limits reached, and he starts to move against me so hard the bed sounds like it's going to break when it hits the wall. I groan as I run my hands over his perspiration covered muscly body. His kisses turn aggressive and I am so overwhelmed at what this man is doing to me I can't even kiss him back. I lie there with my mouth open, groaning into his mouth.

"Fucking hell, Natasha, you fuck me so good." I moan a deep sound that I don't even recognize as he slams repeatedly into me. I can feel it coming. Shit, it might kill me. One, two, three hard lunges and, that's it, I scream out again, the sound bouncing off my bedroom walls as I orgasm hard, my body contracting around his.

"Fuck, yes," he yells as he slams into me, his grip on my behind so hard I think I might bruise. He groans as I feel his hot seed seep into the marrow of my bones, taking with it any reservation I ever had about him. We are both breathless and panting as he drops his head to my shoulder in silence. Tears fill my eyes again as I am overcome with emotion.

"Fucking hell, Natasha, what was that?" he pants. I'm too breathless to answer. I giggle and he pulls me into an embrace and kisses me again. A slow beautiful heartfelt kiss, one that is tenderly equal with the sex we just had. I don't remember anything more, fatigue setting in. But as I drift into an exhausted sleep it is the words he whispered to me that replay in my head. I only have one night with you, I only have one night with you, I only have one night with you. No, I'm sorry Josh, I can't let that happen. I'm keeping you this time.

CHAPTER 9

Natasha

I AWAKE to the glow of the lights in the downtown city beaming through my window. It's dark. How long have we slept? I look at the beautiful man sleeping beside me, out cold and sleeping like a baby. I roll onto my side and smile as I watch him. He's like an Adonis, every muscle in his body on show. Pure male perfection. His dark lashes fan his face, and his large red lips are gently open, his chest rises and falls slowly. I smile again as I note that he has a hairy chest, one of my hot triggers. If I had a magic wand and designed my perfect male specimen, this is what it would look like. His arm is under my head and he is facing me.

My gaze drops to his tattoo, my name down the length of his torso. My twenty–first birthday present. That is some serious heavy shit going on there. My mind retraces the day we have spent together, the love we have made. It's been perfect, everything I could have wished for and then some.

However, one thing is marring my afterglow. The 'we only have one night together' statement. Does he really only want one night? Why in the hell would he have my name on his body if he didn't care? Is it the cousin thing? Surely not. If I don't care, why would he? My mind goes back to the restaurant: I want a woman who loves to fuck as much as I do. A mousy woman who I have to beg for sex won't cut it with me. Think Natasha. Think. What's my plan of attack? I know one thing; I am so not done with him. I want more, much more. I need time, time where he is forced to think about us, time without other females. I watch him sleep for another half an hour with my brain in overdrive. This is where I want to be, naked in bed with him. Even the thought of going to the bathroom is unappealing, as bursting as I am. Unable to hold it any longer I slowly sit up and head to the bathroom. I decide to take a quick shower. If I want to be irresistible, I need to smell good. After drying I don't dress and head back to my bedroom to see him stretching as he gives me a sleepy smile.

"Hi," I beam.

"Where did you go?" he huskily whispers as he wraps me in an embrace.

"I took a shower," I reply as I bend to kiss him. He returns my kiss by pulling me down on top of him.

"Why didn't you wait for me?"

Hmm, I wish I did. "I didn't know how long you would sleep. Did you sleep last night?" He rubs his eyes as he shakes his head.

"Why didn't you sleep, baby?" I nuzzle into his ear as I gently nip it. His eyes close as he shrugs his shoulders and once again smiles sleepily. God, he's adorable when he's sleepy. I could just eat him up.

"Some raving hot bitch got me so worked up. I was too

angry to sleep," he smiles into my neck as he starts to kiss it with an open mouth.

"Raving hot bitch?" I repeat, feigning shock.

He nods again. "I think she needs to be punished for her misdemeanors."

"Mmm, maybe she does," I reply. "I need a cup of tea first."

"Good idea." He jumps up, flicks my side lamp on and strolls to the kitchen completely naked, obviously to make my tea. That was unexpectedly easy. Maybe this won't be so hard after all, he is being very agreeable. Ten minutes later he arrives back in the bedroom with two cups of tea, still gloriously naked. I sit up against my high-backed plush-studded bedhead.

"Why are you dressed?" he raises his eyebrow at me.

"Because I'm cold," I answer.

He bends and lifts my shirt off over my head. "No clothes tonight," he smiles.

"Because you only have me for one night?" I test the waters.

"Exactly," he answers. "So tonight you, my dear beautiful Natasha, will do everything I ask and take your punishment like a good girl. Naked." He sits beside me with his back resting against the bedhead and takes a sip of his tea.

No way, no way in hell am I letting him dominate tonight's activities. Time for action. He wants an assertive woman in bed, well he is damn well going to get one. I put my tea down on my nightstand and turn to straddle his lap.

"That's more like it," he whispers as I start to run my mouth up and down his neck. I stand up onto my knees and circle my hips as I swipe my tongue through his open mouth. His hands fall to my breasts and I kiss him deeply again. With hooded eyes he looks up at me. I lower myself and rub my wet center along the length of his shaft and he exhales in a long slow breath. I rise onto my knees again and his hands drop to my hips. I circle them slowly as I push my breasts into his face. He groans as he tries to kiss me, but I duck away and bite his neck instead. His hands tighten their grip as his cock doubles in size. Oh God, I'm playing with weapons of mass destruction here, do I really know what I'm doing? Once again, I start to rub myself on his hard length that I can now see every vein on. The head large and pulsing. With one sharp movement he cracks his neck hard. He leans his head back against the board, his dark eyes filled with want. I bend and take his nipple into my mouth and gently bite it. As I pull back, he hisses and closes his eyes. So, he likes a little pain with his pleasure— hmm, interesting.

I circle my hips again. "Can you feel me, baby? Feel my need for your cock?" He breathes in on a sharp intake, aahh, he likes dirty talk. I grab his hand and lift it to my mouth and suck his two middle digits. He stays silent, watching the private show made just for him. I simulate a head job on his fingers diving them in and out of my mouth, closing my eyes and moaning for effect. I once again slide my now dripping sex along his pulsing cock. "It's going to feel so good, baby," I whisper into his ear. He closes his eyes and I know I'm getting to him as his breathing has become labored. I rub my hands down from my neck over my two breasts and down to my sex while I rotate my hips.

"Do you see something you like, Joshua?" I whisper. I bend down and he opens his mouth for a kiss but I pull away. I slowly lower my fingers and gently swipe them through my throbbing sex.

"I can feel my pulse here, Josh, it's screaming for you." He grabs me by the hair and drags me in for a kiss, one I can't refuse. This is hot. Who knew acting slutty could be so fun?

"Do I have something you want, baby?" I whisper. I gently start to finger myself as I stand on my knees above him. His mouth drops open and he swallows. His eyes fixated on my sex, he's losing it.

"Almost there, baby, what do you want?' I whisper as I withdraw my fingers and put them in my mouth, ewww, *what the hell am I doing*? He nods, unable to speak and shocked to his core I think, he's never seen me like this. Actually, nobody has, including myself. I go in for another passionate kiss and it gives me goosebumps. He's not the only one who is losing it—I could come just by doing this. "Joshua, you have something I want," I whisper. As I kiss my way down his chest, he grabs my hair again. "If you give me what I want, baby, I'll make you very happy," I whisper into his stomach. I bend and put his cock into my mouth and moan as I suck it as hard as I can on the upstroke and he hisses.

"What do you want, precious girl?" He tenderly cups my face in his hand. "What do you want?" he groans as I once again take him in my mouth hard. I run my hands down his face and across his chest and look into his eyes. I slowly sink onto his waiting erection and we both groan in pleasure. He grabs my hips to still me, obviously closer than I thought.

"I want monogamy."

He frowns. "What?"

"While you're in this country, I don't want you with anyone else."

"Natasha, that's ridiculous," he spits.

"No, Joshua, if you want private access to me, I demand equality. Agree to it and then I want you to pump my tight cunt so full of come that I'll overflow."

He grabs me by the hair. "Natasha, stop talking or I'm going to come."

I give him a wicked smile. "My man like dirty talk, doesn't he?" He stills my hips again and nods. He's trying his hardest not to come. I've found his weakness. "Say the words, Josh, and I'm yours." He closes his eyes as he tries to block me out. "Do you want to blow in my mouth, baby? I can't wait to taste you."

"Fuck. Natasha. Stop talking," he grabs my hips and grinds me forward and we both groan. "Say the words, Josh. Do you want this body to yourself or not?" He closes his eyes as if pained and nods. "Say it out loud," I shout as my orgasm comes dangerously close. He lifts me up and slams me back down on him.

"Yes, monogamy. I'll give you monogamy," he screams.

"For the whole nine weeks," I scream as he pounds into me. "Yes," he yells and, that's it, he loses control. He grabs me by the shoulders and throws me on the bed and starts to fuck me like there's no tomorrow. Fast and furious. And I love it. Never has he taken me like this, so wild with untamed passion. In just a few short moments he roars as he comes and in turn that sets off my own mind–blowing orgasm. We lie scrambling for air, panting. We are both covered in sweat.

"You're trying to kill me," he pants.

I laugh as I pant, coming off the high. "Yeah, you and me both."

I smile as I roll onto my side to face him. I place my hand on his cheek and lean in gently for a chaste kiss, and he cuddles into me. "I've missed you, baby," I whisper.

He gives me a sad smile and whispers, "Me, too."

Trying to save the moment from the sadness in his eyes, I sit up. "So, is this a full-service date?"

He laughs. "Um, looks like it."

"Good. You can take me out to dinner," I smile.

He suddenly looks uncomfortable. "Tash, that's not a good idea."

"Why not?" I snap.

"What if someone sees us?"

"I don't care," I frown.

"I do," he answers.

"Are you ashamed of me?" I'm horrified.

"No, Natasha, I told you it can't be that way between us anymore."

I get up and whip him with my T–shirt. "It's a shame you talk. You're so pretty when you don't open your mouth." His mouth drops open and he bites his lip as he tries to stifle his smile, then he reaches out and smacks me hard on the back-side. I silently high five myself and smile as I saunter out of the room. We haven't bantered for years and I must say it feels good, it feels familiar. Moments later I am in the shower when I feel him get in and kiss my neck from behind.

"Where do you want to go for dinner?" He smiles into my neck as he wraps his arms around my waist. Argument over, I won.

CHAPTER 10

Natasha

NINETY MINUTES later Joshua and I are waiting to be seated at my favorite Italian restaurant. "Table for two, thanks," he asserts to the waiter, without as much as a smile.

"Ah, yes, this way." The waiter motions to the front of the bay windows that lead out onto the street. He looks around.

"We need to be at the back of the restaurant," Josh says as he adjusts his cufflinks. I frown at him, affronted by his rudeness.

"Ok, this table at the back then."

Joshua smiles. "Thank you." Beautiful Josh has disappeared, and Mr. Stanton has come in his place. That became apparent an hour ago when a bodyguard arrived at my apartment with an overnight bag, full of clean clothes for him. After a heated discussion and a small tantrum from yours truly, he finally agreed to the bodyguard travelling in a separate car from us. If I have him for one frigging night I'm not sharing, not a chance. He looks edible of course, jeans, white shirt and a navy blazer.

He oozes confidence and sex appeal—no wonder he attracts so much attention. The forty-thousand-dollar Rolex watch doesn't help the situation either. I am so punching above my weight here. "Why do we have to sit at the back?" I frown, "I wanted to sit near the window." He follows me silently and pulls out my chair for me to take a seat. Oohh, manners. He sits, ignoring my question as he looks around. He calls the waiter.

"I'll have a bottle of Barossa Valley Shiraz, thank you." He turns his eyes back to me.

"Answer my question," I snap.

He raises his eyebrows in silent defiance. "Natasha, I really don't want the paps to find me here. I like privacy."

I huff. "Could have fooled me," I mutter under my breath. "What's that supposed to mean?" he snaps.

"Joshua, I've had a google alert on you, and every time I turned on my computer, I've had to endure every damn date you've been on for the last five years. I would say you thrive on the attention on your love life."

He sits back, obviously annoyed at my challenge. "I do, do I?" He raises an eyebrow.

"Yes, I think you do," I answer. The waiter arrives and pops the cork then pours a little into the glass. Josh tastes it.

"That's fine," he replies, his eyes not leaving mine. The waiter pours me a glass.

"Will that be all?"

"Yes, thanks," I answer. Josh takes a sip and his eyes bore into me as he leans back in his chair. He's pulling a power stance. Give me a break.

"Why would you have a google alert on me?" He tilts his head to the side while he runs the side of his forefinger back and forward over his lip. He's thinking. I've already worked out this mannerism.

"You know why," I answer, slightly embarrassed. Obviously because I don't have one cool bone in my body. "Josh, I've told you my feelings haven't changed. Of course, I want to know what you are doing."

"And what have you found out?" His smugness is starting to piss me off.

I shrug my shoulders, "Lots of things." I take a sip of my wine and look around the room.

"Like what?" he snaps.

"Wouldn't you like to know?" I do wide eyes at him.

"Are you looking for a fight tonight?" His arrogance is seriously pissing me off and I raise my eyebrows at him. He has the audacity to smile and bite his lip.

"It turns me on when you get angry you know." He sips his wine as he narrows his eyes at me.

I smirk, unable to hold it in. "No, I just wonder why you can't be seen with me. But you're more than happy to be seen with every other woman in the United States."

He rolls his eyes. "You can't be serious. Did you ask me to take you out for dinner so you can fight with me about my past?" He takes another sip of his wine, his eyes not leaving mine.

"That depends Josh, is it your past or your future?"

His eyes burn into me. "Both," he replies.

I nod, unable to speak. I didn't expect that answer. I look down at the table and rearrange my knife and fork. Seriously, what am I doing here? I should rip off this band-aid before I get an infection. Maybe I should start with the antibiotics now before it turns septic. He must be able to sense he's hurt my feelings.

"Hey, look at me," he whispers. I drag my eyes to him.

"Natasha, you know we can't be like we were. Why are you

bringing this up now?" I shrug, too afraid to speak in case I burst into tears. What's wrong with me? Talk about how to lose a guy in ten days, try ten hours. Good one Natasha, you fuckwit. I shake my head. "I'm sorry, Josh I just feel...off-center I didn't know this was going to happen." He smiles and nods as if he understands. "Josh, I promised myself a long time ago that if I ever got another chance with you, I would never keep another secret from you again. So, I need to tell you that I can't imagine being with someone else...ever." He stays silent and still, unsure what to say. "Tell me, how have you done it?" He frowns. "How have you moved on? Tell me how to move on, Josh. I don't know how."

"That's laughable," he whispers as he leans into the table. "You're the one that has had two serious boyfriends."

I frown. "And why do you think I broke up with those boys, Josh?"

He shrugs. "Boredom I suspect, the poor bastards."

"I broke up with them, Josh, because I compare everyone to you, and unfortunately no one comes close." He takes another sip of his wine and goes back to his thinking pose, pointer over his lip. Face serious. "No other man gets me crazy like you, Josh... I can't explain it." I give him a sad smile, "Let's just say it's been a lot harder on me than it has on you." There, I said it out loud, no more secrets. He leans forward, narrows his eyes and clenches his hands into fists. Contempt dripping from his every pore.

"If you think this has been easy on me, you have no fucking idea what you are talking about, Natasha. The reason I sleep with so many women is to try and find someone that even rouses a smidgeon of the feelings that I feel when I'm with you, although they always fall short." My heart swells and I smile.

"What do you feel when you're with me?"

"Like I never want to leave. Like the sex I've had since isn't even in the same book, let alone on the same page."

"What sex do you have with other girls, Josh?" I close my eyes. I'm not really sure I want to know the answer. How in the hell did we get onto this topic?

"Empty sex," he sighs.

"What sex do we have Josh, you and me?" I gesture at the air between us. He stays silent as he assesses my question. After two full moments of silence he sighs as he rests his chin on his hand. "The best sex of my life, I never want it to end. It's ridiculous I know."

I smile a victorious smile as our eyes lock. "I feel the same, Josh. It doesn't have to end. Why can't we just spend the next couple of months together?" I grab his hand and give it a pleading squeeze.

"Tash, you know why, it will be just harder to leave when the time comes, and it will end. We both know that."

I blow out a breath in frustration. "But can you please stick with your promise?"

He leans back and smiles. "The one you made me promise under sufferance?"

I smile. "Yes, that one."

"I know what you did back there you know?" he smirks. "Well, desperate times call for desperate measures and I seriously will go postal if you sleep with someone else, Josh. I mean it," my voice is rising.

"Ok, sshh," he whispers, as he looks around. "Why is that so important to you?" he asks. He really has no idea, does he?

"Because if we run into each other, say at the Ivy, can you imagine how it would feel if I'm with someone else?"

He runs his tongue over the top of his front teeth. "I think we both saw how that went the other night," he says deadpan.

I smile and bite my lip. "What did you do to that guy anyway?"

"Nothing until we got out to the back security room and he told me you give a great blow job."

I gasp, "Josh, I've never been with him." I put my hand over my mouth. "My God, what a liar."

He narrows his eyes at me. "Never," he repeats.

"Definitely not," I answer. "He's a dick."

"Why were you letting him touch you then?"

I swallow. This would sound childish, even to my ears. "I was mad with you Josh. I had just seen you with that stripper." I swallow the lump in my throat as the visual re-enters my brain.

He reaches over and squeezes my hand. "So, you were going to sleep with him to pay me back," he murmurs.

"I was going to try," I whisper.

"What does that mean?" he snaps.

"Josh, I have trouble being with... other men."

He frowns. "What do you mean?" he whispers.

I shake my head. "Can we talk about something else?"

"No. You told me no secrets, remember."

This was going to make me sound like the world's biggest loser. "Josh, other men don't..." I shrug my shoulders. "Get me hot for it. I usually get the hell out of there before they even get to first base."

He frowns. "Why?" he questions. "When you are with me, you're gagging for it."

I burst out laughing and choke on my wine. "Gagging for it," I repeat. He smiles and nods. "Josh, you are a born romantic. You should write a romance novel and call it gagging for it."

His eyes twinkle as he smiles warmly. "It does have a ring to it, doesn't it?" he smirks.

"It's definitely a book I would buy." I do wide eyes at him to accentuate my point.

"It would be a real page turner, I suspect."

Our meal arrives and we both eat in silence, lost deep in thought. And as we are waiting for the check, I peek up at the gorgeous man sitting opposite me.

"How are we going to do this, Josh?"

He blows out a breath and rubs his face. "I suppose we are going to want each other from afar and be mollified that the other isn't with anyone else."

"That sounds totally crap. So, I will know at night when I'm alone in my bed that you are alone in your bed and I can do nothing about it?"

He smiles and nods. "I suppose."

"Josh that's torture. It's like...it's like..." I can't think of the appropriate analogy. "Having a Lamborghini in the garage and not being allowed to drive it."

He throws his head back and laughs. "Did you just call me a Lamborghini?" He raises an eyebrow in question.

"I guess I did."

"That's a hot car," he whispers.

"Well, you're a very hot man," I whisper back. He grabs my hand again, his blazing stare burning into me.

"When did you become such a beautiful slut?"

I smile, my chest filling with an unnamed emotion. "When you came back for me and turned on the switch," I breathe. Who knew I would love the endearment 'beautiful slut'. Now I know for certain I'm tapped.

"So, I have you for tonight?" he rubs his finger over his lip, leaning back in his chair, his dominant sitting position makes me feel like a naughty schoolgirl.

"Yes," I breathe as my eyes drop to his finger lingering over

162

his lips, my heart rate rising. His searing stare bores into mine and our eyes lock. I couldn't look away even if I wanted to. I see a familiar tick of the jaw and a much-anticipated crack of the neck.

"Do you have any idea how hard you are going to cop it when we get home?" He smirks as he raises his eyebrows and crosses his legs to readjust his length that I can now see straining in his pants. I swallow a golf ball in my throat and a familiar heat starts to run through me, a fire that has only one extinguisher, a certain gorgeous man in a navy blazer. I smile and lick my lips, and his eyes drop to my mouth.

"I hope it's hard enough to last me a lifetime seeing as no one else can get the job done... Mr. Stanton." He grabs my legs hard under the table, his thumbs nearly at bruising pressure, and leans in to whisper in my ear.

"Be careful what you wish for, precious, you are playing with fire. No one will save you when you scream for mercy."

CHAPTER 11

Natasha

Who in God's name would want to be saved from the fire I have just had for the last four hours? I was right. The man is a frigging Lamborghini, either that or a sex god from another planet. I smile into his chest as we sit on the bottom of my shower, both too exhausted to get up.

"Up, Presh," he whispers. "You're falling asleep."

"Mmmm" I groan. I don't want to get up. He kisses me on the forehead.

"Come on." He helps me off his lap. I slowly stand and he helps me out of the shower and wraps me in a towel, cuddling me in an embrace like a child. His lips gently kiss my temple as he whispers. "I'm sorry, beautiful. I've been hard on you tonight, you make me lose my head and I can't stop." He continues to dry me.

"Mmm," I answer again, too exhausted to open my eyes. My head is resting on his shoulder. "Be as hard on me as you want. My body is yours for nine weeks, remember," I mumble.

I can feel him smile into my neck. "Careful, keep talking like that and you will be on your knees again." He kisses my neck with an open mouth. I don't even have the strength to open my eyes to see if he's serious. He picks me up like a bride and carries me to bed. He slowly removes the towel and lies me down as he snuggles in behind me and wraps his arms around my waist, then he gently starts to trail kisses across my shoulder and up my neck. As I slip into an orgasm induced coma, I hear him whisper the words, "I fucking adore you, Natasha."

When I woke up, he was gone.

Joshua

Cabin crew, crosscheck. I look out the window to my left as my private plane hurtles to take off down the runway. I glance at my watch—6.00 am. She will be waking up soon. I run the side of my pointer back and forward over my lip and close my eyes as disgust twists my gut. What a dog act, sneaking out in the middle of the night. She's going to fucking hate me, and who could blame her? I run both my hands through my hair.

"Can I get you some breakfast, Mr. Stanton?" The blonde stewardess is over-attentive. She has been fawning all over me since I got on the damn plane.

"No, I will just have a Cointreau and ice. Actually, make it a double." I glare at her, silently telling her to back the hell off. She looks shocked and immediately nods and leaves me alone. I look over to see Adrian narrow his eyes at me.

"What?" I snap. He shakes his head and looks back out his window opposite me, his annoyance apparent. I am not in the mood for his shit today. If I want to drink Cointreau for breakfast, then I fucking will. I don't need another mother telling me what to do. The one I've got is enough of a nightmare. I glance at my watch again—6.25 am. I strum my fingers on my table. I'm so worked up I don't think I can sit on this plane all the way to Melbourne.

I stand and walk up the end of the aisle and turn and put my hands on the back of the two opposite aisle seats. With only fifteen people on board for the meeting we have with the Australian Medical Board this morning, the plane is relatively empty. I stand for a while as my mind wanders back to the night before, to Natasha. I can't even bear to be near my colleagues this morning. They are just too... in my space. I check my watch again—6.40 am. She will be waking up soon. I check my suit pant pockets for my phone and then my jacket pockets, shit. I stomp back down the aisle and look on my seat for my phone.

"Lost something?" Adrian asks a little too sweetly.

"My phone," I reply.

"Expecting a call?" he asks. He holds my phone up as he smiles at Ben. "Fuck off!" I snatch the phone off him and storm back down to the other end of the plane. I fall into the seat and rest my arm on the window base. This is a fucking nightmare, a total fucking nightmare. Last night was supposed to bring closure; instead I feel sick to my stomach.

My mind flicks back to when I woke up next to her, and I put the heel of my hands into my eye sockets. What the fuck was that about? I fucking had sex with her while she was asleep. I've hit a new low. I close my eyes, the memory so vivid it is forever burned into my brain. I woke up to the feel of her gentle breath on my shoulder, she was on her back and my arm was draped over her stomach. I leaned up onto my elbow and flicked the lamp on so I could see the time.

What I saw instead was the exact vision of the fantasy I've been having for seven years. Natasha on her back and all mine. I slowly peeled the blanket back so I could drink in her beauty, absolutely fucking breathless beauty. I remove my hand from her stomach and she gently groans and moves her hand around looking for me, then she relaxes as she finds my chest. Instantly my cock twitches. I slowly bend to kiss her breast and instead find her erect nipple in my mouth—so fucking perfect. She groans and her legs fall open, inviting me in. My breath starts to quiver as I slowly run my fingers from her throat down over both her breasts down her stomach and down to her beautiful tight cunt. She groans again and opens her legs further apart. I don't believe this. She's asleep and her body is responding to me. This is every fucking wet dream I've ever had. I wonder if I can feel my semen inside her. I slowly sink in one finger. She groans and spreads her legs again further apart. Her body starts to ripple around my finger—holy fuck this woman is hot.

I add another finger and then another and her body starts

to slowly pump my fingers, begging for more. This is unbearable. Sweat is beading over my body. I don't think I've ever been so aroused in my life. Her body starts to gently ride my fingers and her soft sighs are going straight to my cock. Just the thought of watching her body orgasm as she sleeps is fucking with my head BIG TIME. Every muscle in my body is aching to be inside her, screaming at me in a deafening sound. Her legs fall to the mattress and she moans, her body wanting more. Her tight channel ripples around me and I groan as I put my head into my pillow trying to control myself. Willing myself to stop. Then her words from earlier come back to haunt me. Do what you want with my body, Joshua. It's yours, remember. It's those words that tip me over the edge and I slowly raise above her.

Being as gentle as I can so as not to wake her, I ease myself in slowly. The excess semen makes my entry easy. Her body instantly responds, and I hold myself still. My God, this is too good to be true—she just feels too good. My arms shake as they struggle to hold my weight. I don't move and instantly her body starts to contract around me, milking me and silently begging for my come. Her breathing is labored and she moans a deep sound, one that I haven't heard her make before, and the tingles in my balls force me to start to slowly move. With five gentle pumps she sighs and falls spectacularly into the most beautiful orgasm I have ever witnessed and I gently follow, knowing that I am thoroughly and utterly forever ruined.

Shit, I'm aroused again at just the memory of her... and her beautiful fuckable body. I rub my temples—talk about a total mind–fuck. Cabin crew, prepare for descent. I look at my phone again—7.10 am. She'd be awake by now and she would be spitting nails.

We sit in the limo en route to the hospital and I check my phone for the hundredth time this morning. She hasn't rung —she's definitely pissed. I've fucking blown it. It's probably for the best as I can't have her anyway. What was I thinking? I rub my forehead. I've had enough of this day already and its

7.00 o'clock in the morning. My phone beeps a text and I scramble to check if it's her. Adrian and Ben laugh, and my eyes snap up to them.

"Expecting a call?" Adrian smiles as he deletes the text, he's just sent me.

"Just fuck off, Adrian. I'm not in the damn mood," I snap. "Adrian, I want you to do the presentation this morning," I sigh as I adjust my cufflinks and stare out the window. "I'm not up for it." He doesn't answer. The silence is stifling, and I look up to see what they are doing.

"Josh, this is a twenty–two-million-dollar deal, you can't not do this. What the hell is going on with you?"

"Nothing I just haven't slept and I'm... off."

"Just ring her if it's that important."

"Her name is Natasha, and this has nothing to do with her."

"Josh, you better get your shit together or two years of work is going down the drain, I mean it. Snap the fuck out of it." I rub my forehead and put my head back into the head rest.

This day just keeps getting better and better.

3.00 pm—the meeting went well, and we are having a late lunch in a bar. The techs are on their commercial flight back to Sydney. Ben, Adrian and I are staying in Melbourne overnight so I can see my parents, although I would rather be alone. Not in the mood for socializing... or living for that matter. I order another Cointreau and ice—it seems the only thing that I can stomach today. I'm so tired.

No wonder I feel like shit, I hardly slept on Saturday night after the fight and then last night was a write off. Ben and Adrian are talking nonstop about Sydney versus Melbourne restaurants. I smile at the notion they consider themselves foodies. All I want to do is go to a hotel and take a sleeping pill, knock myself out for the rest of this shitty day. But I have to go to my parents' for dinner. Why do I make these stupid arrangements? It seemed like a good idea at the time. My phone beeps a text.

I'm sore, baby

I immediately smile. It's her. I reply.

Mission accomplished

I leave it for a second and then text back.

And for the record so am I.

I smile again, picturing her reading my text. I look up to find Adrian and Ben silent and utterly shocked in their seats.

"What?" I smirk.

"Are you kidding?" Adrian snaps. "You've been a total ass all day and one text from Cinderella and you are smiling like an idiot."

"Shut up. I am not." But it's true. I am smiling like an idiot.

"I don't believe it." Ben shakes his head. "I never thought I'd see the day."

I frown. "What do you mean?"

"You've done your nuts over this girl," he tuts.

"I have not... done my nuts over this girl." I roll my eyes. "Joshua Stanton, the biggest lady prick in all of America, has been freaking out all day waiting for Cinderella to text him, un-fucking-believable."

Natasha

I smile as I read his text. I bet you're sore, big boy, if my vagina is any indication. So, he is speaking to me. I am in my office between patients, sitting at my desk drinking coffee. I have been overanalyzing him and this situation all day. I was ropeable this morning when I woke and he was gone, coward.

But then I realized he was probably freaked out and I needed to give him space to adjust to this situation, whatever the hell this situation is. I am just as confused as he is. A large lead ball has sat in the bottom of my stomach since I woke up and he wasn't there. It's...annoying. I know we have no future, so why am I trying to prolong this stupid affair? This is just so messed up. Why in the hell is he my cousin? It's not natural to be so attracted to a blood relative. My mind drifts back to last night. He's amazing. I smile again. I know he was right there with me during the sex, the whole six amazing hours of it. No wonder I'm sore, the man is an animal. The kind of animal that has you begging for seconds. I know he lost his head as much as I did, but then he left without saying goodbye. Why? At least I have left the walls for communication open now and he has texted back. Perhaps he's working?

My boss Henry comes into my office.

"Hi Natasha. Just checking that you still want to go with Peter tomorrow?"

I frown as I try to remember what he is talking about. "Where to?"

"Remember he has that appointment at the detention center regarding that bail hearing he's got coming up. He just needs a witness that's all. I can send someone else if you are too busy."

"No, I'll go. I just forgot about it." I smile.

"Ok good, it will be good experience for you, that's all." Henry is my boss. He's kind of wonderful. Although I'm qualified to do this job, I am much younger and less experienced than the other sexual psychologists but Henry took a liking to me in my internship and offered me a position after I finished university. I am still on the relatively easy cases but am learning every day. This job is the opportunity of a lifetime. I'm grateful that he had the faith in me to give me the opportunity.

"Yeah, sounds good. I'm looking forward to it". I smile as he leaves the office. Thank God—a distraction. I need to stop obsessing about Mr. Stanton. If he wants to see me, he will have to ring me. I texted him...now he will have to call me. He better call me.

I stare out of the window of the car on the way to the detention center. My mind is constantly flicking between current events and images of Mr. Stanton making love to me. I'm over it. I need to grow up.

"So, Peter, tell me the drill for when we get there."

He smiles warmly. Peter is in his fifties and one of the most senior qualified psychologists we have. His silver hair is the only giveaway to how old he is, if not for that he could be in his thirties. He really looks after himself. He deals with sexual violence and crimes of that nature. The majority of his clients are male and in prison. I'm interested in why he needs a witness today.

"I'm seeing Coby Allender."

I frown. "Why does that name sound familiar?"

He smiles. "He's the guy that they suspect is a serial killer. He's being charged with fourteen counts of murder."

My eyes widen. "Did he do it?"

He shrugs. "Not sure. The man is smarter than any of us. Has the highest IQ of anyone I have ever met. They think he has an accomplice, so they keep sending me in to try and find out. Don't worry. You won't be in the room with us; you will be in a glass interview room behind a mirror. Although all the sessions are taped, I just need a witness to come with me. Prison policy."

I nod. "Okay. I can do that."

We arrive and we are escorted through the office and searched. The place is unnerving, and my heart rate rises just being behind these walls. We are led down a long corridor which looks like part of a hospital. There we are introduced to two prison wardens.

"This is Natasha Marx. She will be witnessing today." I smile and shake the hands of the two wardens.

They are tall and strong and exactly like I would picture them in my head. The first dark guy shakes my hand, "Nice to meet you. George Hamil." I smile and nod.

The second warden shakes my hand, "Jesten Miller." I shake his hand and am jolted by a shock of sexual energy. My eyes fly up to meet his and he smirks a knowing smile. *Hmm.* I jerk my hand out of his.

"Hello," I stammer, shocked by my physical reaction to Jesten. He's tall, blonde, big and muscular. Looks like Thor or something. Hmm, the mind boggles. We continue down the hall and George and Peter turn to me.

"You go with Jesten. He will stay with you in the witness room." I smile nervously at Jesten and he nods warmly. *Jeez.* Jesten leads me down another long corridor and opens a door.

We both enter. The room is dark and has seats in a row that look onto another interview room. I nervously take a seat, he takes the one right next to me. Bloody hell, he smells good. I smile awkwardly at him as I realize he is the only man other than the beautiful Mr. Stanton that has had a physical effect on me.

"So, your name is Natasha?"

I nod and smile. "Jesten, that's an unusual name."

He rolls his eyes. "Yeah, my mum's a tripper."

I smile and he winks at me. Hmm, he's a little bit cute. He has a naughty boy appeal going on.

"You haven't been here before, have you?"

I frown. "How do you know that?"

"Because we don't get hot psychologists here often." His eyes lock on mine. "And I would have remembered you."

Is he flirting with me? "Um, no I haven't. This is new for me."

"I doubt that."

I frown. "What do you mean?"

"I'm sure you turn on a lot of men you meet."

"Jesten, are you flirting with me?" I bite my lip to stifle my smile.

"Totally. But you dig it, right?" He gives me a cheeky grin.

Hmm, there is definitely something about this guy.

"I might." Shit. Did I just say that? I'm flirting back now.

He smiles and winks again as the interview room door opens. I watch as Peter and George enter the room. Then I watch as a prisoner in handcuffs enters the room, Coby Allender. A cold shiver runs down my back. He's intense and very intelligent, I can tell by the way he looks at Peter. He looks up at the glass and blows a kiss. I sit back affronted.

"He can't see you. He's just trying to fuck with your head," Jesten says.

I nod nervously, "I know." It's working—this situation is freaking me out. For the next forty minutes I watch as Coby Allender manipulates everything that Peter says. This man is very bright and super-frustrating. I find I am intrigued by this interview. It really is interesting. I had considered going back to university part–time to study criminology last year but decided against it. Maybe I should reconsider. Eventually, I am led out of the room by Jesten and we wait in the hall for Peter.

"So, are you going to give me your number?"

I do wide eyes at him. "No, I'm working. This is totally unprofessional." I smirk, unable to hide it.

He smiles back, "You're into me though. I can tell."

"I am not...into you. You're into yourself." I smile broadly at the cheeky hot specimen in front of me.

"Well, I'm into you. Come back for another interview at the prison and we can have another witness date."

I laugh, "Witness date. Did we just go on a date?"

He laughs and nods. "Yep. Hot, wasn't it?"

I laugh again. "Totally hot." I roll my eyes.

Peter comes out, "Ready to go?"

I nod and smile at Jesten, "See you later."

He smiles and gives me a wink. "You can count on it." Hmm.

The problem with being involved with a prickface is exactly that. He's a total prickface who never rings me when I expect him to. It's 9.00 pm Tuesday night and I am waiting for the girls at Oscar's. Abbie arrives first in her work clothes and I instantly feel underdressed in my gym gear.

"Hi, where's Bridg?" She smiles and I instantly feel better knowing that my beautiful friends will put this into perspective for me. I always feel better after talking things through with them.

"Not here yet," I answer. She nods and flops into the leather lounge next to me.

"Have you already had a coffee?" She looks at my empty cup. I nod.

"Yes, I'm trying to keep myself busy."

She rubs my leg in a sympathetic gesture. "So, he still hasn't called?"

I shake my head. "No and I don't think he will."

"Mmm," she answers, "I totally get lesbianism you know. Imagine not having to deal with all this shit we cop from men."

"I know, right?" I answer. Bridget breezes in, oh no, she's back on the love boat. Abbie and I roll our eyes at each other.

"Hi, sorry I'm late. Jim and I just had Thai together," she gushes.

"Don't you mean Jeremy?" Abbie asks flatly.

"Oh yes," she smiles. "I just like to call him Jim," she looks around to the counter and Abbie sticks her fingers down her throat, simulating 'I'm going to be sick'. I stifle a giggle.

"So, Tash, did he call?" she puts her hand on my knee and I shake my head.

"That's it, dump the stupid ass."

I smile. "I don't need to. It seems I have already been dumped, by him."

"What an idiot," she rolls her eyes. "So, what happened on Sunday? I want all the details," she sits forward.

"Well, we went shopping and then we had a fight and then we made up and then we pretty much had sex for the next six or eight hours."

"Eight hours?" Abbie spits. I smile as I take a sip of my coffee. "Hell, is he on Viagra?"

I shrug, "I have no idea. I'm not sure what's normal for him."

"I'm lucky if I get forty minutes," Bridget snaps.

"So, how was it? Is he as good as he looks?"

"Abbie," I snap. "It's not like that," though I smile, unable to hide my glee at being able to report back.

Bridget points her teaspoon at me. "Don't you dare hold out on us. We need details."

"Let's just say, I felt well and thoroughly used on Monday and my throat was sore."

"Sore throat. Oh God, were you giving head all night?" Bridget winces.

I laugh. "No, my throat was sore from screaming. I think he was trying to kill me with orgasms."

Abbie simulates melting down the lounge, while wiping her forehead. "Kill me now. I knew he'd be amazing in the sack. How did you get so lucky, bitch?" she snaps.

I giggle, "Though to be honest, I think I would have rather gone without. Now I know what I'm missing out on and, trust me girls, there is nowhere to go after Mr. Stanton. He's the whole package." I rub my forehead as I contemplate meeting a very mediocre version of man and how disheartening that day will be.

"So, did he say he would call you?"

"No, he told me we could just have one night together."

"So, why are you waiting for him to call?" Abbie frowns.

I shrug. "Wishful thinking probably. I'm telling you he felt it too. He told me he adores me. Actually, no, he said he fucking adores me."

I place my hand under my chin and blow out a deep breath as I swoon at the memory.

"Oh, I forgot, what did he say about the ink?"

"Um, this sounds weird but if you were me it wouldn't." I don't know why but I feel embarrassed to elaborate. "He...he got it on my twenty–first birthday as a birthday present to me."

"Fuck off," Bridget snaps.

"I know, right," I nod.

"He's hot and sentimental," Abbie sighs. "I think I'm in love with him myself."

"Me too," Bridget chimes in.

"Well, that makes three of us," I groan as I lean my head back onto the lounge. "What the hell am I going to do?"

"What drives him mad?" Abbie chimes in.

I shrug my shoulders. "You know was there a point when he lost control?"

"He likes dirty talk," I whisper, a little embarrassed. Both their eyes light up.

"What? What did you say?"

"I'm not going there," I giggle. "But I dropped the C-bomb."

"You're kidding," Bridget laughs. "You hate that word."

"I know," I rub my eyes as I remember how he loved it. "It amped him right up, actually. He totally lost control. He took me to the dark side...and I need to get on a fast train back."

"Well, use your head Tash, if he loses it over dirty talk." Abbie's phone texts a message which she reads.

"You are kidding," she snaps, "I've had enough."

"What's wrong?"

"James hooked up with that tunnel cunt and now he's asking me not to come home tonight so he can make lots of noise. He can forget it."

"Why do you hate this girl again?"

"Because she's after his money."

"How do you know that?"

"The brother of a girl at work hooked up with her a couple of years ago and apparently she gave him six months of terror after the event. She used to be a stripper in an upper-class strip club. It wouldn't surprise me if she's a high-end hooker or something now, and I just don't trust her."

"What does she look like again?" Bridget asks.

"Caramel-blonde, beautiful. A killer body, but I'm telling you the girl is evil. If she hurts him, I'm going to disembowel the bitch with a hairbrush."

We all laugh. I knew if I spent a couple of hours with my friends I could forget about the dread that is creeping over me, the sick ball in my stomach that is telling me I'm just another notch on his bed post, one that he went back to simply for old time's sake.

Wednesday, 12.00 am — I lie in bed on my back while the hot tears run into my ears. I have been lying here since 10.00 pm and still I can't sleep. I haven't eaten all day, and I have a thumping headache. My mind is constantly assessing the situation. Is he in someone else's arms now? Does he have someone in his bed? Maybe he was already seeing someone when he promised me, he wouldn't be with anyone else. Of course, he's with someone else, who am I kidding? My chest is physically hurting.

Thursday 9.00 pm — I am heartbroken after crying on and off for most of the day yesterday. Reality, the bitch, has hit me hard. He's not going to call. He obviously doesn't feel the same. I totally imagined the chemistry we shared, no, actually I felt it. It was just him that felt nothing. I sit on the lounge in my gym gear after devouring a family block of chocolate. Honestly, why bother going to the gym? What's the goddamn point? I feel sick to my stomach and it has nothing to do with the sugar coma I'm just about to slip into. I shower, put on my robe and pour myself a glass of wine. I head out to my balcony and sit on my day bed while I watch the city lights below me twinkle and listen to the hustle and bustle noises, a towel wrapped around my head. What should I do? I know the answer but how in the hell do I forget him? I wish last weekend never happened. It has just brought painful feelings to the surface again, ones that I'm not coping with.

I thought I was stronger than this. My life is a mess.

An hour later, I go and retrieve my phone and glasses to check my emails and return to my spot on the balcony. I stare at my phone for a good thirty minutes. Should I ring him? I know I shouldn't, but what do I do? Am I really going to put myself through this? I would rather he reject me than this waiting around crap, it's killing me. I want to hear him say the words. I need to hear him tell me he doesn't want me. My eyes fill with tears as I even contemplate hearing those painful words. Only then can I move on. Only then will I be able to start to heal. I can't go on like this...I text:

Why don't you ring me?

I suddenly start to freak out, what am I doing? My phone immediately beeps a text.

You know why.

I text back.

Don't you want to hear my voice?

I instantly regret sounding so needy, but I need answers. My phone beeps again:

More than anything!!!

I sit up. What? He wants to hear my voice more than anything... With exclamation marks. For the first time in four days I find myself smiling at my phone. I text back:

I need another night, baby. I can't do this.

Shit, have I gone too far? That's definitely needy. I screw my face up. Oh shit, who cares, I am frigging needy. My phone beeps again:

I can't change my DNA, Natasha.

My heart sinks. It is the cousin thing. That's something I can't change either, no matter how hard I try. My eyes fill with tears. I text back:

You are thinking too much.

I wait for his reply, but he doesn't answer. Fifteen minutes go by and still no answer. I start to pace while ringing my hands. Forty–five minutes later, still nothing. With a heavy heart I text him one last time:

I put a key to my apartment on your keyring.
Please use it.

XXXXX

———

An hour and a half and a second desperately hot shower later, I fall into bed. That's it, I tried. He can't let the cousin thing go and I can't change the circumstances. I give up. It's an exhausting situation, one that I can't change. I am just drifting into sleep when I hear the key go into my door.

Shit, he came.

CHAPTER 12

Natasha

I JUMP up and then I jump back onto the bed. Oh, crap, should I pretend to be asleep? I jump up again, no asleep. I lie back down. I flick my lamp on and I hear him put his keys onto my foyer table and walk towards my bedroom. My heart is in my throat. It is then I feel the intensity of his presence. His body is radiating heat like kryptonite, my body instantly weakening to its strength and softening under his gaze. I roll over and we stare at each other in silence, tension hanging thick in the air. I hold my hand up to him and he takes it and sits next to me on my bed in silence.

"Stop thinking so much, baby," I whisper.

"No," he answers. "You are not thinking enough, Presh. This is wrong, Natasha. We shouldn't be doing this."

"Josh, if it's so wrong, why does it feel so right?" I kiss the back of his hand. He closes his eyes at the contact. "Why did you leave the other night without saying goodbye, Josh?"

He drops his head. "I had a 5.30 am flight to Melbourne, and my brothers are here, remember." I smile a sad smile and nod. That's right, I had forgotten that.

I pull back the covers. "Come and lie with me."

His eyes scan my body, and he smiles a crooked smile. "I thought I told you to throw out the flannel pajamas."

I smirk back. "They're snuggly. I have a good mind to buy you some so we could be matching." He smiles and lies down next to me fully dressed.

"Are you wearing jeans to bed?" I ask.

"No, I'm not staying," he answers.

My heart drops. "Why aren't you staying, Josh?"

"Tash, sshh, stop it. I'm here because you asked me to come. I don't want to fight." I nod as I cuddle him and start to run my fingers through his hair. He relaxes into my arms. I feel him gently kiss my neck as he leans into me.

"Can you stay with me tonight? No sex," I whisper.

"No sex," he repeats.

I shake my head. "Josh, I don't want to be with you just for sex...even though the sex is awesome."

"Awesome," he smiles as he raises his eyebrows.

"What do you want to be with me for, Tash?" I stay silent as I try to think of the right answer. I know the answer to this question is important to him. I can feel it.

"I've missed you, Josh. Just being with you makes me feel better. I can't explain it. You are my medicine, and you calm me. When you're with me, I can stop worrying." He nods as if he understands and snuggles deeper into my neck.

"Just hold me, baby," I whisper. "Don't leave me again tonight. I can't bear it." I gently stroke my fingers through his hair and up and down the length of his neck and gently kiss his forehead. I can feel his body relax. I feel that he, too, is suffering from inner turmoil and that he also feels better just having me near. I haven't truly relaxed since I was in his arms on Sunday night, and it feels good. It feels like home. Truer words have never been spoken—he is my medicine and just having him near makes me feel better.

I continue to run my fingers through his hair and down his neck. His regular breathing notifies me that he has drifted off to sleep— he must be exhausted. He's so tired. Has he not been sleeping well either? A tingle of unease runs through my body as I realize that the man I have with me tonight is a different man to the one I met on Sunday night. The Sunday night man was dominant and confident and in control of his emotions. The man asleep in my arms is gentle and broken and I feel a surge of protective instinct over him. This is the beautiful Josh I remember. The one I fell in love with. He obviously has two very distinct sides to his personality. One strong and one weaker, as we all do I suppose. I myself have two sides: I am strong in every part of my life except when it comes to him.

I wake with a start as the pain in my arm throbs; it's gone to sleep. I must have fallen asleep. Josh is still out cold and asleep in my arms. I smile and gently kiss his forehead again. I slowly peel myself out from under him and head to the bathroom. En route to the kitchen I walk past the foyer and see his phone and keys on my side table. I shouldn't, but I can't help it I walk over and pick up his phone and swipe it on. It's unlocked. *Shit.* I look around, I shouldn't be doing this. I feel like a naughty kid. I go to his messages, the last message he sent being to Ben at 10.45 pm.

I'm at my girl's. Do Not Disturb

I smile, am I his girl? A frisson of excitement runs through me— he makes me feel like a schoolgirl.

I put a key to my apartment on your keyring.
Please use it

xxxxx

I scroll through the next few messages between us.
11.15 am to Adrian.

Get me a coffee while you're out.

I keep scrolling through, nothing interesting here. Monday 7.30 am from Adrian.

Are you expecting a text from Cinderella?

Huh, Monday morning, that's after he left me. Was he waiting for me to call? Surely not. I frown, that's confusing. I exit the messages and go into the images. There is a photo of me asleep. I'm naked so it must have been Sunday night. Hmm, happy with that shot just quietly. Then there are five photos of me from the wedding in which a face–splitting smile breaks my face. A photo of Adrian sticking his finger up at the camera, obviously unimpressed. Ten photos of horses and then there is a photo of a beautiful blonde girl with one of the horses. Who the hell is this? Maybe the photo is of the horse. To my dismay, the next photo is of the girl on her own, smiling. She's... stunning. It's a natural shot taken outside, maybe on a picnic blanket. Another few photos of horses and then another photo of the blonde, on a boat this time. What the fuck? Who is this girl? He told me he doesn't date. Was he lying? Going on picnics and boat rides is definitely a frigging date in my books. There are a total of twenty photos on his phone and this girl makes the cut and now I can't even ask who she is because I'm not even supposed to know she exists.

I click out of the phone in disgust with myself. I tell my clients every day, 'Don't snoop because you will only upset yourself. If you don't have trust in a relationship, then you have nothing.' What a crock. I get my glass of water and drink it at the sink while I calm myself down. She's probably a friend. My gut instincts tell me otherwise. What an idiot, why did I do that? I amble back to the bedroom and walk around to Josh's side of the bed. As I go to switch off the lamp I see Joshua's clothes on the floor. I pretend I don't notice and go to pull back the blankets.

"Pajamas off," he says darkly. I smile and raise my eyebrows. "From now on, our bed is a pajama-free zone," he breathes.

"It is, is it?" I raise my eyebrows. Our bed, I love the sound of that.

"And why can't I wear pajamas?" I slide them off and sit on the side of the bed. He runs his hand from my bottom up my back to my neck and grabs my nape and pulls my head back by my hair. "Because I don't fuck in pajamas," he breathes into my neck as he bites it hard. I close my eyes as goosebumps spread over my flesh. I do so love dominant Mr. Stanton. Thank God he came to visit me tonight. I was beginning to worry.

I wake alone... again. However, I feel a lot more optimistic than I have since last Sunday. At least I now know that I didn't imagine it; there was something there. His brief shutdown of his defenses last night allowed me to see a glimpse of the man I miss. He's struggling with this as well, I think. I stroll out to flick on my coffee machine and find a note on the kitchen counter.

Slept in, early meeting.
Josh xx

I pick up the note and smile. Things are looking up and he gave me two kisses. Maybe there is hope after all, hope for what though I'm not sure. I spend all day daydreaming and reminiscing about the night before, hardly wiping the smile from my stupid face. At work in my break I do the unthinkable, something I haven't allowed myself to ever do. I google cousin relationships. I am astounded to find page after page on the subject. Is this for real? For half an hour I sit transfixed to a website called 'Cousin Love' with tears running down my face. Story after story of forbidden true love. People who have done nothing wrong but fall in love with the wrong person—actually, wrong choice of words, a person their family thinks is wrong. A lot of the stories mirror ours in that they hooked up and fell in love in their teens and tried to suppress it, only to have the feelings reappear in their twenties. Like me, most of the people haven't come out to their families for fear of persecution. I read the list of famous people who married their cousins:

Queen Elizabeth and Prince Phillip
Albert Einstein
Greta Scacchi
Kevin Bacon
Rudi Giuliani Jesse James
Franklin D Roosevelt
Thomas Jefferson
Charles Darwin

Jerry Lee Lewis

Johann Sebastian Bach.

Hmm, some of the most brilliant minds of all time were attracted to their cousins. I'm not a freak. The Queen of England is married to her cousin. Who knew? I leave the website with a heavy heart but feeling somewhat comforted to know I am not alone and that others feel the same. I just wish I knew how Josh felt, I mean really felt. I know he adores me, but is it enough? Adore is not love. As much as I wish it were.

CHAPTER 13

Natasha

"Just pull over up here," Bridget says as she points to the curb. It's 10.30 pm and Abbie and I are dropping her at Jeremy's after our Italian dinner date. I'm exhausted. I yawn. The car is stopped, and she has the car door open talking to Abbie about making fresh pasta or something equally boring. I rub my eyes. "Can you two hurry the hell up?" I frown as I lean my head onto the steering wheel. I'm frigging delirious. They finally finish up and we head down the street. Rhianna's 'Diamonds' blares from my handbag.

"Shit, get that Abbs," I snap.

After rummaging through my bag, she answers. "Hi... No, this is Abbie... um yeah, hang on a sec... Who's speaking please?" She puts her hand over the phone.

"It's Adrian."

"Who?" I frown.

She hunches her shoulders. "Adrian."

"Oh shit. Josh's Adrian." I quickly pull over the car. I snatch the phone. "Hi, this is Natasha." Damn, I sound like a school-teacher.

"Hi, Natasha, sorry to bother you. It's Adrian. Are you busy?"

I frown, that's a strange question. "It's just... I was wondering if you could help me out?"

"Sure, Adrian. Is everything ok?"

"Not really, it's Josh."

My heart jumps in my chest. "What's wrong?" I snap.

"No, it's ok. We have just had a really long lunch and we are in a bar in the Rocks." I smile as I imagine Josh drunk in a sleazy bar. "Anyway, that guy that Josh had that fight with the other night... um, that friend of yours."

"Todd," I snap.

"Yes, he turned up about forty minutes ago."

"Right," I wince.

"They are just glaring at each other at this stage."

"Who is Josh with?"

"His two exec friends from IBM." My mind is going a million miles per minute. Surely this can't be good. "Um, anyway Josh just ordered all of the bodyguards out of the pub and asked me to go home."

My eyes bulge. "Is that abnormal?"

"Well, he's never done anything like this before." Holy fuck, they're going to kill each other.

"I know this sounds lame, but can you come and get him? If he gets into another fight it will affect his visa. This idiot already put him up on an assault charge."

"Ok. I'm on my way. Where are you?"

"Thanks. We are at the Observer in the Rocks." Oh shit. I hang up and start driving like a maniac.

"What's going on?" Abbie frowns.

"Todd, the fuckwit, has turned up at the place where Josh is drinking."

"Oh shit, that can't be good."

"I know, anyway he has ordered his bodyguards out of the Observer Hotel. They are going to get into a fight."

"Oh fuck," Abbie winces.

"I know," I snap. "Ok, come up with a plan."

"Plan," she frowns. "I'm hopeless at plans."

"Just fucking think of one." As I speed up, a taxi pulls out in front of me and I swerve to miss it.

"I want to get there alive you know."

My tongue is hanging out as I concentrate. I hold up my hand. "Ok, I've got it. You're going to take one for the team."

"Huh," she frowns.

"You need to get Todd out of there so, so... take one for the team." She bursts out laughing.

"You want me to sleep with Todd to save him."

I smile at her as I drive. "Please don't grow morals now. I need you."

"Jeez, chill out, will you? I've already slept with Todd and I don't really want to do it again."

I slam my foot on the brake and we both jump forward. "Eeww, you tried to set me up with your sloppy seconds?" I'm beyond mortified.

"Well, how else would I know he wasn't a serial killer?"

"I have no words for you now. Actually, yes I do. You're repulsive." She smiles her sneaky slut smile at me, and I shiver in repulsion. Thank God Josh saved me I shudder to think what could have happened. I would have been scarred for life. We get to the bar and park the car. With linked arms we gingerly approach the bar.

Adrian sees us.

"Oh, thank God you're here," he smiles. It is then I see the three burly bodyguards out front. "Who are they?" I point to the three men with my chin.

"This is Thomas, Josh's bodyguard."

I frown. "Where's Ben?"

"He went home to America for a funeral." I smile and shake his hand. "And the other two are Josh's friends' bodyguards."

"What do Josh's friends do?"

"They are executives at IBM." Abbie rolls her eyes at me as if to signify more ridiculous wealth. I smile and nod, totally understanding her meaning. I look through the window and see Josh walk over to Todd, holy fuck. It is actually laughable to think that a man with as much power as Joshua Stanton, who is probably wearing a fifteen–thousand dollar suit, is in a bar, ready to pub-brawl like a pig farmer. With apprehension I walk into the bar and straight over to the two men. I walk up behind Josh and hear him snap out the words.

"Why in the fuck did you say it then?"

"To piss you off, and it worked, didn't it?"

"Don't push your fucking luck or you will be coughing up a kidney." My heart warms at the sound of my knight in shining armor defending my honor.

I put my hand on his back. "Hi baby." He turns and frowns, shocked at seeing me.

"Tash, what are you doing here?" he slurs. Oh my, he is drunk. I smile.

"I came to take you home, baby," I whisper in his ear. He smiles and leans into me. Simultaneously Abbie grabs Todd's hand and drags him to the dance floor. I give her a wink as she passes me. Todd looks like he is the cat that got the cream and is quite happy to be sidetracked by my beautiful friend.

Surely, it's not going to be that easy, is it? Josh smiles and pulls me into an embrace and starts to immediately suck on my neck. I step back.

"Down boy," I whisper. It is then I notice the two men in very expensive suits across the room. Josh drags me over to his friends.

"This is Natasha," he pronounces as he kisses the back of my hand. His eyes linger on my face with a look I have not seen before. Oh, I like drunk Josh—he's quite charming.

"Showstopper, it's nice to meet you," one of the men says as he puts his hand out to shake mine. I frown and Josh and the other man burst into laughter.

"Showstopper? I'm sorry you have me at a loss," I frown.

"We," he gestures to him and his friend, "have renamed you showstopper." I frown as Josh once again kisses the back of my hand without one bit of embarrassment. Hmm, I definitely do like this cuddly version of my man.

"You are a showstopper because we weren't allowed to go to any strip shows tonight because," he puts his two fingers up to accentuate the quote, "Natasha wouldn't like it." He pokes me in the chest as he smiles at me. Really. This is news. My face turns red as I smile at Josh and he pulls me into an embrace and kisses my forehead. I smile, a little embarrassed and unsure what to say. He's dead on target; I would have gone postal if he went to a strip club tonight. The two men giggle and Josh leans in and grabs my face.

"I fucking adore you." He then grabs me and starts to full-on tongue kiss me in front of his two friends. Ok, not so sure about the cuddly PDA now, way too far. I pull back and do wide eyes at him to signify for him to stop it. He giggles and starts to kiss my hand again. Jeez, he's so touchy and over–the–top affectionate. The two men laugh, and one slaps a fifty–dollar bill into the other's hand. "I told you. I give it six months and he'll be fucking married." Thankfully Josh didn't hear that. He's too busy trying to sex me up in public with my fingers in his mouth. Oh boy, I need to get him home or he will try to go for it on the pool table. I pull him over to the door and out into the cool air and he trips down the stairs.

"How much did you drink, baby?" I giggle and he stumbles.

"Too fucking much."

"We're going home," he announces to the bodyguards and they in turn smile at me as if to say job well done.

"Can you give my keys to my friend please?" Big burly guy smiles and nods and disappears into the pub. Abbie takes the keys and smiles and gives me the thumbs up. She probably will get with Todd tonight. Yuck, so not going there. Josh and I stumble towards his limo with his arm draped around my shoulder.

"I'm going to take you home and fuck you three ways," he slurs into my ear as he stumbles sideways. We both sidestep down the footpath.

"Josh, sshh, keep your voice down," I whisper as I look around to see if anyone can hear him. Jeez three ways, what the hell? My eyes widen. Oohh, shit, I know what he means... surely not. Not when he's in this state. Maybe I should have gotten drunk tonight too. We get to the limo and I open the door and signify for him to get in before me. Instead he pushes me up against the car with the door open behind me. He slowly swipes his tongue through my open lips as his hands hold onto either side of my face. I feel faint as my heartrate picks up. How in the hell can this man bring me to my knees even in this inebriated state? He slowly and gently commands my arousal as he kisses me deeply, his tongue demanding me to give myself over to him. He tastes like Cointreau and his now hard, throbbing length is digging into my hip, my body softening against his hardness. He pulls back and stares into my eyes.

"Do you love me?" My heart jumps and my world stops spinning on its axis. Never in a million years did I imagine he was going to ask that question.

"Yes," I answer without hesitation, relieved that he asked, and I didn't have to spit it out on my own. He smiles the most beautiful smile I have ever seen, and I fall just a little bit harder. How did I get here, so in love with a man that I can't even see straight?

"Get in the car baby, let's go home," I whisper. I don't need to go anywhere in all honesty, as long as I'm with him I am already home. Even blind drunk he has me totally under his spell. In fact, I am the one feeling intoxicated, drunk on his pheromones. He nods and kisses me again.

"Hmm," he whispers as his eyes stay closed.

"Josh...Car," I smile.

"Hmm," he repeats, his eyes still closed.

I slowly unwrap his arms from around me and turn him away from me to face the car. "Watch your head." I put my hand on the top of his head, so he doesn't hit it on the car door frame as he bends to get in. He falls into the limo and I roll my eyes as I hop in after him. To my absolute horror, Adrian is sitting in the limo. He has heard everything we have just said. He must have gotten in when we were still inside the pub. Kill me now.

"Oh hi," I stammer.

"Hi," he smiles. I stay silent as Josh slides across the seat and pats his lap. Oh no, I am not sitting on his lap so I can give Adrian a private sex show on the way home. Josh is totally out of control on the affection tonight. I can't trust him to behave.

"Is it alright if I catch a ride?" Adrian asks me.

"Adrian it's your ride. I'm the one catching a lift," I smile.

"Thanks," he nods. Josh pats his lap again and I shake my head. "Josh, you can drop me off at my house. It's ok. I will see you tomorrow," I speak as if I am talking to a child.

"No, I am staying with you," he snaps. "Come over here. I want to cuddle you," he slurs. I roll my eyes at Adrian who gives me a sympathetic smile.

"Precious, I mean it. Now." He pats the seat next to him.

"Alright," I sigh. "Bossy Boots," I slide over next to him and to my utter amazement he does just cuddle me. He pulls my back to his chest and kisses the top of my head as he sits to the side. The bodyguard comes and gets into the car and we pull away from the curb, and an awkward silence falls over us. Adrian doesn't speak. He just watches Josh, who once again is kissing the back of my hand with his eyes closed. I fake a smile and rub Josh's leg. He puts his head back on the head rest and closes his eyes. After about ten minutes I look up at Adrian and he frowns.

"Is he always like this with you?" I shrug, unsure what to say, and slightly embarrassed. What must he have seen in the past? How many girls has he had this conversation with? I push these negative thoughts out of my mind. Stop it Natasha. Thankfully we arrive at my apartment shortly after and the burly bodyguard gets out and opens the door for us.

"Josh, wake up," I whisper.

"I think we had better help you get him upstairs."

"Thanks, Adrian, that would be great," I gently pat Josh's face and he wakes. "We are home, Josh, get out of the car."

"Hmm," he stumbles out of the car and wraps his arm around my shoulder. I guide him through the foyer and into the lift with the two men behind me, and a horrifying thought crosses my mind. Shit, is my apartment a mess? I can't even remember. I definitely didn't expect company tonight. We get to the front door and Adrian must be able to read my mind because he turns to the other man.

"We should be good from here. I will meet you in the car." He nods and disappears back into the lift. I smile.

"Thanks, Adrian, I really appreciate it." He takes over holding Josh up while I find my keys in my bag and unlock my front door. I flick on the light and silently thank the Lord my house isn't as messy as I envisioned.

"Come in," I gesture to Adrian. He nods as he leads Josh in. I grab Josh's hand and lead him up the hallway towards my bedroom. "Get into bed, baby. I will be in in a minute." He nods and starts stripping off in the hallway in front of us. I smile and turn back to Adrian.

He raises his eyebrows as he puts his hands in his suit pockets. "I've seen a very different man tonight to the one I know, Tash."

I smile. "It's funny you say that, because tonight I have seen the first glimpse of the man I do know." I flop onto the lounge. He sits down next to me and looks around my apartment.

"Nice place."

I smile. "Thanks, I like it. Do you want the tour?"

"Sure," he smiles as he stands.

"This is the living room," I gesture around the room. "Kitchen," I wave my hand around. "Bathroom," as I show him the bathroom.

He frowns. "I am so organizing a bathroom renovation for you tomorrow," he laughs. Ohh, I'm shocked. How rude, my bathroom might be brown nineteen–seventies shit but how dare he insult it. Who in the hell does he think he is, Donatella fucking Versace? He must have realized he's insulted me. "I'm sorry... I just am so used to organizing things. I just assumed that I am your personal assistant too.

Now that you're with Josh." He has the audacity to look embarrassed.

"I don't need a personal assistant," I snap. That came out harsher than I meant it to. I look up and I can see the hurt in his eyes. Poor bastard, he's trying to be nice. You're such a bitch, Natasha. "But I could use a friend," I smile. He smiles back and grabs my hand and pulls me up the hallway. There we see Joshua, spread eagled and naked on the bed like a starfish, asleep. I look down.

"I imagine you must have seen some sights. I mean, being with him all the time." I walk past him back towards the lounge room, uncomfortable with where this conversation was going.

"No, funnily enough I have never seen Josh touch a woman at all." I frown at him. "Josh doesn't date. Girls drape themselves off him, but I have never seen him like he was tonight. He's different with you."

I smile, poor misguided Adrian. "Thanks for trying to save my feelings but I know what Josh is like. He's way too affectionate to not touch girls. I'm not stupid."

He rubs my arm. "I think you underestimate him, Natasha."

I smile. "I wish. Do you want to grab a coffee in the morning?"

He nods. "I will call you."

"Ok, sounds good," and then he was gone. I was alone with my beautiful man, my beautiful, unconscious, smelling like a brewery man who was sleeping like a baby. I take my phone out and snap a photo of him. I smile as I look at it; there's one for the family album.

"Wake up, precious girl," his husky, whispered voice splinters my dreams and brings me into consciousness. "I need you." He kisses my neck and runs his open mouth down its length to my collar bone. I slowly come to and inhale the strong scent of soap and toothpaste. He's showered—what the hell time is it? It's still dark. Why is he even awake? His strong body radiates with need. His arms are straining to hold his weight off of me. I can feel his muscles contract and the overwhelming power emanating from his body. He wasn't exaggerating, he does need me I can feel it oozing from his every pore. "I'm aching for you, aching to be inside you." Hmm, I like this wake–up call. I rub my eyes as my legs fall open.

"Josh, what time is it?" I whisper.

"It's make-love-to-Josh time," he smiles into my neck. His smile is contagious, and I find myself mirroring him like an idiot. "Roll over, Presh. I need you from behind." He rolls my hip so that I am on my stomach and then hitches my right leg up. My knee is level with my breastbone. Then he is on me. He pulls my hair to the side to gain access to my neck. His heavy breathing into my ear from behind sends goosebumps across my body, awakening every cell. His hand runs from my knee to my behind and back again. His fingers gently slide between my legs and he hisses when he feels me. "So wet," he whispers. "You need me, too. Do you know what a turn on that is?"

"Yes," I whisper darkly. This is what his touch does to me: it leaves me vulnerable and begging, submissive even? Before I have time to analyze my thoughts on this, his fingers are inside me. Long, stroking, circular movements, stretching me open. I instantly lift my hips in a silent beg. I need more. My body needs more. As he bites my neck, he slowly sinks his heavy length into my wet sex.

"Mmm," he whispers. His arousal level is off the charts and he's taking me with him. I've never been so hot for it in my life. His open affection for me tonight has opened a can of worms and I desperately want to please him. He pushes in and glides out in a slow movement. He's so good at this. With his hands on my hips he lifts me until I am on my knees and he is kneeling behind me. He strokes my hair.

"Is that ok, Presh? Can you handle it? Tell me to stop if I hurt you." I smile and nod. Even when he is beyond aroused, he is still achingly aware that he is a very large man, and I am a ridiculously tight and inexperienced girl. I nod, too full to speak. He's right, it is a tight fit. He slowly starts to move at a quicker pace and his two hands are on my shoulders pulling me back onto him. He feels so damn good. A sheen of perspiration covers both of our bodies and I feel myself start to quiver.

"Not yet," he snaps. "Let me enjoy you some more." He moves me up until I am sitting on his lap with my knees on either side of his legs. Pulling my head to the side by my hair he gently swipes his tongue through my open lips, and he kisses me with such tenderness I feel weak. My eyes roll back in my head. His hands move, one on my breast and the other down to my clit where he circles with perfect precision.

"Circle your hips," he whispers. "I won't move, take me how you want me." I groan as I feel his hard length move inside me when I circle. This man is hot.

"Baby, why didn't you go to the strip show tonight?" I whisper. He smiles into my neck. "Because you asked me not to."

"Is that the only reason?" I swipe my tongue through his lips again, daring him to give me the truth I so desperately want. He tweaks my nipple and my body shudders in response. I'm close. "Why would I want to watch other women take their clothes off? When you're the only woman I see."

I smile as I kiss him again. "Good answer," I smile.

"Shut up and fuck me," he growls as he starts to lift me and slam me back down onto his brutal length. His mouth is open on my neck, his breathing burning me from the inside out. My head rolls back as I ride his hard punishing rhythm, one that pushes me into a shattering orgasm. I scream into his mouth and my body shudders as he bends me over and puts my elbows onto the mattress. He then really lets loose. A deep, heavy rhythm. Shit. One that I don't think I can take for much longer. I can feel him getting harder and I know he's close. His hands are digging into my hips as he pulls me back onto him with such force, I know I will have fingerprints on me tomorrow and you know what? I love it. He grabs my hips and stills himself, deep inside me, and groans from his stomach. I feel his heat inside me, and I collapse onto the mattress, his sweaty body covering mine.

When I woke up, he was gone.

Joshua

The seagull's cry wakes me from my daydream. Hot sun, beaming down onto my back. My hands drift in the water underneath my surfboard. This is why I love Australia. My morning ritual since being here: 6.00 am surf. I've missed my wave but I'm too relaxed to care. Being out here and being with her are the only two things that ground me and bring me back to reality. I feel like shit and my head is pounding. Why in the hell did I drink so much? The seagulls go wild again as I look to the beach and my stomach drops. Fucking bodyguards. Two of the bastards. Ben will be back tomorrow, thank God. I can't stand having these guys I don't know around me. At least when Ben is here, I just feel like I'm hanging out with a mate. I wish to God they would just catch him so I can have my fucking life back. I feel like a cockroach in a jar, trapped and isolated. Unknown to her, Natasha has been guarded. I smile at the thought of her going off like a firecracker. She'd see it as an invasion of privacy. I catch my last wave in and walk up the beach, shaking the water from my head.

"Let's go," I gesture to the men and I walk towards home.

Brad, one of the Australian bodyguards, laughs. "Your bitch is fuming."

"Yeah, I thought he would be." I smile at the two men with me and shake my head. Adrian is a total prick when he's angry with me. Nobody else is game—he's got guts; I will give him that. He, however, takes pleasure in it I'm sure. I walk in the front door to find Adrian sitting at my kitchen bench reading the newspaper. He looks up and then back at his paper, deadpan.

I sigh. "Out with it." He shakes his head and silently sips his coffee. "Listen, if you came to my house to give me the silent treatment don't bother. Do it from your house. I'm not in the fucking mood."

He holds his hand up. "Do not insult my intelligence, Joshua."

I roll my eyes. "You're being a bit melodramatic don't you think?"

"Melodramatic," he shrieks. "You ordered the body-guards and me out of the pub so you could fight like a frat boy, Josh. Last time I looked you were the CEO of a billion-dollar company. Why in the hell did you get so drunk?" I shrug as I grab the orange juice from the fridge and drink it from the bottle.

"God, get a glass you, behemoth."

"It's my house, get a muzzle. You're hurting my ears." He

narrows his eyes at me. I turn my back to him and make a protein shake, my first of three today.

"What if you had fought that guy and he slapped another assault charge on you? What then huh?" I frown and nod as I rub my eyes.

"Do you reckon he slept with her?" I ask.

"Oh fuck, not this again. You said she told you she had never been with him."

"Yeah, well why would he go to such lengths if he had never slept with her?"

"Josh, you're going fucking crazy."

"Maybe," I crack an egg into my shake. "Anyway, how did Tash know where we were last night? Maybe she was meeting him there and I crashed the party."

Adrian puts his hands on his hips. "You're pathetic, you know that don't you?"

"Shut up." I wince as my brain once again hits the sides of my skull.

"Natasha came because I rang her."

"What? Why in the fuck would you do that?"

"Because you were acting totally crazy."

"What if I was in a fight... and she saw? Don't you remember her reaction when she saw me kickboxing?"

"It was a cage fight, you animal, and I totally support her.

That's not a sport, it's barbaric."

"Whatever," I roll my eyes. "Go home, you're hurting my brain."

"I am going home actually." He turns and walks towards the door. "I'm having brunch with Natasha."

Huh, what the fuck. I jump off the stool and follow him outside. "What did you just say?"

"I said," he wobbles his stupid head to accentuate his point. "I'm having brunch with Natasha."

"No, you're fucking not!"

"Oh yes, I fucking am. Just because you won't take her for coffee doesn't mean I can't."

"You know why I don't take her for coffee."

"No, I don't, I don't get you at all. You're obsessed with her, won't stop talking about her, but you won't let yourself spend any time with her."

"Because I can't, you know that."

"Why can't you?"

"It's fucking incest, Adrian. It's wrong. This is the kind of shit toothless rednecks who live in the damn swamp do, not millionaires and psychologists. It's unheard of. And besides, it is only going to make it harder when I leave, for her I mean."

"Oh yeah sure, harder for her. You're a hypocrite." He turns to walk off again.

"Why am I a hypocrite?" I snap.

He turns and pokes me in the chest. "Who has been my biggest supporter in my sexuality, Josh? Fight for what's right, Adrian. It doesn't matter what anyone else thinks, Adrian. You can't put anyone's happiness before your own, Adrian. You deserve to be happy, Adrian. Little did I know you wouldn't have the guts to practice what you preach."

"It's different," I shout. "And you know that. It's not just me or I would do it in an instant. There isn't a fucking thing I wouldn't do to be with her, but I would never hurt her like that."

"Like what?" He stills.

"Her family will disown her if they know, and I care too fucking much to let her choose me over them. It's a decision that in years to come she will regret, and I know that for a fact."

"You asked her last night if she loves you."

"I did what?"

"You heard me."

I run both hands through my hair again. "This is a total fuck up." I nod and go to walk away.

"Don't you want to know her answer?" He smiles and I shake my head in sad resignation.

"No, I don't," I sigh. I walk back down my steps towards my front door.

"Yes!" he yells. "She said yes."

Oh fuck. What next, how much more am I supposed to take? I just can't take much more.

She's killing me softly.

I stalk back to my kitchen and scull my protein shake without tasting it. One night—I just need one more night. This is totally fucked. I'm like a drug addict waiting for my next hit and she is my drug of choice. I text Adrian.

'I forbid you to go out with her today. If I can't spend time with her, you're definitely not. Trust me, she could turn Elton John. But ask her to meet us at the Ivy tonight.'

This is it. I will just spend one more night with her and then that's it. I will walk away.

CHAPTER 14

Natasha

I'M SO SHITTY. So shitty. How dare he ask me if I love him and not say it back? What was it, a fucking test? Did I pass... asshole. He probably wants to see exactly how pathetic I actually am, and you know what? I'm astounded at myself at just how well I passed. I got a high fucking distinction. He doesn't call me, except in the middle of the night for a booty call. He leaves in the middle of the night, so he doesn't have to do the walk of shame in the morning. He doesn't communicate at all with me unless it's with his damn penis, as lovely as that is.

That's it, I know I've said it before, but I've seriously had enough of his shit. If he does call me, which he won't, but if he does, I'm going to tell him to take a hike. I smile as I listen to my thoughts. Even to my ears I know that's a lie. I put my head in my hands as I lean onto the kitchen bench. I hate having bastard–player–lover syndrome. Aren't you supposed to grow out of this shit when you turn nineteen? I pull on my gym gear and head to the gym—anything to stop me from calling him, calling him and begging for him to come back. At 11 am I receive a text.

Hi Tash, Sorry I have to bail on coffee,
but do you and your friends want to meet
Josh and me at the Ivy tonight?
Adrian x

I press the delete button with such force I'm amazed I don't crack the screen. As if I am going to turn up at the Ivy. He didn't even text me himself. What a wanker. He can wait there all frigging night or go to hell, either way, I don't care.

10 pm

I am in my flannel PJs, the ones he hates. In spite of course, with Abbie and Bridget by my side commiserating and drinking wine. We have decided he can go to hell. If he can't call me himself, well then, he bloody well can't have me. I must say the thought of him at the Ivy with all of those beautiful women and him being, well, himself, is making me jumpy.

"As if he won't pick up tonight," I sigh to Abbie.

"You're such an idiot," she snaps. "I thought you wanted answers?"

"I do," I sigh.

"Well, you are really going to get them here, aren't you?" I shrug my shoulders as I feel sorry for myself and blow out a breath, my head leaning back onto my sofa.

Bridget chimes in. "Natasha, you are doing the right thing.

He's a self-absorbed prick, remember." "What would you do then, Abbie?"

She smiles a sly smile. "I would go and look so unbelievably hot that he would be begging for mercy and then some." I narrow my eyes. "Why don't you go and set a trap?"

"Like what?"

"Arrive and then don't go over and say hello but let him see you. And didn't you say he liked dirty talk?" I nod. "Well, I would get my mouth so filthy it needs disinfecting and then I would go home without him. You watch, he'll be begging for mercy tomorrow. And you know what men do when they are needy?" I shrug—really, I have no idea about men, do I? "They talk," she raises her eyebrows and gives me a wink.

I bite my lip and look at Bridget who shrugs her shoulders. "Hmm, that does sound better than my plan I suppose," I whisper.

She smiles at me, "Lucky you got that Brazilian wax. It's not pretty when girls' pubes hang out the bottom of miniskirts."

"Eeww, you're an animal," Bridget chuckles.

"Hurry the hell up", she snaps. "Time to tart up. Mr. Stanton is going down."

I look into the mirror at my reflection an hour later; ok, yes, it's true. I do look sort of hot. I've got the cleavage happening, thanks to my super duper booster bra, tight wrap, bandage black dress, my shoes that I want to marry, and my hair is straightened to within an inch of its life. I'm even wearing red lipstick. If he can resist me looking as skanky as this then good luck to him, he deserves an exit pass. Now the dirty talk, that's a whole different story. What the hell do I say?

And how far is too far? There's a fine line between hot and downright low, maybe I will just follow his lead all night. See how far he can take me.

11.45 pm

We walk into our favorite bar at the Ivy and I must say the reaction of a few drunken men outside on the street to my dress has given me the confidence boost I so desperately needed. Abbie heads to the bar to buy our drinks and I wait with Brid- get. She knows a group of girls here from uni and one of them has come over to talk to us.

"Oh my, Natasha, you look amazing tonight," she smiles. "Have you lost weight?" I fake a smile and nod. I hate it when girls say that when they can't think of anything else. I haven't lost frigging weight, you silly bitch. My thoughts are anywhere but on this conversation.

"Two o'clock," Bridget whispers. I casually look around and I see them, the Stanton boys, well, three of them and Adrian. Two other men are not far from them leaning up against the wall and I now recognize them as Josh's bodyguards. Josh is in his standard jeans and blazer, but he has a pink checkered shirt on, and he looks frigging awesome as usual. *Bastard.* I turn away instantly, not wanting to be the one that notices him first. Play the game Natasha, play the game, I chastise myself. Cameron notices us and bounds straight over. He grabs Bridge in an embrace and twirls her around.

"How are my two favorite cousins?" He smiles as he kisses her on the cheek. He comes over to me and puts his arm around my shoulder and kisses my forehead. "Sorry about the other night. Josh is a prick." Huh what's he talking about? Oh, the fight night, shit, he doesn't know that I've seen Josh since.

My mind races off in a tangent. He hasn't told them we've hooked up, why would he do that? I know the answer: to protect me. I am suddenly seeing our midnight visits in another light. They have been staying at his house so of course he wants to be home before they wake up. Maybe, and I mean just maybe, I have misread this situation. Abbie returns with our drinks and I take mine immediately, wishing I could drain the damn tumbler in one gulp. From the corner of my eye I see the others join Cam and our group. Adrian kisses me on the cheek and squeezes my hand as does Wilson when he arrives. Joshua, however, stays back and silent but I can feel him watching me and I refuse to look at him. He can kiss my ass.

I keep playing the game, refusing to make eye contact with him while I talk to Adrian.

"So, why did you bail on me today?" I tease.

He shuffles his feet. "I wasn't allowed out to play," he winces.

"Huh, what does that mean?"

He leans in and lowers his voice so that no one else can hear us. "Josh said if he can't spend time with you then I'm not allowed to either."

I frown, not understanding his statement. What does that mean? "Josh can spend time with me—he just doesn't want to," I snap.

Adrian winces and nods. "By the way," he whispers. "Josh hasn't told his brothers about," he points his glass at me. "You know," as he nods his head.

"I thought so. Why not?"

He shrugs. "He's got it in his head it's really wrong."

I scowl. "We are not hurting anyone, Adrian."

He smiles. "I know, I thought you were ok with it. Josh, however, isn't." I take a gulp of my drink without tasting it. Adrian gets his phone out of his pocket and reads the text. He smiles. "I'm going to the bar," he gestures.

"Ok," I smile. I turn back to Cam and Bridget's conversation although I'm not in it. I feel my phone vibrate in my bag and I pull it out to check.

Hello x

It's Joshua. My eyes immediately shoot up to him. He dips his head and gives me a stifled smile. I text back.

Hello

My phone beeps again.

Are you purposely not returning my kiss?

Hmm, what does that mean? Why would he even notice no kiss? This is honestly the most confusing man on the planet. I don't know what to text, so I just look up at him and shrug my shoulders. He gives me a sad smile; he knows I'm cranky. Well, tough titties for him. What does he expect? Bridget thankfully reappears through the crowd with a round of margaritas. Good timing, Bridge. How in the hell am I supposed to stand two meters from him and not talk to him all night? This isn't punishment for him. I'm punishing my stupid self. I look around the club and notice most of the female population eyeing our group of men. I look back at the boys and I smile. Of course, they attract attention. Look how gorgeous the four of them are. They are all very alpha male, even Adrian who's so masculine and good-looking he definitely defies the camp gay boy image. My phone beeps again.

Nice dress

I read the message and smile as I bite my lip, this hard–to–get act is wearing thin on me already. I look up and very deliberately do a pirouette to show him the full package. He gives me a carnal smile, his eyes drop down the length of my body and he cracks his neck. Jackpot, there it is.

Abbie pulls me by the hand. "Come on. We are dancing," she says as she heads towards the stairs.

"I will meet you down there." A bartender walks past us with a tray of drinks, and I have an idea. "Excuse me, can I ask you to do me a favor?" He looks around.

"Sure."

I pull $20 out of my purse. "Do you see that man over there in the navy blazer?" He looks around. "No, over there near the wall." I point with my chin. "Pink checkered shirt."

"Oh yes," he smiles, "he's hot."

"I know," I smirk. "Can you go over and discreetly give him this money and tell him the lady in the black dress and red lipstick would like to place him on layaway?"

He smiles at me as he frowns, "Really?"

"Yes, please." I pull a whiny face at him. He heads off towards Joshua and I stand still watching while he taps him on the shoulder and whispers into his ear. Joshua dips his head to listen and then looks up as the bartender discreetly points me out. He smiles as he takes the money from the bartender and sticks it in his pocket. I smile and bite my lip as our eyes lock. He's giving me that look. You know the one, the one I love. Come fuck me it screams and, boy, it's smoking hot. I head towards the stairs to dance feeling quite proud of myself and halfway down the stairs my phone beeps again.

Layaway Receipt

I smile broadly and stop still. Ow, some idiot bangs into the back of me.

"Watch out," I snap. "Well, don't stop on the stairs, stupid."

Mmm, good point. I walk to the bottom of the stairs and continue reading.

Layaway Name: Beautiful Slut
Layaway Number: 69
Item Purchased: Lamborghini
Pick up time: 1.00 am
Don't be late!

I smile and continue to the dance floor to join the girls and Adrian.

Two hours later, I'm feeling very woozy on my legs when my favorite song comes on. It's a track by Jason Derulo called 'Talk Dirty to Me'. I pull out my phone, smiling, and text Joshua:

Talk Dirty to Me

I smile as I put my phone away. Ok, let's see what he's got. My phone beeps immediately.

Keep thinking those dirty thoughts, precious.
I want that beautiful tight cunt nice and creamy
when I suck on it later.

Holy fuck. He's good at talking dirty; that's absolutely filthy. I smile again. What in the hell am I doing? I am so out of my league here. I text back a lame reply:

It's working, I like it.

My phone beeps immediately.

You will swallow.

Christ, um, what will I write?

Yes.

It beeps again:
It wasn't a question.
Ok, it's official. He's the hottest man on the planet and I find myself feeling rather overheated by his texts. My phone beeps again.

How loud are you going to scream
when you come on my face
with your knees on my pillow?

Shit, ok. That's dirty. I look around, feeling quite embarrassed and flushed. I just know I am going to get some awesome sex tonight. I could come just by reading his texts. My phone beeps again:

Do you have any idea how hard
you are going to cop it tonight?

I smile and shake my head, good God...hard I hope. I text back:

Ok you win, I'm gagging.
Pick up time is now.
I will be up in a minute.

A few more tracks later I turn to find Adrian with another

round of margaritas so, of course, I have to drink. I wouldn't want to waste a perfect margarita; that would be blasphemy. Needless to say, I don't go to find Joshua for about another forty minutes. Adrian and I head towards the stairs together.

"Josh has just texted me," he says, smiling. "I have to take you out to the limo first and he will follow a few minutes later. It will be here in twenty minutes." I frown, not understanding why. "He just doesn't want you two to be photographed together."

"Oh," I nod. "Ok, that makes sense." I smile. When we get to the top of the stairs Adrian takes my hand to lead me through the crowd and I follow, not paying any attention. He suddenly stops and I run into his back.

"Let's get a drink," he says nervously and pulls me towards the bar, huh, why? I look over my shoulder at Joshua and see him talking to a blonde. He's got his hands in his pockets and he's scowling at her.

"Who is Joshua talking to?" I ask Adrian. He starts to fidget in his pockets, looking for money, "Um, not sure," he murmurs without making eye contact with me. He's lying and I don't have to be a psychologist to know that. I look back over toward Joshua and the blonde and I see him mouth the words "Go away". Huh, he knows that girl—I can tell by the way he's annoyed with her. That wasn't a casual brushoff. I go to walk towards them, and Adrian pulls me back by the hand.

"Hey, stay here," he smiles as he pulls his arm around my shoulder. I look back over my shoulder and she is still talking to him. Actually, she looks...familiar. Where in the hell do I know her from? I hope she's not an ex–patient.

Abbie and Bridget come back up the stairs and head straight over to the meeting spot. I see Abbie's back straighten when she sees the girl and her hand goes onto her hip... huh.

She barrels straight over to Joshua and I can see him shuffle on his feet, he's nervous...he's hiding something. I wish I couldn't read body language so well... it's really annoying. I pull out of Adrian's grip which I now know for sure is so I don't interrupt Josh, *asshole,* and head over towards them. Abbie is saying something to her, and I can tell by the way Abbie is talking that she is mad. What in the world is going on? Am I missing something? When I get to them Joshua immediately links our hands and, without making eye contact, whispers into my ear.

"We're leaving." Huh? He turns his back on the girl and gestures for me to walk in front of him. Hang on a minute—how exactly does he know this girl? I pull my hand out of his grip.

"Who is that woman?" I ask.

"Nobody," he answers way too fast.

"Joshua, don't lie to me," I snap. She pushes around in front of Joshua and I see him make eye contact with his bodyguards and nod. This is ridiculous. What in the hell is happening here? She puts her hand out to shake my hand and I take it out of habit of good manners.

"Hello," she purrs.

I frown. "Hello."

"And you are?" she asks as she raises her eyebrows.

"Leaving," Joshua snaps as he steps in between us. He grabs my hand and twists me so I am standing behind him. It's a defensive stance and I know that he thinks she is a threat...to what I don't know. The bodyguards come and stand over her, asking in silence for her to leave. I pull out of his grip and walk back around him. What is his problem?

"Natasha, my name is Natasha," I say.

She looks at Joshua and bubbles up a giggle. "You've got to be kidding. Her name is Natasha; she's Natasha." The blood drains out of my face as realization sets in. Oh fuck, she has seen his tattoo. This woman has slept with him. He grabs my hand again and I snatch it out of his and walk off to the bathroom. Ok, I'm fuming. So, he hasn't stuck to the deal, as if he would. Who was I kidding? Abbie is hot on my heels.

"My God, Natasha, how in the hell does he know TC?"

I stop mid–step and turn. "That was tunnel cunt?" I fume.

She nods and winces. "I thought you knew," she hunches her shoulders. "Mm, sorry."

I bump into a girl coming out as I enter the ladies room. "Watch out where you're going," I snap.

"Ok, sure thing, psycho," she replies. I'm not even kidding when I say I could do some serious bitch slapping tonight. TC... TC... TC...are you fucking kidding me?

"Abbie, how would he know her?" I'm fuming.

"I don't know," she whispers. "But when I got there, I heard him telling her to get out of his fucking sight."

"What! He said that? Just like that?"

"Yes."

"What did he say?"

"He said get out of my fucking sight. What a stupid mole," she winces.

"He's slept with her."

"What, how do you know?" she looks horrified.

"Because she has seen his tattoo and she laughed when I told her my name is Natasha."

Abbie fake punches her fist. "Let's take her out." I smile. That is such an Abbie thing to say. How is it that even in the most intense situations Abbie can make me laugh? I go to the loo, wash my hands and then lean up against the wall.

"I'm going to back–door it, Abbs. I can't be with him tonight. It's making me sick just thinking of him with her."

"This is exactly what the silly mole wants," she snarls.

"What?" I frown.

"She wants you to get the shits and then leave him here and then she will go in for the kill."

"She can have him," I snap. "I'm not settling anymore. He's a player and you know what? I've played right into his hands. He's used me for the last time. He promised me he wouldn't sleep with anyone else. What a joke." I turn and storm out of the bathroom and run straight into the brick wall that is Joshua Stanton.

CHAPTER 15

Natasha

"WE'RE LEAVING" he snaps as he grabs my hand. I snatch my hand out of his.

"Don't touch me," I scowl. He stops and frowns at me. I sigh and put both of my hands up in a stop signal.

"Just go home with blondie, Josh. We both know you've done it before."

He drops his head and rests his hand on my hip. "Tash, don't be like that."

"You promised me, you asshole." Oh no, those stupid tears are welling again. I bite my lip and look down to the ground. He grabs my hand once more and I snatch it away.

"I said don't fucking touch me!" I yell. Okay, donkey on the edge. I'm coming very close to licking the windows here. This could be a scene from *Fatal Attraction* with yours truly starring as the serial killer. "Josh, I'm leaving. Have a nice night, actually life...it's been nice knowing you." I stomp to the front door with him hot on my heels. I glance across the room to catch Bridget and Adrian's eye and give them a wave as I disappear down the stairs and out the door. Outside I immediately lift my arm for a cab as I stomp towards the curb.

"What are you doing?" he snaps. "You're acting totally irrational."

"Irrational?!" I scream as I push him in the chest. "I said go away!" I yell. I really am going for an Oscar here but I'm too mad to care. The limo pulls up, he bends down and in one fell swoop picks me up and throws me over his shoulder and pushes me into his limo. I get in and scowl as I shuffle to the other side to get away from him, but he scoots in after me.

"What's fucking wrong with you?" he yells. I gesture that the driver can hear us, so he pushes the privacy screen button and it goes up slowly. He sits back in his seat and runs his pointer finger over his lips while resting his elbow on the door. I know he's thinking. He runs both of his hands through his hair. He's frustrated. Well, good, because I'm fuming. "If it's not too much trouble, Natasha," he sneers, "please tell me what the hell is the matter with you."

"When did you sleep with her?" He frowns but doesn't answer me. "Josh, you promised me," and that is it, the pathetic dam bursts and I break into full-blown sobs.

"Promised what?" he says gently as he slides over to be near me and he wraps me in an embrace. "Sshh, precious, don't cry. I can't stand it, baby." He kisses my forehead.

"You told me you wouldn't be with anyone else," I sob. "And yet you slept with her." I sound pathetic but I can't even pretend to act cool anymore, I don't have it in me.

"Baby, I'm sorry, it was before I got back with you. I didn't know what was going to happen between us." I stay silent as I process his words, my chest racking with sobs. He runs his hand down over my hair. I shake my head. I'm an embarrass-ment to myself. I have absolutely no self-respect. I put my head down.

"How many times?" I ask but he stays silent. "Josh, how many times?" I repeat...still silence. "So help me, Josh, if you don't."

"Don't ask questions you don't want to know the answer to, Natasha."

"How many?" I sob.

He drops his head. "Three times," he says quietly.

"Three times!" I yell. That's it, I've lost it. I put my head into my hands and weep. He pulls me into his arms and onto his lap. "Shh, stop it, please don't cry," he kisses my face continually as he rubs my leg. We sit in silence all the way home, me too heartbroken to articulate and he too scared to speak in case he says the wrong thing. We pull up in front of my apartment and he moves me off his lap. I slowly get out of the car and walk towards the front foyer area and he walks in behind me. I turn.

"Josh, I don't... I can't do this... not anymore. It hurts...you just hurt me too much. This isn't a healthy relationship for me. I can't deal with this...baggage. You need to let me be." I turn and walk off and he follows again without saying anything. "I mean it Josh, go home."

He shakes his head. "I'm not ending it like this Tash. You can't let that low life come between us. She means nothing to me."

"Three times Josh. You went back for seconds and thirds."

"It was before the wedding. I haven't touched anyone since the first time we kissed at the wedding, I promise you."

Can I believe anything that comes out of his mouth? I'm exhausted. I don't even have it in me to fight anymore. I turn to walk inside, and he waves the driver off and the car pulls away.

We get upstairs and I immediately strip off and head to my therapy of choice, a burning hot shower. This was definitely not the night I had planned. He wisely doesn't come into the bathroom but waits for me in the lounge room with a cup of tea he has made for me. I dress quickly into my favorite nightwear and join him. He smiles when he sees my flannel pajamas.

"What?" I frown.

"I'd never thought I would see the day, but your pajamas are kind of growing on me." I momentarily forget I'm angry with him and look down and smile.

"I told you I would buy you some so we could match." He smiles as he hands me my cup of tea and he leans in and gives me a kiss on the forehead.

"I'm sorry," he whispers. I don't know what to think: is he lying to me? Has he stuck to our agreement? Actually, what a joke. I had to force him to agree not to be with anyone else. Who am I fucking kidding? This isn't a relationship. This is a fuck buddy with benefits. Actually, that isn't even right because at the moment the benefits are a broken heart. I stand up and walk over to my kitchen counter.

"Josh, I need to ask you something and if you have any respect at all for me you will tell me the truth." He swallows and nods.

"How many women have you slept with since you have been back in Australia?" He shakes his head.

"What a ridiculous question," he snaps. "None since you."

"Josh, I mean it." My voice is rising.

"Don't fucking ask questions you don't want to know the answer to, Natasha," he snaps.

Ok, I'm getting outraged. "Josh, stop it. I want to know."

"Why?"

"Because it matters to me."

"Why?" His voice is rising, and his anger levels are starting to match mine.

"You told me three times with that girl."

He scowls at me for bringing that up. "How long are you going to throw that in my face?" he screams. Is he fucking kidding? Throw it in his face? I'm going to be throwing punches at his face in a minute.

"What I mean, asshole, is that if you were with her three times, how many times did you actually fuck her on each occasion?"

He narrows his eyes, finally understanding the question. "Fuck off, that's semantics."

"No, it isn't, we both know how well you...back up, again and again. So, let's see three times is more likely ten to twelve times in Josh language."

"Fuck off, you just want to fight, and I have heard just about as much of your shit as I am going to take. It was before I was with you and that is the end of it. Stop being a fucking drama queen!"

"Drama queen?" I yell. "How many women, Josh?"

"I told you I'm not fucking going there. Now cut the shit or I'm leaving."

"Fucking leave then!"

"Why does it matter to you how many women I have slept with?" he yells. "They mean nothing to me anyway, so who fucking cares?"

"Actually, I do," I scream.

He rubs his eyes. "You know what? I know what you are doing. You're pulling your psychology shit on me, trying to fuck with my head and it's working. You know I have a colored past and that I like a bit of kink so don't act all innocent now. I didn't see you complaining when you were taking it the other night."

Oh my God, he did not just say that. I narrow my eyes. "Bit of kink. What in the fuck is that supposed to mean?" I scream.

He steps back, shocked at my disgust. "I didn't mean... that came out wrong." He suddenly realizes what he just said and is trying to back pedal real fast. I throw an apple at him out of my fruit bowl and he ducks as it goes over his head.

"Well, sorry, I wasn't aware that when I was taking it the other night that I was one of the many you were dishing out your bit of kink to. You fucking sleazebag! Get the fuck out of my house!" I scream.

"No," he yells. "You don't get to choose how this ends."

"I just did," I scream as I storm past him to my bedroom and I slam the door. I hear him coming after me, so I quickly flick the lock.

He bangs on the door. "Open this fucking door!" he yells.

"Go back to the club, Josh, and pick up a few of your harem so you can give them a bit of kink," I scream. "I'm sure they will love to take it!"

The door suddenly smashes, and I jump back from it. I frown. Ok, maybe I should shut up now. I hear my front door slam... And then, silence.

Five minutes later I gingerly open the door and am relieved to find he has gone, my heart still racing at double speed, no doubt from the adrenaline of fighting with such an infuriating asshole. I look at the other side of my door to find a gaping big hole where he has punched it in anger. He is so fucking paying for that.

I head back to the shower.

I didn't get my hot sex tonight, but I definitely got a heated argument. And, quite frankly, I'm too pissed off to care.

CHAPTER 16

Natasha

I AWAKE FEELING kind of stupid. Joshua was right. I was being a drama queen last night, but in my defense I wasn't expecting to meet or know a girl that he has slept with. I wonder what she was saying to him...and it has to be frigging TC, doesn't it. I know I was out of line last night by bringing up his past. The fact that I don't have a past is not helping me move on. If he thinks he can call me a drama queen and punch a hole in my door then he can go to hell. I am so not calling him.

You know the thing about waiting for an apology is that it's stupid. Total torture. I think getting teeth pulled is less painful and definitely quicker. At least you can pop a pill and feel no pain. The worst thing is I am overanalyzing everything to the maximum potential and two days after that dreaded fight, I am seriously debating whether I am out of line and second-guessing myself. When the knock on the door came on Sunday my heart jumped and I ran excitedly to answer it, only to be bitterly disappointed when a handyman carrying another door was standing in the hallway.

Hmm, figures. I know he's not going to apologize. Does he even have something to apologize for? Honestly, I don't even know anymore. I sit at work on Tuesday after devouring yet another packet of biscuits, staring out the window with my coffee. I'm just so sick and tired of being so up and down. I was serious when I said this is not a healthy relationship for me to be in. It's totally toxic. If one of my patients came in and told me about this relationship, I would urge them to end it, it's self-destructive. Why in the hell am I so addicted to him? My heart is aching for him. I have a deep-seated sadness that I know I need to kick, but how in the hell do I do it? I run through the negatives.

He's my cousin.

Our families will disown us. He lives in America. He's rich and famous. He's a total player.

He's playing me...big time. He doesn't call me.

He leaves in the middle of the night. He doesn't put up with my shit.

His will is stronger than mine. Actually, he is emotionally stronger than me which wouldn't be hard though. I've never felt so weak.

We can only be together in secret.

Our feelings aren't mutual. (This one hurts the most and tears threaten.)

He's totally gorgeous. Why can't he be fat and ugly, then I wouldn't have so much damn competition. Why can't my attraction to him be skin deep?

He's too dominant in bed. I smile, who am I kidding? His

dominance is frigging perfect. There isn't a woman in the world who wouldn't want to be thrown around in bed by him.

My mind wanders to the positives.

When I am with him, I forget every damn negative thing about him and get lost in the moment, totally lost to him.

**Hello, milady. It's a beautiful day.
Do you want to go the harbor front and grab some lunch?**

I smile as I read the text from Simon. That's exactly what I do want to do today. Our office is closed for a few days as it is being painted.

Sure, pick me up.

I jump in the shower, already feeling relieved I'm not going to go mad in this apartment by myself all day.

See you in an hour.

Four hours later I am sprawled out on the grass eating a large New York mud-cake waffle cone for dessert after eating my weight in pasta carbonara. I have to say, I'm feeling pretty damn relaxed. It's so nice spending uncomplicated time with my dear motormouth friend. I'm not analyzing or fretting and I'm not horny as hell so I can actually use my brain. It makes for a nice change. 'Diamonds' rings out and I hand Simon my ice cream so I can rummage through my bag for my phone. I really need to clean some of this shit out of here. It's Mum. I smile as I haven't spoken to her in a couple of days.

"Hi Tash."

"Hi Mum, how are you?"

"Good, thanks, darling. What are you doing tonight?"

"Nothing," I reply.

"Oh good, because Margaret and the boys are coming over for dinner and I want you to come."

"Margaret," I gasp. "When did she get here?"

"This morning. She's staying with Joshua and his brothers for a couple of days."

Oh great, there goes the neighborhood.

"Um, I don't know Mum. You know I can't stand Margaret."

"Who can?" she giggles. "I will see you at seven."

"Ok, I suppose." Great, a night with bitchface. I smile at the thought of seeing Josh though. This could turn out ok because now I won't have to ring him after all, seeing as he was never calling me. "Is Bridge coming?"

"Yes, of course. I will see you tonight."

7.15 pm

I pull into my parents' street and see Joshua's Audi parked in my parents' drive. I unfortunately also notice the car on the other side of the road with two bodyguards in it. Why is he being so heavily guarded? My heart starts to race as I check my reflection in the mirror for the hundredth time since leaving home and I have to say for the first time today I am feeling nervous. I've just remembered that Margaret has known about us all along and I'm well aware that this night could end up disastrous. Imagine if she knew it was still going on. A sly smile creeps onto my face. I'm such a bitch. I park the car and walk over to the bodyguards.

"Hi guys." I smile through the window.

"Hi Natasha." They both smile, it's the same two from the pub.

"Do you guys really have to sit out here all night?" They both break into smiles.

"Yeah, it's ok." They laugh. "It's our job and this gig is no different than sitting out front of your apartment all night."

"Huh, you guys watch my place?" They both glance at each other and instantly look uncomfortable and I know they have revealed too much information. "See you later, guys." I give them a wave as I walk back across the road and up to the front stairs of the house. That's confusing. I have to remember to ask him what they are doing here. I stand outside the front door and listen as my heart races. Why am I so nervous? I know why —this is the first time we have been together around our parents since being adults and it's frigging...nerve-racking.

I open the door and Cameron swoops in with one loud roar and puts me into a headlock. He pulls me into the kitchen while I giggle and he announces to the family, "Look what the cat dragged in."

I punch him swiftly in the ribs. "The cat did not drag me in."

He lets me go and as I come up, he gives me a wink. I know he has done it to break the ice—he still thinks Joshua and I are fighting. Well, we are, so he is on the money. I glance around and see Mum fussing in the kitchen being the hostess with the mostess...not.

"Hello, love," she smiles. "Go and pour everyone a drink will you." She's firing orders at Bridge who rolls her eyes at me and I stifle a giggle. I look onto the back patio and I see Dad talking to Joshua and Wilson. Dad is talking and I don't know what he is saying but he has the boys in stitches. I smile as I watch their interaction. Dad has a deep affection for the Stanton boys, I mean who wouldn't? They're polite, good-looking and well-educated. They all have a great sense of humor. Brock is talking to Margaret over in the corner. She has a champagne and strawberry in her hand. Each time I see her I am surprised by how attractive she actually is. Money will do that to a girl. Her deep chocolate shoulder-length hair is salon-styled and she is always dressed to the nines in designer labels. She makes me feel mumsy. She smiles my way and I make my way over to them. Ok, here goes. I smile as I kiss her on the cheek.

"Natasha darling, how lovely to see you," she smiles as she puts her arm around me. Huh? Ok, this is new.

"How have you been?" I ask politely.

"Great. You?" she asks.

"Fine thanks," I smile. I turn and find Joshua, Wilson and Dad all looking our way.

'Hi." I smile. Joshua smiles, his eyes drop down the length of my body and he gently cracks his neck. I silently thank the Lord I wore this white backless maxi dress. It seems to be having the desired effect.

"Tash darling," my mother calls from the kitchen. Saved by the bell.

"Excuse me."

I walk into the kitchen to see Bridget laughing. "Mum has burnt the potato bake," she laughs. "It's now a charcoal bake."

I giggle. "Good one, Mum." She rolls her eyes.

"Honestly, entertaining is over–rated don't you think?" She winks at Bridget. Bridget smiles.

"Yes, why do you think I don't do it?" I get out my phone and I text him.

Hello x

I smile and wait, it beeps.

Hello

Hmm.

Did you purposely not return my kiss?

I wait a few moments. As I look out the back, I see he is talking so I wait. It beeps again.

Did you purposely not apologize?

Damn it. I am going to have to swallow my pride. I knew it.

Sorry xx

I watch him from the kitchen, and I see him smile as he reads it.

And?

Oh jeez, now he wants me to beg.

And you were right, I was acting like a drama queen.

I wait again.

XX

I am beaming like an idiot. I go back to the kitchen and try and help Mum save the potato bake. My phone beeps again.

I missed you today.

Oh my God. My heart stops. What the hell...PROGRESS. This is the first time he has conveyed any type of emotion other than the fact he adores me. My heart swells and I text back.

I miss you every day. xx

I can't help it, an over the top smile beams from my face as I read and re-read the words he has just texted me. I miss you. I am loving myself sick right now.

"Something funny?" Josh whispers over my shoulder. I jump back and do wide eyes at him. For Pete's sake what's he doing?

"Natasha, this potato is catastrophic. Can you go to the shop and get me some more cream, honey?"

"Ok," I smile as I look around for my keys. Poor Mum. Trust her to burn something tonight of all nights. Margaret will love this shit.

"I'll drive you," Josh snaps and before I can retort and tell him that I don't think it's a good idea he grabs his keys and is out the front door. I give Bridge a shrug, and she gives me her best don't fucking do it look. I slowly follow him outside and down the stairs. And then he is on me. Grabbing me by the arm he pulls me around the side of the house. He's kissing me like his life depends on it. My back is against the wall and he is leaning over me, his hands resting on the wall behind me. Excitement starts to warm my blood. I can feel his large erection digging into my stomach, it's promising me carnal things, things that I so desperately want and need. My eyes close as he cups my face in both his hands and tenderly swipes his tongue through my open lips. He grabs my head at my nape and moves me to mould the way he wants me. I can feel a familiar pulse between my legs as he ignites my arousal with his possession.

"Stop fighting with me about shit," he whispers in between kisses.

"Stop sleeping with other women," I breathe.

"You know you have me, what are you worried about?" He kisses me deeply again as he grabs my face.

"Do I have you, Josh?" I question.

"Completely," he breathes. Shit, good answer. My heart melts. Completely. Well, he has me completely under his spell, completely in love with him and completely needing to climb his big, beautiful body and take him inside me.

"Josh, let's just go inside and tell them." He kisses me again but doesn't answer. Our passion turns desperate as he grinds up against me and lifts my leg around his hip so he can gain access to my wet center.

"I want to try and make a go of it. I will move back to America with you." He stills and pulls back to look at me and my leg drops to the ground as he frowns.

"You would do that?"

"Josh, I would do anything to be with you. You have to know that by now." He kisses me again more urgently and rams his hips up against mine. Oh shit, I think I'm going to come just by doing this. His arousal just amped up ten notches.

"Josh, I'm serious, let's go back inside and tell them. They will understand and, if they don't, I don't care. We will deal with this together." He kisses me again and pulls back to run his fingers through my hair while smiling and looking down at me. I can hear my heartbeat in my ears.

"Slow down, precious, let's just see if we can get through a week without ripping each other's heads off before we do anything rash." I smile a shy smile as I gather my senses. What's wrong with me?

"You're right," I whisper. I run my hands up his strong arms and over his broad shoulders. I feel the power emanating from his body. "When will I see you again if your mother's here?"

"I will come over tonight when she goes to sleep," he sighs. "Give me one more kiss to last me till then," he smiles his broad melting smile and I feel my heart flutter. I will do anything to be with this man. We sneak out of the shadows and to Josh's car. I see him make eye contact with the bodyguards and he nods.

"Josh, why are you so guarded?"

"Drawback of having money," he sighs. "Don't worry, it shits me, too." What exactly does that mean? Ten minutes later we are armed with cream and heading back to the house. He holds my hand on his lap the whole time, deep in thought, occasionally lifting my hand to kiss the back of it. I don't know why but all this honesty suddenly has me hoping of a real future with him. Maybe we can do this? Is it really possible? Would I move to America? Who knows and who cares. He's holding my hand and he just told me he's completely mine. Nothing at all can wreck my night tonight.

How wrong can a person be?

We arrive back at the house and I head up while Josh goes and talks to his bodyguards. I'm met by Margaret at the front door.

"Hi," I smile, and she glares at me.

"Is it?" She hisses. Shit, did she just see us? I hope not and an uneasy feeling rips through me. She brushes past me and I walk in the front door. What in the world was that about? I watch her storm across the road to Joshua. Brock comes barreling up the hall and grabs me by the arm and drags me into my old bedroom. Ow, what the hell?

"Brock," I snap as I pull my arm from his grip.

"What in the fuck is going on with you and Stanton?" Holy mother fuck.

"What do you mean?" I feel faint.

"Margaret just went berko on Cameron when she found out you two went to the store."

I swallow the tennis ball and bucket of sand in my throat.

"What did she say?"

"She said you two cannot be trusted. What in the fuck does that mean, Natasha?" Oh crap...crap, crap, crap.

"Um, I don't know," I shrug. "You know she's tapped."

"Is she?" he snarls.

"Of course," I reply. "What do you think?"

"I know what I saw at the wedding and I warned him that night that I would kill him if he touched you."

"You did what?" I snap. "Are you kidding me?"

"I am going to say this once and once only, Natasha. Listen, because I genuinely mean it. I will fucking kill him if he lays a finger on you."

I roll my eyes. "Drop dead, Brock. I'm twenty-five years old. Stop trying to control me. I'm friends with Josh. You and Margaret are as bad as each other. Go back to over-protecting Bridget, because I'm not putting up with your shit." I storm out of the bedroom and back into the lounge room just as Joshua and his mother come in the front door. I hotfoot it straight to the kitchen without making eye contact. This night is quickly turning from hero to zero.

Twenty minutes later we are seated at the dining table. Bridget and Brock are on either side of me and directly opposite is Margaret. Cam and Will are on either side of her and Josh is next to Cam. Mum is at one head of the table and Dad at the other. I don't think I have ever dreaded a family dinner quite as much. Brock is onto us and so is Margaret for that matter. I know I can't lie for shit. I feel like a frigging Russian spy just about to take a lie detector test. I look down. Determined not to make eye contact with Josh or anyone else for that matter. I know he is feeling uncomfortable as well. I can feel it in my bones. Brock is the first to speak.

"So, Josh, I saw on the internet you dated Heidi Mills, that supermodel." Cameron chokes.

"Pass the carrots," Wilson asks me, and I know it's a distraction tactic. I slowly look up to see Josh's reaction. He nods but keeps his eyes cast down. What is frigging Brock playing at? Bridget taps my leg underneath the table.

"She is so...smoking hot." Brock smiles, he lifts his fork in the air en route to his mouth.

"In fact, you seem to date a different glamour girl every week." I look back down at my plate and I wish the ground would swallow me up. This night is becoming very uncomfortable and I know exactly what Brock is doing, *the bastard*. Bridget rubs my leg under the table in a symbol of sympathy.

Margaret smiles. "Yes, Josh sure does well with the ladies, however his heart is taken, unfortunately."

"Oh, is it?" Mum asks excitedly as she takes a sip of her wine. *Shut up, Mum.*

"Yes." Margaret smiles at me. "Her name is Amelie." Will clears his throat and Cam drops his knife and fork, and they hit his plate with a clang. By the boys' reaction I know there is some truth to this story. Ok...I keep my eyes cast down.

"Do tell, Josh." Mum laughs. *Shut the hell up, Mum.*

"Nothing to tell," he snaps.

"Oh Josh," his mother chastises. "Don't be embarrassed." She pats him on the arm. I think I am going to vomit in my own mouth. "She's a veterinarian, a beautiful one at that, and she manages Josh's horse stud for him." My heart drops the blonde from his phone. "Yes, she's an amazing equestrian rider. Josh drives her all over the United States every weekend for competitions, don't you Josh? They go away most weekends she just competes so much." I bet she does. I can't help it. My eyes flick to Josh. I want to see his reaction.

Damn it. He keeps his eyes deliberately down to avoid my glare. Margaret is on a roll. "They have so much in common. They go horse riding together for hours on his country estate. She comes away on holidays with us and sometimes her parents join us as well, don't they Josh? She's English and her family own a castle. She comes from a very well-to-do family. Robert and I visited them last year in their country estate." My cheeks heat and I can hear my heartbeat in my ears. He's lied to me. He told me that he has never dated anyone. Going on holidays with fucking parents is dating, asshole.

"So, is that important to you, Margaret? That your boys marry into a well-to-do family?" Oh shit, did I say that out loud? She fakes a venomous smile. I can't help it. I have to know. She deliberately doesn't answer me. *Mmm.*

"So, how long has she worked for you Josh?" I ask as I bite my food off my fork, smiling at him way too sweetly. He glares at me as he wipes his mouth with a napkin and brushes his tongue over his front teeth, but he doesn't answer. Bridget grabs my hand under the table. He stays silent.

"Five years." Margaret smiles. Fucking bitch, she's loving this. I look back down at my plate. Five years...five years. What in the hell? That's a long time. And I know he has feelings for her because I've seen the fucking photos.

"She's just a friend," Josh snaps as he raises his eyebrows at his mother.

"Oh Josh, stop it. You don't spend every New Year's Eve for five years with a girl, if she means nothing."

"Did anybody see the game last night?" Cameron interjects in a desperate attempt to change the subject. The atmosphere has taken a serious dive and I really want to throw my drink on him or her...on both of them, actually.

"Yes, it was great." Dad smiles and they start to chat about football. I, however, am stuck on the New Year's comment. My mind is going a million miles a minute...don't let her get to you...don't let her get to you. I know this is her aim and unfortunately, she has done just that. I'm totally rattled.

"Joshua, I'm thirsty, darling, I need another wine." He immediately rises to go and pour her a drink.

My mum smiles. "So, tell me, Wilson, I hear you're seeing a new girl."

He smiles a warm smile and it's obvious he likes this girl. "Amy," he answers. "Her name is Amy."

"Oh and, Wilson, I need you to take me to Darlinghurst tomorrow, darling. I am meeting Susan and I want you to join us," Margaret purrs and he nods. She swats Cameron with her serviette, "Don't pick at your food." I sit back and watch their interactions. I don't believe it. How have I missed this? She has these boys totally under her thumb. They all dote on her like she's the fucking Queen of Sheba. Wicked Witch of the West is more like it.

"So, Bridget," she smiles. "How is the travel industry going?"

"Oh good, thanks," Bridge answers happily. "I'm going on a conference to Paris next week." Margaret smiles. "That's exciting." Bridget nods happily. "My boys all speak French, you know." She winks at Bridget and Josh rolls his eyes and shakes his head.

"So, Natasha." She puts her hands steepled under her chin

as she starts to work her venom back in my direction. "What is it you do again?" She knows this, the bitch.

"I'm a psychologist." I fake the biggest smile in the history of human life.

"Oh, in what field?"

"I'm a sexual health psychologist."

"Hmm," she smiles as she takes a sip of her wine. "That figures, what a strange direction for a girl so young to follow." I narrow my eyes at her as I start to hear my pulse in my ears. Pick on me, bitch, and that's ok, but pick on my career and it's go time. "I bet you are really good at manipulating, oh sorry, I mean controlling minds and thoughts." The double meaning is not lost on me. I can't even pretend that she is not pissing me off now, *the bitch.*

"You have no idea," I whisper as I glare at her. Joshua jumps up and starts to clear the table, obviously sensing the tension in the air, and Brock helps him. Mum and Dad go back into the kitchen to serve up dessert. Brock takes the first load of plates into the kitchen.

"Oh, I have a very good idea how well you manipulate," she sneers. I can't hold my tongue any longer.

"Have I done something to upset you, Margaret?" The whole table falls silent and collectively hold their breath. Joshua drops the plates on the table and they clang. He does wide eyes at me, urging me to shut up. Who in the hell is Amelie, you prickface liar? You can go to hell, too.

"No, we will get along just fine, Natasha, as long as you keep your claws out of my son," she sneers. My blood is boiling.

Cameron interjects. "That's enough, Mother." Ok that's it, that's the last straw and I can't hold my tongue any longer. I'm feeling unstable. I stand and lean my hands on the table as I lean my face closer to hers.

"I have absolutely no plans. None! To get my claws into your precious son. But let me tell you this."

"Natasha," Bridget whispers, "that's enough." She grabs my hand and I jerk it out of her grasp.

"*If*, and that's a big *if*, I decided to get my claws into your son, you had better be prepared, because not even the devil himself could stop me."

She narrows her eyes. "Why you conceited little bitch."

Cameron coughs. "Seriously. That's enough, Mother." I look across the table and Joshua is in shock, I think. He looks like he's going to faint.

"Now, I have had enough," I shake my head. "I'm leaving." I stand and throw my napkin from my lap onto the table.

Joshua stands so quickly that his chair falls back and hits the ground. "Natasha, don't go," he pleads.

"Sit," I snap as I point to his chair. "Mummy dearest here wants to breastfeed you and we couldn't have you upsetting her. Get your diaper changed while you are at it. It will save you time later." I hear Bridget and Cameron stifle a giggle.

I walk into the kitchen. "Mum, I have to go. I just got paged from work."

"Oh, that's a shame, darling. Ok, I will call you tomorrow." I don't remember getting into my car. I just know I am off the charts boiling mad.

Josh runs out to the car. "Natasha, don't go. She's just mad."

"Josh, get the fuck away from me, you coward." I poke him in the chest. He steps back.

"Tell Cameron I said thanks for defending me." His face drops at the realization it was his brother who defended me and not him.

"Natasha, please, she's my mother. I was just trying to diffuse the situation."

"And what am I?" He shuffles on his feet as he rubs both hands through his hair. "Don't ask stupid questions," he sighs.

"Stupid questions?" I shriek. This man is a total idiot. "Oh, that's right, I'm your fucking booty call. Go inside. I just lost interest in you...*Big Time!*"

"Tash, please," he begs as he grabs my arm.

"Get your filthy hands off her." Oh shit, it's Brock.

"Not now," Josh snaps at him. Brock grabs Josh by the shoulder and Josh turns to Brock.

"Don't start your fucking shit, Brock, or you will be out cold on the fucking pavement." Brock grabs him by the shirt and Josh slams him up against the car.

"Let me speak to her alone," Josh snaps. "This is none of your business."

"Fuck off," Brock yells.

"Stop it, you idiots," I yell, and the two bodyguards come running across the road. I am too mad to care about either of them and the sudden distraction allows me to pull out and I speed off down the road. Hot tears of frustration pool in my eyes and blur my vision. I don't think I have ever been this mad. 'We will get along just fine as long as you keep your claws out of my son.' The stupid movie screen in my head plays and replays the words again and again, each time with more venom than the last. Who was I kidding—she will never accept us. And then there's Amelie. That's a whole different world of pain and I know it's true. I could see it in his face; he has serious feelings for her. How deep they run I don't know. Have they slept together?

My tears well again and I pull the car over, unable to see the road any longer. I put my elbows on my steering wheel and weep into my hands. My car rocks intermittently as the cars zoom past me at speed on the freeway. They have common interests; she loves horses like him. She lives in his house. They have a bond. He lied to me again. He takes her away and, oohh, the pain slices me again and I sob...New Year's Eve. The lump in my throat begins to hurt as I hold in the tears. He spends them with her...every year. Margaret knew exactly her target tonight and she hit it in a bullseye, attacking my insecurities. My mind wanders back to the past New Years and I break into full–blown sobs. At twelve o'clock every year I have thought of him, wished he was here with me and he was kissing someone else. Spending time with someone else...probably on frigging secluded islands and shit. Someone he cares about.

Out of the corner of my eye I see a man run up to the side of the car and I jump in fright. I quickly start my car and hit the central-locking button. Tap, Tap, Tap. To my horror, a man I have never seen before is tapping on the window. I start to panic until I see Josh's bodyguards standing on the side of the road next to the car, which I now notice is parked behind me. My heart jumps and I quickly look around to see if he's here, but of course he's not. He's with his bitchface mother. I slowly wind down my window and the guy has the gall to look embarrassed now that he sees I'm crying like a baby. He is in his early forties, bald and tough-looking, and has the whole Bruce Willis vibe going on.

"Are you ok, Natasha?" He gives a sympathetic smile at me.

"Fine," I snap as I wipe the snot from my nose on the back of my hand in such a feral manner I even surprise myself. "Who are you?" I demand. He smiles and steps back, making eye contact with the other two.

"Um, I'm your bodyguard," he says quietly in an American accent, as if speaking to a child.

"What?" I scream. "I don't have a bodyguard. Why in the hell do I have a bodyguard?"

"I've been with you for three weeks," he whispers, thinking that would calm me down.

"What?" I scream. "Are you fucking kidding me? Why... how...I mean...are you serious?" I frown. This night has turned into the frigging twilight zone. My jaw is on the ground. "You have been following me for three weeks? I can't believe it. How do I not know this?"

"Mr. Stanton organized it, ma'am."

"Huh, ma'am. What am I, fifty?" My mind goes into overdrive and I get out of the car.

"Why is the security so tight around Joshua?"

He frowns. "I'm sorry. I have specific orders not to divulge that information to you."

"From who?" I snap.

"Ma'am."

"Stop calling me that!" I scream.

"Um, ok. I think you should calm down."

"Calm down...calm down...if you want to know who to guard tonight, guard Joshua, because I am going to fucking kill him."

He steps back and smiles as if he knew I was going to say that. "Let's just get you home safely, shall we, ma'am," he turns me to push me back into my car.

"My name is Natasha, asshole," I scream. "Don't touch me." I yank my arm free of his grip. I get back into my car and slam the door, taking off so fast I rev the shit out of my Honda.

CHAPTER 17

Joshua

As I PULL into my driveway my mother's happy mood is sickening. I don't have the strength to keep quiet much longer. I climb out and hit the lock button as she links arms with Will and begins to walk inside.

"A night of cocktails with my sons, how exciting," she purrs. I roll my eyes at Cameron who puts a reassuring arm around my neck.

"Just keep quiet and don't fight with her. You will only make it worse," he whispers. I walk in behind them and head straight into the master suite shower. I can't be around her at the moment. She makes me sick. How can she be in such a good mood after speaking to Natasha like that? She really does hate her. I blow out a breath as I put my head under the water. I hear the door shut and my eyes shoot up to see Cam sitting on the side of the bath with a beer in his hand. I turn my back to him and start to soap up.

"Do you mind?" I snap. I'm not in the mood for his shit either. He takes another swig of his beer but stays silent. He comes over to the walk-in shower and leans on the wall of the entrance with his shoulder, his face impassive. Obviously, he has something to say to me but is trying to word it correctly in his head.

"How long?" he asks. I drop my head and continue washing my legs, deliberately ignoring his question.

"All along... have you always been seeing her?" My eyes shoot up.

"Fuck, no," I snap.

"Since when then?" he questions. "Why didn't you tell me? I thought we told each other everything."

"Cam," I sigh. "This is fucked-up shit that I don't want anybody to know about."

He sits back on the side of the bath and takes another sip of his beer. "I want to know since when?"

I sigh and drop my head. "Since we had that fight at the fight night." He nods and takes another sip of his beer. I stay silent as I wait for him to start going off at me, but he doesn't. He stays silent which is worse... much worse. I turn the water off and get out and start drying myself while he sits in silence watching me.

"Do you love her?" He takes another sip of his beer.

I wrap the towel around my hips. "What do you reckon?"

He raises his eyebrows and smirks. "Well, as I sit here and read her name written down the fucking length of your body, I would say yes." I raise my eyebrows at him and shake my head. "It's not that bad you know." He sighs.

"Huh, what do you mean?" I walk into my room. He follows me and sits on my bed. I drop the towel and head into my walk-in closet.

"Being with her, it's not that bad."

"Fuck off," I snap. "It's woeful."

"Twenty percent of marriages worldwide are between first cousins you know."

I frown. "How do you know that? That's bullshit," I snap.

"Seriously, it's not that bad."

I shake my head. "No, it is that bad, you are just desensitized to this shit like her because you're a doctor, well soon-to-be doctor, whatever."

"What does she say about it?" he asks.

I shrug. "She wants to come out and move back to America with me."

He raises his eyebrows and takes another swig of his beer. "Shit. Have you forgiven her?" I frown, unsure what he is talking about. "For cheating on you."

I smirk a sad smile as I pull my jeans up. "She didn't. She lied so I would go to America and not throw away the opportunity."

His eyes widen. "Fuck," he whispers.

"I know." I sit on the bed to put my shoes on. "Are you going out?" He frowns.

I nod. "Yeah, I have to see her. I have some serious explaining to do."

He nods and smiles. "You seem scared, what, is she a ball-buster or something?"

I smile. "You have no fucking idea—we fight nearly every time we see each other."

"Seriously?"

"She doesn't put up with my shit which is," I shrug, "refreshing I suppose. Without wanting to sound conceited I am pretty used to women doing anything I say."

He listens and I can see him thinking. "Do you think that's what the attraction is, the defiance thing?"

I shake my head. "I wish it was just that." I flop back down on the bed as I try to articulate my thoughts.

"I've never been with anyone remotely like her. She's funny, beautiful and smart." I rub the heels of my palms into my eye sockets. "And the sex." I shake my head and blow out a breath. "She fucking blows my mind. You have no idea how hot the sex is. It's... ridiculous. And it's intimate which is new."

He frowns. "Intimate, what you mean?"

I shrug and stand back up. "If I knew how to turn it off I would have done it seven years ago."

"Do you think that maybe it's just that she was the first girl you loved that you are so stuck on her?"

I smile and nod. "I did think that, but since I have been with her again, I've fallen harder for her again. It's totally fucked. I have absolutely no control over her or my feelings when I'm with her and it's fucking with my head. I've lost six fucking kilos since I got back. She makes me so crazy I can't even eat."

He winces. "This whole situation sounds shit. Just don't tell Mum until...," he shrugs, "... you know if it's going to work out. Don't put yourself through it," he smiles. "Actually, don't put me through it. She will go fucking apeshit when she finds out."

"Just tell her I've gone to bed then, will you? And then tell her I've gone to work early in the morning."

"Are you not coming home at all?"

"Probably in half an hour. She's going to kick my ass when I get over there, but hopefully I will be staying." I quickly throw my work gear into an overnight bag. He watches me silently as I move around my room.

"Going somewhere, Joshua?"

Fuck, it's Mum. I don't need this shit. How did she hear us? "Yes," I keep my eyes down as I keep packing my gear in my bag.

"Where are you going?" One of her eyebrows rises as she waits for my answer and her arms are crossed in front of her.

She knows damn well where I am going so, I don't answer. Cameron interjects. "Come on Mum, where's my cocktail?"

She holds up her hand. "In a minute, Cameron. Give us some privacy, please."

I glare at Cameron, warning him not to go anywhere. "Cameron can stay, Mother. I have nothing to hide from him. What is it you want to say?"

She walks over to the window with her back to me and pulls the curtains back and stares out at the view. "What is going on with Natasha, Joshua? And don't you dare lie to me."

Cameron does wide eyes to me, signaling silence.

"I'm still attracted to her," I answer as I close my eyes and wait for the backlash.

She turns and smiles at me. "I know you are attracted to a lot of women, Joshua. God knows you've slept with more than your share." I bite my lip as I listen to her. "You realize that if you allow her to persuade you into her bed, you will disgrace the family." I smile. The fucking gall of this woman, I really have had enough of her shit for one night. Cameron shakes his head at me, again signaling my silence.

"Natasha would never have to persuade me into her bed. I

would go there willingly." She narrows her eyes at me, and I cross my arms in front of me in defiance.

"Tell me Mother, does Dad know you use your money to intimidate people?"

"What is that supposed to mean?" she snaps.

"Natasha asked you tonight if it mattered to you if your boys married into money."

"And?" she snaps.

"You totally ignored the question."

"Of course, I want my boys to marry into money. Any self -respecting mother would want good breeding for her grand-children."

I stand up and start throwing my things into my bag again. "That's funny, because if I know the story right , Dad's parents didn't accept you because you came from a poor family. Yet you have the audacity to judge Natasha."

"Natasha is a self-absorbed social-ladder climber, Joshua, and even if you were not related to her, which you are, I would not approve. The girl repulses me." That's it. I pick up my bag and sling it over my shoulder. "Where are you going? Put your bag back down immediately until you tell me where you are going."

I turn slowly. "Josh, just go," Cameron urges.

"You want to know where I am going, Mother?" I have never been so angry. She glares at me "Do you really want to know?" I whisper again.

"Enlighten me," she growls.

"I'm going to Natasha's and then I am going to beg for her forgiveness for letting you speak to her like a piece of dirt tonight."

"Don't you dare apologize for me. I meant every word I said," she screams.

"I won't be home tonight," I snap as I grab my bag.

"Joshua, no, you can't sleep with her again. She's bad news," she says frantically.

"No, Mother!" I scream. "Natasha is the only thing that is good! I have been holding myself back from her out of respect for you. But seeing you don't respect her, or me, it's on, and you can blame yourself."

"You can't be serious."

"Totally!"

She runs and grabs my arm. "Cameron, talk some sense into your brother. Joshua, no. Don't leave. This is what she wants, to cause trouble between us."

"What? You can't be serious. I am going to spend the night with the one woman in the world who doesn't love me for my money. The one woman who I have no doubt can make me happy."

"You're a fool, Joshua. She will break your heart again and deep down you know that. This can never have a happy ending. As soon as her family finds out, she will leave you again and then who will pick up the pieces?" I storm out and grab the keys to my car, trying my hardest not to punch something. I've had enough of this shit. Why is everything so fucking hard?

The apartment is too quiet when I enter. I used my key because I know she wouldn't have opened the door if I knocked. She must be asleep. I walk into the bedroom and see her lying with her back to me. She hasn't moved so I'm assuming she's asleep. I watch her for a few minutes in silence. My heart aches just to touch her, to soothe her, to tell her everything will be alright. I just wish I knew if it will be.

Probably a good thing she's asleep. I'm too fucking angry with my mother to even talk to Natasha now. I will only end up fighting with her again which is exactly what my bitch of a mother wants. I can't believe she brought up Amelie...that's low, even for her. How in the fuck am I going to explain that one? She might be the one punching holes in the door this time.

Natasha

I hear the key in the door and I quickly jump under the covers. I am way too mad to speak to him but he's damn lucky he had the guts to come. He walks to the bedroom door and I watch his reflection in the mirror. He doesn't say anything and blows out a breath as he walks back into the lounge room while running his hands through his hair. I hear the jug flick on and then fussing about in the kitchen. What is he doing? The toaster pops. What in the world? He's making toast and a cup of tea. I hear the television flick on. Now I've seen it all. Actually, I'm hungry, too. The wicked witch of the west killed my appetite at dinner. How does she live with herself?

I lie in bed and try to think of this evening's events from his side. It wasn't his fault his mother was a bitch, but then he didn't defend me either—it was Cam who told her to shut up. Was Josh really just trying to diffuse the situation? This is a mess. And the Amelie thing. My heart aches as I ponder this one; he has lied to me again. Even if they are just friends, she obviously has a hold over him if he drives her everywhere for horse stuff. She lives in his country estate and she's a veterinarian. I can't compete with this shit. I hate horses with a passion. I roll over for the hundredth time and punch the pillow. A depressing thought crosses my mind. Even if Josh and I have the guts to come clean about our relationship or whatever this is between us, our lives are just so different that we might not work out in the long run anyway. Do we even have anything in common? I mean, honestly, apart from sex what do we have other than memories? A lump forms in my throat as I try my hardest to suppress my tears. How do I walk away from him without this hurt? I need to get out of this relationship—it's going to break me I just know it. It's not healthy for either of us. An hour later he comes into the bedroom. It has taken all of my strength not to go out into the lounge room and demand answers, but I know I can't fight with him tonight. I don't have the strength. I will end up crying like a baby. I feel weak and it's an emotion I have become way too familiar with lately. I have never felt so weak in my life. It's true, I feel better with him here and if we fight and he leaves I will just put myself through hell again anyway. If I just act asleep maybe, we will both actually get some sleep and maybe I will calm down enough so I can actually articulate what I want to say. What do I want to say? He pulls the blankets back and silently slips in behind me, pulling me into an embrace. I pretend to be asleep.

"I hate these fucking flannel pajamas," he whispers as he cuddles into my back. I smile on the inside. He gently kisses my hair and blows out a breath. "We will talk about it in the morning, precious," he whispers. "That's if my balls haven't exploded by then." I smile as I hear the last words he has spoken. I must admit, all this dirty talk and no action is about to explode my ovaries as well. Glad I'm not the only horn-bag in the house. I stifle a giggle as the last thought runs through my head.

"You find this funny?" he whispers, and I roll over to face him.

"No," I pull a sad face and he leans in and kisses my cheek.

"Sweetheart, I'm sorry." He gives me a sad smile.

"I'm mad at you, Josh."

"I know," he whispers, and he runs his fingers up and down my arm. We stay silent, both lost in our own thoughts while looking at each other. "I can't handle fighting with you tonight. We haven't spoken in three days. Let me stay and we will talk about it in the morning."

I narrow my eyes as I sum up his words. He acts like he cares. Does he truly care or is it an act?

"You won't be here in the morning, Josh. We both know that," I sigh.

"You know why I never stay with you, Presh?" My eyes tear up and I shake my head. I can't say the reason I know out loud because it just hurts too much. He can't even bear to look at me as he does the walk of shame. He's just that ashamed that we have been together and every time I think of this reality my heart breaks just that little bit further.

"Because I can't handle saying goodbye to you," he whispers. "I never want to say goodbye. This is not easy on me either you know." His voice betrays a deep sadness, much like the one I'm feeling myself. The tightness in my throat hurts as I try to suppress the tears that threaten again. Stop saying things like that. You're fucking with my head.

"Baby, don't cry," he whispers as he wipes a lone tear that rolls down my face.

"Josh, we are not going to make it, are we? The hill is just too steep. We have too much against us". My heart rate picks up as I try to grip the reality of the situation, my lip quivers and I sob out loud. There is no way out of this. If I stay, I get hurt. If I leave... I can't even face that reality and pain laces through my chest. I already know what awaits me. He stays silent as he sums up my words and he leans his forehead in to touch mine. I run my fingers through the sideburns of his hair and down his jawline along his heavy stubble and his eyes close at the contact. He has an air of resignation about him. I can feel it. I know, because I have it myself. "Can't you just shut up and look pretty?" he whispers as he bites his lip. I stifle a giggle. I did not expect him to say that but it's frigging funny. Trust him to put our saying into that context. I know in my heart I don't have him for long. In fact, tonight is probably going to be our last night together. Once I give it to him an ultimatum tomorrow, and I will be. I know he won't hang around, that's if I even hear from him after I wake up alone. We both know it's only a matter of time until his mother gets to him.

"Josh, I think you are probably better suited to be with Amelie," I whisper. "You should go home to her." My heart breaks as I close my eyes. I mentally kick myself. I swore that I wouldn't do this tonight, but I'm not strong enough to stop myself. He grabs my chin and rips it up to his face.

"You listen to me," he growls. "You are the only woman I want. I don't want Amelie. I. Want. You."

My eyes tear up again. "Baby, I can't do this...this casual thing. We are either together or we are not. It's messing with my head too much, Josh. It's breaking my heart."

He swallows and nods. "Mine too." I frown at him—he says the most confusing things. What does that mean?

He stays silent. "Then let's be together," he whispers. "I want to be with you, Tash. Do you want to be with me is the question?"

My eyes meet his. "Yes, you know I do." He gently grabs my face with his two hands and passionately swipes his tongue between my lips.

"Then, be mine." The finality in his tone sends my pheromones into overdrive and goosebumps scatter over my body.

"Are you mine, Josh?" He smiles.

"I told you already. Completely." There is that word that I love again. Completely. He kisses me again more urgently. "If I rip these pajamas will you throw them out?" he smiles into my neck.

I giggle. "Then what would I wear to bed?" He grabs my behind and grinds his hips forward, circling his pubic bone against my clitoris.

"Me." I smile, hmm, I do like the sound of that. "You think you want to be my girlfriend but there are stipulations you know."

I smile as I listen to the words he is saying. Girlfriend, I like it, I like it a lot.

"Like what?" I whisper.

"Definitely no pajamas, and I need a lot more sex than you have been giving me." He has that look in his eyes that I love, the one that makes me scream in ecstasy. "You've had me on rations and I'm not coping. A man's not a camel you know," I smile as his oral assault moves lower.

"Tell me something. As your girlfriend how often will I be given sex? I mean, you're not the only one who has a healthy appetite."

He smiles at me. "You will be well fed, put it that way." I frown and smile, how are we not fighting? Just when I think I can read how a situation is going to go, it goes the other way. My hands run over his strong large shoulders.

"What are you going to feed me?" I run my fingers roughly through his hair, desire starting to take me over as my legs fall open wider. He rolls me onto my back and bites my neck.

"Cock," he whispers. Mmm, I get a rush of moisture to my core. "Tongue," he kisses me slowly, his tongue demanding arousal, and again my blood heats. "Fingers and toes," he smiles again into my neck.

"Toes?" I giggle. He nods as he starts to slowly unbutton my top as his mouth follows his hands. First one nipple in his mouth and then the other. He grabs my other breast roughly in his hand and pulls my top open to his searing gaze.

"I can't get enough of your body." He cracks his neck. From the lounge room his phone beeps a text. "Fuck off," he whispers into my stomach at his phone. I smile up at the ceiling like an idiot and then it beeps again. He growls and keeps sucking on my breast, his hand sliding down my pajama bottoms. "These are going in the fucking garbage," he smiles.

"Ok. I will buy a onesie."

He lifts his head to look at me and frowns.

"I forbid it," he snaps, and I giggle. His phone beeps again. "Just fuck off," he whispers at his phone again into my stomach.

"Baby, go and switch it off. It's annoying me," I whisper as I raise my hips to meet his hip roll, my eyes half closed with desire. He gets up and switches the side lamp on and I wince under the light. "Why are you turning that on?"

"Because I want to watch you come," he kisses me again chastely and saunters naked out of the room to get his phone. I lie on my back with my shirt open, smiling at the ceiling. I'm aching for him. I need to orgasm like... now, hurry the hell up. I've been aroused since Saturday when he was dirty texting me. What's he doing? I can hear him on the phone, and I sit up to listen.

"I don't care... No, I just talked to her about that. Just tell Mother I am with Natasha and I won't be home any time soon." He goes silent as he listens. "I don't give a flying fuck. She can like it or lump it. Cam, I mean it," he listens again. "No, of course not." Shit, he told his mother that he was with me. I jump out of bed and start to shake my hands, a bad habit when I'm stressed. "I have just spoken to Tash and we are going to try and make a go of it." I jump up and down excitedly like a little kid, holy shit is this really happening? "Tell her what you want. I don't care, see you tomorrow." He hangs up and I dive back into bed so I can pretend I didn't hear the conversation he just had. My heart rate is thumping in my chest as excitement pulses through me. He is so getting laid tonight. My arousal just hit an all–time high. I lie on my back with my legs bent at my knees and the blankets pooled around my waist trying to calm my breathing and wipe the stupid smile off my face. He slowly walks into the bedroom and stands at the end of the bed, unashamedly naked. His dominant stance doesn't go unnoticed. He's taking no prisoners tonight and a rush of cream once again rushes to my core as I anticipate the pleasure, he is about to bestow on me. With hooded eyes he takes his long length in his hand and gently starts to stroke himself while watching me, his jaw slackening with the contact. I sit up and watch as my legs involuntarily fall open onto the bed. He is just so fucking hot. He puts one of his feet up onto the bed and continues to stroke himself heavily as my arousal starts to pump in my ears.

"Here's the thing, precious," he huskily whispers. "I don't want to have I–missed–you sex tonight."

I frown. "You don't?" I whisper, puzzled.

"No," he shakes his head as the strokes get stronger and the muscles in his shoulder flex at the contact. I would pay good money to watch him pull himself to orgasm. This is off-the-charts arousing. "I don't want to have make-up sex tonight." I swallow as my eyes flick to the visual in the mirror behind him to see this Adonis from the rear angle. His whole back is flexing as he jerks his hand with such velocity. My mouth goes dry. "I don't want I-love-you sex tonight."

I frown and bite my lip. "I might, how does that go?" I whisper. He smiles as he continues the hard, punishing strokes and I start to worry I am going to miss out on that beautiful cock.

"You've already had it," he smirks.

Huh, which one? Damn. I missed it. "What do you want, baby?" I sit up onto my knees and pull him forward so I can lick off the pre ejaculate that is oozing down his thick, heavy length. He cups the back of my head gently. I take him into my mouth — he tastes good. He hisses and gently cups my cheek in his hand as he takes my top off and gently cups my breast. He strokes in and out of my mouth a few times. He pulls my hair back to pull himself out of my mouth. It releases with a pop, my suction is so deep. I look back up at him.

"What do you want, baby? Your wish is my command." He smiles a slow sexy smile at me.

"I want to fuck." His mouth drops open as he gently strokes the back of my head. "I want to fuck you until you're raw." I swallow, shit that sounds painful. A frisson of fear runs over me followed closely by a rush of cream. Why do I respond to fear like that?

"Please me. Let me have my way with you." Huh, hasn't he been doing that for three weeks? What in the hell is he talking about?

"Oh ok," I nod nervously. My body wouldn't let me get out of this bed even if I tried—my ovaries are screaming at me at a deafening pitch.

"Pants off," and in one fell swoop I am naked. "On your knees," he snaps.

"What... What do you mean?" Shit does he want anal sex? He's too big; he will rip me in half. I hesitate and he must be able to sense my fear.

"I won't hurt you, precious girl, trust me." He puts his hand gently on my lower back and I give him a shaky nod. "I mean on your knees in the middle of the bed and resting down on your elbows." I move into position and he walks around behind me, still stroking himself. I can see him through my legs. "Legs wider apart." His voice is husky with arousal. I wiggle my knees further apart. I am leaning on my elbows and knees naked. My legs are spread as wide as they go, and he is behind me. He hisses again, ticks his jaw and cracks his neck as he continues to stroke himself while looking at my open, weeping flesh.

"You're fucking perfect, do you know that?" I smile as I bite my lip. Thanks to a bit of bleach and wax I think to myself. He bends and I am expecting his tongue on my sex, what I am not expecting is his tongue on my rear entrance. *Oh fuck.*

"Josh," I tense and try to pull away.

"Don't move," he snaps as he grabs my hips. He licks me again gently and all of the blood drains from my head. Dear God, I put my head into my pillow, he can't do that to me. It's not...right. He slowly runs his fingertips through my swollen dripping lips as he continues his oral assault on my back rosette. He slides one finger into my sex and slowly makes time with his tongue, fucking me slowly with his finger. He adds another finger, twisting his hand as he enters, and my knees start to buckle.

"Josh, I can't...I can't do...I can't hold my weight."

"Don't come," he whispers into me and the vibrations send me into a spiral and an orgasm I don't think I can stop.

"No!" he snaps and pulls his fingers out. I whimper at the loss. He waits for me to settle. He pushes three fingers into me as his tongue once again softens my rear, spreading saliva. God he's good at this. He is definitely God's gift to women, without a frigging doubt in my mind. I feel uncomfortable letting him do this to me, but I can't stop him. It just feels too good. Then he's up, leaning over me as he continues to fuck me with his fingers and kisses me over my shoulder. A deep hungry tongue kiss. He bites my lip as I feel his thumb pressure my rear entrance. I hold my breath and my mouth is open as I feel the pressure he is putting on my opening.

"Relax, Presh. Let me in," he whispers. His breathing is heavy as he tries to control his arousal. I drop my head as I close my eyes and then he's in. His thumb is pulsing into me in time with his fingers into my swollen sex. *Oh dear God!* I instantly start to groan as my hips drop by themselves towards the penetration.

"That's it," he kisses my back. "It feels good, doesn't it?" He bites my shoulder blade. I start to quiver, and he stills his fingers. "Don't come," he whispers into my back as he tries to control his breathing. "I can't wait to take you here," he smiles into my back. "I'm aching for it." I moan a sound that, if I hadn't made it myself, I would swear came from a beached whale. I feel like I am having an out-of-body experience. This level of arousal is new to me. I pant in anticipation as I nod, unable to speak.

"You're going to fucking love it. Love my cock buried deep in your beautiful, tight ass." Holy shit, if someone had told me I would actually like this, I would not have ever believed it. Not in a million years. This is unexpectedly intimate in a new and raw kind of way. "But you're not ready yet, Presh. I have to get you ready. And I'm not ready," he whispers as he gently kisses my back again. My orgasm fog temporarily lifts.

"Why aren't you ready, Josh?" I know for certain he likes a bit of kink—why wouldn't he be ready?

"Because once I take you there, we are playing for keeps." He pumps his fingers hard again and my eyes close and I moan.

"Do it, Josh. Take me, now," I whisper. "I want to be yours, I need to be yours."

"Not yet," he smiles into my back and he picks up the pace and strength, so the bed starts to rock. Holy shit, that's it. I start to quiver, and he whispers into my ear.

"Come for me." I convulse into the most violent orgasm I have ever experienced, and I fall onto my stomach. He puts his hands under my hips and pulls me up. "Back on your knees," he snaps. He slowly feeds his thick length into my swollen sex, pulling my hips back onto him. He holds my hips up as he slowly sinks into me. He groans. "You're such a hot fuck," he snaps as he slowly pulls out and then slams back into me. "You are so addictive," he whispers as he repeatedly drives into me. Oh no...can't be. I start to quiver again.

"Josh, I can't come again, I...I...it's too much," I whimper. "You can and you will," he bites out in a husky voice. He

reaches around and with precision swipes the tips of his four fingertips over my clitoris and I convulse into another earth-shattering orgasm. I scream into the mattress but before I can relax, he's pulled out and is around on his knees in front of me. What the fuck?

"Open," he whispers. I go to speak but, before I can, he has me by the hair, pulling my mouth onto his cock. *Holy shit.* I'm not sure about this but one look at the arousal level in his eyes has me begging to please him.

"Suck," he yells. I start to deep-throat his large, engorged cock. I feel so out of control, so unlike me, but I've never felt so alive. He pulls back and rides my open mouth as he grips me by the hair.

"Tash, you fuck me so good," he whispers. "I'm going to blow so hard, baby."

On the sixth stroke he stills and jerks as he comes in a rush, flooding my mouth with his seed. It hits the back of my throat with such force that my gag reflex kicks in and I automatically retch.

"Swallow," he whispers as he pants while throwing his head back and gently rubs the back of my head. I nod as I swallow and follow the clean-up with gentle laps. He is gasping for air as he holds my shoulders for balance. Perspiration covers our bodies. My eyes meet his as I rise from my kneeling position and he smiles and falls back onto the bed with his eyes closed, pulling me with him. He kisses my forehead and pulls me into an embrace.

"I fucking adore you," he smiles.

I smile as I sink into his embrace. "Josh."

"Mmm, baby," he answers with his eyes closed.

"You can add porn star to my resume. That was porn-star sex."

"Hmm," he smiles with his eyes closed. "That was hot sex and it had my favorite ending."

I frown. "What do you mean?"

"The happy ending."

"Doesn't all sex have a happy ending?"

He shakes his head. "Some endings are happier than others."

I giggle as I cuddle into him. "Josh, I need a drink and a shower."

He kisses me on the forehead. "I'll get the drinks; you run the shower." I nod as I lean up onto my elbow.

"Leave the soap on the floor," he smirks.

CHAPTER 18

Natasha

I ROLL over and hit a brick wall. My eyes shoot open at the unexpected lump in my bed. To my utter disbelief, I am lying next to a naked sleeping hunk of a man. I smile as the realization that Joshua stayed sinks in. He's out cold on his back with his arm under my head. My body is draped half over his, our legs entwined.

I'm amazed when I stop and look at him how utterly gorgeous he is. His dark–chocolate hair, dark lashes and olive skin are a stark contrast against my white bed linen. His swollen red lips gently open and close as he breathes. I know I have said it before, but I am totally punching above my weight here. He is just so... out of my league. My eyes drop to his tanned rippled torso. My name firmly branding his body, goosebumps scatter me every time I look at that tattoo. It means so much to me. The fact that he got that at a time when our love was so distant. And yet he still committed, without knowing if we had any kind of future together. I will forever be grateful that our limited time together previously meant as much to him as it did to me.

For the first time in seven years I am proud that I didn't give into desire and that I kept myself only for him. I haven't told him that fact yet, I'm not sure if I ever will. At first, I kept the secret so that he wouldn't be worried about hurting me when we had sex. I didn't want to be lacking or for him to have a preconceived idea that I was inexperienced in bed. But after last night I'm pretty sure he's not being gentle anymore. Actually I'm sure of it. The man's a deviant and the thought brings a satisfied smile to my face. Our relationship is complicated. My darkest fear is that we are not going to make it. But I owe it to myself to try. I could never move on knowing I didn't give it my best shot. I just wish we didn't have so many things against us; it's exhausting. I want to be with him when he wakes but nature is screaming at me and I need to go to the bathroom.

I gently rise from bed and his arm feels around the bed for my body warmth. I smile as I rise from the bed and gingerly tiptoe to the bathroom. After the quickest wee in history I brush my teeth and sprint back to bed. He is still out cold. I lie and watch him for nearly an hour, my mind deep in thought. I don't want him to fight with his mother over me. That's the last thing I want. She's trying to protect him and, in all honesty, if my son was embarking on a relationship like ours that was so passionate and volatile, I don't know how I would react either. It's obvious she thinks I am going to hurt him again. I wonder if he told her I never cheated on him all those years ago. I doubt she would have given him the chance to elaborate.

What about Brock? I wince as I remember that he is onto us. I wonder what happened last night between him and Joshua outside. Did they fight? Surely the bodyguards would have stopped it, wouldn't they? That's right, what's with the body-guard claiming to be mine? Seriously, that's just way too much NCIS action, who in the hell would want to hurt me? Joshua has been watching too many movies. My eyes go back to the Adonis in my bed and I smile as I watch him. Am I the only woman deeply in love with him? Is Amelie in love with him? Is he in love with her? He told me last night that he is completely mine.

Please let that be true. He hasn't told me how he feels about me, apart from the adore thing but then adore isn't love. We only have three more weeks together and we need to decide our future. I just wish we had more time to work this mess out.

He gently starts to wake, and I can't help but smile, it's like Christmas morning. He opens one eye and smiles a sleepy smile at me and pulls me into an embrace and kisses my forehead.

"Good morning, beautiful," he whispers in a husky voice. "Morning," I lean in and kiss him softly on the lips. He

smiles and keeps his eyes closed. I lie waiting for him to wake up but he's still half asleep.

"Why are you so tired, baby?" I whisper.

"Hmm," he smiles, still half asleep and absentmindedly starts to run his fingers through my hair. He smiles and kisses my forehead once more, still with his eyes closed.

"Why are you so tired?" I ask again.

He smiles and huskily whispers. "This hot raving bitch I know keeps fighting with me about everything and I can't sleep. I've hardly slept since Saturday."

I smile a sad smile. "Joshua, why didn't you just come over here?"

"Because I'm not putting up with your shit, that's why." He smiles, his eyes still closed.

My heart skips a beat. Am I torturing this poor guy with my dramatics? "Do you want coffee?" I ask.

He nods again with his eyes closed. "Yes, please."

Fifteen minutes later I am seated at my breakfast bar when he saunters out in the hottest black underpants known to man and takes his coffee from the counter and sits on the breakfast stool. I take a sip, unsure how to broach this subject and totally distracted by his beauty. Underpants is a definite unfair advantage. I am painfully aware how easy our conversations turn into full–blown arguments.

"Does your mother know where you are?" He puts his head down and nods. "Josh, I don't want you fighting with her over me."

"Well, I am. So, too late."

"Did you tell her?" he nods, and I wince.

"How did she take it?" He shrugs, obviously not wanting to continue this conversation.

"Is Brock ok?"

He smiles and nods. "Yes, but he is seriously pissing me off."

"Me, too," I shrug. Silence falls and we both sip our coffee. I have never felt so unsure of what to say in my life. I'm walking on eggshells. This conversation is awkward. I feel like I'm interviewing an errant teenager. He sits down next to me but stays silent. I am not bringing up last night until he does. He bloody better bring up last night or he will be seeing that raving bitch again, sooner than he would like.

"What are you doing today?" he says, smiling.

"My office is closed for renovation. I have the rest of the week off. You?"

"I'm training interns all week."

"Oh, what do you teach them?"

"Fun stuff you wouldn't understand," he smiles into his coffee cup.

I smile. "I know what you're doing," I whisper.

He raises his eyebrows. "Really, what am I doing?"

"You're being evasive. Making me talk first."

He smiles and bites his bottom lip. I am so onto him. "Got something you want to say, Presh?" He raises his eyebrows and smiles. I roll my eyes at him, "What?" He smiles.

"You don't think we should talk about last night?" I sigh.

"I said everything I needed to last night. I want you. You want me. Case closed."

I frown at him. "Josh, please, if we are to have a future."

He cuts me off. "Have you changed your mind?" I frown. "Don't you want this anymore?" he snaps.

"Of course, I do, you know that I do. I need some truths from you first," I breathe. He goes to speak but I hold up my hand in a stop signal gesturing for him to give me silence. "Please understand I can forgive anything and understand everything as long as I am told the complete truth. Honesty is imperative to me, Josh. It's a deal breaker."

He nods and I can see him sum up the weight of my words. He narrows his eyes at me. "Can I have a truth of my own?" I nod. "Were you serious when you said you would move to America with me?" He licks his bottom lip in anticipation for my answer.

I smile. "Yes, but couldn't we live six months in Australia and six months in LA?"

He shakes his head. "No, it won't work. I've already thought of that."

I frown. "Why not?"

"Because of my horses. The quarantine laws getting back

into Australia are too stringent. I wouldn't be able to do it. It's either here or there, not both."

I nod. Those horses are going to be the death of me. Everything about those fuckers and their vet spell unparalleled trouble. "Would you move to Australia for me?"

He smiles. "Yes, but I'm contracted in America for at least the next five years, so it would be impossible for me to move at this point."

"But, after that, would it be up for negotiation?"

He puckers his lips and raises his eyebrows as he thinks. "Perhaps"

"Josh, I need to be sure we are going to work, before I would leave my job and move to the other side of the world."

"And how will you be sure? I don't have a crystal ball, Natasha. I can't promise you anything other than the fact I will look after you and try my hardest to make you happy." His wide eyes search mine.

I melt into his gaze. "That's enough, Josh, that's all any girl could ask for."

He smiles and pulls me into an embrace where I am rewarded with a gentle sweep of his tongue through my lips. This man is just...beautiful. Everything about him melts my heart.

I pull back to look at his face. "Can you promise me monogamy, Josh?"

He smiles warmly. "Of course, what man wouldn't be loyal to you? I'd have to be a fucking idiot to stuff this up now." This conversation is going better than I expected.

"Can I have my truths now?" I ask. He frowns and releases me from his cuddle. He walks around behind the bench and places both of his hands wide on the bench and I know he's feeling vulnerable. It's a defensive tactic to have something between us. "Do you have feelings for that blonde from the club?"

He smiles and shakes his head in relief. "Definitely not."

I nod, "How do you know her?" He swallows and looks down while he thinks. "Josh, please. Honesty, remember."

"Here's the thing Tash, if I tell you how I met her, I face you getting the shits. If I don't tell you, I know you are definitely going to get the shits. So basically, it's a no-win situation. Promise me if I tell you, you are not going to kick me out." I fake a smile. Shit, do I really want to know this.

I nod as my heart rate picks up speed. "Fire away."

"The day I arrived in Sydney my friend Carson sent me around a housewarming present to the house."

I frown. "Who's Carson?"

"My friend from LA."

I nod and frown again. "So how do you know her?" He blows out a breath, obviously hoping I will fit the puzzle together.

I frown again. "Am I missing something?" I ask.

He frowns and rubs his two hands through his hair. "She was the housewarming present." Horror dawns. Oh fuck, this is worse than I thought. You could knock me over with a feather. I sit back on my chair as I process what he has told me.

"She's a prostitute," I gasp. He hangs his head and nods.

"I see." My eyes must be the size of saucers. He comes around behind me and cuddles me. He's right. I really want to kick his sorry ass out right now...*deep breaths...deep breaths*. Why did I promise to not get the shits when I so clearly have a reason to?

"So, you can see I have no feelings for her and don't need to worry, baby." He's talking way too fast...*deep breaths*.

"How often do you see prostitutes, Joshua?"

He winces and goes silent. "Don't call me that," he whispers.

"It's your name, isn't it?" I snap.

"Yes, but you only call me that when you are shitty if you haven't noticed." Hmm, I hadn't noticed, actually.

"Josh, I told you I won't get the shits, but I need to know what I'm up against here."

"You're not up against anything. You know I only care about you. Please don't make any more of this than it is."

I look at him deadpan. "Answer the question."

"I don't like to date, Tash, and you know I have a...high sex drive." He swallows and is tripping over his words. "It's not something I can control, the sex drive thing."

"Why don't you like to date?"

"You know why."

"No, I don't." My voice drips with sarcasm. "Please elaborate." He starts to run both hands through his hair. I know he is feeling out of control of this situation.

"Women I date always get...attached and well... My heart is already taken...by you." He reaches for me and I pull my arm away instinctively. I am not supposed to be getting emotional here... *deep breaths...deep breaths.*

I put my head into my hands. "How often?"

"Tash, please, baby, it doesn't matter. It is in the past." "Joshua! So, help me. Answer the goddamn question or I am going to be wearing your balls for earrings."

He stifles a smile and raises his eyebrows. "Really. Earrings?"

I do wide eyes at him. "Really. Don't push it. I'm great with a butter knife." I pull out the drawer. "And I have a few handy here you know." He smiles again. "Please, Josh, just tell me. I thought we discussed honesty. I need the truth."

He looks down and ticks his jaw. "At least once a week."

FUCK... I was hoping for once a year.

I close my eyes and pinch the bridge of my nose. "We haven't been wearing condoms. Am I going to get an STD?"

He looks mortified. "I'm always safe. You're the only person I would ever go bareback with. How could you think such a thing?" I frown—is this the frigging twilight zone? He tells me he has sex with prostitutes all the time but I'm out of line for asking about STDs.

"So, you have never had sex without a condom with anyone else?"

He shakes his head. "No, and I don't want to. Only you, who I can't stand to be separated from." He pulls me into his arms and goes in for a kiss, but I keep my lips tightly sealed shut.

He pulls back. "You're mad."

"No," I lie.

"Yes, you are, I can tell."

"I'm disappointed, Joshua."

"Stop frigging calling me that, call me baby," he whispers. I smile...why does he have to be so damn cute. "Isn't that a song?" he smiles and blows out a breath.

"So, you see my, precious girl, you have nothing to worry about. I will never see any of them again. They were all high-class prostitutes though."

I frown. "Excuse me, idiot. There is no such thing as a high-class prostitute." He nods quickly, realizing he has said the wrong thing. "Josh, how in the hell am I supposed to keep you sexually satisfied when you are used to...you know...such variety?"

He tenderly cups my face and gives me a gentle loving kiss. "Tash, you are all I see...all I want, you mean everything to me, and I have missed you desperately for seven long years. In fact, I think I have fallen for you harder all over again. I fucking adore you. Give me a chance to prove myself. I am not going to fuck it up. I promise."

I smile a weak smile. Ok, I can live with that...for now. I reach up and run my fingers through his stubble.

"I just feel out of my depth here," I whisper. "I have no sphere of reference for this level of debauchery."

"Thank God," he whispers with his lips against my temple. "I can't stand the thought of you with anybody else. It kills me." Guilt hits me and I know I should elaborate. Should I tell him? No, he will think I'm an idiot. Actually, I am an idiot, who am I kidding.

"Why do I have a bodyguard, Josh?" He frowns.

"Because if you want to be my girl you have to be protected."

"Why?"

"You just do, and I don't want to fight about that. In fact, I need to ask you another truth. How do you feel about my money?"

I pull back to look at his face and I frown. Of all the nerve. "I don't want you for your money, asshole. How could you even think that?"

He smiles. "No, I mean, are you going to leave me because of my money?"

I frown again. "You think I'm going to leave you because of your money?"

He nods. "Why?"

"I am a very wealthy man, Tash, and I live a very expensive life. I have been very careful not to expose you at all to it because I didn't want to frighten you off."

"How wealthy are we talking?" He shrugs.

"Around about?" I raise my eyebrows.

"Nearly a billion." *What?*

"Fuck off—you're a billionaire?"

He winces. "Nearly," he whispers. I stare at him open mouthed.

Holy shit, this is unimaginable.

"Joshua Stanton, you are a total mind fuck, do you know that?"

He smiles. "I'm your mind–fuck if you'll have me."

"That depends." I smile as I cross my arms in front of me.

"On what?"

"On whether you're going to show me how that I–love–you sex you mentioned last night goes."

He smiles and kisses me. "Does it have a happy ending?" he whispers into my neck. I bite my lip as I smile.

"Yes, but this time the happy ending is going my way."

An hour later, we are in the shower and Josh is soaping up my back with deep massaging strokes. My eyes are closed, I am leaning onto the glass and am deeply relaxed. In all honesty, I just want him to myself for the day. Bang work I say.

"Can't you stay home with me today?" I know I sound like a whiny kid, but I don't care. I turn and kiss him as I put my arms around his neck.

"No, you've already made me late." He pulls my hips into his by my behind. He smiles down at me tenderly. I find myself returning the goofy grin.

"What?" I frown.

He hunches his shoulders and bends to kiss me softly, his tongue swiping through my lips. He grinds his hips into mine and once again I feel his beautiful length against my stomach. "Do you know how long I have dreamed of having you like this?" he whispers into my neck. I smile as I drop my head back to allow him greater access to me.

"Like what?" I smile. I know exactly what he means.

"Wanting me as much as I want you." I smile again.

"How could you have ever thought anything else, you big dope?" He grabs me hard on the bum and I squeal with laughter.

"Big dope," he growls as he bites me hard on the shoulder. "I will show you just how big I am." I giggle as I hunch to escape his attack. "Tash," I look up at the serious tone in his voice. My eyes close at the contact of his lips to mine.

"Hmm."

"Our adult relationship starts today, ok?"

I frown at him, not understanding his meaning. "What do you mean?"

"I mean, to me, our relationship of being scared of being found out and unsure of each other is over. I want to start again." Tears well in my eyes at the sincerity in his face and the meaning of the words. It's true that I have felt torn, guilty and unsure about our relationship since the day it began. What we have is beyond beautiful, how could it be wrong? It's impossible and, he's right, we need to start acting like adults and take our future into our own hands.

"I would like that, too," I whisper as I lean in for another gentle kiss. With his lips pressed to my temple I hear the gentle words.

"I fucking adore you, precious girl."

These words are very quickly becoming my favorite thing in the world to hear. Chicken soup for my soul.

Eleven o'clock and I am on my way home from the gym. I may as well try to lose the twelve pounds I have stacked on since Mr. Orgasmic came back on the scene. It does seem like I am naked a lot of the time lately. It's only a matter of time before hail damage strikes. A song comes onto the radio. It's a new track by Katy Perry called 'Dark Horse'. I heard it the other day and it gave me goose bumps. The words are exactly the situation between Josh and me and, seeing as we are literally the dark horses of the family, a pubescent idea comes into my brain and I laugh at the thought. I stop off and grab a coffee and text the girls.

Five o'clock Oscar's Coffee Catch up

They both reply immediately, and I smile as I appreciate the two most beautiful friends any girl could wish for. I remind myself to ask them about their stuff tonight. I have been so self-absorbed lately I wouldn't have a clue what's going on with them or Jeremy or army guy. It seems every time we talk lately, I'm rambling on about myself and my problems. I'm a bad friend. I didn't even talk to Bridge at Mum's the other night. I was too busy fighting with Mole Patrol to even notice poor Didge. I make a pact to myself to not turn into one of those bitches that only needs friends when she's single. I hate those girls. I've had them as friends before. They get a new boyfriend and, poof, you never see them again—they drop off the face of the earth. I know I need my friends. They keep me sane and make me laugh. Mostly at myself.

As soon as I get home, I download the song 'Dark Horse' and send it through as a message to Josh's phone. I smile when I imagine him opening it. I frown as the thought that he might open it in front of someone crosses my mind—how embarrassing. Surely, he wouldn't be that stupid? It seems all this sexing up definitely wears a girl out and I shower and flop into bed for a well-deserved nana nap. No doubt the frigging nymphomaniac will hit me full throttle again tonight...not that I'm complaining.

I awake with the sound of the keys in the door and smile that my beautiful man has surprised me with an early visit home. I amble into the lounge room in my undies and tank top. To my horror the face I'm looking at is Bruce Willis, my new body-guard. *What the fuck.* I scream and run back into my bedroom to cover up.

"Sorry, Natasha," he calls out. "The delivery guy couldn't get you and I was getting worried." I chuck on some clothes and return to the lounge, fuming mad.

"Why do you have a key to my apartment?" I demand. He nods and moves to the side to allow a delivery man with a huge bouquet of red roses to step out from behind him. Oh shit, I'm a total bitch. I rub my forehead in frustration. The delivery guy speaks.

"Natasha?" I smile and nod. "Can you sign here?" He pulls out a delivery docket and pen. I sign and he passes over the biggest bunch of red roses I have ever seen and then disappears back out the door to retrieve something else. I sheepishly look at Bruce, embarrassed by my rude outburst. I am not going to get used to this invasion of privacy—it's doing my head in. The delivery guy returns with a big black gift box with a beautiful satin cream bow. I smile as I take it and put it onto the table.

"Thank you," I smile, and he disappears down the stairwell. "Can you tell me your name please?" I whisper to the bodyguard.

"Max," he smiles. "Sorry about barging in, I thought you might be in trouble."

I frown, is this a joke? "What trouble could I possibly get

into in my apartment, Max? I was having a sleep." He nods, also feeling a little embarrassed. "Max, I don't need a bodyguard. Josh has officially lost his marbles."

He smiles and steps back. "Excuse me for talking out of line here, ma'am, but I have been guarding Mr. Stanton for four years and if you are close to him, you are in danger, and you do need protection."

"Danger, what kind of danger?" I frown.

He shrugs as he walks toward the door. "Speak to Joshua, Natasha. I can't elaborate." I frown as I close the door behind him. How very odd. Talk about dramatics. I turn to the table and pick up my roses—they are beautiful with the biggest buds I have ever seen. And the perfume...I inhale deeply. They smell divine. I put them back on the table to remove the card written in Joshua's handwriting.

Yes, I want to play with magic
X

I jump up and down on the spot like a five-year-old. This is the first time in my life that I have received flowers from someone that I actually love. He wants to play with magic. He must have liked the song that I sent him. I clap my hands together in glee while feeling very proud of myself. He sent me roses. I feel like I am sixteen again, actually no, I don't. I feel like I'm seventeen since that was the last time Joshua made me feel like this.

I turn my attention to the gift box. For some reason I feel nervous about opening it. He has never bought me anything before... it feels weird. I slowly undo the ribbon and inside is thick cream tissue paper. I slowly unwrap the contents. My heart stops. Inside is the most beautiful black satin corset, suspender belt, stockings and the briefest satin and lace under-pants. They are stunning with a cream satin ribbon entwined through the lace around the top and bottom of the corset. Tiny cream ribbon bows are around the tops of the sheer thigh–high stockings and up the boning in the corset. My eyes drop back to the box and I pull out a gorgeous black evening dress that does up at the front with a trail of intricate black ribbon bows. He's dropped a pretty penny on these babies. I swallow a lump in my throat. Ok, so he wants to play with magic, and I think I am supposed to wear these. A sudden thought sends panic through me. Shit. I grab my keys and run out the door. I had better get myself to that beautiful behind salon *like now*. And I don't give a flying fuck if Max is following.

5 pm

I am at Oscar's waiting for the girls. I'm excited to see them. I have news and it's good news. Bridget and Abbie arrive fifteen minutes late and walk over to our low sunken leather lounge deep in conversation.

"So, then what did you say?" Abbie hunches her shoulders.

"Hi, what's going on?" I ask. Abbie flops into the lounge, blows out a breath, throws her head back and closes her eyes.

"What's going on?" I wince.

"Tristan wants to be exclusive."

"Huh, who's Tristan?" I frown.

Abbie points at me. "Exactly," she snaps.

Bridget does wide eyes at me. "Army guy," she snaps.

"Oh, of course." I frown. I probably should have known that. "What happened?"

Abbie pulls a sad face at me. "He said he wants to be exclusive or he can't see me anymore."

I narrow my eyes at her. "And?"

She throws her arms in the air. "You know I can't do that." Bridget and I frown at each other.

"Ok," I whisper.

"Why in the hell not? You can't fuck around for the rest of your life," Bridget snaps.

Abbie scowls at Bridget. "Watch me." We all fall silent as the waitress comes over and takes our order.

"Change the bloody subject. I'm not discussing this." Bridget rolls her eyes at me and I nod.

"So, what's happening with Mr. Stanton?" Abbie smiles.

I lean back onto the lounge and swoon, "He's amazing."

Abbie pulls a disgusted face at Bridget. "He's not that amazing—he slept with TC." I shiver at the mention of her name. "What did he say about that?"

"He 'fessed up that he slept with her."

"Fuck off," Bridget snaps.

I nod, "I know, gross huh."

Abbie fake–punches her hand. "I swear I am going to take that bitch down. First James, now Joshua. Who's next? Jeremy?" We all nod and agree at the disgusting turn of events.

"What did he say? Oh shit, that's right, what did he say about his frigging mother?" Bridget puts her hands up to her cheeks.

"Nothing. He told her we are back on."

"Holy shit," Abbie whispers, wide–eyed.

"We've decided we are going to try to make a go of it." They both smile beaming smiles at me which I can't help returning. "He sent me roses and lingerie today and said I will be picked up at eight by my bodyguard."

They both frown at me. "Fuck off," Abbie snaps. "You have a fucking bodyguard now?"

I frown and nod. "Apparently, I need one."

"This is James Bond shit and, trust me, you are no Bond girl."

I laugh. "You've got that right." A little girl walks up to us while her mother orders.

"Hello," Abbie smiles.

The little girl glares at us and walks off. Abbie hunches her shoulders and laughs.

"Getting clucky, Abbie?" I ask.

"God no," she winces. "I don't cluck, I fuck." We all burst out laughing.

"What about you, Bridge? How's Jeremy?" She smiles and fake bats her eyelashes.

"Perfect," Abbie does cross-eyes and lurches to simulate throwing up. Hmm, I nod. How do you go from thinking a guy is cheating to being totally in love in the space of three weeks?

Bridget grabs my arm. "Oh shit, I forgot. What did Josh say about Ivy?"

I frown. "Who's Ivy?"

Bridget rolls her eyes. "The frigging vet."

I pull a disgusted face. "You mean Amelie."

She nods, "Yeah, that's her."

I shrug my shoulders. "I didn't ask him."

"Why in the hell not?"

I blow out a breath. "At that point of our massive argument I was more worried about TC."

"Oh shit, what did he say about her?" Abbie is seated on the front of the chair with bated breath waiting for my answer.

"I'm actually embarrassed to tell you." I wince as I imagine their reaction. Too bad I'm not lying to cover his sleazy ass. "She's a prostitute that he had sex with."

"Fuck off!" Bridget snaps. Abbie's eyes are the size of the saucers. "No way"

"Unfortunately, yes." The girls both sit in silence with frowns on their face. I sip my coffee, acting totally unaffected that my boyfriend uses prostitutes.

"And you're ok with this?" I hunch my shoulders.

"Seriously, you need to change your job. You are so desensitized to this shit, it's frigging scary."

Is that true? I smile to myself—of course it is. Every second male I see is a sex addict who frequents prostitutes. In fact, I think prostitutes do a great service to the community. Imagine the rape crimes if unstable men had no other way of getting their needs met. I shrug my shoulders.

"As long as he is loyal to me now is what matters in this early stage of our relationship."

Abbie rolls her eyes. "Who are you convincing—us or yourself?" I pull a sad smile and hunch my shoulders again.

"You're right," I whisper. "This is messed up, but I don't really know how to deal with this so I'm going with denial."

"Idiot," Bridget snaps.

"Totally," I whisper.

The driver opens the door of the car and I nervously slide out. I am pimped to the nines in the lingerie and sexy dress Joshua has bought me and I'm wearing sky-high stilettos. The dress is stunning and it's a perfect fit. When did he have time to buy it? Max walks me through to the desk and announces to the three ladies behind the desk, "Mr. Stanton's guest." They all look at me up and down and smile.

"Second elevator on the left." The blonde one smiles. "Fourth floor." A guard comes over and accompanies us to the lift and pushes the buttons for us on the outside of the lift. I think this is strange until I realize there are no buttons on the inside. This place is very exclusive. As we enter the lift a horrifying thought crosses my mind. Do they think I'm a prostitute? Probably... stop thinking. Max stays silent next to me in the elevator and my heartrate is jumping through my chest. This place is probably the most luxurious hotel I have ever been in. It's breathtaking. Is this what he was talking about with the expensive life thing? Is this normal for him? I shake my head.

"How the other half live, hey," I sigh to Max. He smiles and nods, understanding my meaning. We walk up a wide corridor. Exclusive artwork lines the walls and the carpet is plush underfoot. Large fresh flowers adorn the antique benches. Beautiful chandeliers hang low. The sheer grandeur of this place only adds to my nerves. We finally arrive at the door.

"I will be out here for you, ma'am, if you need me."

I frown, "Are you staying out in the corridor all night?" I'm mortified.

He smiles. "No, Mr. Stanton has booked the whole floor. Ben and I have our own apartments too." He winks at me and I smile. There has to be some perks to guarding a billionaire. He steps back to allow me privacy to knock. Why in the hell am I so nervous? It's because I am feeling out of my league here in this exotic place. I feel like bloody Bridget Jones in a Hollywood blockbuster movie.

The door opens and there he is. The finest male specimen on earth in a black dinner suit. My heart stops; I have never seen him in a dinner suit and black tie. He looks breathtaking. He stands back to allow me to enter and nods to Max in appreciation for getting me there safely. I enter and gasp at the sight.

The room is half dark with only the lamps and a row of gentle spotlights around the perimeter of the roof. The back wall has a breathtaking view of the Sydney skyscraper lights, Sydney Harbour Bridge and the Opera House. He closes the door behind me. My eyes shoot back to Mr. Stanton. That's who he is tonight. I can feel the dominance oozing from his every pore.

My throat is dry as I look him up and down. The sexual tension in the air is thick with anticipation, my heart racing. His eyes hungrily scan from my head to my toes and back up again, and he cracks his neck. *Hmm, there it is.* He holds up his hand for me as he smiles affectionately. I take it and he wraps me in an embrace. He retrieves something out of his pocket and points it at the wall and a loud beat fills the space. I smile—it's the song I sent him today. 'Dark Horse', the sexiest song I have ever heard.

He starts to move his hips in time to the beat and pulls me close, so we are dancing a slow sensual dance, backwards and forwards. He pulls something out of his pocket and points it towards the wall and three huge screens light up around the perimeter of the room, all with different angles of us. My eyes shoot back to his in realization of what's going on here and he smiles a slow knowing sexy smile. His head is on an angle as he waits for my approval. He tenderly grabs my face with his two hands and swipes his tongue through my lips hungrily, as his hips keep dancing. I can't help it. I get lost in his kiss and the provocative dance he has me dancing here.

"I missed my beautiful girl today," he whispers into my neck. Warmth spreads through me at his intimate words. I could get used to this. As he is dancing, his lips follow down the length of my neck and he gently sucks me, all the while gently dancing the erotic dance with his hips. I look over his shoulder and reality sinks in. *Holy shit.* There are three cameras around the room on tripods. One is angled toward the double ottoman in the middle of the lounge room where a spotlight is also angled. He kisses me again more deeply, more passionately and I know I had good reason to be nervous. My gut feeling was onto something. I know what's going on here.

Josh's kink is coming to life... We are making a porno.

CHAPTER 19

Natasha

As KATY PERRY'S velvety voice sings the seductive words to 'Dark Horse', the addictive sexy music fills the room and my senses through the sound system.

We start dancing to the sensual words that are being sung. Ok, how did I end up in an exclusive hotel? In what is definitely no celebration dinner. This is a planned seduction, and you know what? It's working. I'm totally seduced. This beautiful man dancing sexily up to me, grinding against me and pulling me onto his erection in a black dinner suit. His erotic demanding kisses and the pure dominance in his stance has me begging to be part of his kink world, begging to please him.

The words are hypnotic...applying just to us. The beat turning me inside out.

He keeps our hips dancing to the slow beat. His eyes penetrate mine as his hands gently start to move up my legs, lifting my dress for the cameras. He runs his finger along the garter strap as he rests his lips on my temple. He twirls me around suddenly to the music and I laugh out loud. His lips are on me again, his teeth grazing my neck as his arousal level amps up a couple of notches. He lifts one of my legs and hooks it around his hip. I find I am holding my breath as I feel a rush of cream to my core and my nipples harden under his expert hands. His hand rubs from my knee up to my behind and he grabs it hard, grinding himself onto me. His pupils are dilated, and his mouth is open. He cracks his neck. My eyes drop to his lips.

He turns me so my back is to his front and he continues the slow circular hip sway. I could come from just this. This man is the maestro of seduction. His hands caress my breasts and follow my body and he gently starts to lift my dress. He kisses my neck and whispers into my ear.

"Watch." My eyes drift to the screen before us and I am openly shocked at just how hot we look. His arousal level is off the charts, I can see it in his eyes. Not surprisingly, I look like I am about to burst into orgasm at any second. I can see through my lace panties and my thighs as he lifts my dress. He raises my arms, so they are around his neck behind me as his hands drift up and down my body, each time lifting my dress and exposing my lingerie just that little bit more to the cameras. I can feel the pulse between my legs as I watch the two of us in IMAX erotically dance in time to this sexy music. The song finishes and starts again, and I smile as realization hits that it is on repeat. He bends at the knees, so he is lower than me and opens my legs to the cameras, slowly sliding his hands up my inner thighs.

"I'm aching for my precious girl," he whispers into my ear. "I need to be inside her." He runs his fingertips over my lace panties and feels the shape of my most erotic core. "You're so wet for me, baby...dripping. Do you know hard you make me?" *He's good alright.*

"I can't wait to taste you," he whispers. My eyes flick to the screen and he runs his fingers around the rim of my garter belt and bites my neck hard. Oh shit, I don't believe this. I whimper as an orgasm gently pulses through me. He kisses me passionately again and he turns and pushes me up against the wall.

"Fucking perfect," he whispers. The orgasm fog temporarily lifts, and I think to myself, fucking embarrassing more like. I can't believe I came without him even touching me. He steps back from me, still while moving his hips to the music. He's such a good dancer. He gently starts to undo the bows of my dress one at a time. He is concentrating on the bows, looking down, and I pull his chin up to my face level. I need him to see what he means to me. His eyes meet mine and he stops what he is doing to put his hands on either side of my head on the wall.

"Do you know how much I fucking adore you?" he whispers, and tears fill my eyes. He speaks the truth. I can feel it. He doesn't just adore me, he loves me. This isn't a sleazy stick film we are making. This is a declaration of our love. My tears start to flow freely as I grab him by the face and kiss him with everything I have. I need him to know how much I desperately love him, how desperately I need him.

"Don't cry, baby," he whispers. "Just know that this is it for us." He kisses me deeply. "We will never be apart again...I promise you." I bite my bottom lip and smile as he gently wipes the tears with his thumbs from my eyes then releases me again to continue untying the bows. I come to an internal decision. You know what? If it's kink, my man wants, then it's kink, my man is going to get. He deserves my best and if he wants to watch this film again tomorrow and the day after that then so be it. Hell, he can put it on the national news for all I care.

We keep moving slowly, dancing erotically against each other.

My dress drops to the ground and I am standing before him in my corset, suspender belt, panties, stockings and stilettos. His eyes drop hungrily down the length of my body and once again he ticks his jaw and cracks his neck. He grabs my hand and walks me back to the middle of the room where he pulls me into an embrace and gently starts to dance with me again, his hips demanding attention.

He is really moving to the beat now and I know for sure that every time I hear this song in the future, I will probably orgasm by picturing him just like this, dancing to this song. I reach up and start to undress him. I first remove his jacket and I throw it on the back of the lounge. Our hips are still swaying in time to the sensual beat. I slowly take off his tie and put it around my neck as I go in for a swipe with my tongue. He starts to lose control. I know he is tempering his arousal by sheer will alone. His hands grab my behind as he pulls me into his hard length and my eyes close at the contact. I remove his shirt and am rewarded by the sight of his rippled torso. My name branding his body, I bend to kiss his tattoo. He gently rubs the back of my hair and pulls me back up to a standing position.

"Not tonight," he whispers. Huh, he doesn't want my mouth on him...that's different. Then I remember the cameras. He doesn't want me giving him a head job on film and I fall just that bit deeper in love with him. Even in this he is thinking of me, putting my needs before his. He doesn't want this to appear smutty. I undo his pants and he kicks off his shoes and removes his socks. I slowly peel him out of his pants and we gently start to sway to the music in sync with each other.

We keep dancing and I have lost track of how many times my new favorite song has played. Our kissing has turned desperate and I can tell just by his breathing how close he is to orgasm, his fingers digging desperately into my behind. My hands are clutching his head, dragging him down to me. His beautiful length is becoming painful against my stomach. I need him inside me. He turns me towards one of the cabinets along the wall. I know a camera is situated on top of it. He bends me over it, and I place my two hands on top of it to hold myself up as he kisses my neck from behind. He drops to his knees behind me and slowly peels my panties down my legs. He pushes my torso forward and starts to gently lick me from behind. My mouth is open as he takes his time pleasuring me on his knees. I'm close again. Why am I so damn responsive to this god? Slowly he pushes two fingers into me with a twist of his hand and I groan and close my eyes. He starts to take over my body as he slowly fucks me with his fingers, each stroke stronger than the last. My hair is everywhere, and a sheen of perspiration covers our bodies.

His mouth is open on the small of my lower back, his breathing is labored and I know he's going to come soon, very soon. I look up into the camera and he pushes me hard forward with his fingers and I throw my head back at the delightful sensation, my mouth falling slack. I look directly into the camera and mouth the words.

"I love you."

The toxic rhythm of the beat sounds loud in our ears. I want him to watch this film and feel my euphoria at his touch, the depth of my love for him. I want him to have it on film as a silent witness. He twists his fingers again and I groan and fall into another intense orgasm. I am overtaken. I slump forward and he leans over me and pulls my hair over to one side of my neck and kisses my shoulder blade, his breath quivering. He needs me to take care of him. I turn and dive my tongue into his mouth and with renewed vigor I mouth the words to him.

"Get on your back." His eyes bore into mine and dilate and his neck cracks. He takes my hand and leads me over to the double ottoman in the middle of the room which I now realize is covered in a white sheet. I smile, this was his plan all along. He wants me to take him, dressed like this in my corset, suspender belt and stockings. I slowly peel his boxer shorts away and am greeted with his mouth-watering erection, the thick veins coursing its length. I have never seen him so hard. It's hard not to taste him, I'm dying to. He lies down on his back and I step over him, my hands on his shoulders. Slowly but surely I slide my wet core along the length of him and he hisses in approval as he closes his eyes. I lift my hips and grab the base of him to lower myself onto his waiting cock. I groan at the intense pressure as his body possesses mine. My mouth is open as I work my way down onto him. Our gaze is locked and I'm having trouble taking him this way up first. He's so large. I'm moving side to side to allow my body to loosen and he stills my hips with his hands as he lurches forward. I pant and look into his dilated blue eyes. He's trying to stop himself from climaxing. Trying to hold it together. I mouth the words, "Fuck me."

He smiles a slow, seductive smile and starts to move. His eyes flick to the screen as his mouth hangs open and he looks back at me and mouths the word, "Watch."

My eyes shoot up to the screen. He's right. This is the most erotic thing I have ever seen. My body taking his, his hands on my hips controlling the way I move. The black satin corset with cream ribbons to match my stockings, my hair wild and my skin flushed from orgasm. I can see every muscle on his torso ripple as I ride him hard. I slowly start to unclasp the front eyelets of my corset to expose my breasts to his gaze and he closes his eyes again, he's trying to block the visual. I know to stop the oncoming orgasm. I remove the corset and throw it over my shoulder as I lick my lips and suck on my fingers and that is it. He loses control and jumps up and throws me down onto the ottoman to swap positions. He is then riding me hard, slamming into me in deep long strokes. He picks up my legs and puts them over his shoulders as he holds his weight up on straight arms and open mouth kisses my inside lower leg. Perspiration is running down his back. He circles his hips while deeply slamming into me. He starts to suck on my inner ankle and I moan a deep sound and he slams into me one, two, three more times and he cries out and I feel his hot semen burn me from the inside out. Oh shit, not again. I start to ripple inside, and I know what's coming. His jerking cock deep inside me spirals me into yet another orgasm and I scream as I am wrung dry. I can hardly breathe, my heart is racing so fast. I am absolutely worked over, and on film no less. The camera never lies.

Two hours and two orgasms and a very hot shower later, I walk out of the bathroom in my hotel–supplied white robe to find my Adonis. I locate him on the outside deck leaning on the handrail and looking out over the harbor at the stunning view. He has poured us both a glass of champagne and has a platter of chocolate–covered strawberries waiting on the table. The dinner we have just devoured was amazing, as is the service. The Park Hyatt at the Rocks definitely knows how to please; this place is beyond swanky. He is wearing nothing but a white towel around his waist. His olive skin is a stark contrast to the white towel and with the way he is leaning on the railing I can see every muscle in his broad back. I smile, arrested by his beauty. I can't resist, the temptation too great.

En route to him I pick up my iPhone and take a picture of him from behind. It looks like it has been photo–shopped, nobody could be that perfect. I quickly shoot it to Abbie and Bridge with the text :

Just enjoying the view
with my champagne and chocolate strawberries.
Xxxxx

I immediately get a text from Abbie.

Fuck off. I hate you.

I smile a bratty smile and my phone beeps again. It's a message from Bridget:

How in the fuck did you get him?

I laugh out loud. My friends are just so...bilingual, cursing of course being their first language. I am busted. He turns and smiles as he walks towards me and hands me my champagne. "Why are you taking photos of me?" his eyes question.

I smile. "Because I can." He leans in for a tender kiss and his eyes linger on mine. Something has changed between us tonight. I know he's impressed that I let him film us or maybe it's the fact that I realize I trust him enough to let him film us, I'm not sure. But I know he feels it, too, and I need to get something off my chest. The plan was to let him see my I–love–you message on the movie and let it go from there, but he might not watch it for years, who knows. Actually, what in the hell is he going to do with that movie? The mind boggles. He pulls me into a gentle embrace and rubs my back. "Do you know how much I adore you?" he whispers into my hair. I nod and smile. "Yes," I answer. It's true, I do feel truly adored.

He returns the smile, looking down at me. He's so much taller when I have no shoes on. His eyes hold mine again and I can't keep it in any longer. I want this night to be perfect, more perfect than it has been already.

"Do you know how much I love you, Joshua?" I whisper as I run my hand down the side of his face. His eyes widen and he leans in and gently kisses me. He breaks into a full blown, swoon worthy smile. "I just need you to know how I feel about you," I whisper. "I have never stopped loving you, Josh, it's always been you. You complete me." My eyes tear up again. What's going on with me lately, frigging crybaby? He nods and swallows but doesn't say anything. His eyes glow with a warmth I haven't seen in them before.

"Come to bed with me and show me how much you love me back, baby," I smile. He kisses me again with such passion my heart stops and he throws me over his shoulder and marches me off to the bedroom. And just like that the chocolate coated strawberries and champagne are forgotten...what a waste.

CHAPTER 20

Natasha

I AWAKE SLOWLY and immediately feel the exhaustion of a tired body. I feel second hand, maybe even third hand. I feel the weight of someone watching me and I slowly open my eyes. Hmm, what a beautiful sight to wake up to. Joshua is naked and lying on his side next to me, leaning up on his elbow. He smiles and leans in gently for a kiss and his lips linger on mine.

"Good morning, beautiful. Did you sleep well?" I smile and nod, still too sleepy to find my voice. I rub my eyes and roll onto my back. I try and will myself to wake up. He stays silent, watching me, and after about ten minutes of watching me in silence I turn back to him.

"What?" I smile. He looks at me as if he wants to say something but is trying not to. I raise my eyebrows.

"Well," I answer again. "Spit it out."

He smiles and then swallows. "Are you going to leave me?" he whispers nervously.

I frown. "No dummy, are you going to give me a reason to leave you?"

"What exactly classifies as a reason to you?" he answers.

I close my eyes and start to absentmindedly run my fingers up and down his arm. Why are we talking about this shit first thing in the morning? Give me a break.

"Being with another woman, Josh, is the only reason I would leave you."

He nods and smiles. "What about when your parents find out, are you going to leave me then?"

I frown. "No, I wouldn't have come this far if I planned on leaving you, you big dope."

His eyes widen. "Big dope." He grabs me hard. I giggle and roll to get away from him as he goes to bite me on the leg.

"My precious girl, you just got yourself a one-way ticket." I laugh again as he grabs to tickle me, and I make a dash to get off the bed.

"To where?" I yell.

He pulls me by the foot back towards him and I giggle.

"To pound town," he snarls. I laugh out loud and squeal as I try desperately without success to escape.

"Pound town?" I repeat.

"Yes, you're gagging for a one-way ticket." I squeal as I am dragged underneath my powerful man in a fit of giggles.

It seems I quite like destination, pound town. I would suggest you take the scenic route.

We are in the shower and I am very relaxed. I can't remember feeling so...sleepy. I have told him I love him, and he hasn't run for the hills—things are looking promising. Although I did notice he didn't say it back.

"What are the plans for today?" I ask. He kisses my shoulder and continues washing my back. "I have to do some training. I have a fight tomorrow night." My eyes widen and I jerk around to face him. "Fight... Josh.

I don't want you fighting anymore. I don't like it." He frowns at me. "Tough shit," he replies. "I do."

I'm shocked. "Tough shit," I reply as my face drops. He nods to confirm that I heard him right. I quickly wash the soap off and exit the shower. I'll give him tough shit...tough shit, he really should keep that big mouth of his shut more often. I quickly dress and walk out onto the balcony. He, however, takes his time and doesn't join me for at least twenty minutes. By that time, I am fuming. I am not dating a fucking cage–fighter. No way in hell. What does he think this is? An episode of Conan the Barbarian? Annoyingly, he walks out onto the balcony holding our breakfast tray, looking like he doesn't have a care in the world. Why would he? I have just been fucked every which way in a porno...which he produced. I'm an idiot. He smiles warmly at me as he sits down at the table and starts to remove the trays for breakfast. I cross my arms like a petulant teenager.

He raises a brow. "Are you eating?" Is he deluded? I shake my head. He hunches his shoulders and starts to tuck into his breakfast. I scowl again. He's so annoying. He doesn't even care I've got the shits. I walk over and pour myself a coffee. I really am starving, and he knows it, the asshole.

"Don't you care that I'm pissed?" I snap.

He continues chewing his food and shrugs his shoulders. "Not really." He smiles as he swallows. My mouth drops open, of all the arrogant...I do wide eyes at him and he has the audacity to laugh. I'm so mad but for some stupid reason I find myself mirroring his stupid smile.

"What's funny?" I snap.

"You are," he smirks.

"What planet are you from? I'm not dating a cage–fighter, Josh. End of story." He scowls.

"What planet are you from if you think I'm going to put up with your shit? You are not telling me what I can and can't do, Natasha. Just because you love me doesn't make you the boss of me," he snaps.

I scowl again. Oohh, touché idiot. Trust him to throw the love-you-thing in. "Why in the hell do you want to do this anyway? I don't get it."

"Sit and eat your breakfast," he sighs as he points at my chair with his knife. I sit and start to eat my breakfast in silence, and he smirks at me.

"Seriously, Josh, I'm going to have a shiny new pair of earrings in a minute," I hold up my butter knife and he laughs.

"Calm down, psycho, I do it for exercise and the challenge," he says.

"Challenge," I repeat. "What's that supposed to mean?"

He shrugs. "Apart from you, I don't really have any challenges. Without sounding conceited, most things come easy for me. I love technology. I would do it for free, but it has paid me a lot more than I feel I deserve. That money has allowed me to buy the thoroughbred horses I love, so I find polo easy as well. My cars, houses and women. Everything comes easy. But when I fight it doesn't matter how much money I make, or what my brain can do, or how I look. It just doesn't matter, it's just me and my opponent and the ring and if I can't fight then I'm going to get beaten and that feeling of being equal gives me a massive adrenaline hit. I love it." I narrow my eyes as I listen. "I know it sounds like a head trip but that's how it is," he says deadpan. I suppose that does make sense. I can only imagine how it feels to be so successful. I should be so lucky. I know I'm not going to win this argument and it's true I don't want him to have to change to be with me.

"Fine, but I'm not supporting this. There is no way in hell I am going to another fight."

He smiles and picks up my hand and kisses the back of it. "Deal," he whispers. "I have no wish at all to tell you what you can and can't do." He raises an eyebrow.

Margaret Stanton arrives at her lawyer's office just after nine. She has travelled to Sydney to see this lawyer. She couldn't trust anyone in Melbourne. They all know her husband. She is shown into his office by his secretary and she nervously takes her seat.

"Can I get you a coffee, Mrs. Stanton?"

"No, thanks, dear," she smiles. The tall grey lawyer enters and shakes her hand.

"Mrs. Stanton," he smiles. "Yes," she whispers.

"What can I do for you today?" he asks. She pulls out a large envelope that is sealed with a wax seal and her nerves are obvious, even to a stranger.

"I need you to put this in a safety deposit box for me," she says nervously.

Her lawyer frowns. "You came all the way from Melbourne to put something in a safety deposit box?"

She nods. "Yes, I need your utmost discretion and my husband knows too many lawyer in Melbourne."

"I'm intrigued, Mrs. Stanton."

"Please call me Margaret."

"Ok, Margaret, what are your instructions?"

She swallows the large lump in her throat. "If I go missing or am found dead, I want you to deliver this envelope directly by hand to my eldest son, Joshua Stanton. Make sure he is alone when he reads it." The solicitor frowns.

"Do you think your life is in danger, Margaret?"

She smiles. "I don't think so, but I am concerned about a current relationship my son is having and if it continues it could be."

"We must call the police. What exactly is in the envelope? I assure you it will not leave this room?" he breathes.

"No police...please no. I don't want to draw unnecessary attention to this matter. If I do go missing, I am just covering all bases. After Joshua has read the contents please pass it onto the police."

"Margaret, this is highly irregular, and I have concerns. What exactly is in the envelope? Are you involved in criminal acts?"

She smiles. "No, nothing like that. It relates to my son's... paternity."

He smiles and nods. "I see."

She smiles a nervous smile at him. "If this information gets out, it will destroy the lives of my husband and son, but it will be catastrophic for a very powerful man who stands to lose everything."

"How would this information put you in danger?"

"My son is deeply in love with his... first cousin. I have kept this information from him for twenty-seven years but if this relationship continues, I will tell him. I will not let him live a life of guilt when he doesn't deserve to."

"Maybe this affair will end," the solicitor kindly smiles.

"We can only hope. He has been in love with her for seven years and they have recently reconnected. He is not letting her go this time. That I am positive of." The solicitor writes the necessary instructions and walks Mrs. Stanton out of his office.

"My discretion is assured. Thank you for your trust." She smiles and wipes the tears from her eyes. She hopes to God her son never has to see that letter. It will break his heart as he idolizes his father. Pain lances through her as she realizes Joshua is going to lose either way. The love of his life or his father. Either way it's a loss she doesn't know if he will be able to bear and definitely not one that he deserves.

You know what the problem with dating a very intelligent man is? Just that. He's a smart son of a bitch. When he agreed that I didn't have to go to his stupid fight I did have an inkling that it was all a bit too easy—he was too agreeable. So why was I surprised when Abbie, Bridget, Cam and Adrian came around to my house tonight to pick me up to go to the fight? And when I refused, drank wine with me until I was tipsy enough to be talked into anything? Diabolical. So here I am, three hours later, at the bar in Luna Park Convention Centre wincing as I watch the big screen. Thankfully, Adrian and I are staying at the bar boycotting the activities. It seems Joshua made Adrian come too because he knew I would come if he did. Thankfully, we are having a really good time and we are very tipsy.

"So, tell me, Adrian. What goes on with you? Do you have a boyfriend?" I point my wine glass at him.

He smiles and rolls his eyes dramatically. "No, sort of, yes."

I raise my eyebrows. "What does that mean?"

He shrugs, "To be honest I don't even know. My stupid boyfriend's phone calls are getting fewer and fewer. When I first got here, he rang me twice a day and now it's down to once every three days." He shrugs and talks into his wine glass. "He couldn't even wait three months."

I give him a sympathetic smile and he smiles and shrugs. "Josh hates my boyfriend."

My eyes widen. "How come?"

"Josh knew him a long time before I met him; he's on his polo team."

I nod and raise my eyebrows and take another way too large gulp of my wine. "And," I prompt.

"Josh thinks he is after my money."

I choke on my wine. "Don't tell me you're fucking rich, too." I giggle as I wipe the wine from my chin.

He laughs and shakes his head. "I'm only rich because of your over generous boyfriend."

I frown. "What do you mean?"

"Josh bought me a condo and a Corvette and pays me three million dollars a year."

I choke again. "Fuck off."

He nods and smiles as he drains his glass. He nods an over exaggerated nod. "Don't you talk. I think he paid off your mortgage yesterday."

"What?" I snap. "Tell me you're joking."

"You know how over generous he is." I frown. Weirdly enough I don't. I point my wine glass at him again.

"So why does he hate him?" He rolls his eyes.

"Josh is just overprotective because I don't sleep around."

I frown, not understanding. "What do you mean?"

"Shit, you really do psychoanalyze, don't you?" I raise my glass and clink it with his, raising my eyebrows as I smile. I really should stop drinking; I am feeling very inebriated. "I am not your normal gay guy, Tash. I hate camp with a passion, hate feminine men. I find most gay men sleazebags and can think of nothing worse than going to a gay bar where everyone is wearing next to nothing and eyeing up their meat for the night."

I nod an exaggerated nod. "Hear, hear," I yell way too loud.

"So, basically, I'm a gay man who loves everything heterosexual. All my friends are straight, I prefer straight bars, straight... everything," he shrugs. "Except women."

I give him a sad smile. "That must suck."

He nods. "Totally"

"So how did you meet Josh?" He smiles a broad warm smile and I know how much he cares for him.

"I had just finished college."

"What did you study?"

"Politics and Economics." I nod, impressed. "Anyway, I got my dream job as an intern at his company. But I was only there for three weeks and both of my parents were killed in a plane crash, my mother immediately and then my father four weeks later from his injuries."

I grab his leg. "Oh Adrian, I'm so sorry."

"Me too, they were... are really missed. Anyway, I had six months off to get my shit together and when I finally came back Josh kept me in the office next to him to keep an eye on me." I smile as I imagine the scenario, he is setting for me. "Anyway, I started doing more and more for him and then he offered me the position of his personal secretary and then two years later he promoted me to his communications manager." I nod and raise my hands to signify more drinks and the bartender smiles and nods.

"What does a communications manager do exactly? I mean how do you earn so much frigging money?" I laugh and cover my mouth for being so intrusive.

He laughs out loud. "I run the company. I handle all of the

staff management, the programming timetables, the equipment and of course all of the public speaking."

I frown. "Of course meaning?"

"Well, you know how shy Josh is. Public speaking is his worst enemy." I screw up my face.

"Is Josh shy?" How do I not know this?

He frowns at me." Are you kidding? He's painful. Haven't you ever seen it?" I shake my head. "Oh shit," he smiles as he puts his hand over his mouth. "You two have always known each other, he wouldn't be shy around you." I pull a face and shrug. This information is weird. In fact, there is a lot of things that we don't know about each other. I would never have said he was shy but then I really haven't seen him in the company of strangers.

"I can't imagine big burly Josh being timid."

"Trust me, he's not timid. We are here watching him cage fight remember?" I nod and screw my face up. "He comes across as arrogant but it's just because he doesn't really mix with people he doesn't know."

I nod as I process the information. "Obviously, he has no trouble talking to women." I scowl.

"Obviously" He raises his eyebrows and we both sit in uncomfortable silence contemplating that last comment. The screen comes back on and another fight begins, the crowd going wild.

"Remind me what we are doing here?" I laugh to Adrian.

He shakes his head. "I don't know." Adrian is suddenly grabbed from behind in a headlock that nearly knocks him off his chair.

"What are you doing here, man?" A very happy Cameron smiles as he messes up Adrian's hair. "Will you two stop being such boring fuckers?"

I dramatically roll my eyes "Sorry if I don't like watching people get the shit punched out of them." Cameron laughs and swoops me off my chair and throws me over his shoulder.

"Cameron, put me down." I grab Adrian's arm for stability, and he laughs and walks along behind us. "Cameron you're scaring me. You're too drunk to carry me." I punch him in the back. "Cameron, put me down!" He laughs and starts to run down the stairs to our seats. I am in fear for my safety here. Cam is way too drunk to pull this off.

"Do you know how dead you will be if you drop her?" Adrian smiles at Cam. He must take that warning seriously because he laughs again and slides me down, back to the safety of the ground. We get to our row. I am appalled to see Bridget, Abbie and Ben all standing on their seats with giant foam-fingers on their hands. Oh dear, I have embarrassing friends. Adrian grabs my hand and pulls a disgusted face at them. I nod as we walk along to our seats. The crowd goes crazy again and everyone jumps from their seats. I look at the stage to see a man get kneed to the head.

"Oh shit." I cover my eyes. The crowd roars again. I really don't want Josh to do this. It was bad enough last time, and we weren't even together then. I start to freak out at the violence of the situation. How can my beautiful Josh be so brutal? Why does he like this? I mean if he's so bloody bored, he needs to do this. What in the hell is going through that pea brain of his?

The crowd is really getting animated and I hate to admit it, but my two friends are right in the thick of things. Abbie is jumping up and down screaming and Bridget is pointing her foam finger into Cam's face trying her hardest to annoy him. Ben has his hands in a funnel around his mouth yelling at the stage. This place is barbaric. The fight ends and my heart is in my throat.

Oh no, I see him. Joshua is on the side of the ring in a cape.

A fake name is called by the announcer and I see his opponent enter the ring, and the crowd all scream. I can hear my pulse in my ears as I am gripped with anxiety. Adrian pulls me next to him as he puts his arm around me. Josh enters the ring and the crowd roar. I can see his trainers talking to him as he jumps around, trying to keep warm. The bell rings and I sit down and put my head in my hands. I don't know if I can take this. I feel sick to my stomach. Cameron shuffles along the row of chairs until he gets beside me. He gives me a sympathetic smile as he pulls me from Adrian's grip and puts his arm around me.

"Calm down. It's ok," he whispers into my temple. I look up at the ring as Josh connects a massive kick to his opponent's torso and he doubles over in pain. I scream and put my head back down to try and block out the visual of my boyfriend taking such pleasure in beating someone to a pulp. Cameron suddenly stands and the crowd goes crazy. Shit, what's happening? Ben starts to yell, "Get up...get up." I stand and peer at the ring to see Josh on the ground and the other guy laying into him. Oh my God. I go to run down there to stop this craziness and Cam and Ben both grab me to hold me back.

"Stop it," I yell. "Let me go."

Cameron shakes his head. "Just give him a minute." I sit back down and put my head in my hands with my heartrate thumping in my ears. How can they watch him get hurt like this?

"What if that maniac kills him?" I scream at Ben. "Aren't you his frigging bodyguard?" He smiles and shakes his head and Adrian is now standing on his seat yelling at the ring.

"Finish him off, finish him off." Good grief—finish him off.

Now I have heard it all. I grab Adrian's shirt and yank him off the chair so fast he nearly falls over.

"Shut up," I yell. The crowd screams again, and my eyes flick back to the ring. To my horror Josh has a bleeding nose and is going berserk on this guy. He punches him, his head snaps back at the contact and then follows through with another knee. Blood is on both of their faces and I don't know whose blood is whose. The blond guy seems to be losing it and they start to really let loose on each other and the ref steps in and grabs the blonde guy to stop the fight, obviously because of the blood. Blondie pushes the poor ref, and he falls down. The crowd all stand and go wild. He then turns his attention back to Joshua as he kicks him hard in the stomach.

I stand. "Oh my God, get down there," I scream at Ben and Cameron. This isn't entertainment anymore. They are actually fighting for real. Ben and Cameron stand and start to run down the stairs toward the ring. An abundance of people are now down there, trying to break them up. I see Josh's trainers in the ring. I can't see or hear a thing because everyone in the arena is going ballistic, jumping up and down. Is this place a sick frigging joke? Abbie now has her hands over her eyes and Bridget is trying her best to calm me down before I start to hyperventilate. Josh runs and tackles the blond guy to the ground and starts to repeatedly punch him in the head. Suddenly there is a crowd rush in the corner of the audience to the left of the ring and everybody screams again. Holy shit, there is a fight in the crowd.

"What in the hell is going on?" Bridget screams. My eyes go back to the ring and I see Josh and the blond guy surrounded by about fifteen men trying to break them away from each other. They manage the task and I look down to see Joshua being held back by two arms, the look on his face murderous as he glares at his opponent. A cold chill runs down my spine, he looks evil. Completely evil. He is covered in blood and is still trying to get free to try and continue killing this other man with his bare hands, who I might add looks more than happy to repay the favor. He spits blood onto the ground. Who is this man? Definitely not the polished rich boy I know. Do I even know him at all? This is the part of his personality that I cannot reconcile. The fight in the crowd continues and I see Ben climb beneath the ropes into the ring. Joshua looks at him and starts yelling. I see Ben nod; he then turns and sprints back up the stairs toward us. Joshua and blond idiot are led out of the ring and backstage, both being held tightly with their arms behind their backs to prevent them from attacking each other again. I sit down and cover my face with my hands.

"Holy shit," I whisper.

"Fuck. That was intense," Adrian murmurs.

"You think," Bridget yells back.

"See why I hate this," I snap. "Over my dead body is he doing this again." Adrian, Abbie and Bridget all nod. This is not a sport. This is thuggery at its lowest point. Ben walks along the row of seats and back to us.

"What did Joshua say to you down there?" I ask. He doesn't answer and looks at Adrian and shrugs his shoulders.

"What did he say?" I repeat. He looks annoyed at my question. "He went off at me for leaving you alone." *What*? This man is un-freaking-believable. He's covered in blood and fighting a suspected psychopath in front of twenty thousand people but is worried about me sitting in the frigging grandstand without protection.

"Now I've heard it all," I snap.

Adrian raises his eyebrows and shakes his head. "Me too"

. . .

An hour and three cocktails later we are waiting outside the exit door of the fighter's locker rooms. Cameron never came back from the ring so I suspect that he stayed with Joshua. Ben is hanging with us but is not drinking at all, obviously on duty. Adrian and the girls are far beyond tipsy; they are downright drunk. I, however, have sobered up considerably since witnessing Rocky Balboa on the rampage.

Adrian has a giggling girl on either side of him and he has his arms around both of them. They are finding everything hilarious as they rock from side to side. Abbie is raving on about looking for the father of her children, still infatuated with that Italian stallion we saw fighting here last time, and Bridget is talking it up how some guy at the bar asked her for a quickie. Adrian is laughing out loud at the shenanigans of my crazy friends. I smile as I realize this would be new for him. I take my friends' sense of humor for granted. They are funny and you don't have to be friends with them to have fun around them as they make everyone feel comfortable.

The door opens and the blond guy that Josh had the fight with exits with two security guards. Oh shit, my mouth drops open. I know him, he's the prison warden from my visits in jail —the hot one. He smiles at me and walks past to a short and slutty Barbie on my left. Honestly, doesn't she own a mirror? My eyes follow him as I try to remember his name. What is it? Japer? J something. He looks like he has a broken nose with two oncoming black eyes. He will be a mess tomorrow. His eyes also stay on me and I know he is trying to think where he has seen me before. Shit. I hope he doesn't remember me; this looks so unprofessional for me to be here. The door opens again, and Joshua exits, flanked by two security guards and Cameron. He walks over to me and bends to give me a peck on the cheek. I would really like to punch him in the face for putting me through such stress, but I don't think now is the time or place. He nods at Ben and takes my hand and turns toward the parking lot.

Abbie and Bridget start shuffling on their feet with their hands in fists up to each other, play–fighting. They start to wrestle Adrian into a headlock as he giggles out loud.

"Hey, Natasha," a voice calls out from behind us. Oh shit, it's the prison warden guy. We all turn together, and he winks at me.

"Think of me tonight when you're having sex. It will get you over the line quicker."

CHAPTER 21

Natasha

MY EYES BULGE from their sockets. Oh, tell me he did not just say that. Everybody collectively takes a breath and Cameron and Ben quickly grab me and put me behind them. Josh drops his bag. "You really want to die tonight, fucker, don't you?" He walks over and punches him straight in the face. They grab each other and slam into the wall behind them, and security starts to run from everywhere to separate the two. Adrian and the girls are all in silent shock, as am I.

Cameron turns to Ben. "Get Natasha to the car."

Ben nods and grabs my arm. "Let me go." I yank my arm out of his grip. "Joshua," I yell. They continue fighting.

"Joshua," I yell again. He seems to remember I'm here and backs off from the kamikaze who is obviously on a death wish. He shakes his head. The guy is still being held by security. Joshua turns and takes my hand and starts to storm towards the car. Abbie and Bridget and Adrian are practically running to catch up.

"Oohh! Smell that adrenaline. It's frigging hot," Abbie slurs. "Your vagina must be on fire, Natasha." Abbie giggles. "All these hot guys fighting over you". Everybody bursts out laughing and Cameron laughs but turns and puts his finger up to his lips to signify silence. I turn around as Joshua drags me forward by the hand like a naughty child. I do wide eyes at the girls, signifying for them to shut the hell up.

Bridget nods. "Yes, from now on you will be called Dr. Flaming Vagina." Everybody burst out laughing again.

Joshua stops and turns. "Enough," he yells. Even I am having trouble stifling my giggles and the three stooges drop behind us to laugh out loud at their stupid flaming vagina joke. Cameron wisely stays straight faced and with us.

"How the fuck do you know him, Natasha?" Joshua snaps.

"Um, he's a prison warden at the jail I visit through work."

He stops still and Cameron and Ben both turn to see what he's doing. "You go to the fucking male prison?" I swallow and nod. "You will be handing in your resignation on Monday!" he screams. His order to leave work is like waving a red flag in front of a bull to me, but he is way too mad to even think about fighting with him now.

Cameron must sense my agitation and steps in.

"Josh, mate, let's just get home in one piece, huh." I am grateful I have Cameron here to calm him down.

Cameron turns to Ben. "You go to the Ivy with them and I will go with Tash and Josh. I will meet you there in about an hour." Ben nods and then pulls out his phone and texts someone and, in a few seconds, the two Audis come around the corner. The four others pile into the first car and Josh, Cam and I get into the second. Cam squeezes my hand reassuringly as I get into the car. We sit in silence on the way to my apartment and I come to the realization that Cam has come with us to make sure Josh isn't so mad he starts to fight with me. He's making sure I'm safe or maybe making sure Josh doesn't go out and continue fighting, either way I'm impressed with his loyalty. We get back to my apartment and Josh bales straight out of the car and storms towards the door. Cam looks at me and smiles as we both slowly climb out of the car. "I would ask you to come out with us but we both know he won't let you come without him and if he goes out tonight, he will definitely get into trouble." Cam raises his eyebrows and gives me a sympathetic smile.

I blow out a breath and nod. "Is he going to try and fight with me now?"

"I don't think so. He hates fighting with you."

"How do you know that?" I'm puzzled to find out how much Joshua tells Cam, how deep their friendship is.

"Because he doesn't eat or sleep when you're fighting with him and he follows me around, stressing me out."

I smile, oh crap. Cameron does know everything. "How much does he tell you Cam?"

He smiles. "Probably more than you would like." I nod again as we enter the lift. Josh has obviously stormed up without us. I suddenly feel uncertain about the info he has on me and Cameron must be able to sense my apprehension.

"Don't worry, Tash, you've got him by the balls. I smile and link my arm through Cam's and roll my eyes.

"Really. Balls? I'm honored. Here I was thinking that maybe I had him by the heart."

He laughs. "That too," he winks as we enter my level and approach my wide–open door. I look at the door and frown at Cameron.

He shakes his head. "It's just the adrenaline, Tash. He would still be full of it. He will be back to normal in the morning." I nod. This is ridiculous, I am dealing with a tantrum throwing two-year-old here. I can hear him in the shower, and I flick the jug on. "White and one," Cam says as he bites into an apple out of my fruit bowl.

"So, Dr. Stanton? Hey," I tease.

He smiles. "Yep, three months to go."

"What are your plans when you finish?" I pass him his tea. "I'm moving to LA as soon as university finishes in November."

My eyes go wide. This is news. He laughs. "Don't worry I'm not moving in with you and Josh." My eyes drop to my tea. Shit, if I was a better person, I would tell him it's ok to move in with us, but the reality is I want Josh to myself. "I got offered a job six months ago in LA Public Hospital and as Josh has been trying to get me to move over for years, I thought it was now or never."

I give him a sad smile. "Am I wrecking your plans?"

He shakes his head. "No, I'm just glad you two are working your shit out. I will probably live with Murph, that's if he gets rid of his wanker boyfriend."

I frown. "Murph, who's Murph?"

"Adrian, his last name is Murphy."

"Don't you like his boyfriend either?"

"I can't stand him. I think I hate him more than Josh."

"Why do you all hate him so much?" He shakes his head as he drains his cup.

"Spend some time with him and you will see. I don't get what Adrian sees in him. He's not even a good sort." I smile. The boys really are good friends with Adrian—their affection is obvious. Joshua walks into the kitchen with a towel around him and saunters up to me as he gives me a lopsided smile.

"Sorry baby," he runs his thumb over my bottom lip and

314

bends down to give me a tender kiss. I temporarily forget that Cam is here and return his kiss.

Cameron puts his hands up to his temples. "Fuck. It's spinning me out seeing you two together. I know you're together, but I haven't seen you together, together."

Josh rolls his eyes. "Aren't you going out?"

Cam smiles. "Yes. I'm going to find a certain kind of Mrs. Tonight." He winks at me.

I frown. "Mrs. Stanton?" I ask and Josh laughs. "God no... Mrs. Give–Me–Head, Baby."

My bulge. "Oh, right. How stupid of me. Have fun," I smirk.

He raises his eyebrows. "I always do." And within a second he is gone. Josh blows out a breath and gives me a resigned smile.

I go to speak but he puts a finger up to my lip. "You don't have to come again. It was a mistake making you go. But in my defense it isn't normally that bad." I nod as I listen. "How do you know that guy?" he asks.

"I told you he's a prison warden at the jail I go to." Josh listens and then narrows his eyes.

"I want you to resign."

I smile. "I am anyway, dopey." I roll my eyes. "I'm sort of moving away with this thug I've started dating." He looks relieved and smiles.

"So you are." He yawns as he goes to my freezer and removes a bag of peas.

"Are you hurt?" I ask.

He gives me a sly smile, "Yes, and I need nurse Natasha to give me some tender loving care." He grabs me roughly on the behind.

"Are you hungry?" I ask.

"Starving."

"I don't have any food so I'll order some Thai takeout. Go to bed and ice your knee and I will be in after I shower." He nods and bends to give me another gentle kiss as he leaves the kitchen. Twenty minutes later after I shower, I walk into my bedroom to find my beautiful thug fast asleep in a towel on top of the bed complete with frozen peas. I imagine cage fighting must be exhausting. Actually, you know what? Watching it is too.

I wake to feel two eyes on me, and I roll toward him. To my surprise he isn't in bed with me. He's sitting on the side of the bed drinking a protein shake.

"I made you breakfast." He smiles as he gestures to my bedside table. I look over to see a chocolate protein shake in a large glass with ice.

I frown. "Is this a sick joke?" It's too early for this superhero workout shit. "Josh, I would like two eggs on toast, please."

He frowns. "You don't like protein." I look at him deadpan. "No"

He shrugs his shoulders and smiles. "Tough shit. That's what I'm making today, and we have to go to my house for a while. I want to check on Adrian."

I smile. "Aren't you supposed to be fussing over me and stuff like in all the romance novels? I never heard anyone say tough shit to their girlfriends in my books."

His eyes twinkle and he raises his eyebrows. "Yes, but remember that the book about you is called 'Gagging for it'." I slap him on the arm, and he dives over me to hold my hands above my head.

"What are you wearing to the wedding today?" I ask. He pulls back in horror.

"That's today?" I nod and smile.

"We don't really have to go, do we? I hate weddings."

"Since when?"

"Since I don't know anyone there." I smile. This is the shy thing Adrian was talking about—it's kind of endearing that he has such a hang up.

"I'll be there, Josh. It can be our date night."

He frowns. "That's a shit date. If you want to go on a date, I can arrange something, like the other night." He smiles a sly smile. "Actually, let's stay home and watch a movie. I have a really good one that I planned on watching this weekend. It's called, let me see, 'Beautiful Slut'." Oh crap, I know what movie he is talking about. The frigging porno staring yours truly.

"Let's not," I snap as I get out of bed. I shower and am thoroughly peeved to find that I have my period. How annoying it really is, a fault in the female body. And on the weekend, that's just rude. Half an hour later we pull up out the front of Josh's and as we get closer to the wide–open front door I can hear the boys all laughing loudly and bantering with each other. I haven't been here before and I am feeling a little nervous and out of my comfort zone. The house is huge and impressive, and it looks like it backs onto the water. There is a stone table out the front and two security guards are sitting playing cards. I turn and look at the car pulling up behind us to see another two bodyguards pull up who have obviously been following us. How do I keep forgetting we are being followed everywhere? Josh nods as he walks past them and I hang back, a little unsure about whether I should have come. Joshua must sense my apprehension and he turns and walks back towards me.

He frowns and smiles at me. "How could anyone as perfect as you ever intrude on me." I nod and give him a shy smile. He's right. If I am going to move to the other side of the world with him, I have to get used to his friends. We walk in and my eyes go straight to the beautiful high ornate ceiling. This place is stunning. He follows my eyes to the ceiling and smiles.

"Nice ceiling, huh? The rest of the place is pretty dated though. I'm not really a fan." I raise my eyebrows, if he doesn't like this place what in the hell is his house like? "Actually, can you get a week off work the week after next? I want to take you to LA to see a few houses."

I frown. "What's wrong with the house you have?"

He smiles and puts his hands in his pockets. "Nothing. I just want to start our new life together in a new house, one that you pick. I want you to be happy."

My heart swells. "As long as I'm with you, baby, I'll be happy," I breathe.

He smiles and bends to run his lips gently over mine. "Me, too," he whispers. We walk through large double doors out into a massive kitchen and lounge area. Adrian is sitting on a barstool at the kitchen bench in a pair of board shorts. Cameron is lying on the lounge in a pair of boxer shorts and Ben looks as though he has been for a swim and has a towel wrapped around his waist. Jeez, these guys are buff. This could easily pass as a scene from Magic Mike. Josh grabs me by the hand as we enter.

"Hi." He smiles at his friends.

"Oh yeah. Mike Tyson is back," Cameron laughs in a husky I've–had–too–many–tequilas voice. He's talking really loudly, obviously still a little deaf from the loud music last night.

Adrian smiles as he walks over, puts his arm around me and kisses me on the temple."Good morning, beautiful. How did you put up with this idiot last night?" He smiles and winks at Josh.

"Ha, ha." Joshua fakes a smile as he pulls me from Adrian's

grip and sits me up on the counter. His little burst of possessiveness doesn't go unnoticed and I have to say I kind of like it.

"The girls are coming over to go out for breakfast," states Adrian.

Joshua frowns. "What girls?" he asks.

"Bridget and Abbie. I like your friends, Tash. They're good value."

I roll my eyes. "Of course, do you think I would have boring friends?"

Joshua laughs. "Why not? I do." Adrian whips him with a tea towel. Cameron is lying on the lounge with the back of his forearm over his face. I never realized how hot he actually is. He has the same olive skin as Josh, same height, same dark eyes, but his hair is longer on top with a bit of a curl to it. He's not as big as Josh and he doesn't have the tattoo—that tattoo that I love. But jeez he could definitely hold his own. I smile at the thought of all the poor women out there that end up having Cameron as their doctor. They don't stand a bloody chance. Abbie and Bridget come through the door laughing and Abbie trips over her own feet and stumbles into the kitchen.

"Crap," she snaps.

"How did you go last night?" Joshua smiles at the girls but continues his conversation with Cameron.

Cameron shakes his head. "I went to bed with a ten and woke up with a two." Everyone laughs. "I'm not joking, man. I couldn't get out of there fast enough when I woke up this morning. I left my fucking shoes there."

Joshua laughs out loud. "What was so bad with her?"

"It was total false advertising. When a girl bats her eyelashes at me, I kind of expect them to be real. She must have been really good with the make-up shit because the girl I went to bed with looked nothing like the monster I woke up with." He scrubs his hand over his face and does a fake cold shiver.

Adrian winces. "I hate to break it to you, but those beer goggles you had on last night didn't help." Cameron screws up his face and nods with his eyes closed.

"Oh my God!" Cameron yells way too loud. "How big were that dude's balls last night telling Tash to think of him when she had sex?" Everybody, including myself, laughs out loud. I do have to admit it was pretty ballsy.

"That fucker is going to die next time I see him," Josh says deadpan.

Bridget walks over to Adrian and affectionately cuddles him. "Thanks for getting me home safely." He smiles and kisses her temple. "No worries, baby."

"Abbs, what went on with those two guys last night fighting over you?" Cameron asks as he makes his way over to the fridge. Joshua has now settled in between my legs as I sit on the edge of the counter. He discreetly pulls my hips towards his groin and gives me a sly smile. I do wide eyes at him. "Stop it," I mouth. Abbie rolls her eyes.

"What? Tell me what happened?" I ask, the shock in my voice evident.

Abbie scrubs her face with her hands. "Number four challenged number one."

I narrow my eyes at her. "Who won?"

"Army guy," Bridget chimes in.

"So what number is he now?" I ask, confused.

"One. Definitely one," Abbie snaps.

Cameron frowns as he opens his bottle of water with his back to the girls but facing Josh and me.

"How many do you have?" Cameron asks as he makes eye contact with Josh and takes a drink of his water.

"A few," Abbie answers. Cameron smiles and raises his eyebrows at Josh. Josh glares at him and mouths the word "No." Cameron smiles and shrugs as he goes back to his position on the lounge. Hmm, that was an interesting exchange, is Cam interested in Abbie? I'll have to remember to ask Josh later. Everybody goes into the lounge room and flops onto the chairs as they start to reminisce about last night's shenanigans. Joshua leans in and lifts my chin to give me a gentle kiss and I put my arms around his neck and breathe in his beautiful scent. He always smells so frigging hot.

"Oh God!" Cameron yells in that damn tequila voice. "They're all kissy and shit." Everyone's eyes shoot back to us on the bench.

"I went to bed with a ten and woke up with a twelve. Why wouldn't I be kissy?" Joshua snaps as he leans in and kisses me again. I smile into his face. This man really is all kinds of wonderful.

We walk into the reception venue and Joshua goes over to look at the seating arrangements. The church service was beautiful and thankfully short. I don't know many people. Alyssa and I went to university together but have not mixed much since. It's one of those weddings that you go to because you have to. It would be rude not to attend. However, in hindsight, Josh's offer of a hot date does seem like it would have been a better option. He has done well so far and has managed a few strained conversations with people. I can't believe I didn't know he was shy, is he shy or is he just rude and not wanting to talk to people? Who knows? I haven't quite worked that one out.

He points toward a table in the middle of the room and we go and take our seats. Joshua looks edible of course in a navy suit, white shirt and grey tie. I am wearing a black draping dress. I had planned on wearing a pale pink tight dress, but my bloated tummy made me feel too uncomfortable in it and I hate being self-conscious when things are too tight. To Josh's amusement our table guests have all started arriving. All eight single girls of them. Is this a set–up? I'm here with the most gorgeous man on the planet and we are seated with eight single girls. I can see their eyes light up as he introduces himself to them. I don't see any sign of shyness now, *prick*. The chair next to him is still empty and a blonde in a white lace dress comes over to our table. Shit. She is stunning and equipped with the best set of boobs I have seen. They are hanging out, her dress is damn near indecent. Didn't she get the memo about not wearing white to a wedding? The rude bitch. She makes eye contact with Joshua and puts out her hand.

"Hi, Tatiana Richards," she purrs. I roll my eyes, Tittiana more like. Joshua shakes her hand and introduces himself and turns and smiles at me.

"What?" I roll my eyes.

"Maybe this wedding won't be as boring as I thought." He smiles at me with a twinkle in his eyes. I fake smirk at him. The thing is, I know he's trying to make me jealous and guess what? It's working. She introduces herself to everyone on the table and they all start their usual crap talk. Josh runs his hand up my thigh. "Do you want another drink, baby?" He leans in and kisses me underneath my ear.

I smile. "No, thanks." I have to remember to not show him any sign of my unease. There is nothing worse than an insecure girlfriend. I know, I counsel their boyfriends all day long.

"So, Joshua, I'm a social network analyst. What do you do?" Tatiana purrs.

His eyes light up and he smiles. "I design software."

"Really?" she smiles and puts her hand on his forearm. "What a coincidence that we should be seated together." Oh, get off it, you stupid bitch, social network analyst my ass. Anybody can count how many likes they get on their selfies. Joshua moves his arm away from her grip and he grabs my hand under the table. I try to calm my jealousy; she is so making a play at him. "Are you American?" she asks.

He shakes his head. "No, Australian living in America."

"I see." She smiles. I look over and see a girl I used to go to school with and we wave at each other over the crowd. I'm not sitting here and listening to desperate and dateless make a play for my man, I might as well mingle. I pull my chair out and Josh grabs my hand.

"Where are you going?" he asks.

I fake a smile. "Over here to see my friend. I'm sure Tittiana here won't mind amusing you." He narrows his eyes. En route to my friend I glance out to the balcony and stop dead in my tracks. Oh my God. It's Christopher. I haven't seen him since he asked me to marry him and I consequently broke up with him. My heartrate immediately picks up. Holy fuck, this is a disaster. I pull out my phone and text the girls.

Wedding is going great.
Dolly Parton cracking on to Mr. Stanton.
And Christopher just turned up

I continue walking to my friend and I glance back to see Joshua's eyes firmly on me. He's not happy I left him there but seriously I'm just not in the mood for Tatiana tonight. Don't mess with a hormonal woman has always been my mantra. And if she had any sense, she would take the tip. My phone texts a message from Bridget:

Shit, what did Christopher say?
Is he still gorgeous?

I get to my friend Tracey and give her a kiss on the cheek. She continues to babble about the flowers in the church or something. My eyes flick back to Joshua and he is still deep in conversation with the Bimbo central table. I look towards Christopher, his beauty is arresting. His black wavy hair and dark features stand out above the crowd. He's tall, maybe about six foot one and built in a lean sort of way. I met him at university; he's an orthopedic surgeon. I did love him, just not in the way I love Joshua.

It's sad because if we had met in any other lifetime, I have no doubt he could have made me very happy. In the end, I had to let him go. It was selfish of me to let it carry on as long as I did. I had no idea he was going to ask me to marry him. He was desperately in love with me and I was desperately in love with Joshua. Shit, I don't know what to even say to him. Why in the hell didn't I stay home and watch that porno? Hell, I would have bought popcorn. Tracey babbles on a bit more and I feel an arm go around my waist and I turn, expecting to see Joshua. My heart sinks, it's Christopher and I'm hit with the pain of guilt. He was too good for me; he deserved better.

He bends and kisses me on the cheek. "Hello, Natasha," he smiles. My eyes flick to Josh who is now watching me like a hawk. I swallow again.

"Hi, how have you been?"

Christopher raises his eyebrows. "You mean since I asked you to marry me and you broke my heart instead."

I drop my eyes. "Christopher, I'm so sorry. I didn't mean to hurt you. You have to believe me, I'm not the girl for you."

He bites his bottom lip, "Not really what I wanted you to say, Tash. You haven't missed me at all?" I drop my head.

"Christopher, we wanted different things." I'm getting uncomfortable with this conversation. Josh will go apeshit if he hears this and after last night, I can't risk his temper. He's displaying psycho tendencies. I couldn't bear it if he hurt Christopher. He goes to grab my hand and I pull it away and go to turn and slam straight into Josh who is standing behind me. I feel faint. This is the worse timing ever. I haven't run into Chris since we broke up. Why tonight? Joshua looks at me and raises his eyebrows in a silent question.

"Um Joshua, this is Christopher. Christopher, meet Joshua, my, my boyfriend." Joshua narrows his eyes at my awkward introduction and Christopher glares at Josh. "Boyfriend—I see it hasn't taken you long too move on." He glares at Joshua. Oh, for the love of God, please shut up.

Christopher smiles at Joshua. "Commiserations, my man. I'm the ex-boyfriend and she's a hard act to follow." He smiles a devious smile. "Although, I have no doubt you will find that out for yourself soon enough." He storms off. All of the blood drains from my face and I look up at Joshua and grab his hand.

"Can we go?" I plead.

"No," he snaps and storms back to the table, practically ripping my arm out of the socket. He sits at the table and immediately drains his champagne glass.

Tatianna titties puts her hand on Joshua's shoulder. "Where did you go?"

I glare at her deadpan. "He came to find me, seeing as I'm his girlfriend," I snap.

She smiles. "Of course," she replies. Seriously, this night is turning very ugly indeed.

"How long were you with him?" I have butterflies in my stomach, and I don't want to have this conversation.

"Josh, it doesn't matter. It's over. I didn't know he was going to be here."

He glares at me. "How long?"

I swallow. "Two and a half years." He runs his tongue over the front of his top teeth as he glares at me.

"Is he the guy who asked you to marry him?"

"Yes."

"And you broke up with him?"

"Yes," I answer. The entrée is served, and I am now desperately wishing these stupid women would make some kind of interesting conversation to keep Joshua's mind occupied and off Christopher. I wonder if paying someone to take their top off in this situation would be acceptable. Joshua pushes his entrée to my side.

I frown. "Don't you want it?"

He shakes his head. "I just lost my appetite." Hmm, that's funny because I just found mine, bloody stress eating is back with a vengeance.

"What does he do?"

"It doesn't matter."

"Answer the question." His eyes bore into me. "

He's an orthopedic surgeon."

He fakes a smile. "Of course he is."

"Would you rather he be a prostitute that slept with me for money?" I snap.

He scowls at me. "Yes, I would. At least then I would know that you were never in love with him."

I smile a sad smile at him and grab his hand under the table.

"Josh, I love you. Please let's not fight about this. You already knew about him. It's in the past," I whisper. He nods and cast his eyes down onto the table. My heart breaks a little. It would hurt me to know if he had been in love with someone else. It's bad enough knowing he had sex with everyone in America. I can't imagine what it would feel like if he actually cared for any of them. The main meal is served and once again Joshua just picks at his food. I wish I didn't eat when I was stressed. If no one was watching I could happily devour both his and my meals at this moment. The speeches have finished and Tittiana is beginning to really piss me off. I'm finding myself imagining pouring my drink happily over her head. Her open flirting with Josh is grating on my nerves. I pull my chair out and Josh grabs my leg.

"Where are you going?" Gently he kisses the back of my hand.

He's loving watching me get jealous. "I'm going to the bathroom."

"Can I come?" he smiles.

I narrow my eyes. "No," I whisper.

He leans forward and whispers into my ear. "Let me rephrase that, I need to come." He raises an eyebrow.

"Josh, I'm out of action for a week," I whisper. He frowns, not understanding my meaning. I raise my eyebrows, waiting for him to catch on. He doesn't. I shake my head and smile as I stand from the table and walk past the dance floor and head toward the bathroom. Ten minutes later as I am walking back to the table I am accosted by Christopher.

"Natasha, do you ever think of me?" God, this night is going from bad to worse.

"Christopher, we are over, and I have a new boyfriend. This is inappropriate." I go to walk off and another of Christopher's friends comes over and puts his arm around me. "The beautiful

Natasha, we have missed you." I smile as I try to hurry the conversation along, but I can't be rude. It's another ten minutes before I return to our table to find Josh missing. I take a seat and eat his untouched chocolate cake. After what seems like an eternity Josh is still not back, I start to feel a little unsettled and start to look around for him. To my horror he is slow-dancing with Tatiana. *What the hell*? Is this a joke? He looks totally smitten and she is grinding herself up against him, not that he looks like he minds. He wants a reaction from me and I am definitely not giving him one. I probably deserve him to be pissy, but this is going too far. What will I do without causing a scene? I must admit seeing Christopher tonight has rattled me. It's made me realize how many people my relationship with Joshua has caused hurt to, myself being the main victim. I have to get out of here before the dam bursts. I'm going to leave. I pack my bag up and am just about to stand when Christopher comes over to the table. My heart drops again, he looks determined.

"I want another chance."

I close my eyes. "That's impossible, Chris. I am in love with someone else."

He glares at me. "Who? That douche bag who's dancing with the stripper?" My eyes drop in embarrassment. I've got no answer to that. He's right; Josh is acting like a douche bag.

"That's him," Joshua snaps. Oh shit, where did he come from? "Not that it's any of your business who I dance with."

Christopher rolls his eyes. "Go back to your whore, pretty boy." Joshua runs his tongue over the front of his top teeth and glares at Christopher. Christopher returns his angry gaze. I start to panic.

"Chris, just go please, I don't want any trouble."

He grabs my hand. "Please, Tash, I need another chance. I can't get over you. I'm totally fucked." Joshua stands back and waits for my reaction and I can feel the fury emanating from him. This is the most uncomfortable conversation I have ever had, breaking my ex–boyfriend's heart in front of my new boyfriend.

"Christopher, please, you know why we broke up. Our feelings aren't mutual. You deserve better, Chris. I'm sorry, I'm not that girl."

He pulls a disgusted face at me. "You make me sick, Natasha."

Josh steps forward. "Careful," he growls.

Christopher turns to him. "Has she told you that she loves you yet?" Josh continues glaring at him but doesn't answer.

"I take it that's a yes." Christopher laughs. "You poor bastard. You're next. I met up with the ex-ex-boyfriend the other day and she did the same thing to him. Expresses undying love and then poof...up and left without as much as a hint of guilt. Don't say I didn't warn you, mate. She's the fucking ice queen." Joshua glares at him and I grab his hand.

"Take me home, Josh." He nods.

"When your fucking heart is broken into a million pieces remember this warning," Christopher snaps. I'm appalled. I have never been so embarrassed. Is that true, am I an ice queen? Hot tears start to run down my face as we walk down the outside steps towards the car. Josh opens the door and I get in and break into full–blown sobs. I have hurt two beautiful men because I was too selfish to let them go, knowing all along in my heart that I could only ever love Joshua. Josh gets in and starts the car in silence, not looking at me. We drive in silence for fifteen minutes. I continue to cry and put my hand on Josh's leg for comfort and he picks it up and flicks it off his leg. I frown at him.

"Am I fucking next Natasha?" he screams.

"Huh, what are you talking about?" I sob.

"It seems to me there is a pattern here. You've already broken my heart once. Is that it? Or are you planning on doing it again? You make men fall madly in love with you and then..." He shakes his head unable to articulate his words.

"What's with dancing with that girl tonight, Josh? Are you trying to send me insane?" I snap.

"Who are you kidding? You didn't even care I was dancing with her; you were too focused on your ex." I roll my eyes and my tears start again.

"Don't start with the fucking waterworks. If anyone should be crying it's me. I already know what's coming for me as soon as you get bored. You will leave me just like that and move onto your next victim," he yells.

"I would never leave you. You know that!" I scream.

"You already left me and I'm still not fucking over it," he screams back. I wipe my eyes angrily with the back of my hands.

"Don't you dare throw that in my face. I broke up with you for you. I had to save you from yourself; you were going to give everything up to be with me and I loved you too much to let you do it." He pulls up out the front of my building.

"So, what's the excuse with the other poor bastards? I suppose you had to save them from themselves?"

I glare at him. "I broke up with them because I was still in love with you. You asshole. God knows why." I get out of the car and slam the door. He is hot on my heels. I look over and see the two bodyguards wisely staying in their car. God, what must they think? It's like frigging Jerry Springer around here. We enter the lift and I hit the button, he stays silent, his arms crossed in front of him, glaring at me. We get to my floor and he gets his keys out and opens the door. I storm in and head straight for my therapy of choice, a boiling hot shower, and he follows me.

"Get out!" I scream.

"No!" he screams back. He sits on the floor outside the shower and I turn my back to him.

"Why are you so mad at me? I'm the one who's mad," he snaps. I frown. "I'm mad because you think you know everything about me and you know nothing. I'm mad because you dare even compare our relationship to any others, I have been in. I'm mad because I have given you the best years of my life and you throw it in my face continually." I can't help it I break into full blown sobs. "How in the hell have you given me the best years of your life? We only just got back together." Oh my God. I grab a bottle of shampoo and hurl it at him.

"I said, get out!"

"No. Why is our relationship so different to others? You're talking shit." He blows out a breath as he links his hands on top of his head.

"You really want to know? Do you?" I scream. "While you were whoring around the United States of America, I was here waiting like the absolute idiot that I am. I have never slept with anyone else, Josh. You're the only man I've ever let make love to me." He steps back, stunned. "So, when you dare compare what we have to the platonic relationships I had with other people, I find it insulting."

His eyes widen. "I don't understand."

"No, you wouldn't, because you've slept with anyone with a pulse." I start crying again, frigging hormones.

"Why haven't you slept with anyone else?"

He really is stupid. "Because I belong to you, Josh. My body belongs to you and I could never betray you. When I said that I loved you, I meant it. Unfortunately, my love has had to be unconditional, because you never loved me with the same depth that I loved you. I told you once, once, that I slept with someone else and you believed it, and you never came back for me. That's not love, Josh. Trust me I know love, you have no fucking idea. Every goddamn morning my google alert would tell me about the tenth girl you slept with that week. And I, being the stupid fuck that I am, would cry myself to sleep every night missing you and still deny myself the intimacy that you got from everyone else. Because I couldn't betray you!" Hearing myself state the pathetic truth hurts and I slump to the floor and burst into full-blown sobs. It's true. I have given him the best years of my life and he doesn't love me the way I have always loved him. He showed me that tonight on the dance floor with that girl.

Joshua

My God! I'm shocked. Surely, this can't be true. She sits on the bottom of the shower sobbing. I have never felt like such a total prick in my life. It's true, I have fucked my way around the United States...and she's never...I put my hand over my mouth. I feel sick to my stomach. Tears fill my eyes, but I quickly blink them away. It's not...possible...is it? I don't deserve her. Brock is completely right; she is out of my league. My eyes flick back to her as she sits hysterical on the bottom of the shower. What do I do? How in the hell can I ever make this up to her? And here I am accusing her of planning to break my heart when I've been breaking her heart all along. I walk into the shower fully clothed, drop to the floor and pull her onto my lap.

"Baby, I'm so sorry, I didn't know. Why didn't you tell me?"

I gently kiss her forehead; her chest is racking with sobs. We have put each other through hell. My denial of intimacy with another woman. Her denial sexually with another man. My heart breaks as I watch her sob in despair. I don't know what to say, I feel helpless. The lump in my throat is back. Why in the hell are we related? I close my eyes in pain. We deserve an easier path. I have never felt such deep regret. I have always loved her, but deep down I couldn't forgive her for betraying me and now I find out that she never...God, what a mess.

"Precious, why didn't you tell me? When we got back together, you didn't tell me." She continues crying and doesn't answer me. We sit in silence for fifteen minutes as she continues crying. I'm so fucking angry with myself I could punch a hole in the wall. The feeling of raw guilt brings bile to my stomach.

"At first, I didn't want you to be easy on me...sexually," she whispers.

My eyes widen. "Oh God, did I hurt you?" My stomach drops as I remember how hard I was on her the first few times and I close my eyes. FUCK. What's wrong with me? I should have been able to tell.

"And then I was embarrassed to tell you," she whispers.

I frown. "How could you be embarrassed to tell me that? It's the most fucking perfect thing I have ever heard!" She slowly calms down as I continually kiss her forehead. "Come on, baby. Let's get you up and dressed." I stand and take my wet clothes off, then I wrap her in a towel. She's distraught. I'm such a fuck up.

She looks up at me. "I love you, Josh." A lump in my throat forms and I am unable to speak. It happened the other night in the hotel too. The sound of Natasha's voice. Hearing her speak those words. It makes me weak.

"I... I love you, Tash. I never stopped. Please forgive me. I will never doubt you again." She reaches up and runs her hand down my stubble.

"Don't leave me," she whispers with tears in her eyes. Unable to speak, I shake my head and bend to take her lips tenderly in mine.

Seven years...seven long years...I've waited for this and now I realize the sick truth is that I'm undeserving of her love. My heart breaks. It's been five days since we got back together. Five days she has taken to break down my defenses and I have never been more in love in my life. I'm in serious trouble.

CHAPTER 22

Natasha

I WAKE to find Josh not in bed. I sit up startled. Is he still here? I hear the toaster pop and I smile. He's making me toast, not protein. That makes for a nice change. He walks in and smiles at me before pulling me into a gentle embrace as he kisses me. "Hello, my beautiful. Are you feeling better this morning?"

I smile and nod.

"I've made you breakfast," he announces. "Come to the table." He smiles warmly as he pulls me up by the hands. I look down at myself and smile. I notice he hasn't said anything about my flannel PJs. I must be allowed to wear them when I have my period. I walk out to the table and frown. It looks like the buffet breakfast that hotel had where we stayed the other night. Croissants, bacon and eggs, muffins and toast and three types of juice. Ok, he's lost it. I screw my face up.

"So, yesterday I got tough shit because I wanted an egg and

today I get this," I gesture to the table. He smiles a little embarrassed.

"Yesterday I was a prick." I smile as I walk over and give him a gentle kiss and I stroke his face.

"I happened to like you yesterday," I smirk. He smiles a proud of himself smile. "Sorry about last night."

He frowns at me. "What for?"

"The whole drama queen thing."

He puts his toast down. "You are not a drama queen. I was thinking about it while I made you breakfast. If I was you, I think I would have killed me by now."

"Lucky you're not me then. What are we doing today?" I smile.

"Whatever you want."

Five o'clock after a day of kissing and cuddling and sleeping I wake up toasty in our bed. Josh is lying facing me and I smile as we lie and stare into each other's eyes. The emotion between us is palpable. As if in silence we have both realized how deeply in love we are and how much we need each other. He holds my hand and gently picks it up and kisses the back of it.

"I know you saved your body for me, but you must know I saved my heart for you. I love you more than anything." He kisses my hand again and I smile a shy smile. We hold hands as we lie facing each other not speaking—no words are needed. I have never felt so deeply connected to another human being. Nothing has ever felt so right. He leans and tenderly swipes his tongue through my open lips.

"Thank you," he whispers.

I frown. "For what?"

He smiles. "For waiting for me." My heart swells and my eyes tear up.

"You're worth the wait, Josh. I would do it again." He runs his hands through my hair and kisses my forehead.

"How long do we have to wait? I need to make love to you, desperately," he whispers as he rests his forehead against mine. How is it a twenty–seven year old man does not know about women's cycles?

"How do you not know this?" I tease.

He frowns. "I've never had a girlfriend, Tash. How would I know these things?" He does wide eyes at me. I smile, I know we could but I'm going to make him wait the week out. Let him suffer for a change. And boy is he going to suffer.

It's Wednesday lunchtime and I am in the lift on my way up to Josh's office. We have had the most wonderful week together. Josh has been attentive, loving, funny and hot as hell. Ridiculously hard the whole time. It's a wonder he has any blood left in his body. I have been at a conference this morning and have the afternoon off. I purposely dressed in a tight, black, high waisted pencil skirt and silk white blouse with the top button undone and high closed in heels, my hair up and my glasses on. I know Josh loves me in naughty secretary get up. I had a business suit on when he picked me up from work on Monday and he stopped the car twice on the way home to try and molest me. I had to smile when he asked me if I was deliberately prick teasing him. He's going to kill me when he finds out I have been. It's just too delicious watching him beg. The lift opens and I am confronted with wall to wall marble and amazing views. There is a large reception area on the left with two pretty blondes sitting behind the desk. I tentatively walk to the desk.

"Natasha Marx to see Joshua Stanton," I smile nervously.

The girls glance at each other and buzz the intercom. "Yes," Adrian's bored voice comes through the speaker. "Natasha Marx is here to see Mr. Stanton."

"I'll be right there." The girls frown at each other. Is that not normal? I stand awkwardly on display as the girls look me up and down. Adrian bursts through the security door.

"Hi, baby," he gushes and wraps me in an embrace and kisses me on the temple. Way to embarrass me in front of the staff. He smiles and pulls me toward the doors. "Show's over, ladies. Back to work," he snaps. The two girls immediately put their heads back down and start to look busy. Shit, Adrian's a mean boss, who knew. I thought he was a butterball. He pulls me by the hand through a large room that is surprisingly empty with only about fifteen desks with computers and men sitting behind them. They are typing so fast it looks like they are pretending. "What are they doing?"

Adrian shrugs. "Some are designing, and some are hacking."

I frown. "Hacking? Do you hack? I thought this was a reputable business," I ask.

He smiles. "We are just checking facts, medical stuff. Nothing important." Some are dressed in suits and some are in jeans and hoodies. Hmm, what is the dress code for this place? I am then led through another set of double doors to a huge office. The whole back wall is glass with an amazing view over Sydney. There is a huge desk in the middle of the back wall facing the door.

"This is my office." Adrian smiles. "Nice" I nod, impressed. "Josh is just training. He will be about ten minutes. Do you want to go into his office and watch?" I smile and nod. I walk through another set of doors and into the most impressive

338

office I have ever seen, holy shit. Another huge glass wall looking over the city adorns the space. There is a conference table with at least twenty seats on one side of the room, a desk at the back and then to the left is a glass wall looking into another room. And there he stands, my prince. Looking unbelievably hot in a grey pin striped suit and, I have to say, unbelievably smart. He is standing in front of about twenty students, writing on a whiteboard. A huge computer screen hangs behind him, erected on the wall. They are all in front of computers and are following his instructions. Every now and then he grabs his mouse and shows them on the large screen what he is doing as he talks into a microphone thing attached to his ear. Intelligence is just so...sexy.

"Who is he training?" I ask.

"He runs these competitions where computer kids from around the world have to hack into traps he has set and uncover the hidden formula."

"Why does he do that?" I frown.

Adrian smiles. "Because he likes to set the traps more than they like to do them and it exposes him to the most talented computer geeks on the planet." Ah, the penny drops.

"He's recruiting?" I ask.

Adrian smiles. "Yes, they think they are here to learn, and they are, but what he hasn't told them is that the top five will get internships with us."

"And an internship is valuable, is it?" I frown.

"Learning from Josh is like winning the frigging lottery. The man is a genius." My mind goes into overdrive and I ask the question I have been dying to.

"Adrian, why is Josh so heavily guarded?" He gives me a sympathetic smile.

"Josh has a lot of jealous people around him, Tash. It's not so much him that they are after, as his mind." I frown as I try to comprehend what it must be like to be that smart. I shrug my shoulders and smile. Guess I'll never find out. I sit on his desk. A smile plays on my lips as I imagine him in this office when we first started hooking up.

Now that I know him better and am fully aware that he had feelings for me all along I know he would have been unbearable to be around during those first few weeks. Poor Adrian... and Cam. What did Cam say the other night? Hmm, that's right, Josh follows him around stressing him out. I smile at the thought...why do I find that funny? I look back to my Adonis in front of his class and I feel a familiar pull towards him; never have I been so attracted to another human being. No other male even exists when he's in the room. As I sit in his office hanging off his every word, his eyes drift over to where he spots me sitting on his desk. Our eyes lock across the room. I can hear what his body is saying to mine, my body instantly softening under his gaze. Preparing itself for his onslaught. He looks me up and down and immediately cracks his neck. Bingo. I smile and he calls for lunch and wraps up his class. He walks into his office, grabs me by the hand and pulls me around the corner away from the sight of his class and pushes me up against the wall. Then he is on me. His powerful kiss leaves me breathless as he grabs both sides of my face.

"Jesus, what the fuck are you wearing, Miss Marx? Are you offering me yourself on a platter? Just looking at you is driving me crazy with lust. But you already know that, don't you?" He smiles into my neck as his lips fall down to where my shirt meets my shoulders, his mouth hungrily running over my goose bump covered flesh. I smile and pull his mouth back to mine. It has been five days since we made love and I have to say in all honesty I am gagging for it, his words not mine. His hard erection digs into my thigh and he grabs my behind to pull me onto it. I won't even make it to lunch at this rate.

"Josh, we are going out for lunch remember."

"I'll have you for lunch," he whispers, smiling into my neck.

Hmm, that does sound more appealing I have to admit. "We can't. I invited Adrian."

He immediately pulls back and frowns at me. "Why? I wanted you to myself."

I smile. "Because I need to get to know him seeing he is probably going to be my only friend in LA."

"You have me, and I can be a friend with very, very..." he pumps his hips into me, "good benefits." He runs his lips down my neck again and my eyes close at the contact. I can't even play hard to get, who am I kidding?

"And Cam, you will have Cam." He raises his eyebrows as if talking to a child.

"Cam's going to be a doctor doing shiftwork at a hospital and when he's not there...Let's face it, he will be playing Dr. Dreamy in bed. Besides I have a lot in common with Adrian." He smiles and nods as if understanding my point.

"Come on then," he releases the tight hold he has on my body and I feel the loss of the contact. "Let me give you a tip, Miss Marx," he growls as his eyes drop to my skirt and then back up to my breasts. "If you want to make it through lunch without being fucked on the table, you had better change clothes. This whole secretary thing you have going on," he waves his hand up the length of my body, "is making me so hard I might break you."

I smile and bite my lip. "I didn't bring any spare clothes, Mr. Stanton. I hope I don't get into trouble, sir," I whisper darkly. Two can play this game. If he wants to play bosses and secretaries, he had better well be good at it. He smirks a smile and does up my top button. His eyes linger on my lips.

"You're a beautiful slut." He turns me so my back is to his front and pulls me against his erection. "I can't wait to fuck you with those glasses on." He bites my neck hard from behind and smacks me hard on the behind as he pushes me forward.

We walk out through the lobby to wait for Adrian with our hands linked and I am immediately made aware, by the amount of attention we are getting, that the staff have never seen Joshua with anyone. All of his workers are doing a double take at the affection between us. The two female secretaries literally swoon at the sight of him, so much so I don't think they even notice I am actually on the other end of his arm, silly bitches. Hmm, mental note, watch out for secretaries; he seems a little too interested in secretary get up for my liking. Adrian joins us and the three of us head to lunch together with our three bodyguards trailing behind us. Is this necessary? It all seems a bit dramatic.

We go to a place a few blocks from the building and head into the reception. We are greeted by a waitress whose eyes linger a little too long on my two lunch dates. She doesn't even look at me, how annoying. Honey, wipe the drool from your chin, it's kind of embarrassing. While we are waiting to be seated a bustle comes through the restaurant. A group of reporters have just spotted someone and are rushing towards him as he leaves the restaurant. I turn to see who they are looking at and I see my boss Henry walking towards me.

"Hi, Natasha, you guys having lunch?" I nod and smile and turn to introduce Adrian and Joshua when I am literally stunned to silence. My absolute guru, Nicholas Anastas, is walking up behind Henry. My eyes literally pop from their sockets and luckily Henry knows what's going on in that messed–up head of mine and takes over the introductions.

"Hi, I'm Henry, Natasha's boss, and this is Nicholas Anastas." Joshua shakes Henry's hand first.

"Joshua Stanton." He smiles and then shakes Nicholas's hand.

"Joshua Stanton." He smiles again. I am standing, stunned to my core. This man is the most brilliant psychologist on the planet and has written the very bible of psychology. He is a world-famous author. I am totally dumbstruck—I have no words.

"This is Natasha Marx who works with me."

Nicholas shakes my hand and smiles. "Hello Natasha."

Oh my God, he touched my hand...freaking out right now.

"Hello," I nervously smile. He then turns his attention to Adrian and they shake hands.

"Nicholas Anastas." He nods and smiles.

"Adrian Murphy." Adrian smiles. They stay shaking hands a little too long and I have to say the chemistry between them is off the charts. Nicholas is an older, maybe fortyish, European, six foot two, gorgeous man and in perfect physical condition. He is wearing a charcoal suit and I am a little in awe of his beauty. He is so much better looking in person than I ever imagined. He has a presence, like Joshua and Adrian. I think all powerful and dominant men have it. His and Adrian's eyes are locked on each other. What the hell? Adrian's eyes widen at the contact and Nicholas frowns as he looks down at their hands.

Shit, what is going on here? Adrian pulls his hand out of Nicholas's grip a little too quickly and looks nervously at me as he swallows.

Henry smiles. "Nice to meet you." Then he walks toward the door.

Nicholas, however, stands still on the spot, his eyes drilling into Adrian.

"It's been very nice, Adrian," his husky voice whispers, he nods and is out the door.

Joshua frowns. "What the hell was that about?" he asks Adrian.

"I have no idea." He wipes his forehead in frustration.

I do wide eyes at Adrian and link my arm through his. "Oh my God, the hottest man on the planet just totally made a play at you." I giggle. Joshua turns and looks at me deadpan.

"I mean second hottest man on the planet after you, of course, baby." I smile.

He fake smiles back and nods his head. "Sure you did," he mouths at me. We take our seat.

"Who was that God?" Adrian asks me wide eyed.

"Only one of the most intelligent men on the planet. He's a psychologist. You're right. He is a god and a bloody good author, not to mention smoking frigging hot."

Josh puts his menu down and rolls his eyes at me. "Down low on the frigging hot," he snaps. I smile and grab his hand. I have to say I am loving jealous Mr. Stanton a little too much, he's just simply too delicious. I am interrupted by a man who comes through the crowd to our table.

"Excuse me, Mr. Murphy." Adrian frowns. It is then I notice Adrian's bodyguard coming up behind the man.

"Can I help you?" he asks the man. The man looks at the bodyguard and then at Adrian, unsure of who he is. Adrian looks a little embarrassed.

"I'm a friend of Nicholas Anastas," he says. My eyes must light up because Joshua squeezes my hand so tight, he nearly breaks a bloody finger.

Adrian turns to his bodyguard. "It's ok, Sam." The bodyguard backs off and the man narrows his eyes as if summing up the situation and turns back to Adrian.

"Mr. Anastas asked me to give you this. He said to tell you he would have come back himself, but the photographers were following him, and he didn't want to embarrass you." He passes Adrian a business card, dips his head and walks away. Adrian looks at the business card and frowns and then turns it over to read the back, he then bites his lip and smiles at Joshua. Joshua is sitting watching Adrian with his elbow on the table, running the side of his pointer back and forth over his lip, his thinking position.

I, however, am just about to wet myself. "Oh my God, Adrian, what does it say?"

He passes me the card.

Let me take you out for dinner
Call me +441.695.8720
Nicholas

"Holy crap, Adrian. He is asking you out for dinner. Oh, and I love the wording so...dominant and sexy." Anyone would think he was asking me. I'm like a little kid.

Josh smiles and gets out his phone. "That was very Hollywood, don't you think?" He smiles at Adrian as he raises a brow. Who, I think, has been rendered speechless.

"It was, wasn't it?" he whispers, wide–eyed.

"He looks like that dude off *True Blood*," Josh says as he tries to think of his name.

"Who?" I frown.

"You know, the hot ripped guy...European."

"Yes, Jo Manganiello. He does, Adrian," I snap. "Oooohh my

Goooddd, I looove Jo Manganiello." I wipe my forehead to accentuate my point as I grab Adrian's hand over the table.

Adrian frowns. "He was a bit of a Greek god, wasn't he?"

"Are you kidding—no contest." I smile.

Joshua starts to read to us from his phone; he has obviously just googled Mr. Anastas.

"Ok, here are the facts." He raises his eyebrows at Adrian. "Greek, forty–two, gay, successful author, estimated wealth at two hundred million." He frowns as he reads the next bit of the information and pauses, "Tragically his husband died in a snow–skiing accident eight years ago." We all go silent.

Adrian eyes widen. "He was married?"

Josh nods. "Apparently to a French lawyer." Hmm, that's interesting. I had no idea he was even gay. What in the hell did we do before Google? Josh smiles at Adrian and raises an eyebrow. "The marrying type, hey." Adrian rolls his eyes at Josh. "You're calling him," Josh announces.

Adrian frowns. "No, I'm not...I'm in a relationship, remember." Joshua goes to say something but glances at me and holds his tongue. I know he wants to say the words but doesn't want to appear like he'd condone infidelity. I smile as I watch him internally struggle with what he wants to say and what he wants to reveal around me. I must say if Adrian's boyfriend is as big a dick as everyone keeps telling me I also think he should call him, but I won't say that either just quietly. An hour later the three of us exit the restaurant.

"I'm not coming back to the office, Adrian." Adrian frowns. "I've already organized for Tom to watch the students this afternoon," Joshua remarks. Adrian frowns again and pulls out his phone to check an email.

"Why, what are you up to this afternoon?" Adrian is concentrating on his phone, sending a message to someone. I look at

Joshua. Yes, what is he doing this afternoon actually? I have to wonder.

He grabs my hand. "Miss Marx has been pulling misdemeanors all day and she needs to be punished." Oh my God, he did not just say that in front of Adrian. I do wide eyes at him and I want the ground to swallow me up. My eyes shoot to Joshua as he cracks his neck, his dark eyes bore into mine and I know he wouldn't care if the pope was standing with us. He's too aroused to have his mouth to brain filter on. Adrian doesn't even look up from his messaging as he smirks and raises his eyebrows.

"Too much information, Stanton." He then winks at me and gives me a kiss on the cheek. "Catch you later, baby." And with that he is gone into the crowd.

Nicholas Anastas sits in the back of his chauffer driven car as he watches the three friends leave the restaurant. He is ruffled. He hasn't felt such an attraction to anyone like that for a very long time, and to an American no less. And why do they have security with them? Who are they? How odd. It was very unexpected and disarming meeting him.

"Peter, I want as much information as you can gather on Adrian Murphy. I'm not sure of where he...actually he was with a Joshua Stanton so check...maybe they work together. I want a criminal record check and past partners, or actually, is he in a relationship at the present moment?"

"Yes, sir," Peter responds as he pulls into the traffic.

Joshua

It's Sunday morning, 5 am, and I am sitting on the end of our bed putting my running shoes on as I prepare for my run. My eyes roam up the beautiful body that is asleep like an angel next to me, her dark long hair spread over my pillow. She's naked, her beautiful curves calling me back to bed. Thank God, she kept her shape, I hate thin women. It may be fashionable to be thin but for me as a man I need a soft lush shape for the testosterone to kick in. Not muscular either... I like the female form in as natural state as it comes. And boy has she got the whole package. Dark long hair, olive skin and those fucking dimples. I can see them even as she sleeps. I smile as her large brown eyes that can see right through me flutter as she tries to refrain from waking. She calls to me deeply on a subconscious level and any thought that I could have a future without her in it is gone. A distant memory. She is so ingrained in my psyche that she is as necessary as air. This is how contentment feels...calm. I have never had such an overwhelming sense that I am where I am supposed to be. This is right. I smile as the realization hits me: I have never had it and now that I have I am not letting it go, no fucking way. Wild horses couldn't drag me from her side.

CHAPTER 23

Natasha

"GOOD MORNING, Presh. How did my girl sleep?" His velvety voice rasps down the phone line. I smile as I stretch and listen to the sexy voice on the other end.

"Hmm, fine thanks, where are you?" I say with my voice still husky from sleep.

"I trained this morning, remember, with Murphy and we are now having breakfast in a café." I rub my eyes as I try to bring them into focus.

"That's right, come home and come back to bed, baby. I don't like waking up without you."

I can hear him smiling down the phone line. "What time will you and the girls be at my house?" I roll my eyes. Josh's friend is coming in from America today with his family to take his kids to the Great Barrier Reef. They have stopped off specifically in Sydney to see him and Josh has organized a lunch at his place for them. I don't know who this friend is, but he must be important to Josh as he has been on my case about not being late since Friday. Abbie and Bridget are coming, as well as the usual boy crew.

"Is this my wakeup call?" I smile down the line.

"Yes. I want you at my house in an hour."

I roll my eyes. "Not happening, Stanton. It's Sunday. I won't be there until eleven."

I can almost hear his eyes bulging. "No. I said I want you here early."

I smile. "And I said I will see you at eleven." I am so not going over there in an hour, tough shit as he would say. He stays silent and I smile. I've got him. He knows I am not going over before eleven and there is nothing he can do about it.

"Fine but so help me, if you're any later than that...you're going to cop it."

I smile. "Oohh, I hope so baby. Copping it is my favorite pastime. You know I'm naked right now, don't you?" I purr.

He smiles down the line and I can hear him walk away from the others. "Behave, my beautiful slut, I want you here early so I can have you to myself for an hour before anyone else gets here." I smile. I know that's not the reason. He's nervous about me meeting his friends. Their opinion must matter...a lot.

"Who is this friend Josh? And why is it so important I'm there early?"

"No reason. Just get here. I'm going. I will see you soon." And he hangs up. He didn't like the last question I threw him, hmm, interesting. Mr. Stanton really is a confusing puzzle, one that I am having fun working out.

"And this is Natasha," he presents me to his friend and his wife three hours later like a prized pig with his hand at my lower back. I smile, feeling uncomfortable. Ok, now I wish I had gotten here earlier as they arrived before me, awkward. Joshua is not impressed with us being an hour late but, in my defense, Abbie is having a crisis. She thinks she is falling in love with Tristen the army guy and was practically hyperventilating when we got to her house. We had to stop for emergency caffeine and a pep talk. Well, that's my story and I'm sticking to it. If he wants to date a puppet, he's with the wrong girl.

I smile a nervous smile. "Hello." I shake both of their hands. The wife is about thirty two at a guess and stunning. I think she might be Italian or something. She has beautiful dark features and a figure to die for.

"This is Maria." Joshua smiles. "And this is Sean. Sean and I play polo together and he and Maria are probably the only friends I have who are happily married."

Oh. I frown. "Don't you have any other friends who are married?" I ask.

He nods. "Yes plenty, but most of them hate each other." We all laugh.

Sean gives me a warm smile and shakes my hand. "Lovely to finally meet you, Natasha." Oh boy, what does that mean? How long has he known I exist? I nervously look at Joshua who is smiling at me with a twinkle in his eye. I smile back and have an inkling I am forgiven for my lateness. Then I am accosted by three little girls who run around my legs as they chase each other.

"These are our children: Bonita, Francesca and Allegra." I smile and shake the girls' hands; yep, definitely Italian judging by the names. They're adorable and I can't help but like them.

"You're pretty," says the little one.

I smile and hunch my shoulders. "Thank you."

"Mummy says Uncle Joshua loves you." I laugh out loud

and Maria hushes the girls as she tries to control their giggling behavior. Josh rolls his eyes.

"Are you giving away my secrets, Bonita?" He bends and tickles the little girl who has just divulged his information. She screams as she tries to escape. This is going well. So they know about me and Maria thinks he loves me. Maybe this day won't be so bad. Cameron walks around to the backyard, looking like what the cat dragged in. He looks dreadful and Abbie winces as she sees him.

"You look terrible. What time did you go to bed?"

He looks at his arm where his watch should be. "Far out, I left my watch there...um..." He scratches his head. "I haven't been to bed yet."

Josh smiles and shakes his head. "You're hopeless."

Cam smiles at Sean and then shakes his hand. "Hi Sean." He then looks affectionately at Maria.

"How's the best sort in America?" He walks over and kisses her cheek, and she slaps him on the arm.

"You, Cameron, are a flirt," she teases.

"You love it, Ree." What the hell? How does Cameron know these two so well? I had no idea; maybe I should be nervous. Did he bring them here to judge me? Why in God's name was I so late? I might kill Abbie later for that one. I don't know what to talk about, so I decide to go and help Abbie and Bridget who are supposedly hard at work helping in the kitchen...as if. I walk in the door to find Bridget lying on the counter and Abbie lying on the lounge and Adrian sitting at the counter eating a carrot.

"So, why is this a problem?" Adrian asks.

Abbie rolls her eyes. "I told you he's in the army."

He frowns. "What does he do in the army?"

"Special forces," she says deadpan.

Adrian fans his face. "Mmm, that's hot. What is it about Special Forces that gets the imagination going?"

"I still don't get it, what's wrong with that?" Bridget asks. "There is no way in hell I am going to be a war widow, Bridget. Even if he doesn't get killed, he will be away most of the time. I need a man in my bed not on my mind." We all nod.

"This is true," Adrian says. "However, imagine how hot the homecomings would be."

Cameron walks into the kitchen looking like death warmed up. "I'm so fucked. I'm sneaking off to bed. Don't tell Josh, he's on entertaining crack or something. He's killing me."

We all laugh; it's true Josh is on entertaining crack and we are his crack whores. Ben walks into the kitchen.

"Josh wants you all to go out and socialize." Everybody groans and I smile. It is becoming increasingly apparent that Josh bosses everybody around like he does me. Even Cameron does what he says.

Joshua

Sean and I are sitting by the pool. The girls have been having a ball this afternoon. Tash has had the music on, and they have been having dancing competitions which Adrian and Cameron have been forced into judging. I look at Cameron and laugh—he really does look like shit. It must have been a total bender for him to be this bad. He usually is ok the next day. And to think I am making him help me entertain. I smile. I'm evil. Then I look at Natasha who is now piggy-backing Francesca around and pretending to gallop like a horse. With a few wines under her belt she has loosened up and is finally being herself.

"She's beautiful, Josh."

I nod. "You have no idea."

"What is going to happen when you move home?" he asks. "She's coming." I take a drink of my beer. He nods as he listens.

"This is the girl you have loved all along, right?" I nod and I smile at him. Apart from Cameron and Adrian, Sean is my closest friend. We never go out together drinking or anything like that. We play polo and train in the gym together but if I see him it's usually with his wife and kids. We have a normal friendship. The kind of friendship I don't get from my party friends. He tells me the truth and doesn't want anything from me in return. He's had money all of his life and is not seduced by its trappings or impressed by easy women. He's had his time doing that and it holds no interest for him at all anymore. I respect his opinion most out of everybody because he says it like it is, nothing is sugarcoated with Sean. And when you have most people sucking up your ass constantly it's very refreshing, although sometimes a little harsh. His parents, wife and I all get on very well and we do spend a lot of time together. They all breed horses as well. He's a good husband and father, the kind of husband I want to be, devoted. I don't know why any of my other friends even bother getting married as they sleep around all the time.

"Forgive me for intruding but isn't she your cousin?" I rub my hand through my hair. Fuck, when did I tell him that? He must sense my horror. "You told me one night when you were drunk." I nod, feeling more than stupid. I told him that when I didn't think they would ever meet and now they have. God, how must this look from an outside perspective?

"Do me a favor and keep that on the down low, will you?" I ask. He smiles and nods.

"Of course, you have my word."

"This is a fucked-up situation, isn't it?" I sigh, he nods and stays silent.

He looks at me as he takes a drink. "Tell me, Josh. How is this going to go? Have you thought about this? I mean really thought what this will mean for her?" I take a swig of my beer as my eyes wander to Natasha who is dancing with Francesca by the pool and I smile.

"Yes, I am fully aware she will have to move to America to be with me, but she wants to. She offered first." He narrows his eyes as he listens.

"How much do you love her?" he asks as he takes another drink. I break into a full smile as I shake my head. "Man, the sun sets with her. I'm done. This is all I want; all I'll ever want. The last seven years have told me that." He listens and I can see him thinking as he watches her dancing with his daughter. I raise my eyebrows, waiting for him to speak and when he doesn't, I ask the question. "Spit it out. What do you want to say?"

"I just don't think..." he stays silent. I frown as I try to work out what he is saying. "I just think I love Maria too much. I couldn't let her sacrifice so much to be with me."

I frown as I try to work out his meaning. "What do you mean?" I ask.

"She has to give up her job, her family, her friends and her country to be with you."

"I know but I told her after five or ten years we could come back here."

"Are you really prepared to take motherhood from her, Josh?"

I frown. My eyes shoot to Natasha who is now wading in the pool with Bridget and the three girls. "Josh, you know you two can't have children together, right?" My heart drops.

"What do you mean?" I ask, panicked.

"Josh, it's cross breeding. You can't do it. The children will end up sick." My eyes widen as I take in the information he has just given me. My eyes flick to Natasha again. Why in the hell did I not think of this before? Fuck!

"Look, I don't know man. It's none of my business. But you had better be sure before you strip her of everything is all I'm saying." He looks at me deadpan and takes another swig of his beer and I know he is completely serious.

Maria comes over and grabs Sean by the hand. "I'm stealing my husband, Joshua." And with that she drags him away. I sit still, stunned to my core. I am so fucking stupid. My heart drops as I watch Natasha's uninhibited laughter, like she doesn't have a care in the world. She deserves better than I can give her, all the money in the world cannot replace motherhood or her family. I close my eyes and consider the serious ramifications for her if we stay together. In years to come I know she will regret the choice to give up a family to be with me—anyone in their right mind would. I'm not worth the sacrifice. Not with my baggage. She should be with someone like... Christopher. He can give her what I can't. He still loved her, and they weren't even sleeping together. Pain lances through my chest as I realize she is better off with someone else, someone for whom she would not have to sacrifice. Someone who I know would look after her. Someone who loves her as much as I do. Her words come back to haunt me. I had to save you from yourself, baby, you were going to give everything up to be with me and I loved you too much to let you do it. I put my head in my hands as I think. I honestly don't know if I can do it. I'm not strong enough to walk away. Am I?

Natasha

On the way home I am holding Josh's hand on my lap. "Are you tired, baby?" I ask and his eyes flick to me and he frowns. "You hardly ate any dinner and you're so quiet."

He smiles a shy smile at me. "Yeah, I guess I am." He picks my hand up and kisses the back of it. His eyes are then on the road and he is deep in thought again. What is he thinking about?

"Do you think your friends liked me?" I ask nervously.

He smiles broadly at me. "There isn't a person on earth who wouldn't like you, Tash."

I smile. "Except for your mother," I tease.

He bursts out laughing. "Yes, she is the exception." He rolls his eyes. We get home and I get into the shower and Josh stays in the kitchen and puts the kettle on. Twenty minutes later I get out of the shower wondering where my shower buddy got to, fully expecting him to be asleep on the lounge. I look up the hall from my bedroom and I see Josh pacing in the lounge room with both hands linked on the top of his head. He does that when he is upset. I've seen him do it before. What's the matter with him? What is he thinking about? He seems worried about something. I stand in the hall watching him. I have to say he's acting strange. I walk out as I continue drying my hair.

"Josh, what's wrong?" His eyes search mine. "Are you sick?" He pulls me into an embrace and kisses the top of my head.

"I love you Natasha, you know that, don't you?" I smile and nod as I kiss his chest, what is this about?

"I love you Josh, you know that, don't you?"

He smiles nervously and nods. "Sit down, Presh, we need to talk."

"Ok, what about? Are you going to take me to pound town, my beautiful Lamborghini?" I raise my eyebrows as I go to drag his shorts down, but he stops me. His face drops and he looks like he is about to burst into tears.

I frown. "Josh, what is it? You're scaring me. What's wrong?"

He swallows and goes to speak but nothing comes out and he closes his mouth again.

"I, I just have a head... headache that's all," he stammers. I smile a big smile at him.

"You big dope, why didn't you tell me? I will get you some aspirin." I jump up and return with a glass of water and his tablets and he pulls me down onto his lap and cuddles tightly.

"Bed, baby," I demand. "I can't stand seeing you like this."

As I lay in bed four hours later, I am achingly aware that Josh is wide awake next to me thinking about something. I can hear his mind ticking from here. Something has happened today, something that has upset him. Maybe he spoke to his mother on the phone and is upset about it or maybe his friends didn't like me. I don't think that is it though. I can't put my finger on it but being a psychologist sucks sometimes. I wish I couldn't read people so well or try to analyze why they are thinking so much. He said he had a headache, and I should just believe him. Unfortunately, a tiny voice deep down in the pit of my stomach is telling me something is seriously wrong with my beautiful man and it's a problem that he doesn't want to share with me. Maybe tomorrow will bring new light.

I woke alone this morning, no note left from Josh and it is now four o'clock in the afternoon and I haven't heard from him at all today, which is very unusual. He hasn't left while I slept since we started seeing each other seriously and it has left me feeling uneasy all day. I called him to see if his headache was alright, but he didn't answer or call me back. He has usually called me at least a couple of times or texted me long before this. I walk outside to my car in between my patients to try and find Max. I find him sitting in the park.

"Hi, Max."

He smiles and nods. "Hi, Natasha."

"I was wondering if you know if Joshua is at work today."

He looks uncomfortable. "I believe so, ma'am," he nods. Hmm, what in the hell does that mean? He's obviously not sick, yet he hasn't called me back. Maybe he's getting cold feet about our relationship. I try to calm my nerves and the sick feeling in my stomach. I hate depending on someone so much and we have come too far to be playing games now.

"Thank you, Max." I march back inside with renewed purpose and ring Adrian who answers on the first ring.

"Hi, Tash."

"Hi," I snap. "Can you put Joshua on the phone, please?"

He stays silent and after a minute whispers, "Sure, baby, I will get him." I hear him hold his hand over the phone and walk into Josh's office. "It's for you."

Then I hear Josh's angry voice snap, "Stanton." I stay silent as I listen to the anger in his voice. What in the hell is going on with him?

"Josh, it's me."

He inhales and I can hear he's shocked that I have tricked him by ringing Adrian's phone.

His voice softens. "Hi precious, are you ok, baby?" He's not angry with me, I can hear it in his voice.

"What's going on? Why haven't you called me back?" He stays silent. "Josh, I asked you a question. Answer it."

"Natasha, I'm very busy. I can't talk."

"Don't you dare very busy me. What the fuck is going on?" He stays silent and I know I have shocked him with my screaming anger. "What time are you coming over tonight?" I ask. Again, silence. Ok, I am getting seriously pissed off now. Who in the hell does he think he is? "Answer my question."

"Tash, I have to work tonight, I'm not coming over." Now it is my turn to stay silent. He doesn't want to see me—my stomach drops. "Tash, just…just know that I love you and I only want what's best for you, ok." I frown, he's talking riddles. What is that supposed to mean?

"What's best for me, Josh, is to not be away from you." "That's debatable," he whispers.

"Just come over when you finish work and we can work it out baby, ok?"

I can hear him thinking. "Bye, Tash." And he hangs up the phone.

It's twelve o'clock and I am wide awake, heartsick but awake. Joshua hasn't called me or come over and I am beginning to think the worst. If I wasn't waiting for him to come over, I would be driving around spying on him. Where is he? What is he doing? And what has changed so dramatically between us that he can't talk to me and tell me what's going on? I hear the key in my door, and I lie still with my heart trying to pump through my chest. He came. He fusses around in the kitchen for a few minutes and I hear him put his keys and wallet on the side table. I'm not angry anymore, I'm freaking out. I don't want to be a drama queen, but my gut feeling is that something is seriously off between us. He walks over to the side of the bed and turns the side lamp on. I lie still as I watch him, unable to pretend that he hasn't upset me. He gives me a sad smile and bends to gently kiss me on the lips as he brushes the hair back from my face and sits next to me.

"Hi, my beautiful girl," he whispers. That is all it takes and I grab him into a tight embrace. "Josh, please talk to me, you promised me honesty."

He nods. "I know, Presh." I frown. He bends and gently kisses me again, his tongue lingering in my mouth. "I love you," he whispers. "That's the honest truth, does that count for anything?" Tears fill my eyes.

"Are you mad at me, Josh? Have I done something to upset you?"

He smiles at me. "No, baby, you have done nothing wrong. Stop worrying. I'm here now."

I cuddle him tighter. "Baby, you're scaring me, you're acting weird."

He nods and smiles. "I am weird. Are you just figuring that out?"

I giggle as I hug him just that bit tighter. "Take your clothes off and get into bed, Josh. I've missed you today."

He smiles into my neck. "Same," he whispers. He takes off his clothes and lies on his back next to me and I look at him with a puzzled face. Is he not touching me?

"Make love to me, Tash. I'm going to lie still. I want you to touch me like you love me."

I smile. "That won't be hard, Josh. I do love you." He gently swipes his fingertips over my lips as he looks at me. Maybe things are not so bad, perhaps I am just being a drama queen. I bend down and gently kiss him as my hands wander down his torso over his ripped stomach. He sticks to his word and lies motionless as he watches me, his breath catching as I run my tongue up his beautiful long length. Our eyes lock as I take him deep into my mouth while sucking, his mouth hanging slack, weak from arousal. His hands gently run through my hair. I love it when he does that to me—runs his hands gently through my hair while taking pleasure from my mouth, it turns me on big time. He grabs my hands and links our fingers so he is holding my hands. The memory of the first time he went down on me and he did that runs rampant through my mind. I love the intimate gesture of holding my hands. It's so simple, but it means so much to me and he knows it.

"I can't wait for you, precious. Mount me."

I frown and smile. "You know I can't take you like that without you warming me up first, you're too big."

He smiles and pulls me down for a kiss and his tongue dives into my mouth as he demands intimacy.

"I know. I want you to try. I want to feel how perfectly tight you are around me. I need to have it burned into my brain."

I frown, he's talking riddles again. "I am not going to be tight for much longer, Josh. I have a taste for this now."

He gives me a sad smile and nods. "I know," he whispers as he closes his eyes as if in pain. I stand up onto my knees as he holds the base so I can mount him and I was right, it's too big. He won't fit so I need him to stretch me first. "Tash, kiss me and take it slow. I know you can take me." I nod again and start to kiss him deeply. With each lash of his tongue I open just that little further and within ten minutes he's completely in. I don't know whether he's in heaven or hell because his face is showing indicators of both. I start to move, and he stills my hips with his hands.

"Slow...I need this slow," he growls. With our eyes entranced on each other he gently rides me to orgasm and I feel him swell inside me. His quivering breath tells me how close he is. He rolls me over while still inside me and starts to gently move as he kisses me deeply, never breaking precious contact. With one, two, three pumps I feel his hot seed burn me from the inside out and he buries his head into my neck and stays perfectly still while trying to catch his breath, and then I feel it. Something hot runs down the side of my neck and drops onto my shoulder. That was a fucking tear...not mine but his. What in the hell is going on here? That was the gentlest loving sex we have ever had, so why in the hell is he crying? I have a lump in my throat and am unable to speak as I try and process what to say. What's wrong? He kisses me again, this time more urgently and, that is it, he's reached his gentle limit. He withdraws and starts to really warm me up, until I don't think I can it take anymore and then we are hard at it. My hands are being held up above my head and he is making love to me like his life depends on it. Strong, powerful strokes where the bed is hitting the wall and I am gasping for breath.

I think I fell into an exhausted sleep after round five and then I think I woke hours later to find Josh tenderly taking me while I slept as he whispered how much he loved me into my ear, but I can't be sure if it was a dream or reality. Either way it was perfect.

When I woke up, he was gone, and I was left with a sick uneasy feeling in my gut.

It's seven pm and I haven't heard from Joshua all day and have decided I'm not ringing him. I don't know what his problem is, but I do know for certain he loves me. He proved that last night. He will call me, I hope. At one am I fall into an exhausted sleep hoping I will be awoken by the sound of keys in my door. I don't and when my alarm goes off at six I feel like I have been hit by a truck. I drag my fat ass around, feeling sorry for myself, and end up getting to work late. Shit. I have a booked–out morning but thankfully a slow afternoon so I chastise myself not to think about him until then.

I read through the case notes of my next appointment.

Client: Aaron Marks: Referral: Dr Parker
Symptom: Erectile malfunction

Aaron is a new client that I haven't seen before. I show him in, and he takes a seat nervously on my couch.

"Hi, Aaron, my name is Natasha Marx. I will be looking after you."

He nods and looks down unimpressed. "Ok. I did ask if I could have a male therapist."

"Oh, I'm sorry. You have been booked in with me for some reason. I can see if a male psychologist can see you. That's fine. You are here because of erectile malfunction, am I right?"

He looks down and shakes his head. "No, I lied to my doctor to get a referral to see you guys."

I frown, "Ok, what is the problem Aaron? So, I can recommend the right person to see you."

He lifts his head and looks at me, "I'm not talking to a female child about my problem. Is there a male here or not?"

Mmm, cranky pants. I smile. "That's fine, come back through to reception and we will get someone else to see you." He grunts in response. I show him to the reception and arrange for him to see someone else. Every time my confidence rises a little at work, I encounter a client like this, and I am quickly reminded of my age and lack of experience. Apparently, it happens to everyone in this field when they first start. It's bloody annoying.

At one our receptionist knocks on my door. "Excuse me, Natasha, but your sister has called for you six times. She said it's urgent."

I frown. "Thanks. I will ring her now." I dial Bridget's number and she picks up first ring.

"Tash, baby, are you ok?"

"Yeah, why wouldn't I be ok?" I ask.

She stays silent down the line. "Tash," she whispers with tears in her voice. "Turn your Google on, honey." A sick feeling drops in my stomach as I click onto my Google page and my google alert drops. I click onto the link to Joshua. Oh my fuck. I put my hand up to my mouth in shock. A barrage of images hits me like a cement truck and the tears start to freely run down my face. Images of Josh kissing a brunette outside a strip club and then getting into his car with her. Joshua was with someone else last night.

CHAPTER 24

Natasha

"I...FUCK, Bridget, I have to go. I will see you tonight."

"Are you ok? Have you seen it?"

I nod. "Yes, I see it. I will call you later." I hang up the phone. I angrily swipe the tears from my eyes as I process this new information. How dare he do this to me and who in the hell does he think he is? I try to focus through the tears as I stare at the screen. I don't believe it. I know I see it in front of my eyes, but I still don't believe it. Am I that stupid that I didn't see this coming? I run to my bathroom and dry retch into the toilet. I'm such an idiot. I slide down the wall and sit on the floor and sob. I waited for him last night and he was with a dirty whore. He had sex with someone else. My stomach rolls again. After half an hour I peel myself up and return to my desk. I need to know what happened. My psychologist's capacity for detachment kicks in and I scroll through the photos one at a time, studying each one and analyzing it. My pen taps double time on my desk as I think. He's smoking as he leaves the club which indicates to me that he was drunk.

However, he looks too together to me to be drunk. I've seen him drunk and that is not how he looked, not even close. I enlarge a photo of the girl. She's fucking ordinary, give me a break. I scroll down to the end and back to the top again. What's wrong with this picture? I look at the number; there are thirty-two photos in all. I think back to how he has been acting the last few days...like he's distracted about something, regretful even. I scroll to the top of the page again, so the photos run from when he leaves the club to outside when he kisses her and then, as he puts her into his car. I scroll back to the top... he's alone. He has a different security guard with him, one I haven't seen before. I frown, what does that mean? He never goes anywhere without his entourage or group of friends or whatever it is. That in itself is highly irregular. I then go back to the five kissing photos; something is wrong with the body language. I narrow my eyes as I try to pin it down...what is it? I tap my front tooth with my fingernail as I think. He hasn't had paparazzi follow him at all while he has been in Sydney, so why now? Talk about bad luck... or is it? I sit back on my chair and cross my arms as I think while staring at the screen.

Joshua Stanton, stop fucking with my head. It's pissing me off. I stand and walk over to my window and I see Max sitting in the park reading the paper. Why is he still here protecting me? Joshua apparently doesn't care about me, so why should Max? I grab my keys and go down to my car to pretend getting something out of it as a ruse to talk to Max. Maybe he has some answers for me. I walk to my car and Max rushes over.

"Hi, Natasha." He looks nervous, probably expecting a neurotic head case. An idea suddenly comes into my head and I get into my car pretending I am going to drive off.

"Where are you going, Natasha?" he asks a little panicked. I smile at him and get back out of the car.

"Crazy," I reply as I do wide eyes at him.

"Is everything alright?" he asks. He obviously knows what's going on here. That makes one of us. "Everything is great, Max, why wouldn't it be?" I answer too sweetly. He narrows his eyes at me, and I can see his brain ticking as he assesses the situation.

"You can go, Max, I don't need protecting anymore."

He smiles at me. "I've been assigned to you for three months, Natasha."

I fake a smile. "I'm pretty sure Joshua's mind has been changed, so you can ring him now and tell him I will be just fine, and I will not be accepting any protection." He nods and looks uncomfortable. "Go on, I want you to ring him while I stand here." He frowns at me. "Go on," I urge. He tentatively takes out his phone and dials Joshua's number and he answers on the first ring.

"Hi, it's me. I'm with Natasha...yes...yes." His eyes flick to me. "She's...fine." Hmm, Joshua just asked how I am. "I'm not sure. It doesn't seem so." And he looks at me again. Joshua has just asked if I have seen the Google alert. He turns his back to me. "No, nothing has been said. Anyway, she said she doesn't want protection anymore and asked me to ring you and ok it." He holds the phone out from his ear, and I know Joshua has just screamed at him.

He can take it up the ass if he thinks I am going to put up with one more minute of his shit. I'm done. This relationship is taking more energy than it's worth and I intend to rectify that situation right here right now. You've fucked with the wrong girl, Mr. Stanton. I smile at Max and turn and walk back into the building. My work here is done. Joshua is yelling at him over my non-reaction. He wanted me to see the Google alert. Does he really think I'm that stupid?

As I walk through the office I say to the receptionist, "Can you let Henry know I am going home sick?"

She frowns. "Is everything ok?"

"Yes, I just feel a migraine coming on and I need to leave. I will let him know about my plans for tomorrow." I walk back into my office and bring up the pictures again and click on their website and google their phone number.

"Hi, this is Megan Jones from Joshua Stanton's office. I need to make a payment for some work that was posted yesterday."

"Oh, ok, I will put you through to accounts," the bored voice replies.

"Hello, accounts. This is Tanya." Boy, she's chirpy, an exact opposite to the receptionist.

"Hello, this is Megan Jones from Joshua Stanton's office. You posted some photos for us yesterday and I need to pay the account."

"Ok, hang on a sec, I will just check." I can hear her keyboard buttons being tapped double time and my heart is in my throat. If my suspicions are correct, I already know what she is going to tell me. At least I hope I know what she is going to tell me; please let me be right.

"No, that's all fine. The account was paid for yesterday in full."

I smile... Gotcha. "That's unusual, can you please tell me what method was used to pay?"

"Yeah, sure," she replies. Once again, I hear her keyboard buttons. "That was paid on a credit card yesterday at 10.50 am." I shake my head as my anger flies into uncharted territory, 10.50 am. He has thought long and hard about this. I'm going to fucking kill him with my bare hands.

"What was the name on the credit card, Tanya?" I ask innocently.

"Joshua Stanton," she replies.

"Thank you, Tanya, you have been very helpful."

The thing about being so angry that you can't see straight is that you become unpredictable and embarrassing. I storm through the foyer of Joshua's office and straight to his door. One of the dumb and dumber receptionists speaks.

"Excuse me, you can't go in there."

"Fuck off," I snap. "Try and stop me." She frowns at the other secretary and I see her push the security alarm button under her desk. This is going well already. I push through the doors and head straight to Adrian's office. No one is in there. I then push through to Joshua's office and my eyes narrow as I lay eyes on Adrian sitting at the desk and Joshua standing looking out the window with his hands in his pockets, his back to me. I storm in and Adrian jumps up, obviously shocked at my arrival.

"Natasha," he gasps.

"Get the fuck out, Adrian, before you witness a murder," I scream. Ok, donkey on the edge here. I'm getting embarrassing but I am way beyond caring. Joshua turns deadpan as if he has been expecting my visit.

"Adrian, don't go anywhere. It is Natasha who's leaving." That's it. I explode and walk over and slap his face as hard as I can. The crack echoes around the room and Adrian's face is full of fear—for me. I don't think he witnesses psychotic women every day. I know Joshua is going to lose it at my anger, but he can bring it the fuck on. He was looking for a fight and guess what, he found it. Who in the hell does this conceited prick think he is? I go to slap him again when I get no reaction and he grabs my hand midair.

"If you hit me again, expect a return," he growls. I step back and the bile rises in my throat. I have never been so angry, angry at him, angry at myself for letting him get to me so badly. "Do you think I'm stupid?" I scream. He runs his tongue along his front top teeth under his lip as he puts his hands back into his pockets.

"Natasha, I'm sorry it had to end like this but the whole relationship thing is...boring for me and it was time to end it." His ice-cold stare bores into me. "Sorry, if I hurt you; it was unintentional." I shake my head as I hear Adrian's audible gasp at what Josh has just said.

"You dumb ass, who do you think you are talking to?" I scream. He turns his back to me again and I know it's to hide his face from me. "You can cut the act, Joshua. Don't try and fuck with me; I'm a psychologist, remember. I know how your brain works better than you do."

He turns and glares at me. "I don't know what you are talking about," he snaps.

"Oh really, you haven't just tried to pull the ultimate deceit on me?"

He narrows his eyes. "I couldn't help myself. She was attractive." Ok, it's official, I am going crazy. I burst into laughter.

"You think this is about the other girl?" I laugh. He frowns at me but doesn't speak. I walk over to him and go up close to his face.

"I know about the premeditated inception, you dumb fuck!" I scream.

He steps back in shock that I am onto him. "Inception?" he frowns.

"Inception means to plant an idea in another's mind. What

are you trying to plant in my mind, Joshua?" I angrily tap on the side of my head.

"Stop it," he yells. "You don't know what you are talking about!" he screams. I walk around him with my arms crossed in front of me, sizing him up. He looks like he's about to run.

"You see, Joshua, you insult my intelligence if you think I don't know what you have done." He glares at me but doesn't speak. "What are you trying to plant in my mind, Joshua? Hmm, let me think." I run my pointer finger over my lip...Ok, I'm going for an Oscar...I frigging deserve one that's for sure. "You're unworthy of my love or you're a sleazebag or maybe that you are just not good enough for me, huh, what is it?" He looks at me mortified as my words sink in. "Speak," I yell. "Are you really that much of a coward that you can't face the truth and you would rather force me to leave you?" He frowns and Adrian smiles and winks at me from where he stands behind Joshua. I bite my lip to stifle my smile. Ok, I'm on the right track. Adrian just confirmed it. "What are you afraid of, Joshua? That I will leave you? That your stalker is going to kill me?" He frowns and I know hearing that point has made him unsettled. "You gutless prick. Even when I call you out you can't tell the truth." He glares at me and I know he wants to fight but is holding it in. If I can just push him that bit further. I smile a knowing smile.

"Actually, I know what happened, Mummy dearest got to you, didn't she?"

"Shut up!" he yells. "Leave her out of this."

I smile a conceited smile. "Yes, that's exactly how it went, Margaret rang you and you run to make her happy. Once a mummy's boy always a mummy's boy. You make me sick. Did she pay for the photos?"

"Get the fuck out Natasha!" he yells.

I smile a sad smile. "And to think I actually thought you

would protect me from her. What a joke. Come on, we are going home." He frowns and looks at Adrian.

"Move!" I yell. I see a bottle of water on his desk and pick it up and unscrew the lid as I talk.

"I told you. We are over, Natasha."

"We are over when I say we are over and not a minute before, asshole. You don't get to say how this ends and I will not be played into breaking up with you," I snap as I start to pour the water on the keyboard of his computer. Adrian and he both scramble to get to me. "Is this computer important, Joshua?" I do wide eyes at him as I start to pour it on the monitor. "I'm not going anywhere until you come with me and I could do a lot of damage in here. You might want to think about that."

"Just go, man." Adrian smiles as he slaps him on the back.

"Fuck off!" Joshua yells. "Get out of my fucking head, Natasha. I know what you are doing."

"Does it feel good to protect your mother, Joshua?"

He glares at me. "This has nothing to do with my mother."

"Yes, it does," I scream.

"I'm protecting you. You raving bitch," he yells. Silence fills the room. His eyes widen at the realization I have just tricked him into getting angry so he would speak unguardedly. I sit on his desk and smile.

"There it is. Bingo. Adrian can you leave us, please." Adrian smiles and walks over and kisses my forehead.

"Bye, baby, love your work." He grabs my hand and squeezes it before he leaves through the door. I lower my voice and pat the desk next to me.

"Come sit with me, Josh. What are you protecting me from?" He looks at the floor and won't make eye contact with me.

"I'm not having this conversation, Natasha."

"Then I'm not leaving. Come home with me and we can fight in private. You do realize that your workers are listening, right?" He frowns as he looks up to the door and realizes that I'm right. I smile as he puts his jacket on.

"Come," he holds his hand out for me and I grab it like an olive branch. The embarrassing thought that I have to go back through the office where I have just screamed fuck off to the valued employees makes my stomach turn and I pull back on Josh's arm. He frowns at me.

"What?" he snaps.

"I just yelled fuck off to your receptionists."

He smiles. "Why are you such a firecracker? Isn't slapping my face enough aggression for one day?" Oh God, he had to bring that up, didn't he?

"Josh, if I see you kissing girls, I can't be held responsible for my actions." He gives me a sad smile and nods.

"We need to talk, Presh, because we can't be together anymore." My heart drops.

"Don't say that, Josh. Just take me home."

He gives me a heavy smile and nods. "Let's go then."

We sit in silence on the way home. We stand in silence in the lift, and I have to say I'm feeling very nervous. I thought when I caught him out with the deception all would be ok. But it is becoming seemingly more likely that it won't, he's too controlled and too silent. We walk into my apartment and are immediately greeted by the sight of my new suitcase sitting in the center of my living room. He frowns and looks at me.

"Going somewhere?"

"Um, yes, I'm going to LA on Friday to pick out a new house remember, or have you forgotten that, too?" He nods and sits me on the lounge chair. He turns and faces the window as he puts his hands in his pockets.

"Natasha, I want you to go back to Christopher."

Horror dawns. "What?" I gasp.

"I know he loves you and he will look after you."

I immediately stand. "Josh, I don't want Christopher, I only want you." He keeps his back to me, and I know it's so I don't see his face. I walk over and cuddle him from behind.

"Josh, what's this about? Talk to me, I don't understand." He turns and cuddles me as he kisses the top of my head.

"Tash, I'm going to be honest with you because I love you and I want what's best for you. I want you to hear me out before speaking." I nod.

"I wasn't with that girl last night. I was in the strip club for about ten minutes, picked her up and left. It was totally premeditated that the photos were taken. I didn't realize that you knew me as well as you do and in hindsight it was a bad decision but I still think that we should break up." Ok, now he's scaring me.

"Josh," I whisper as tears fill my eyes. "Don't say that, baby."

"Hear me out, I can't give you everything that you deserve. You have to give up everything to be with me," he says deadpan as if running on autopilot.

I frown. "Josh, moving to the other side of the world is not giving up everything and besides I told you already as long as we are together, I don't care."

"Tash, you have to give up your job, your friends and your family." He looks down to the ground. "Motherhood," he whispers. My eyes turn to saucers.

"This is about children?" I gasp. His haunted eyes come back up to meet mine and I know immediately that's the

375

reason. He needs to be admitted, what in the hell is he on about? I burst a giggle and he looks at me in disgust.

"This is not funny, Natasha, not even close."

"Josh, we have every opportunity to have children. There is only a one per cent increased risk in first cousins and the younger I am the risk goes down. I have researched this for years, you stupid man. Besides, I don't care if we adopt or use a donor egg, whatever. As long as I get to mother your children I will be happy." He swallows the lump in his throat but doesn't speak. "Josh, it is not your role to protect me from you, I am not a high school girl giddy on love. I have thought long and hard about our relationship and I will not be with anyone else as long as I know you love me. So, if you push me away in some hero act you will only be punishing me with a broken heart."

"Tash, you don't know what you are saying," he whispers. "Wouldn't you prefer to be the man who looks after me and loves me and tucks me into bed every night?" My eyes search his. Nodding, he drops his eyes as he thinks.

"Josh, I am not letting you go. I love you too much to do that and you can't ask that of me. It's not fair that you have made this decision by yourself when it involves my future, what were you thinking? We have fought too hard already to be pulled apart now." I grab his arms and wrap them around me and finally he relaxes into me and cuddles me, then he bends down to gently brush his lips over mine.

"Tash, I just need us to break up now if we are going to. It will break me in a few years if you decide that you hate America or the life I live and leave me. I won't be able to handle it."

I smile a broad smile. "Do you honestly think that you won't be making any sacrifices to be with me?" He frowns, not quite understanding my meaning.

"No women or strip clubs and by the way, if you pull a trick like you did last night I will kill you with my bare hands and a smile on my face."

He smiles warmly as he pushes the hair off my forehead and nods. "Deal," he whispers.

"I mean it, Josh, postal. Like Silence of the Lambs–style killing." He laughs out loud.

"Ok, I get it. Natasha, I didn't know what to do, I knew I wasn't strong enough to leave you and I knew you wouldn't let me. You're right. I am gutless. I tried to take the easy way out." He hangs his head in shame.

"Yep," I smile. "Totally," I reply as I do wide eyes at him. I frown as I sum up the events.

"Why are you even thinking of babies and me, Josh?" I pause and smile. "Are you going to ask me to marry you?"

His eyes twinkle as he smirks, his head on an angle to the side as he watches me. "No, it doesn't mean I am going to ask you to marry me."

I frown in disappointment. "This is probably one of those times when you should shut up and look pretty then, Josh."

He laughs. "Are you saying you want me to ask you to marry me?" He raises his eyebrows.

I smile and bite my lip. "No, I don't want you to ask me to marry you."

He fakes a cranky face. "Now you can shut up and look pretty."

"Actually, I already look pretty and I think you need to be punished," I smirk.

His eyes shoot up to mine. "Punished," he repeats.

"Yes, I just told you I'm not a giddy schoolgirl and you didn't bat an eyelash, are you saying I'm an old boiler?"

He laughs again. "Old boiler," he repeats as he raises an eyebrow. I nod as I smile, and he shakes his head. "I'm not saying that at all. What I am saying, though, is that you're a beautiful slut who is too good for me," he whispers as he runs his whiskers down the length of my neck. I bite my lip to stifle my smile.

"Way out of your league, Stanton." He smiles.

"And do pray tell who is in your league, Miss Marx?" His hands run down the length of my body to my behind and he pulls me onto his rock–hard erection. His eyes drop to my lips as he cracks his neck. Why do I find that so damn arousing?

I shrug and act nonchalant. "I don't know, Jo Manganiello or Henry Cavill, Thor, James Bond you know the type, all dominant and hot like."

He licks his lips and then smirks. "Are you gagging to be punished, Miss Marx, by teasing me with interest in other men?"

I open my mouth to feign shock. "Me?" I smile.

"Yes, you. If it's domination you want then I'm only too happy to serve it up," he growls and picks me up and throws me over his shoulder. "Out of my league, let me initiate you into *my* league, Miss Marx." He marches down the hall to our bedroom and he kicks open the door. "There's a reason your name has an X in it," he growls as he slaps me hard on the behind before he throws me onto the bed. I lie back as he rips my pants down and my shirt over my head so violently, he nearly rips them. I am panting as anticipation seeps through my bones, my head lies back as he spreads my legs and looks down at my glistening sex, his mouth slightly open. He cracks his neck hard. *Mmm.* He looks up at me and without taking his eyes off mine he slowly undresses.

His body is hard everywhere and my eyes drop to his perfect manhood and my name burnt into his side. This is desire...pure unadulterated lust. I feel the familiar rush of mois-

378

ture as he opens my legs to his gaze and swipes his fingertips through me, his breath catching at the contact. How did I get here? So totally in love and lust with this magnificent beast. And he is a beast, even if I wanted to back out, I know he would take me anyway. Just the thought of his domination over my body has me weeping for him and eager to please him. He bends and runs his whiskers up the inside of my thigh until he gets to my center and without taking his eyes from mine he runs his tongue through my creamy arousal. He lifts my legs over his shoulders and then he is in me, his tongue unleashed. Oh damn, he's good at this, my eyes close and my head rolls to one side as I watch him, my hands running through his hair.

He reaches up and links my fingers with his as his tongue dives deep into my body, long deep licks. I'm close and I start to quiver, he releases my hand and pushes three fingers into me and I jump. He sits back and watches me as he fucks me hard with his fingers, my eyes closing and my body finding a rhythm of its own and bearing down on him hard. "Oh yes, that's it, precious girl," he whispers. "Squeeze me and warm yourself up for my cock." He starts to move his hand quicker and I can't help it. I start to jump, my body flying headfirst into a hard orgasm and I scream out loud. He leans in and then slides into me as he lifts my legs over his shoulders, his open mouth on my inside ankle. His hooded eyes watch me as my body tries to accommodate him. God, it's too much. I'm too sensitive, too swollen.

"Josh, wait," I whisper. "I can't...wait a minute." I gasp.

He slams into me harder. "You can and you will. Squeeze me and suck out my come, it's yours." I close my eyes as I ride the deep punishing rhythm, each stroke harder and deeper than the last until I can take it no longer and I scream into his mouth as another powerful orgasm rips through me. He stills and then it's one...two... three pumps and he growls into my mouth as he kisses me hard. We both pant, covered in sweat, as our hearts beat out of control.

"You're going to kill me woman." He smiles and I gasp for breath.

"Not if you kill me first."

It's six o'clock and Joshua and I have had awesome makeup sex for approximately three hours and I'm ready to go to bed to sleep. I haven't really slept since Sunday when Josh started acting weird. We are both wrapped in towels fresh from bed and yes, I feel even closer to him now that we have crossed another hurdle, how is that possible? Joshua is in the kitchen eating everything he can find, because if I know him at all he has hardly eaten since Sunday and it's now Wednesday. I can hear ice banging in the shaker as he makes another chocolate protein shake. God, how does he stomach those things? The keys sound in my door and I turn as Bridget comes in carrying the biggest McDonald's paper bag in history.

"I bought supplies, chick," she smiles. Oh shit, this is not going to go down well. I forgot to ring her back. She walks through and puts the bag onto my coffee table.

"Big Mac, extra-large fries and coke and an apple pie for added cellulite." She puts her hands on her hips and beams at me, feeling proud of herself. I stand still as Joshua comes around the corner, oblivious, in a towel. Her eyes turn into saucers as she sees him, and she turns and scowls at me.

"Are you fucking kidding me?" she snaps. I squirm uncomfortably under her glare. She turns to Joshua.

"Get out sleazebag, before I tip this coke over your head." He looks at me and I gently shake my head signifying for him to keep quiet and thankfully he does. "Start talking, Natasha, because you can't be this gullible. A picture tells a thousand words and the picture me and the rest of the world woke up to this morning was Joshua Stanton doing another stripper." I bite my lip. This does look bad. Joshua doesn't like that last comment and folds his arms in front of him as he rests the bottom of his foot against the shin of his other leg while he looks at her deadpan. She glares at him. "Speak, asshole!" she yells.

"Not that it's any of your business what goes on between my girlfriend and me but."

She cuts him off.

"None of my business? Are you fucking kidding me?" Ok, she's losing it.

"Calm down, Bridget, it's ok. He was trying to protect me." She looks at me like I have just grown another head.

"Seriously, if you pull your psychology shit out now, I am going to frigging kill you. Your boyfriend slept with a cheap stripper last night and you saw the photos and here you are in a towel playing happy families with him. What in the hell is the matter with you?" I wince as I sum up the situation from her perspective. She's right, this does look bad.

"I didn't sleep with her," Joshua snaps. She turns on him like the devil himself pointing her finger in his face.

"I don't care if she fucked you up the ass with a broomstick, you kissed her and that's cheating! She waited seven fucking years for you, Josh, and this is how you repay her? Shaming her in public?"

He drops his head again in shame. "It was a bad decision, I will admit."

"Oh, how big of you to admit it. You loser!" she screams.

He scowls at me and I know he wants to fight with Bridget

but is holding back for my sake only. It's not in his nature to handle someone being so aggressive toward him without snapping.

"I'm going to take a shower," he growls.

She glares at him. "Don't slip on the soap and break your neck, you asshole, I couldn't handle it." He narrows his eyes at her and comes over and runs his hand down the length of my spine and gently kisses me on the lips. It's a power play, he's showing her who's the boss. He's lucky she doesn't kill him on the spot; at this point I wouldn't put it past her. She glances around the living room and notices the suitcase.

"Why do you have a suitcase out?" Oh God, not now Bridget. Why is she so good at playing the bitch? My eyes drop to the ground, this is not the way to tell her.

"Natasha's moving to LA with me." My eyes snap up to him and he raises an eyebrow in defiance. I can't believe he just said that. *Bloody bastard.*

"What?" she screams, "Have you lost the plot, Natasha? Over my dead body are you moving anywhere with this asshole."

Joshua glares at her. "That could be arranged, Bridget. Don't tempt me."

"Is that a threat, Stanton? Because I swear to God it will be go time if it is." Jeez this is getting out of control.

"Bridget, honey, calm down. Joshua, get in the shower. Now!" I throw him a dirty look and he frowns at me as if not understanding what he has done wrong. He storms towards the bathroom and she pulls me into an embrace.

"Natasha, please...don't put up with this...he's frigging brain-washed you or something. Let's leave now. You can stay at my house."

"Bridget, Bridget, Bridget," I sigh as I hug her back. How do

I get around this? "Bridget, I believe him and if that makes me an idiot so be it. But I can't go against my gut instinct." Bridget pulls back and frowns at me.

"You know you have always had a dodgy digestive tract." I laugh out loud.

"Can you trust me, please Didge?"

She scowls at me. "What would you say if this was Jeremy in that photo? How would you be acting?"

I give her a sad smile. "Exactly like you are, thank you for being a great friend." She nods and flops on the lounge chair and blows out a deep breath.

"Fine but if he thinks he's having any of this McDonald's he can fuck off." I laugh again. I love Bridget. She has such an articulate way with words.

"I fucking adore you, precious," he whispers as he withdraws from my body and rolls onto the mattress next to me. His open lips linger on mine. I lay panting, still trying to catch my breath. Honestly, he couldn't get any hotter. Sex between us is incredible. The sheen of perspiration thickly covers us, and I can still feel his heart beating heavily against my body. I smile against his neck. He hasn't said that to me for a while and I have to say I've missed hearing it.

"What's so amusing?" he smirks.

"You are." I smile.

He frowns. "Why am I amusing?" I bend up and kiss him with an open mouth, my lips holding onto him. "Of all the things you say to me, that means the most."

He frowns. "The most, of all the things I say to you? I fucking adore you means the most?" I smile and bend and kiss his shoulder and rub my cheek on his chest.

"It sounds crazy I know, but it was my olive branch. When we first started hooking up you always said it to me. It gave me hope that somewhere deep inside on some level, you still loved me." My eyes tear up.

"Baby," he whispers as he kisses my forehead. "How could you ever think anything else? I will always love you. I've loved you since I was a nineteen year old boy. When I saw you at the wedding I started freaking out because I knew instantly that I wasn't strong enough to stay away from you." I get a really large lump in my throat and my eyes tear up again.

"Josh, you nearly broke us. How could you throw me away so easily?" He closes his eyes as if in pain.

"Presh, I love you. Of course I wanted to put your needs before mine. I saw you with those little girls on the weekend and I know you will be a great mother. I couldn't take that from you. You did the same for me, remember, when you were seventeen." I roll onto my back and tears run into my ears.

"Josh, I put myself through self–inflicted torture. You have no idea the amount of remorse and guilt I felt. It nearly killed me, and I wouldn't wish it on my worst enemy." He lies silent as he stares at the ceiling.

"Do you want to know what I did after I kicked that girl out of my car around the corner the other night?" I nod and roll onto my side to face him.

"I ran on the treadmill for six hours, had a fight with Cameron and crashed my car."

I frown. "Why in the hell did you have a fight with Cameron?"

"Because he told me I was a gutless prick and deep down I knew he was right and then he told me you were too good for me anyway. I just snapped. I couldn't help myself. We got into an argument and he told me to marry a stripper, seeing that's all I deserve. I disgust myself." He puts the back of his forearm over his eyes. I put my hands over my face.

"Josh," I whisper. "Have you seen him since?"

"Yeah, we made up late last night, but the guilt I felt knowing you would be heartbroken this morning had me going insane and, he's right, I don't deserve you. Everything he said was completely true." He goes silent. "Tash, please don't let me mess this up. I can't explain it, but it fucks with my head big time knowing I depend on one person so much for my happiness."

I smile a sad smile. "I feel it too, Josh, and you're right, I depend on you for my happiness. So, man up and make me happy, dickhead." He growls and rolls me onto my back as he holds my hands above my head.

"You just got yourself a ticket," he smiles into my neck. I giggle. "To where?" I ask too sweetly.

"Pound town," he smirks as he bites me hard.

CHAPTER 25

Natasha

CABIN CREW CROSS CHECK. We are seated in Josh's private plane bound for LAX Airport and I have to say I'm pretty damn nervous. Cameron and Adrian have come along for the ride, Cameron to check out the hospital and living arrangements and Adrian to catch up with his boyfriend. After not seeing him for eleven weeks he jumped at the chance to go home for a week. They are sitting together three seats behind us. Max and Ben and, what's his name, Adrian's bodyguard, are seated at the back together already playing cards, obviously used to extensive travel. To think it's only been nine weeks since I started seeing Josh again and already, I can't imagine my life without him. I blow out a breath and close my eyes. I hate flying. I've watched way too many episodes of Air Crash Investigation to sit back and enjoy the ride, who knows what the hell is going on in that damn cockpit? Half the time I don't think the pilots do.

One thing I do know for sure is that they don't tell the passengers anything is wrong until they have approximately five seconds to live.

I frown at Josh. "Who is this pilot again?" I ask.

He smiles and shakes his head as he closes his eyes and leans his head back on the rest.

"Will you chill? Do you think I would let a pilot who can't fly, fly the freaking plane?"

I frown as I take his hand for comfort. "Did you check his references?"

Josh opens his eyes and frowns at me. "Is that a joke?"

"Josh, this is serious. We have precious cargo on board you know. Namely me." I bat my eyelids to accentuate the point.

He gives me a swoon-worthy smile. "Very precious cargo," he repeats as he leans in and kisses me gently on the lips. "Why don't you read a book? I have work I have to get done and then we can have sex and a sleep later?"

I frown at him and my eyes shoot around the cabin. "Sex in here, with everyone on the plane?" I gasp. He mischievously smiles and nods as he does wide eyes at me. I lean in to whisper, "I know you're an exhibitionist but there is no way in hell I am having sex on this plane." He smirks. "Handbrake," he whispers as he does wide eyes at me. Oh, I'm shocked.

"Did you just call me a handbrake?" I ask.

He smiles and nods. "Totally" The plane speeds down the runway and I brace myself for take-off. Joshua senses I am scared and puts his arm around me for comfort. I always feel so safe when he's around. It's like I'm in a safe bubble when I'm with him and I know it's a false sense of security, the last week has shown me that. My mind wanders back over the last few weeks. The strip club when I saw him with the blonde stripper.

I hated that night. And then seeing his tattoo at the fight, this brings a smile to my face. What about when he told me he fucking adored me the first time? I swoon at the memory. And to think I am on my way to LA with him to pick out a house for us to start a future in together. Could he be more perfect? Hmm, unfortunately, yes he could. The horrible memory of TC enters my head. The amount of sex he has had with other women is definitely a fly in the ointment. The stripper he was kissing the other night. I close my eyes and rub my forehead in frustration. Is Bridget right? Is he really just covering his ass with an elaborate story? Is he the world's biggest player? Have I turned into one of those pathetic girlfriends that make excuses for my philandering boyfriend?

My eyes roam back over to him in the seat next to me and I melt again, his beauty arrests me. Never have I seen such an attractive male and he doesn't even try to be, that's what is so sexy about him. That and his sexual confidence. I suppose I can't begrudge his sexual history because it has made him an incredible lover and... I blow out a breath as I try to articulate my thoughts. If he still wants me after all that he has been exposed to, that's saying something surely. Isn't it? I wonder if sex with another man would be as good. I smile and bite my bottom lip. I'm naughty. I can't even imagine what it would be like.

"Why don't you take your top off?" he whispers.

My mouth drops open. "Joshua, behave." I smirk as I lean into him and kiss his beautiful lips.

"Frigid," he whispers as he pulls back and winks at me.

Frigid, I am not frigid.

"Joshua, so help me, if you don't shut up and look pretty for the rest of this flight, you are going to cop it."

"What about in the bathroom? Can we have sex in the bathroom?" he smiles.

I frown at him. "No, definitely not. In your bed tonight when we get home, if you are lucky." He smiles and leans back in to me and grabs either side of my face as he tenderly takes control of my mouth with his tongue. I feel that familiar pulse between my legs as he kisses me deeply. Hmm ok, this is going to be a long flight.

Exactly fourteen hours later I wake as I feel Joshua stand and fuss around in the overhead luggage hold.

"What are you doing?" My half-asleep voice sounds husky as I speak.

"Just getting changed, Presh. Go back to sleep." I nod and snuggle back into my pillow and blanket and then it dawns on me, why does he have to get changed? Did he spill a drink on himself or something? I open my sleepy eyes to see him in the aisle in just underpants as he unzips a suit bag. What in the hell is he doing?

"What are you doing?" I frown as I ask again.

He leans over the aisle and give me a kiss. "I'm in my underwear, feel free to molest me."

"Josh, get your mind out of the gutter. I mean, why are you putting a suit on?" He smiles a sad smile.

"I can't...I mean I always wear suits in public here, baby." I frown.

"Huh, why?"

He shrugs his shoulders. "I just do, you will get used to it." How strange. I mean the man rocks a suit but to put one on to land at an airport...that's just crazy talk. Ben walks up the aisle to us.

"Joshua, what are the arrangements?"

Josh bites his bottom lip and glances at me. "Natasha will go with Adrian, you and Max in the first car and Cam and I will travel with Jim in the second."

Ben frowns. "I think I should stay with you."

"No, I want you with Tash. We will be one minute behind you, it will be fine." What are they talking about?

"How come I can't come with you?" I ask.

Joshua grabs my hand and squeezes it. "Because we can't be photographed together until we tell your parents." I slump down in my seat like a naughty child.

"Oh, right. Who would be at the airport at this time anyway?" He smiles and nods and for the first time since we have been together, I see an emotion in his eyes I haven't seen before...pity.

Adrian grabs my hand as we walk across the tarmac with Ben in front and Max behind us. I turn and look at the plane.

"Isn't Josh coming?" I ask.

Adrian lifts my hand up and kisses the back of it. "He will be out in a few minutes, Tash. Just don't act like you know him if you see him." Huh, why in the hell not? As we walk out of the airport through customs and towards the glass screen, I nearly stop dead in my tracks. There must be fifty photographers lined up against the glass, all waiting. I hesitate and Adrian jerks me forward.

"Act normal or they will know." Ok, what in the hell is he talking about now? Have I missed part of the conversation? I nod and continue forward to the black Audi wagon parked outside. Adrian ushers me to the car and opens the door for me to climb in, hmm, smell the leather. This car is new; it has that new car smell. I scramble over the seat and look out of the dark tinted windows toward the airport hoping to catch sight of my honey. Adrian and the boys are putting all the luggage in the trunk and I sit in silence trying to sum up the situation. Is Josh really this protected in America that I can't even be seen with him? This is ludicrous. Does he think I'm going to live in a cupboard hidden from the world? We are so telling my parents when we get home. Adrian jumps in and grabs my hand again.

"Drive," he orders the driver without saying hello. *How rude.* The driver pulls out into the traffic, but it is backed up and we are standing still, and then I see it. My heart drops. A media frenzy, where photographers are running backward to try and get the shot. Joshua is walking through the airport and every one of the photographers is chasing him and screaming out his name. I sit still, frozen on the spot, as I stare out the window in horror. This is why he got changed. He knew that they would be here, waiting for him. I am brought back to the present by Adrian squeezing my hand again and I look at him bewildered.

"Is this normal?" I frown at Adrian.

He smiles and nods. "Unfortunately, yes. Now we find out what you are made of, Tash girl." I frown as his words sink in.

"I hope you have a strong stomach," he whispers as he puts his arm around me. "You're going to need it. Joshua Stanton's world can be pretty harsh."

The luxury car maneuvers between the busy traffic, but my mind is far from sightseeing. I am stuck with the 'see what I am made of' comment from Adrian. What did he mean by that? Does he think I am not going to last in Joshua's world? I put my head back onto the headrest and close my eyes. What am I made of? And what of the 'Joshua's Stanton's world can be pretty harsh' comment? What the hell does that mean? Does he mean the other women in Joshua's life are going to make my life a living hell? God, I'm so out of my depth here. Am I really considering giving up my safe little haven to move to...whatever the hell I am moving into?

My mind then moves to Josh, beautiful Josh, and I smile. He's so worth the fight, any fight. You know what? I would move to the moon to be with him. So, if someone wants to make my life hell... then bring it on bitches, I'll be waiting. I just have to promise myself that I won't let anyone put it over me. Stay true to myself. Yes, that's the only way I have any chance of surviving LA, LA Land and its Botox beauties. I glance down at my faded jeans and slouchy off–one–shoulder black T-shirt. Is this even acceptable in Josh's world? I'm the world's biggest dag. I make a mental note to get my shit together and buy some new clothes- funky ones that kick ass. Hmm, yes, good plan. Adrian smiles and grabs my hand again. "You're quiet," he smirks.

"I suppose," I answer. "This is all very new to me, Adrian. I'm feeling out of my depth." He smiles a sympathetic smile and nods. "Will you promise me something, Adrian?"

He nods. "Anything"

"If I am put into a situation where you think I will be with someone who I can't trust, will you tell me?"

He smiles an honest smile, "Of course, Tash."

I nod, feeling better. "What will you say?" I ask.

He frowns. "What will I say?"

I nod and smile. "Yes, code for snake."

He laughs out loud. "You want to have a secret code for someone you can't trust?"

I smile and pick up his hand and kiss the back of it. "Exact- ly." I narrow my eyes as I sum up my diabolical plan. "So the word for snake is?" I ask.

He smiles again. "Cinderella" He giggles.

I frown. "Cinderella, that's a pretty lame code word. I was thinking Mole Patrol or Booby Trap." He bursts out laughing.

"If I say the word Booby Trap, I'm pretty sure Joshua will catch onto our plan."

I nod. "Oh right, good thinking. But why Cinderella?" I ask.

"That's what Ben and I used to call you before we met you," he smirks. My mouth drops open.

"Why would you call me Cinderella?" I ask.

"Because Joshua was besotted with you and we used to tease him." I frown as I sum up his words, hmm, I like that piece of information. My confidence gets a much-needed boost and for the first time since leaving the airport I feel a little excited about seeing Josh's house. We enter a road with beautiful trees and get to what looks like a guard station. The driver slows down and the gates are buzzed open and we drive through.

"What was that?" I ask.

"This is a gated community, otherwise Joshua would be hounded night and day by photographers." I nod again, feeling stupid. The car turns a few corners, and the houses are all amazing. We slow and pull into a driveway with massive sandstone gates, the driver punches in a code and the gates slowly open. Shit. This can't be his house, surely? It looks like something out of a magazine only a thousand times better. There is a massive circular driveway that joins onto a huge, and I mean huge, dark charcoal rendered space–age palace. Fuck. The gardens are impeccable and have beautiful lights shining up into all of the trees. There is a huge water fountain in what looks like a trop- ical heaven. Jeez, this is opulence at its best. There are a few cars parked in the parking bays to the left and Ben looks around at Adrian and raises an eyebrow.

"We had better wait in the car until Joshua gets here."

Adrian nods. "Good idea" Huh, whose cars are they? And why do we have to wait here?

"I would like to go in please," I announce.

"No, we will wait for Joshua," Ben snaps and I frown at Adrian.

"Is Cinderella inside?" I whisper. Adrian winks and nods. Right, that's it. I barge the car door open and start marching up the stairs towards the front door. Adrian bungles out of the car behind me.

"Natasha, stop now." This only infuriates me more. What, is the house frigging full of Penthouse bunnies or something? I can hear music and laughter coming from the house as I get close to the huge metal double doors.

Adrian catches up with me. "Tash, I'm not playing Cinderella anymore if you are going to act crazy every time I say it and trust me you will hear it a lot." I scowl as I open the door and march in. I stare open mouthed at my surroundings. There is a massive foyer with a beautiful pendant light lighting up the area. The floors are all dark polished concrete and the walls all stark white with massive abstract art adorning them. The place is so modern it looks industrial almost.

A red–headed lady in her fifties comes around the corner and gives us a loving smile.

"There's my boy," she laughs in a German accent. She pulls Adrian into an embrace and gives him a cuddle, which he returns. "Where is my other boy?" she asks as she looks out the front door for Joshua.

"This is Brigetta, Joshua's housekeeper. He is on his way. Brigetta, this is Natasha." I smile as I shake her hand. Her eyes shoot to Adrian, he smiles and nods.

"Speak to me, child." She smiles.

"Um, hello, nice to meet you," I stammer. She laughs and claps her hands together and holds them under her chin as if praying.

"Australian, so you're the beloved Natasha." She pulls me into a cuddle. Yep, I like her already. Anyone who calls me beloved Natasha is in the good books. A man's voice echoes from the room next door.

"Brigetta, where's my drink? I'm not a fucking camel." Adrian rolls his eyes and Brigetta shakes her head. I frown.

"Who is that?" I snap.

Adrian gives me a sympathetic smile. "Carson," he says deadpan. "He's Josh's best friend."

I narrow my eyes. "You're his best friend, Adrian." He smiles and grabs my hand.

The voice echoes again. "Brigetta, is this a fucking joke?" Brigetta goes to walk off but I grab her by the elbow.

"Why don't you two wait here?" Adrian frowns, not understanding my meaning. I storm into the next room. Oh shit, this is worse than I imagined. There are five men in the lounge room all sitting on the biggest leather lounge I have ever seen. They are all drinking and have a tray of what looks like frigging cocaine on the coffee table. Is this for real? Adrian walks in behind me and the boys notice him and all start yelling.

"Murphy, you're home. Where's Stan? We thought we would host a little welcome home party. Brigetta, drinks...fuck." Oh my God, he did not just yell at her to get him a drink. I cross my arms in front of me.

"This is Natasha," Adrian says. They all ignore me and go back to their conversation. Ok, I have had enough of this shit. I am fuming. Who are these losers? I walk over to the stereo and turn the music off and they all look up to see what happened.

Carson speaks first. "Brigetta, you speaka de English? I want a drink."

I glare at him. "And I want you to treat Joshua's staff with some respect. Please get your own drinks."

Adrian grabs my arm from behind and I snatch it away. "Don't," I snap. Carson looks up at me.

"Who the hell are you?" I cross my arms.

"Who the hell are you?" I snap.

He narrows his eyes at me. "I'm Joshua's best friend and I don't take orders from bimbos. So, fuck off."

I smile a sarcastic smile and raise my eyebrows.

"Did you just tell me to fuck off?" I asked way too sweetly.

Adrian steps in. "Carson, this is Natasha...you know Natasha, Natasha." He widens his eyes.

Carson stands up. "I don't care if she's the fucking queen of England. I don't take orders from anyone. And there is no way in hell I'm listening to her."

I smirk. "We'll see, asshole," I snap. Brigetta puts her hands over her eyes and leaves the room as Joshua comes in the front door. He looks around the room and quickly sums up the situation. The animosity in the air is stifling. He puts his arm around my shoulders and kisses my temple as he pulls me into him. The boys all jump up and run to Joshua to shake his hand.

"Stan the man...you're back." Oh, get off it, you losers, so fake.

"Boys, this is Natasha, my girlfriend."

Horror dawns on their faces and you could hear a pin drop. I smile at the boys. "Nice to meet you, now get the fuck out," I snap.

Joshua coughs in shock. "Natasha," he gasps.

"They go or I do Josh. There is no way in hell I am staying

here with these drug-fucked assholes." His shocked eyes shoot to Adrian.

"What's going on?" he asks him?

"Your mate Carson just told me to fuck off, so you can stay here with him and I can stay at Adrian's or they can leave and I will stay, have it your way," I snap.

He frowns at Carson. "Is that correct?" he asks.

Carson glares at me. "I don't take orders from chicks, you know that. And I am not going anywhere, she can leave."

Oh God, I hate this man with a passion. Joshua looks at him deadpan and runs his tongue over his top front teeth. He's annoying him too. Good.

"Natasha is not going anywhere. In fact, she's moving to America and in with me, so you will show her respect in her own home. Go home. I will call you all tomorrow." Joshua then walks over to the staircase and starts to go up to his bedroom. "Ben, can you show the boys out?" he calls from the stairs.

I stand still on the spot and cop the full wrath of Carson's evil glare.

"I give you two weeks. He won't put up with your shit," he snaps.

I smile a little too sweetly. "Such a pleasure to meet you, boys, pity you had to leave so soon." I think Bridget's bitchiness is contagious. I head into the other room to find Brigetta and locate her in the kitchen.

She grabs me in an embrace. "Natasha, Natasha," she whispers. I giggle as I return her cuddle.

"Brigetta, don't put up with their shit. Joshua isn't like that. He won't let them speak to you like that." She nods nervously.

Adrian comes into the kitchen and picks me up and spins me around. "You're a tough little thing, aren't you?" he smiles.

I roll my eyes. "Maybe I'm stupid. I think I just made hating me all that much fun."

He nods. "Baby, all of LA is going to hate you. You have just nabbed yourself one of the world's most eligible bachelors. They don't know your history with Josh, and they will try to test you but tonight you passed with flying colors."

He smiles as he rubs my shoulders and gives me a wink. "Mission accomplished."

CHAPTER 26

Natasha

CAMERON WALKS through the front door carrying the bags. "What the heck just happened? Carson is fuming."

"Tash just told him to get the hell out," Adrian smiles.

Cameron's eyes drop to me in mortification. "Fuck. What did Josh say?"

I shrug my shoulders. "Nothing really." Actually, that is strange, where is he anyway? I walk out into the lounge room and head toward the huge staircase that splits in two and turns into two separate staircases from the landing. My eyes stare at wonder at the opulent room. It's so modern, no wonder he didn't like the last house. It looks like a museum compared to this swanky pad. I gingerly walk up the stairs and look left down the massive opulent hallway. It's so wide that there are beautiful Balinese benches along the walls outside each bedroom with beautiful hanging pendant lights above them. It has a real resort feel, although it doesn't feel like a vacation at the moment. The light at the end of the hall is on and I hear drawers slamming shut inside. That must be Joshua's bedroom. I walk in to find him decked out in training gear and sitting on his bed putting his running shoes on. I stand at the door and watch him. He's angry. I can tell by his body language. His eyes lift to mine and without showing me any emotion they drop back down to tying his shoes. He can't be angry at me... surely? I walk over and put my hand on his shoulder, and he shrugs it off.

Joshua

Just fucking go back downstairs before I tell you to fuck off, Natasha. I blow out a breath and try to calm myself. If she thinks for one minute, I'm putting up with her shit she's going to be sadly mistaken. How dare she kick my friends out of my fucking house... if anyone is going. "Are you mad at me, Josh?" she asks as she runs her hand up my arm. I quickly shrug it off.

I stare up at her. "Is that a joke? I walk into my house to hear you tell my friends to get the hell out. Use your imagination, Natasha. I'm fucking thrilled with you."

She looks at me as if shocked. "But you said downstairs that this was my house, too."

I frown at her. "It is your house and that's why I backed you up. But the whole throwing down the gauntlet, I stay if they go shit. What in the hell was that? If the first time I met Bridget and Abbie I told them to get the fuck out of your house what would you say?"

Her face drops. "Carson was rude to Brigetta, Josh. I had to stand up to him."

I shake my head as I stand up. "Carson is rude to most

people, Natasha, and it is my place to pull him up—not yours," I snap.

"He told me to fuck off, Josh. Please don't tell me you condone that."

"He thought you were a bimbo I just picked up. He had no idea you were important. He would never have spoken to you like that if he did."

She glares at me. "Oh right, how stupid of me. I keep forgetting that you constantly pick up bimbos. You fucking sleazebag!" She storms through to my bathroom and slams the door. I am not taking this shit for one more minute. I storm downstairs and through to my gym.

En route I pick up my phone to text Carson.

Misunderstanding tonight, mate.
I will call you tomorrow.

I blow out a breath. How in the hell do I explain this situation? What a fucking bitch. Who in the hell does she think she is, fucking sleazebag? She has no idea. A text comes back from Carson.

What time is your operation tomorrow?

Huh, what in the hell is he talking about?

What operation?

A reply immediately bounces back.

The one to get the thumb print on your forehead surgically removed.

401

Fuck. That's it. I'm fuming. I throw my phone onto the lounge with such force it bounces back onto the floor and I storm to my gym.

I set the pace on high and start to run for my life. If I stay on here long enough, I might just calm down enough to be able to go to bed. What I really feel like doing is ringing the boys to come back and pick me up and hitting the clubs where the women don't speak or call me a fucking sleazebag, or tell my friends to get the fuck out. But I know I will regret it in the morning. I always do. I've worked too damn hard to get her back here to fuck it up now. She's got me between a rock and a hard place, and she damn well knows it. I'll stay on this treadmill all night if I have to, anything is better than getting into bed with that raving bitch.

Two hours later, I am exhausted and dripping wet as I leave my gym and head out to the pool. I strip off and dive in and swim a couple of laps. It's good to be home, I've missed my house. I love this pool. It's a twenty meter lap infinity pool at one end and the other end has a beach area for kids and a swim-up bar. The overhead trees are all lit up with fairy lights and there are ground spotlights scattered everywhere in the garden. It's huge, it took them eight months to complete but I love the whole resort feel going on, and it's great for entertaining. I purse my lips, hmm, there's a question. Will I ever be entertaining again? I knew my life would be different when I moved back with her, but I didn't expect the change to be rammed down my throat. I trudge up the stairs from the pool and grab a towel out of the cupboard and wrap it around my waist. I head to my inside bar to pour myself a Cointreau and ice. I open a packet of darts and take the bottle and the cigarettes back out to the deck chairs near the pool. I need to clear my head.

I am on my second glass when I am asked from behind. "What are we drinking?" I put my head up and see

Natasha sinking into the deck chair next to me with an empty glass full of ice. She probably wants to grill me about smoking now too. She holds her glass out to me and I give her a small smile and fill it.

"Cointreau," I reply.

She nods as she takes a sip. "I like it with coke—do we have any?"

I frown. "You like Cointreau?" I ask, quite shocked.

She smiles and rolls her eyes. "Yes, but with coke." I raise my eyebrows.

"I think there is some in the pool bar fridge," I reply. She rises from her seat and I watch her walk around the pool and down the steps into the pool bar. She fills her glass, puts some ice in her cup and walks back around to sit in the deck chair next to me. I look at her as I bite my bottom lip.

"Nice place, Josh, I like it." I smile, still unsure what to say and nod. "I'm sorry about before, you're right I shouldn't have told your friends to leave. They just caught me off guard, that's all. I won't do it again." I take a sip of my drink as I look straight ahead. I know I should tell her it's alright, but I can't. It's as far from alright as you can get.

"Tash, I have been single all of my life," I reply.

"I know, baby, I forget that sometimes. But I won't take shit from your friends and you need to talk to them as well."

"I told you I would but if you could just hold that temper down a bit. It would be very handy." I smirk at her as I take another sip. She picks up my packet of cigarettes from the table. Oh God, here it comes. Another lecture. To my utter amazement she opens the packet and takes one out and lights it. What the fuck, she smokes. I sit still in amazement as she sits back in her chair and takes another drag. You could knock me over with a feather. I did not expect her to just do that.

"You smoke?" I ask.

She shrugs her shoulders. "Not really. I probably would though if I knew it wasn't trying to kill me."

I smile and nod. For the first time in a while I am seeing her in a different light.

"You?" she asks.

"Same" I nod. She smiles as she raises her glass and clinks it with mine.

"Let's not kill each other on our first day. Do you want to call a truce?" she asks.

I nod. "Yeah, I suppose." I am riveted to my chair as I watch her blow the thin stream of smoke up into the air as her eyes lock onto mine. Why in the hell is that sight so arousing? It's just so unexpected, sort of good girl goes wild thing going on here.

She picks my hand up and kisses the back of it. "You're staring," she smiles. I shake my head and smile into my glass. This woman is a total mind fuck. One minute I hate her, the next thing I want to fuck her into next week. I can't keep up.

Cameron walks out of the back doors. "Natasha Marx smoking, that's a little bit hot," he states as he walks over.

"Shut up, Cam," she smiles. "Pull up a seat."

He sits down and takes a sip of his beer. "Am I interrupting?"

I state the word, "Yes."

At the same time Natasha says, "No."

"Josh," Natasha snaps, "don't be an ass." I nod as I take

another drag of my cigarette. "What are your plans for the week Cam?" she asks.

He shrugs. "I suppose go to the hospital and try and check out where I am going to live."

She nods. "Why don't you live here with us?" she asks. What the fuck, she wants Cameron to live with us? That's a new revelation. Cameron's eyes shoot over to me in question. I already told him if Natasha came, he couldn't live with me.

"You want me to move in here?" Cameron asks her.

"Yes, why not? I think Josh and I will need someone to referee our fights, don't you think?" she smirks into her glass as she drains it. Bitch.

"Josh, what are your thoughts on this?" he asks.

"I told you I don't want Natasha waking up to three strange girls at the breakfast table." Both he and Tash laugh out loud.

"I've only ever done two at a time, idiot," he snaps. "Three is still a work in progress. I'm working up to it."

Natasha looks at me. "Have you done three at a time, Josh?" Oh shit. Don't ask these fucking questions. I look at her deadpan. "Don't ask questions you don't want to know the answer to, Presh." Cameron laughs at my answer and Natasha rolls her eyes.

Cam sits back on his deck chair. "So do tell. Natasha Marx, what is her sordid history?"

She smiles as she pours another drink. "I've only ever slept with your brother Cam, no sordid history."

Cam's mouth drops open and his eyes shoot to mine. "Fuck off," he snaps.

She nods. "True story." I bite my lip and smile. I can't believe she told him that. I've been dying to.

"You waited for Josh, for seven years?" He sits up in his chair, his eyes the size of saucers.

I nod. "Unbelievable I know." I smirk.

Cameron is in shock. "I didn't think girls like you existed."

He looks over at me in mortification. "How the fuck did you get her?" he asks as Natasha giggles. I smile again as I shrug my shoulders and shake my head.

"I'm fucking blown away. You two are like...in love...in love," Cameron whispers.

Natasha laughs again. "No, tonight we are like... in hate... in hate," she states. I choke on my drink as I laugh and so does Cameron. She stands up and lifts her top over her head and drops her shorts to reveal the skimpiest gold bikini on record. Fuck, she's hot.

"Let's go swimming. It's heated, right?" she asks as she dips her toe into the pool. She walks around to the other side of the pool and starts to walk slowly down the steps. My eyes shoot to Cameron, whose mouth is literally hanging open.

"Fucking hell, Josh, when did she get that body?" he whispers.

I smile into my glass and shake my head. "She's always had it. I told you I didn't stand a chance."

He points his thumb to her. "She looks like that, and she has never slept with anyone else but you," he repeats in shock. I nod.

"Josh, how in the hell do you get out of bed? I wouldn't let her leave the bedroom."

"Fuck off," I snap. "Keep looking at her like that and I am going to put my cigarette out on your eyeball."

"Getting out of bed is not without hardship I tell you," I add dryly.

He looks down at his beer as he shakes his head. "Fucking hell man, if you blow this with her, I swear to God I am going to kill you."

I run my hand over my face. "You and me both, now be a good roommate and run along. I have some extra testosterone I need to get rid of." He smiles and shakes his head as he rises from his chair. "Oh, and can you move your bedroom to the west wing?" I ask. He frowns at me and I raise my eyebrows. "I don't like it when she's quiet," I smile into my drink.

He smirks and nods. "Yeah sure, lucky prick."

I watch her swim through the water in silence. Her body is calling to mine on a higher level I don't understand. Sex with her isn't a want, it's a need. A need that I so desperately want. I stand and head to the main light switch and turn off the lights surrounding and inside the pool area. Bringing us into darkness and providing us with privacy. I then take my shorts off and walk around to the steps and slowly enter the water. Her eyes are locked onto mine and she slowly swims towards me. I've dreamt of having her here, like this. Alone with me and in the darkness. I feel the blood rush to my cock as it hardens at the feel of her approaching through the water. My neck gets tight and I crack it to release the pressure.

She wraps her arms around me and kisses me, her mouth open and wanting. I can't help it, my tongue takes over. We are perfectly sexually suited. It's my natural nature to dominate and take over and it's her nature to submit to me, to let me take her the way I want to. I have no control over it, I never have with her. It's why we are so good together. Where

I am hard...she is soft...and wet...and wanting...and begging to be fucked. Even when she's not saying the words, I know what she's thinking. I know what she needs. And at this moment, she wants my cock, and she wants it hard. Our kissing turns more desperate and she runs her hands down my abdomen toward my penis and I step back and lift myself up, so I am sitting on the side of the pool.

She smiles and comes between my legs. I gently cradle her head as she takes me to the hilt in her perfect mouth. Oh fuck. She sucks me so good. I look down at her as her head bobs up and down in the shadows, her hands clutching my hips and running over my stomach muscles as they flex under her suction. Jesus, I'm close already. I need some...oh shit...we need to stop because I can never last long in her mouth. She's too good, fuck...I need to come already. I pull her head back by the hair and kiss her deeply as I lower myself back into the water. I grab her legs by the ankles and bring her knees up to under my arms and I put my fingers beneath her bikini bottoms and slowly swipe them through her hot wet flesh. Her eyes close at the contact. I push into her with one finger and then two and place my hand on her behind to push her onto my fingers, giving her guidance to fuck them. She groans and starts to ride them hard, circling as she pushes down. Her eyes are dilated and she is watching my lips. I love it when she's like this...like she will die if I don't fill her up...so hungry for me and what I can give her.

The fact that I'm the only one who has seen her like this, seen her beg for me and an orgasm, is like a fire to my libido, it's almost too much to control. It blows my mind. She rolls her head to the side and I bite her neck hard. Our kisses turn frantic and she pulls back to rip her pants down and I smile into her neck. I turn us so that she is against the side of the pool and I lift her legs again and wrap them around my waist. With one hard thrust I'm in...Oh God, she feels so fucking good. My eyes close at the intimacy as my heart races out of control and my breathing catches. I can feel every beautiful muscle contract in that beautiful tight cunt.

"Josh," she whispers in a hoarse voice.

"I know, precious," I whisper. The feeling between us when we are like this is too much. Too intense. Too perfect. Unable to control it any longer I start to move into her, and she groans with pleasure.

"I need...I need it harder, baby," she whispers into my ear. Fuck. So do I, but the water is between us and I can't get any friction. I pull out and she whimpers at the loss of contact.

"Come to the hot tub, Presh. Ride me, milk me." Her eyes widen and she smiles and nods as I lead her through the water. I sit in the hot tub and she kneels over me, kissing me deeply and, if I'm correct, stalling. She's trying to calm herself, so she doesn't come on entrance. Too fucking bad! I need what's between her legs and I'm taking it now. I grab her hips and pull her down onto me with such force that she cries out at the brutal force of penetration. Our eyes are locked as I lift her and grind her back down, rubbing her clitoris onto my pubic bone. This is what I need...what I love. Our bodies are so in sync with each other I feel sometimes as if I am just here for the ride, my body on autopilot. My heart is racing, and my breathing is labored, as is hers. The driving urge to fuck takes me over and I start to move her harder against me and she groans a deep groan as she closes her eyes—she's close. I can tell by the tone depth in her voice, by the way her body is trembling. Shit I'm not going to last, she just feels too good. I feel the familiar ripple of her inner muscles and I hold her still and deep and she convulses and screams into my mouth. I will never tire of this. Every time with her just gets better. Her orgasm is my green light to let go and I start to slam her down onto me, my hands on her shoulders from behind for leverage, her knees around my shoulders. Our bodies were made to fit together. Each thrust deeper than the last, her core is still rippling around me, sucking me in. Oh yes! My eyes close and I slam one...two... three more times and I explode into a mind–blowing orgasm. We stay still...panting as we try to catch our breath. This is the part that brings me to my knees every time, the after-math. The intimate prolonged kissing and the way she looks at me, like she can see right through me. She looks at me like she loves me and is as blown away by this as I am.

"I fucking adore you, precious," I whisper into her neck as I kiss it again. She smiles her beautiful smile complete with dimples.

"That's good because I fucking love you," she whispers. I feel myself harden again and I just know it's going to be one of those nights when I can't stop.

"Saddle up, baby. We're going for a record tonight."

I wake feeling groggy. I haven't drunk recently and those drinks I had last night on an empty stomach have made me feel like shit. I need a protein shake and something to eat. Natasha is draped over me and sound asleep, obviously suffering a bout of jet lag. I watch her for a minute in silence. I have never seen such a perfect woman, infuriating but perfect. I could look at her all day. I could fuck her all day. In fact, I might just do that today. My mind wanders back to her in the hot tub last night. Shit, she's a hot fuck. The way she rides my cock sends me into overdrive, never have I been with someone where the chemistry is so raw and untamed. She blows my fucking mind, every goddamn time. I smile as I think of what I will have her doing when she wakes up. She can start by sucking my dick, hmm, I feel myself getting harder at the thought of those beautiful lips surrounding my cock. I narrow my eyes as I feel my arousal grow. Yep. That's what we are doing today. International oral sex day in the Stanton household. I stumble out of bed and throw some boxer shorts on and head downstairs to the kitchen.

"Morning, lovely," Brigetta smiles as she kisses me on the cheek as she walks past. Brigetta has become my surrogate mum since she came to work for me five years ago.

"Morning," I mumble in response.

"Where's Natasha?" she asks.

"Still sleeping," I reply.

"She's beautiful, Josh." I nod as I get my powder out of the cabinet and make my shake.

"She is," I reply.

"Tell me something, Joshua, how long have you known this girl?" I know where she is going with this. I blow out a breath and reply.

"Since I was nineteen and yes, she's the girl in my tattoo." She puts her hands together under her chin as if praying and her eyes light up like the fourth of July.

"She's the one then?" she asks nervously.

"Yes, she's the one alright," Cam casually remarks as he walks into the kitchen and kisses Brigetta on the cheek. She slaps him away.

"I asked your brother," she snaps, and her eyes shoot back to me.

I put my hands on my hips, "Yeah. She's the one, as

annoying as that is," I sigh. She jumps up and down on the spot in excitement and Cam laughs as I slump onto the breakfast chair.

"Don't look so excited," Cameron remarks as he slaps me on the back.

I frown and blow out a breath, "Being in love is fucking annoying, Cameron, you have no idea."

He does a fake cold shiver. "Yes, I can imagine, that's why I'm not planning on doing it for at least...ten years." I roll my eyes.

Ben walks into the kitchen. "Can I see you in the security room, Josh?"

I frown. "Sure." I follow him out of the room and down the corridor. "What's this about?" I ask and he looks at me uncomfortably.

"I have been running the security tapes this morning and I found something very interesting at Murphy's house."

I frown and gesture to the screen. "Run the tape." He puts it on and my stomach drops. I watch in slow motion as Adrian's boyfriend Ross drives into the driveway of Adrian's house in Adrian's car. He's not alone, he has another man with him, and it is nighttime. "What time is this?" I snap.

"Two am," he replies. I rub my forehead in frustration. Fuck, I know where this is going. We both sit in silence as the tape plays, he goes around and opens the car door for the guy and pulls him out and then he is pinning him up against the car kissing him... Adrian's fucking car...at Adrian's fucking house. I stand still with my legs wide and my arms crossed as I watch. I am fuming. That sleazy fuck.

"That's not it," Ben says, and my eyes widen.

"How many?" I ask.

He winces. "I'm up to twelve and we had only been gone

eight weeks, there is another four weeks to go through yet." Contempt drips from my every pore, never have I hated anyone like I do Ross. And unfortunately, I now have the proof of what I have known all along. I feel sick. How am I supposed to tell Adrian this shit? He deserves better. I blow out a breath and return to the living room to get my phone and I text Adrian.

Hi Murph, can you come over now?

I wait for him to reply and a text beeps.

Not really. What's up?

I text back.

Where are you?

A text beeps back.

I'm at home but I am going to Ross's soon. Can't I see you later? Is it really that urgent?

I fume again at the mention of that prick's name.

YES, this is a matter of urgency. Get here now!

I wait for his reply.

You're a pain in my ass, Stanton. See you soon.

I turn to Ben.

"Bring the car around, time to pay lover boy a visit." He nods, understanding my meaning.

"Sure thing."

I walk up the stairs with renewed purpose. He's fucked with the wrong person if he thinks I will let him do this and get away with it. I walk into my room to quickly get dressed and there she is. Lying naked in the middle of my bed smiling up at me. My God, those dimples are beautiful. I lie down on the bed next to her and gently kiss her lips as I push the hair off her forehead.

"Morning beautiful, how did you sleep?" She gives me a mussed up sexy smile.

"Fine thanks, but you know I hate waking up alone.

Where have you been?" she says as she stretches her arms. I kiss her again and smile. "Can you do me a favor?"

She smiles and nods as she runs her hand up my legs to my shorts. "Hmm, I like the sound of that," she purrs.

I wish. "No, not that, can you keep Adrian busy for an hour or so? I need to organize something for him, a surprise, and I don't want him to know. Could you do that for me, Presh?"

She frowns. "You want me to babysit Adrian?"

I smile and nod. "Exactly, thanks, baby. I will make it up to you later." I jump up and start pulling on my clothes in a hurry. I need to leave before Murph gets here. I give her a peck on the cheek and dart towards the staircase, pretending not to see her disgruntled face.

We pull up out the front of Ross's house and both sit in silence as we weigh up the situation. I slowly get out of the car and Ben follows me up the path in silence. He's going to be sorry and begging for mercy by the time I've finished with him. That's if I don't kill him first. I don't know if I have ever been so furious in my life.

Knock, knock, knock.

Ross opens the door and his face lights up.

"Joshua, nice to see you." He looks around for Adrian and I continue to glare at him. "Come in," he gestures with his hands.

My eyes flick to Ben and I murmur the words. "Guard the door."

We exchange nods and he steps back into his position. I walk in and close the door behind me. Time to pay, fucker.

Natasha

He's odd. I rub my eyes as I try to remember what he has just told me. Is it Adrian's birthday or something? I hear the sound of people talking downstairs and I get up and shower. I suppose I had better get to my job, whatever that is. Fifteen minutes later I enter the kitchen to find a very annoyed Adrian speaking to Cameron.

"Well, why would he summon me over here and then frigging take off?" Oh shit, I need to think quickly.

"Hi, Adrian." I smile and his eyes flick to me. "Hi Tash, where did your nutjob boyfriend go?"

"Um, I asked him to go and get something from the store for me." He and Cameron both frown at me.

"Joshua doesn't shop, Natasha," he snaps. Boy, he's angry. "Um, no...I ahh...I needed something specific." They both frown at me again. Oh shit, what am I going to say?

"Um, he went to get me my pill prescription for me." They both frown and look at me as if I'm crazy.

"He doesn't particularly want a baby and I told him no sex until he got my tablets for me...you know taking one for the team and all that." Oh shit, that was the lamest excuse in the history of lying. Josh is going to kill me.

Adrian shoots his eyes to Cameron and they both burst out. Cameron holds his hand up and Adrian slaps it in a high five.

"What the hell have you done to Joshua Stanton? He's like a fucking lovesick puppy." He puts on a fake Aussie accent. "No sex for you, Joshua, until you get me my pills," Adrian says to Cameron as he points his finger at him.

I roll my eyes and flick the coffee maker on. Josh is right. I'm a totally shit liar.

CHAPTER 27

Natasha

AN HOUR later I hear Joshua's deep voice echoing throughout the house. He's home. I bound up to the bedroom to change into my bikini which are still hanging on the towel rack in the bathroom before I go and find him. I am trying to tie up the top when I notice something on the bottom of the shower that wasn't there when I had a shower an hour ago. I pick it up. It's Josh's T-shirt. I hold it up to see why it is in the bottom of the shower and to my mortification it is covered in blood. What the hell. Who has he been fighting? I head downstairs to find out what in the hell is going on. I hear Adrian speaking outside on the phone to someone and Joshua and Cameron are in the kitchen deep in conversation. I sneak closer to try and eavesdrop. I hear Cameron's voice rise.

"How bad is it? Do I need to go around there? Does he need a doctor?"

I try to act casual and waltz toward the kitchen. I hear

Joshua's hushed voice as I walk closer. "Don't tell Tash, she'll go postal."

Hmm, he plans on keeping it a secret. How do I play this? Adrian comes through the back door in a huff, obviously pissed off about something, and I smile and link my arm through his as we walk into the kitchen.

I walk in and smile at Josh. "Hi baby, did you get my pills?"

I kiss him on the cheek, and he raises one eyebrow at me. "Your pills," he repeats. Silence falls on the room. I do an over accentuated nod.

"Yes, you know how I needed contraceptive pills and you went to get them so we could have sex without producing an heir." He frowns at me and I bite my lip to stifle my beaming smile. It's so fun making him squirm.

He narrows his eyes. "Um, yes I...I got them."

Cameron winks at me from behind Josh and I know he's enjoying my joke as well.

I hold out my hand. "Give them to me then." He frowns as he looks at my outstretched hand. I can see him thinking what the fuck is she talking about. I see Adrian and Cameron stifle their giggles in the background and I bite my own lip to stop the smile from splitting my face.

He frowns and then grabs me in a headlock, and I squeal out loud. "Very funny, Miss Marx," he growls, and we all laugh. "Don't even mention heirs."

I pull out of Josh's embrace and turn to Adrian. "Are you ok, honey, I overheard you being annoyed with someone?" I ask.

He shakes his head. "It seems I just got dumped."

"Dumped?" I'm shocked. Who in their right mind would break up with gorgeous Adrian? This Ross must really be a dick.

"Yeah, I was going to break up with him anyway, it seems he beat me to it."

My eyes flick to Joshua and I catch him make eye contact with Ben. I bet any money Josh had a fight with Adrian's boyfriend today. *What is going on here?* Everyone falls silent as they wait for Adrian to say something. My experience tells me he needs to be distracted.

"I'm going shopping, want to come too?" His eyes flick to Josh for approval.

"Don't look at him, look at me. I asked you if you will take me shopping," I murmur.

He smiles and shrugs. "What do you want to buy?"

I shrug. "Don't know, maybe lingerie or something. I thought I would give Rodeo Drive a run for its money."

Josh and Cam both smile. They know exactly what I am doing. "Go, Murph." Josh pats him on the back and then looks at me. "Show him how hot lingerie is, on the mannequin of course." He does wide eyes at me.

Adrian frowns. "Eeww, are you that stupid you think I would want to look at your girlfriend in lingerie?"

Josh shrugs. "You're only human."

"Tash," he whispers in my ear from behind. "I need to show you something." I smile into my teacup, knowing exactly what he wants to show me.

"In a minute," I whisper back.

"Now," he growls into my ear, sending goose bumps scattering down my arms. He pulls me out of my chair by the hand. We have just eaten a beautiful three course dinner and I am quite exhausted from shopping with Adrian all day. I have acquired some very naughty little outfits and Adrian has vented all day about hating men. Of course, I have made him come and stay with us, who knows what a scorned boyfriend could do? It seems I was right. Joshua told me the whole sordid story this afternoon. Adrian's boyfriend is totally a dick. Josh grabs my hand as Adrian and Cam grab their beers and head out to the pool.

"I want to give you a tour of the house." Josh smiles. Oh, he really did want to show me something, that's unexpected. We walk through the kitchen and he opens a door and there is a staircase down a corridor. We go down two flights and Joshua flicks a light switch. Shit, a massive wine cellar is lit up like a Christmas tree. He gestures his hand around the room. "Wine cellar," he announces, and I smile. It seems Joshua is proud of his wine cellar.

I nod. "Very impressive" He kisses me quickly on the lips and heads back up the stairs. We head down the corridor to the left of the kitchen and walk past the dining room and the lounge room. This house really is stunning. Joshua's decorating style is a little sterile, but the house looks too beautiful to be real. The high ceilings combined with the polished concrete and the amazing light fixtures give the house a luxury feel.

"It looks like a resort, Josh," I remark.

"That's the look I have gone for." He winks at me. He opens a door on the left, "Games room." A massive pool table and bar complete with twelve bar stools are in here, complete with three big screen televisions. My eyes flick back to him as I remember our night of movie making and he smiles, knowing exactly what I am thinking of. We continue walking down the hall and he opens a door on the right. "Part...pool room," he murmurs. Why did he just correct his speech? He was going to say party room, but he corrected himself. He quickly closes the door as if he doesn't want me looking in. Hmm, mental note, I need to investigate this room tomorrow and find out why he's uncomfortable with me in it. We continue down the hall and we get to a huge glass wall. "Gym," he smiles. Ah, he's proud of this room and I mirror his smile. There is a huge flat screen on the wall and every damn machine I have ever seen. I just know I am going to end up hating this torture chamber. Now I won't even have an excuse not to get to the gym, how annoying. We continue down the hall and it occurs to me to wonder why he wants to leave this house when he is so obviously attached to it?

"Josh, why do you want to move?" I ask.

He stops dead in his tracks. "I want you to be happy, Tash, and I want you to pick the house you want to live in."

I smile and pull him close for a cuddle and I kiss him on the lips. "Josh, I just want to live with you...in your house and if that's a humpy in the damn desert then I will be happy. I don't need a new house, Josh. This house is amazing. What is it about this house that makes you think that I won't want to live here?"

He frowns as he considers my question. "It's not that you won't want to live here, Tash...it's me. I have been single a very long time and," he's trying to articulate his thoughts, "everybody in LA knows this house as a party house. I would like to live in something that...I don't know. You and I are the only ones that see... certain parts of the house."

I give him a sad smile. "You want to move so I'm the only one that has seen your bedroom." He bites his lip, and his eyes drop to the floor. I hit the nail on the head; he has too many memories here. Memories of other women. I pull him into an embrace.

"Josh, I'm not afraid of your past. It can't hurt me unless you let it. I want to stay in this house for a while. At least until...I don't know...down the track when Cam moves out and then if we find an amazing house we can move then. I have enough to worry about moving here than making you sell your beloved house."

He smiles and nods. "I wasn't going to sell it. I was going to give it to Cam."

My mouth drops open. "You are going to give a house worth... what?"

"Twenty mil," he cuts in.

My eyes bulge from their sockets. "Twenty million. This house is worth twenty frigging million dollars?" He nods and smiles. "And you are going to give it to Cam?"

He shrugs his shoulders. "Yeah, why not, unless you want to keep it for guests and stuff." This man has lost touch with reality. I shake my head as he continues pulling me up the hall to the end door and he opens it. "Garage," he smirks. My mouth drops open, holy fuck. This room is like a parking lot of a dealership. A massive hall with two rows of sports cars that are all black or white. I frown at him.

"I collect cars," he smiles.

"No shit, Sherlock," I whisper wide eyed. He pulls me down the huge walkway through the center of the cars and my jaw is on the ground. Ok, I am getting the feel of his money now. This is extravagance...extreme extravagance.

"Aston Martin," he points. "Corvette," he points again. "Lamborghini," he smiles. I stop dead in my tracks.

"You have a Lamborghini?" I smirk.

His eyes light up as he nods. "Yes," he smiles. And sure enough, a beautiful black Lamborghini comes into view.

I laugh. "And here I was thinking you were my Lamborghini," I whisper.

He smiles again and kisses me as he places something in my hand. I frown and look down and there in my hand is a silver engraved keyring with a single key on it. I hold the keyring up to inspect the inscription:

Always, Joshua X

Huh? What is that supposed to mean? I turn the keyring over and the initials:

N M S

What do the initials stand for? He kisses me.

"Welcome home, baby. This is your housewarming present." He can't be serious. "Joshua, you're giving me a Lamborghini as a housewarming present?"

He smiles and nods. "Not just any Lamborghini, this is my most prized possession apart from Jasper."

I frown again. "Who's Jasper?"

"My horse," he whispers as he does wide eyes at me.

"Oh, of course," I mutter. I cringe that I didn't remember that important piece of info.

"When I first made real money, I bought this. It's very sentimental to me. So, when you started calling me your Lamborghini..." He breaks into a full beam smile and I swoon at the sight of him. "I knew I wanted to gift it to you because it was sentimental between us," he whispers.

My eyes drop to the car. "It's beautiful, Josh, very black."

He laughs out loud, "I give you a Lamborghini and you tell me it's very black." I smile as I bite my lip and shrug my shoulders. I walk around the car. It looks like something from space. I don't even think I have seen one in real life before. My eyes drop to the gold number plates:

N M S

Oh shit, Natasha Marx. He has put my initials on it but,hang on, what does the S stand for? I frown as I look at the number plates and I break into a full smile.

"You put slut on my number plates?" I ask in mock horror. He laughs out loud again and then goes silent, so silent that I look back up at him to see what he's doing.

"The S stands for Stanton," he whispers. Did he just say that or is my overactive imagination playing tricks on me?

"Natasha Marx Stanton," I whisper. He nods and gives me a nervous smile.

"Has a nice ring to it, don't you think?" he says as he grabs my hand and kisses the back of it. His eyes searching mine. My heart started beating out of control and I think I have stopped breathing all together.

I shrug. "I would probably drop the Marx," I say as I bite my bottom lip.

He raises his eyebrows in surprise. "You would drop the Marx?" he questions.

"In an instant," I breathe as my eyes tear up. "A millisecond," I murmur.

We both stand still in silence, staring at each other. I wish I could freeze this moment in time. If I could just bottle this feeling I would. Then he is on me, kissing me like his life depends on it.

His hands are in my hair, pulling me closer to him. "Natasha...I fucking love you," he murmurs and the emotion in his voice nearly breaks my heart. This man is perfect, and he loves me. Daggy Natasha from Sydney who loves McDonald's fast food. He nearly rips my arm out of the socket as he pulls me towards the door and up the staircase. "I am taking you to bed for a very long time, Miss Marx...saddle up."

True to his word, we have hardly left our bedroom for two days. Joshua has put himself on a self–imposed sex ban. I winced this morning at breakfast when I sat down and the look of horror on Josh's face when he realized I was sore was price-less. I got the giggles, much to his annoyance, and he announced that we wouldn't be having any sex for at least two days. Yeah right, I will believe that when I see it. He has gone out to meet up with his friends for lunch and Cameron has gone to the hospital. Josh tried to get Adrian to babysit me, but I insisted that I need to get used to being at home alone if I am going to move here.

What a joke...home alone. Brigetta is in the kitchen. Max, my bodyguard, is in the backyard talking to two other security guards. A couple of gardeners are roaming about and there seems to be some activity in that room Josh didn't want me looking at the other night, painting or building or something. I head down the hall to investigate. I open the door and am relieved to see that the workers are not in here. I walk in and pull back the curtains to get some light. This room is massive. To my surprise it opens with massive bifold doors out to the pool area. Another huge bar and stereo speaker system line the walls.

Seriously, how many bars can one house have? I look around at the room and it seems...off. A huge space but only one leather lounge against the wall. This room is different to the rest of the house. What is it? I look at the floor and I realize that except for the bedrooms this is the only room that is carpeted. That's odd for a room that I imagine would be used for parties. Hmm and I can smell wet paint. Why is it being repainted? A young blond painter comes through the bifold doors from outside. He is about twenty and quite good looking. He is wearing a tank shirt and work shorts and is tall, probably six foot two and very well built. His eyes scan down my body and he looks shocked to see me. I look down at myself, oh shit, I'm in my bikini with a towel wrapped around my chest. I wasn't expecting anyone to be in here. I thought they had left for the day.

"Hello." I smile.

He smiles back. "Hello." Oh, he's English...I do love an English accent.

I look around the room. "Nearly finished the work?" I ask.

He shrugs. "Yeah, I suppose, just a patch–up job really. Not as urgent as I was told, God knows why it was a priority job." Hmm, that's interesting.

"Why was it priority?" I ask. This guy might just be dumb enough to tell me.

He shrugs. "Don't know, my boss got a call from Australia saying this room had to be remodeled in three days and he is paying my boss, like, five times the quoted price."

I nod and act uninterested. "When did your boss get the call?" He shrugs. "Don't know, last Wednesday night I think." Hmm, that's about the time Josh and I sorted our shit out and made arrangements to come here.

"So, you have nearly finished the work?" I question. He smiles and nods.

"Yeah, we just had to patch the ceiling and carpet and repaint the room." My eyes flick to the patched wet paint on the ceiling.

"What was on the ceiling?" I ask innocently.

"Don't know. It had all been removed by the time we got here, but there were some pretty massive holes where some big screws had been taken out." He points to where the screws were. "And we patched the carpet in the same spot." I nod as my mind races.

"You've done a good job on the paint." I smile.

"Yeah, all five frigging coats of it."

My eyes widen. "Five coats...why five coats?"

He frowns as if I'm stupid. "Black walls are hard to cover with white paint."

I frown again, not understanding why this room would have been painted black.

"Can I help you?" Joshua snaps as he enters the room. His eyes scan down my body in the towel and I instantly feel uncomfortable. He throws me a dirty look and I shrivel under his glare. "I'm paying you to work, not chat up my girlfriend!"

"Joshua," I stammer. My God, how embarrassing, this poor guy was just returning my questions, not chatting me up.

"Um sorry, Mr. Stanton," blond guy stammers in shock.

Joshua glares at me again.

"I will see you out," he gestures toward the door and poor blond guy walks out with his tail between his legs. I stand with my hands on my hips as I sum up the situation. So, there was something on the ceiling. I walk over to the wall and notice four large indents on the carpet in a huge square. What leaves a mark like that on carpet? And then it hits me. This is bad, really bad. The only thing I know of that leaves a mark like that is a massive bed. I walk over to the scrap pile of carpet and pick up the piece that has been cut out. A hole has been cut with two screw holes either side of it. What screws to the roof and the floor? Think, damn it, think. Oh my fuck. A pole, the kind that strippers use, and I know what's been removed from the ceiling... mirrors.

This is Joshua's fuck pad.

CHAPTER 28

Natasha

JOSHUA STORMS BACK into the room. "Why the fuck are you in a towel?" he growls. How do I explain this?

"I was walking past, and I thought that the workers had left for the day and I came in because I was nosy." He glares at me.

"Joshua, what was in this room?"

His face drops and he pulls me by the hand out of the door. "I'm hungry. We are going out for dinner. Go and get some fucking clothes on," he growls. "If you want Cameron to live with us, not to mention my fucking staff, you will goddamn wear more clothes around here."

"I asked you a question...answer it!" I repeat as I pull my hand out of his clasp.

He scratches his head in frustration. "Don't ask questions that you don't want to know the answer to, Natasha," he snaps.

"This was your fuck pad, wasn't it?"

He stills and turns to look at me. "It is in the past—it doesn't matter what this room was for. I never professed to be an angel, Tash," he says in monotone.

I glare at him and fold my arms. "Just how many girls have you slept with, Joshua?" I ask in a sarcastic voice.

He swallows and looks uncomfortable. "Don't start your shit, Natasha! I'm not going there, I've told you before," he yells.

I storm down the hall in front of him and I turn and point my finger in his face.

"You... asshole, are taking me house shopping tomorrow. There is no way in hell I'm living here." I turn and stomp off and I hear him yell after me.

"Like I said...you raving bitch. And put some fucking clothes on."

Four hours later we are on our way home from dinner, our fight long forgotten, when his phone rings in the car. He presses a button on the steering wheel to answer it.

"Stanton," he says, void of emotion.

A woman's English accent sings through the speaker. "Darling, you're back...I've missed you." Joshua immediately picks up the phone so I can't hear what is said. *Bastard.* I sit still as I watch him squirm. It's obviously Amelie on the other end of the line. She's missed him...what in the hell is that supposed to mean?

"Hi Am," he smiles. Am now, is it? Give me a break, I want to puke. His eyes flick nervously to me. "Yes, I'm back. I brought Tash home to pick out a new house...no, we have to go back for two more weeks," he replies. Hmm, so she knows about me. I frown as I sum up the situation. He isn't acting guilty—is this all in my head? He laughs out loud, "Yeah, probably," he answers. Hmm, how annoying. He's laughing and carefree with her. I'm green with envy. "No, I'm glad you rang. I was going to call you tomorrow." *I bet you were, asshole.* I sit still, nearly craning my neck as I watch him. He's happy to hear from her, in fact he's acting like he missed her.

Stop it, Natasha, you jealous psycho, you haven't even met her. I rub my eyes in frustration. He frowns as he listens to her. "Yes, and then what happened after you gave her the antibiotics?" He nods. "Yes," he answers and then listens again. "I will come down tomorrow to check it out." His eyes flick to me and I give him a deadpan look. "I will bring Natasha to meet you." He smiles, "Yeah, me too." She just told him she can't wait to see him...I just know it. "I'll see you tomorrow, Am, bye." The tone in his voice is the same tone he uses with me: gentle and cajoling and I have never heard him use it with anyone else. Ok, I can handle this two ways, either do what I want to do and scream and demand he sack her and look like a neurotic jealous girlfriend that I am or I can play it cool and pretend I am not threatened at all by an English veterinarian who has spent every weekend with my boyfriend for the last five years. Who he obviously has feelings for and she has feelings for him. I hate her already, but I pretend to know nothing. He gives me a megawatt smile and does wide eyes at me.

"Looks like we are headed to Willowvale tomorrow." I frown. "Willowvale, what's that?" I ask.

He rubs his hand up my leg. "My favorite place on this earth, my horse stud farm." He gives me a broad grin.

"On earth," I repeat. "That's a big call," I remark.

He nods. "I hope we can live there one day. That's the plan anyway." I frown. I thought he was going to move back to Australia with me one day. Is that the plan: to move me here and never take me home? Am I really going to leave Australia and my friends forever if I move here? A sinking feeling of dread starts to form in my stomach. Black brothel rooms, asshole best friends who take cocaine, horses that come with vets from hell, no more Oscar's with Abbie and Bridget, no more Sydney, no more me. I look out the window as I fall deep into thought. This move is going to be harder than I ever imagined. My eyes flick back to Joshua who is oblivious to my thoughts. He is chewing his thumbnail, his eyes on the road in front. Don't hurt me Josh, I won't be able to handle it. I am literally giving up everything in my life to be with you.

"This is it." He smiles. We are driving up a sweeping road with sandstone block fences. The driveway to Willowvale. The road is lined with massive old beautiful trees on either side. Joshua is as excited as I have seen him.

"Over there are the stables for the thoroughbreds." He points and smiles. "And this here is the stable hand quarters."

I frown. "That is the help's house?" I ask in shock.

He nods and smiles again. "Josh, they are bigger than most houses and made of sandstone."

He smiles and nods. "I know, awesome huh?" Hmm, I hate to admit it, but this place is pretty damn heavenly, green rolling hills, huge sandstone buildings and fences. Adrian's comment when we were leaving of packing my glass slippers has only heightened my nerves. He obviously thinks Amelie is a threat if he's giving me Cinderella jokes. I'm nervous, why am I so nervous? We turn the corner and my mouth drops. There on the hill is a castle...I'm not even joking... a huge sandstone house, a castle–size house. It looks like Mr. frigging Darcy's house from *Pride and Prejudice*. Holy crap, I am definitely out of my league here. My heart starts to thump in an uneven beat. We pull the car up and a man comes out and shakes Joshua's hand. He smiles and nods at me. "She's in the stables, Josh." Josh's eyes flick to me nervously and I smile innocently. Josh's first question when he pulls up is obviously where's Amelie? He grabs my hand and leads me inside, blissfully unaware of my inner turmoil. He leads me around the castle, I mean house. It's breathtaking; he's right, I do love it. He leads me up the stairs and along a wide corridor to a bedroom where he puts our cases on the end ottoman.

"This is my room, I mean our room." He gestures around the room and I nod and smile. "There are ten bedrooms in all," he continues.

"Is this the master suite?" I ask.

He frowns. "Um, no...Am...I mean Amelie has the main bedroom, you know, since she is here all the time." I nod again. He's talking too fast, too panicky. Yep, he's just as nervous having me here as I am being here. We walk back downstairs, and Josh shows me around the frigging King Henry the Eighth castle. It's a wonder it doesn't have a damn moat. My mind is everywhere but on his tour guide skills.

"Come on, we will go up to the stables." He gestures to the back of the house. I nod and follow him out the door to where he gets into a huge Range Rover utility that is waiting at the back door. I will never get used to having this kind of money; it's just so ridiculous. Who has spare new cars sitting on farms? We sit in silence as we drive on the dirt roads over another set of hills. I have never felt like such a fish out of water. Horses and I have a hate-hate relationship. I hate them and they hate me. We pull over another hill and I am shocked; my jaw literally hits the floor. Rows and rows of stables and I can see at least ten workers around, doing different things.

The car pulls up and they all come straight over to us. It's remarkable how differently Joshua treats his staff out here, as if they are all his friends. Maybe they are. I am being introduced to all of them, one by one, when I see her and my heart drops. A beautiful natural blonde comes out of one of the stables, wearing navy jodhpurs and a pink checkered shirt and riding boots. *Oh my God*, she looks like frigging Grace Kelly... I'm so screwed. And she looks good in jodhpurs. Nobody looks good in jodhpurs. If I put a pair on, I would evacuate this whole establishment, everybody would run for the hills. I can't compete with this shit. Her hands are dirty, and her hair is in a low loose bun. She has no makeup on, and her skin is flawless. Damn those English girls and their perfect skin. She is naturally stunning. Her eyes light up when she sees Joshua and she laughs out loud and runs over and cuddles him. He returns her cuddle and then seems to remember that I am here and pulls back.

"This is Natasha," he says nervously to her.

She gives me a warm smile. "Lovely to meet you, Natasha." Oh God, her accent is lovely. Another nail in my fucking coffin.

"Hello," I stammer. Witty... good one Natasha, you horse hating freak.

"I would shake your hand but I'm terribly dirty. I'm sorry." She smiles. Jeez, she's nice too. *How annoying.*

"Ok, what's the verdict?" Joshua asks. She starts talking horse jargon and they walk together deep in conversation toward the stable. I stand still on the spot, unsure if I am meant to be going with them or not.

Joshua turns to me. "This way, baby." He holds his hand out for me. I nod and give him a weak smile and follow him, he puts his arm around me and kisses my temple as we walk.

Ok, now I'm confused, he's not acting like I think he will, maybe this is all in my head. She smiles another warm smile at me, totally unaffected by my presence.

"Sit up here, Presh." He lifts me so I am sitting up on some high gates away from the horses and I give him a thankful smile. He remembered I'm scared of horses. Why in the hell didn't I do riding lessons when I was a kid? There is a horse on the ground lying down and they both kneel next to it.

"So, she has had a temperature for the last couple of days and I thought she had an infection or something so I put her on antibiotics, but then when I came to check on her through the night she was down and couldn't get up."

Joshua frowns and pats her.

"Sh, sh," he says to the horse in a calming voice. I sit detached from the situation. It is blatantly obvious how passionate Joshua is about this farm and his horses. I sit and watch them in silence for an hour deep in discussion, and seemingly innocent, and finally my legs are asleep, and I go to jump down.

Josh jumps up. "You ok, babe? Do you want me to take you back to the house?" he asks. Amelie is writing in a notebook and googling something on her iPad.

"No, it's ok. I can get someone else to take me back if you want." I smile.

He shakes his head. "No, I will take you back. I want to spend some time with you."

I smile and nod. Ok, I think this is totally in my head. He wouldn't say that in front of her if he had feelings for her.

"Am, why don't you come home, and we can come back together later?" he whispers. Hmm, I'm not sure if I like the sound of that.

She smiles. "No, thanks. I will stay here, just get someone to bring me some dinner later tonight. I will call you if there is a change."

He smiles as he stands and puts his hand on her shoulder. "Thanks." He smiles.

"Bye darling," she says. Josh bites his lip as he realizes the slip of her tongue and his eyes flick to mine. I instantly look down... don't be the jealous girlfriend...don't be the jealous girlfriend. It's really hard not to be, when I so obviously am. He grabs my hand, and we walk back to the car and head back to the house. We ride in silence.

"You're very quiet, Presh, you ok?" I nod. Don't say it...don't say it. It's like a volcano that is poisoning me, and I blurt out the words.

"Josh, why aren't you with Amelie?" He puts his hand on my leg and sighs. He knew this question was coming.

"Because I'm in love with you."

"Have you ever been with her?" I ask.

He frowns and shakes his head. "Amelie is not the kind of girl you be with, Tash. She's like you. It's all or nothing." I bite my lip and look down. Not the answer I was looking for.

"So why has it been nothing then?" I ask. He shrugs his shoulders.

"Because I have never let myself...let it go there because I was still in love with you, and it wouldn't be fair to her." I nod... fair to her...not that he's not attracted to her.

"So, if we were over you would probably be with her?"

He gives me a sad smile and squeezes my leg. "Don't do this to yourself. I am with you and I am staying with you and we are planning a future together and Am knows that. She's fine with it." Oh my God...she's fine with it.

"Does that mean that she has feelings for you?" I ask.

He shrugs. "She would if I were single," he sighs. "Can we not talk about this, please? Amelie is a dear friend who has been with me for a long time when I have been very lonely. She doesn't have a deceitful bone in her body and she will respect our relationship. I have spoken about you for years to her, and she knows what you mean to me. She wants me to be happy, Tash." I smile and nod and internally swear to myself I will never bring this up to him again. He is under her spell and in all things in Joshua's world I have been wary of.

I know I have just met my only competition.

Joshua's phone goes off at two in the morning and he jumps out of bed.

"Hi," he answers and then he listens. "I'll be right there." He hangs up. He starts to pull on his clothes. "Freya is really sick, baby, and I'm going to help Am. Go back to sleep. I might be all night."

"Ok," I whisper sleepily.

He bends down and kisses me. "Love you. Max is here in the room next door, so you are not alone," he whispers and then he is gone.

I wake with a start. I'm still alone. Joshua didn't come home. He must be still at the stables with Amelie and the horse. My stomach sinks, what have they been doing all night? Stop it, you idiot. Without trust you have nothing, the words I have preached to clients for years are coming back to haunt me with a vengeance. Why has he been gone so long? I am determined not to go to him, so I make myself some breakfast and sit on the steps in the sun with a coffee.

Three hours later, at ten o'clock, still no word from Joshua. I'm starting to become unsettled. A girl rides up on a horse and I hear her tell one of the other workers.

"They lost her. She died about half an hour ago." Oh shit, the horse died. I walk inside and find Max.

"Can you take me to the stables please?" He nods and finds the keys and drives me in silence to the stables. I wish he would talk more. It would be handy having his insight on things. He parks the car and stays outside. I walk up to the stone building and my heart is in my throat. Why hasn't he come looking for me? As I turn the corner it becomes very apparent why. Amelie is in Joshua's arms crying; she is obviously devastated. He is comforting her and talking softly into her ear as he cuddles her and kisses her temple. They look good together. There is a deep connection between them. I can feel it from here. I stand still, rooted to the spot in shock. Out of the corner of his eye Joshua sees me and jumps back from her...a guilty response if I ever saw one. My gut twists as I stand still.

"Tash...we...we lost her," he whispers.

I nod. "I know, I'm sorry. I will give you some privacy," I stammer, and I turn to walk out. "Natasha, don't go," Josh calls as he sprints out after me. I feel like I have just witnessed and interrupted something private between the two of them.

"Tash, I want you to stay. Amelie has to wait for the autopsy guys to come and I don't want her waiting alone. Just stay here with us. It won't be long." He grabs my hand and kisses the back of it. My eyes flick to Amelie and she quickly looks down at the ground and bites her bottom lip to hide her hurt at his open affection towards me. My blood runs cold and my gut instincts kick in. At this moment in time I am absolutely certain of three things.

Amelie is in love with Joshua and I am in love with Joshua. And Joshua is in love with the both of us. His past has met with his present but which one of us will he choose in the end? And when it is all over, who can make him the happiest? I'm afraid of the answer to that question because in all honesty I just don't know.

After everything we have been through, am I going to lose him anyway?

He sighs as he puts his head into the crook of my neck and kisses it. I can feel his heart beating in his chest, his body still inside mine. We are back in my bed in the afterglow of love making, having arrived back in Sydney yesterday. I'm not myself. I haven't been since meeting Amelie.

"Natasha, so help me God...what's wrong, baby?" he whispers as he lifts up onto his elbows so he can look at my face.

"Nothing, I'm fine," I breathe. He bends and tenderly kisses me again, his eyes searching mine.

"Tell me why I just made love to a completely different woman then?" I swallow the lump in my throat and look away, his piercing gaze too much for my fragile nerves.

"What do you mean, Josh?" I whisper as he kisses me again. "When we fuck...we fuck. But when we make love...I can feel it. Every cell in my body can feel how much you love me. You have never detached from me like that before. It felt like you didn't even know me." My lip starts to tremble, and tears threaten. Do we have to have this conversation when I am emotionally weak from orgasm and he is still inside me?

"Maybe I don't, Josh," I whisper as my eyes fill with tears.

He frowns. "You feel like you don't know me? What does that mean?" he whispers as he pulls out of me and rolls me on my side to face him. Tears roll down my face and I am appalled at my own insecurity. I am getting a firsthand lesson that one of the most destructive emotions in a relationship is the poison of insecurity. I am frozen with fear.

"Baby," he whispers as he pulls me into an embrace and kisses my face. "What's wrong sweetheart? I can't fix it if I don't know," he whispers.

"I know Josh," I sob, and he frowns. "I know you're in love with Amelie," I whisper.

He gives me a sad smile and nods. "It's true I do love Amelie," he whispers. I start to sob uncontrollably. *I knew it.* "But I'm not in love with Amelie. I'm in love with you. I don't want to be with Amelie, I love her like a friend. I have no sexual attraction to her whatsoever. We have common interests, Tash. We both live in a country without our families. I feel very differently about her than I do you." He cuddles me close as I listen to his words. "It's different between us, Presh, you know that. Actually, you even told me that you loved your ex boyfriends, but it was missing something because it wasn't me," he whispers. I listen, that is true.

"Do you feel like...?" How do I articulate what I want to say? "Do you feel like our relationship is holding you back from her?" I whisper. He actually has the hide to laugh. He bends and kisses my lips again.

"You're so fucking perfect, you know that, don't you? I could never be loyal to Amelie, Tash. She's not strong enough to hold me and I'm not sexually attracted to her. I would be playing up within a week and I know that—she knows that. Trust me I have slept in that house with her in the bedroom next to me for five years and never once have I wanted to go in. Whereas just the mention of your name makes me rock hard and ready to fuck. Besides," he grabs me on the ass, "I like witty brunette beautiful sluts who are gagging for it." He smiles. I punch him in the stomach, and he laughs out loud. He pushes the hair off my face and kisses me tenderly again.

"I know it's not going to be easy moving with me, Tash, but I promise you Amelie is not going to be the problem. I have even asked her to move out of the main house and into the farm next door. I knew you were uncomfortable with her there and seeing I love it so much I want you to love it, too."

I give him a sad smile. "Do you think I'm being a drama queen, Josh?" I whisper.

He gives me a broad smile and does wide eyes at me. "Totally...a raving bitch even," he whispers as his lips trail down my neck.

I smile and giggle as he bites my neck.

"Do I need to be punished Mr. Stanton?" I smile as he bites me again and comes over me. He rubs his hard length through my core.

"Fucking oath," he growls as he slams into me.

CHAPTER 29

Natasha

TODAY IS THE DAY, the day I have been dreading for seven years. We are telling our parents. Josh has flown his parents to Sydney on the false pretense of a business deal he is doing. I have been vomiting with nerves all morning and Joshua hasn't eaten in two days. We feel sick and distraught because we honestly don't know what reaction we are going to get...we could both be parentless tonight. But seeing as we leave for LA in a week the time has come. Cameron and Bridget are coming for moral support and by the sounds of it they are as nervous as us. They are having breakfast this morning together to discuss possible outcomes. I find myself pacing and shaking my hands in my bedroom while freaking out about what to wear. Joshua is dressed in a suit and leaning over the balcony rail on his elbows. He hasn't been to bed yet and it's seven am. I watch him out the window...poor love, I have never seen him so stressed. I walk out to try and comfort him. I smile and kiss him on the neck.

"Stop worrying, baby. We can do this. Just think of it as we are coming out as gay. They will be shocked at first and then they will be angry and that's when we leave and in time they will have to accept us. We are not doing anything wrong, Josh, it is legal in most countries for us to be together," I smile.

He frowns and shakes his head. "Stop talking, you're making it worse," he snaps.

"We had better get going." I smile.

He nods and stands to face me and takes my two hands in his. "Promise me one thing," he whispers and I nod. "Promise me that whatever happens we will leave your parents' house together today." I smile and nod and give him a tender kiss while cupping his face in my hands.

"I promise you we will leave together today and then we will go out for dinner to celebrate our bravery, followed by awesome hot sex." He gives me a nervous smile and nods.

"Sounds like a plan."

Walking up the steps to Mum and Dad's house is the most terrifying thing I think I have done. Joshua is as white as a ghost and the tension on Cameron's face is priceless. But this means we can finally be together in public. We walk into the lounge room, oh shit, Brock is here. Joshua and I quickly glance at each other, knowing exactly what the other is thinking.

"Come out the back, everyone," Mum calls from the kitchen in her best entertaining voice. Ok, this is it...*it's go time.* Cameron and Bridget are sitting on a stone bench and Joshua's mum and dad are sitting at the table with my mum, Brock and Dad. Holy fuck. I feel like I am going to vomit. Joshua runs both of his hands through his hair and I stand still on the spot. I give him the nod symbolizing now.

"You are probably wondering why I have brought you all here," he stammers. "I...we have something to tell you," he continues.

"Joshua, no...stop," Margaret snaps. He swallows and ignores her and continues,

"Natasha...Natasha." He looks at me and I can't stand it any longer. I stand and grab his hand.

"Joshua and I have fallen in love." The room falls silent. My eyes flick around the room to see five sets of shocked eyes staring at us.

"What do you mean?" Joshua's dad snaps.

Joshua swallows the lump in his throat. "We have been seeing each other and we have fallen for each other," he stammers.

Brock breaks the silence. "You're a fucking prick, Stanton."

My mother yells. "Brock, enough."

I need to speak quickly—everyone is just too quiet.

"We fell in love when we were seventeen and only just got back together. We couldn't stay apart any longer."

"He was with a fucking stripper just a week ago, Natasha," Brock yells. Oh shit, he did have to see that, didn't he? Joshua glares at Brock and I grab his arm signifying for him to calm down.

Joshua's dad stands. "Back up—did you say seventeen?" I frown. "How old were you then, Joshua?" he asks. Joshua bites his lip, knowing what's coming.

"How old?" he screams. Oh shit, this is getting out of control and Cameron stands up and walks around next to Joshua as if to signify support.

"Nineteen," Joshua answers.

"So, Natasha is the girl you nearly didn't go to America for?" Josh hangs his head. "And she is the girl in your goddamn tattoo?" he yells.

"Yes," Joshua sighs as he rubs both of his eyes with his hands. Margaret, Joshua's mother, bursts into tears and my mother stands and starts pacing.

"You're cousins," she screams. This is bad...worse than I thought.

I look to my dad to see his reaction and he picks up my hand. "This is wrong, baby girl...you can't do this," he whispers.

My eyes tear up. "Dad, nothing has ever felt so right. Don't say that."

Joshua gets a new bout of bravery. "Natasha is moving to LA with me," he announces.

"Over my fucking dead body," Brock screams.

Joshua glares at him. "Don't temp me, Marx," he snaps.

Brock jumps up and knocks the chair over and runs at Josh and Cameron steps in the middle. Brock punches Cameron with full force and he falls over and everybody starts screaming for them to stop it. Joshua loses control and grabs Brock off Cameron and then punches Brock in the face. Bridget and I are screaming.

"Stop it now...Brock, no."

From behind me I hear Margaret yelling. "John, John. Oh my God...John." We all collectively turn to see my father slumped in Margaret's arms and clutching his chest. Oh dear God.

"Call an ambulance," I scream. Joshua and Brock still have a hold of each other, slamming into the wall, and the table tips over as they fall into it.

"Stop it now. Call an ambulance," Joshua's dad yells. Suddenly the room spins. What's happening? I feel like I am having an out of body experience. I am in shock with no emotion. My dad is on the ground and Cameron is doing CPR frantically. My mum and Margaret are crying and holding each other. Bridget is screaming down the phone for an ambulance.

"What's the address?" she screams. "What's the address?" Even though she has lived at the house her whole childhood. Joshua is pacing with both of his hands on top of his head.

Cameron screams to Bridget. "Tell them it's a heart attack. We need defibrillators urgently." Oh dear God...please, no. I drop to my knees and pray.

"Please God, let him be ok...please God, let him be ok... please God, let him be ok."

The ambulance finally arrives, and I run out to the road to show them the way. Cameron quickly fills them in on the situation and they run him to the ambulance. They shut the doors and I can hear Cameron call from inside... "Clear"... "Clear"... Oh my God, they are trying to shock him back to life. I start to hold my head and scream "No...No... No...This isn't happening."

The ambulance driver yells to my mum.

"Royal North Shore Hospital," and they scream off. Everybody starts running to cars, my family in one and Josh's family in another. Josh comes over to me and puts his hand on my back.

"I will drive you," he whispers.

"No. You stay away from her and the hospital. You fucking caused this," Brock screams. "I swear to God I will kill you if you come anywhere near the hospital."

I look at Joshua, my eyes wide with shock.

And this is the moment...you know the one in the front of the book. When I said the next thing, I was going to do would change the course of my life, and would I still do it knowing heartbreak was imminent?

I know what I want to do. I want to go with Josh to the hospital but my family is all screaming at me to get into the car and Brock is so mad. I look again at Josh who is holding his hand out for me.

"Natasha, you promised we would leave here together," he whispers. I am crying hysterically with snot all over my face. This situation is totally out of control, totally fucked up. I hold my head, what do I do? I can't handle this. My poor dad. I shake my head at him and get into the car with my mum and brother and sister and we scream away. I look back to see Joshua alone in the middle of the street...alone...I left him alone.

It's been six weeks, six weeks since my beautiful father died. A death I caused. Blood is all over my hands.

I am in a living hell with no escape. I killed my own father, my own flesh and blood. I was in bed for a month, the pain too much to bear. I don't even remember the funeral. The doctor had me so drugged up for stress, I was a walking zombie. I have stayed with my mother since Dad's death. I don't want her to be alone because of me. I have made her lose her soulmate and in turn I have lost mine. I haven't spoken to my love, Joshua, since the day Dad died.

My life is a living hell and I have no one to blame but myself.

I wish I had died instead of my dad. It would be easier than living without him and my beautiful Josh. Crying myself to sleep every night. Dry retching myself through every day. Grief... guilt...what a horrible, lonely combination of emotions.

It is true, what they say. A broken heart really does hurt your chest. I feel like I can't breathe.

I hope I don't wake up tomorrow. I can't go on like this.

It's been eight weeks and I have finally gone back to work. Bridget, Abbie and my mother haven't left my side since that dreaded day that is burned into my memory. My boss, Henry, and Simon have visited me daily and Henry offered me my job back. I was supposed to be moving to LA and had resigned. Cameron has also visited me every day since it happened. He has just sat at my bedside while I wept...sometimes for hours, or I lay and stared at the ceiling with no words. He too is suffering at the loss of his first patient, his uncle. I refuse to talk about Joshua. My father's last words to me were, "This is wrong, baby girl, you can't do this" and so I haven't. I killed my father so I will do as he asked, even if it kills me. I have no doubt that it will. My mother has begged me again and again to go to Joshua, saying that Dad could not have borne seeing me like this. But I can't do it, even though it's killing me. It's twelve o'clock and I am about to go to lunch when the receptionist comes in.

"Excuse me, Natasha. A Margaret Stanton is here to see you." I roll my eyes. I don't even have the strength to fight. "Send her in," I whisper.

Margaret walks through the door and takes one look at me and bursts into tears.

"Natasha, my dear girl. Look at you. You're so thin." I smile and nod and gesture for her to sit. She shakes her head and continues standing. She's nervous and she has a good reason, I have absolutely no patience for this bitch anymore.

"Excuse me for intruding but I need to tell you something. Something that involves you and Joshua."

I roll my eyes. "Margaret, your boy is safe. I won't go near him again."

She tears up again. "Please don't say that. He loves you, Natasha. With all of his heart."

The nasty caustic tears start to burn as they run down my face.

"And I love him, but I will respect my father's last wish." I stare deadpan at her. I have nothing left. She puts her head into her hands.

"You and Joshua are not genetically related."

I frown. "What do you mean?" I ask.

"I had an affair and Joshua is another man's child. He doesn't know, of course." I step back from her in shock. *Oh my God.*

I drop into my seat.

"Joshua and I are not cousins," I repeat, and she nods.

Horror again.

"*JOSHUA AND I ARE NOT COUSINS!*" I scream again. She nods and starts to cry uncontrollably.

"I'm so sorry. If I had told you, my life would be in danger. But I fear Joshua's life is more in danger. You must go to him, Natasha. I have never seen him like this, he is not coping. He hasn't been to work for a month." I stand still, rooted to the spot, shock coursing through my body.

"So, you knew all along how in love we were and you kept us apart?" I scream. She cries into her hands and nods. I scratch my head and start to pace.

"You said Joshua doesn't know. Why are you telling me?" I ask.

"Because I know that it is the only thing keeping you apart. Now that your father has passed your father would know the truth, Natasha. He knows now you are not related, and he would give you his blessing." I step back in shock wide eyed as I sum up the words just spoken. I lunge forward and slap her hard across the face.

"Murderer," I scream. "You killed him with your lies... I fucking hate you. Get the hell out of my sight."

Cabin crew, cross check. I am on a flight to LA with Max. Joshua left him behind to watch over me. I stare out the window as adrenaline courses through my body. It's hard to sit still. Hold on, baby...I will be there soon. I sit back in my chair and for the first time in eight weeks I smile, and I have hope in my heart. I'm coming, my love...I'm coming.

Joshua

Katy Perry's voice rings out to her track 'Dark Horse'. I am in bed watching Tash in the movie I made of the two of us. I have had it on repeat since I got home on Friday...it's now Sunday. I have a drink in my hand and a tray on my side table. I know every ripple of her muscles. I hear every sigh that she makes and every smile, complete with her beautiful dimples. I watch the back angle as her perfect body takes mine again and again. I sit forward each time she whispers the words 'I love you' to the camera and my heart breaks just that little bit more.

I'm low...I've never been so low.

I can't seem to snap out of it. The guilt is eating me alive. I blow out a breath as I lean my head back against the headboard. She is supposed to be in this bed with me, curled around me. Starting our life together.

I have had too much...I know that. I just needed a little something to give me a lift. It's just not fucking working. I go to reach for my Cointreau and my arm doesn't move. What the fuck? I swing my legs over the side of the bed, and I fall.

Shit, what's happening?

The room starts to spin, and my body starts to convulse.

Oh fuck. What have I done? I go to call out, but my mouth doesn't open. I hear Adrian's voice scream out.

"Joshua, dear God. HELP...HELP...BEN. Jesus, what the hell are you watching? Turn off the fucking television."

"Call an ambulance... He's taken an overdose."

"Joshua, hold on, baby. It will be ok."

"NOOOOOO. Dear God, no." Panic...Fear... Darkness...Nothing!

Continue reading for a sneak peek into the next book on Natasha & Joshua's story, Stanton Unconditional...

STANTON UNCONDITIONAL
EXCERPT

AVAILABLE NOW

Adrian

"Hi Brigetta. How is he today?"

"No change, love. He still hasn't left his room. He's been locked up there since Friday. Go and drag him out."

I shake my head in disgust. He needs to snap the hell out of it, it's been weeks. I knock on the door.... knock.... knock.... knock. No answer. I open the door, expecting to be told to go away, just like he has told me every day for the last week. My eyes flick to the television. Jesus, he's watching porn. Actually, that's a good sign, maybe he's returning to some normality. I can't see him, so I look back down the hall and into his bathroom. No, nothing. My eyes are drawn to the television again as I hear the girl's voice.... Australian. I narrow my eyes at the screen. Shit, that's Natasha! He is on his back and she is on top and topless ... Oh fuck. I don't want to see this shit. *Why do they film themselves?* Then I see it: a bare foot coming from behind the bed on the floor. I frown and walk around to the other side of the bed. To my horror Joshua is lying on the floor, unconscious. My eyes scan the room and I see a tray of cocaine on his side table.

My eyes widen as I put the pieces of the puzzle together.

Oh fuck, he's taken an overdose!

"Ben! Help! Call an ambulance!" I scream. I drop to my knees beside him. "Ben!" I scream again.

Ben casually walks to the door eating an apple. "What's up?"

"Joshua has taken an overdose! Call an ambulance." Ben's eyes scan down Joshua's body. He stands still, eyes wide with shock. "Fucking move, Ben!" I yell.

He snaps out of it and runs down the hall, yelling to Brigetta. "Call 911, the stupid fuck has overdosed." I hear Brigetta scream and at the same time Joshua starts to convulse.

"Oh my God. Hold on.... Joshua, hold on." I start to panic as fear grips me, then I try to roll him onto his side.

Ben runs back into the room. "Get him on his side," he yells.

"What does it look like I'm trying to fucking do? Help me," I scream. We both work together and roll him onto his side, and he has what seems to be another small fit. "What's happening?" I yell.

Ben shakes his head, "I don't know."

I put Josh's head in my lap as I start to hear my heartbeat in my ears. What the hell do I do? "Go and find the fucking ambulance!" I scream through my tears. Ben nods and runs back out of the room. "Josh.... stay with me. Wake up. You can't die....*What the fuck were you thinking?*"

Brigetta runs into the room and drops to her knees beside him. "Joshua, my boy, it's going to be alright. You need to be strong, the ambulance is on its way." She takes his hand and holds it up to her lips and starts to pray as she wipes the hair from his forehead. "How much has he had?" she asks Ben.

He hunches his shoulders, "I didn't even know he had any drugs in the house. Carson must have left them here."

"What's taking so damn long?" I shout. Ben starts doing CPR and I hold my breath. I hear people running in the hallway outside and I realize that the whole house is in an uproar. All of the staff have come inside and are freaking out. I finally hear the ambulance sirens and I put my head in my hands and burst into tears of relief.

They are led into the room by Murray, Joshua's gardener, and the paramedics immediately start to work on him. I am pushed to the back of the room as they take over. My heart is in my chest and Brigetta and I are crying uncontrollably. We embrace and sob into each other's shoulders as Ben runs from the room and vomits in the bathroom. Within seven minutes Joshua is on a stretcher and being wheeled through the house and into the back of the ambulance.

And we are left in shock.

Natasha

'Cabin crew, crosscheck'.

I sit back in my seat and brace myself for the takeoff. Jeez, I hate this. I sort of thought I would be used to this extreme sport by now, but my stomach is in my throat. I don't know any other twenty-five-year old girls who act like a two-year-old when flying. Max, my right-hand man, is sitting next to me. I have made him sit next to the window just in case.... you know. Glass smashes on impact, so I hear. I give him a weak smile. I have grown quite fond of dear old Max in the last two months. He has been by my side during the most traumatic eight weeks of my life. Joshua left him to guard me when he went back to America. At first, I think it was to guard me from myself and then it was to guard me from Brock, my brother.

I smile as my eyes flick to him, he did that job well. Max and Brock have been hating each other for weeks. Brock blames Joshua for Dad's death and every time Brock even brings up Joshua's name, Max shuts him up with just a look. I'm having a hard time dealing with Brock myself. I blame *him* for Joshua leaving and Dad's death. If he hadn't made it so hard for us, Joshua would have come to the hospital with me on that dreaded day. He would be here with me now and we would be dealing with this mess together as it should be.

I had an affair and Joshua is another man's child.

I frown as I go over the words Margaret spoke to me just yesterday. We are not cousins. We do not share DNA. At first, I was ecstatic and hopeful and now the hard cold reality has started to sink in. Joshua is going to be devastated, because he idolizes his father. He is not biologically a Stanton. For him it might be better if we were cousins.

My heart is heavy. I wish to God that Margaret the bitch hadn't told me about her sordid previous life, but then, on the other hand, I would not be on my way to him if she hadn't. I'm so damn confused. It's like his loss is my gain and I feel guilty and torn. I shouldn't be relieved that we are not related ... but I am, in fact I'm ecstatic. I haven't slept but am displaying promising signs. I have been comfort-eating for China since that dreaded meeting in my office yesterday. I have hardly eaten a thing for two months, so this is good, this is real progress. Why have we had to sacrifice both of our beloved fathers to be together? I know my father had an undiagnosed heart condition and that he was a ticking time bomb, but I pulled the pin. I know that, we all know that. It is just not fair and so unrealistic. Talk about a beautiful, tragic love story, ours takes the cake. Loving each other for so long from afar, fighting our social restraints and conscience to be together, trying desperately to resist a deep natural desire.... it doesn't make sense. I've never heard of a couple with so many barriers, not any that have made it anyway. I blow out a breath as I pop two sleeping tablets into my mouth and take a sip of water.

"Wake me up if the plane is going down," I yawn to Max. He smirks. "Sure thing," he replies.

"Meh, actually. Don't. I would rather be asleep as I drown.... or catch on fire." I frown as the disturbing thought rolls through my head.

He pats the back of my hand. "Sleep, worrywart." I return his warm smile and nestle into position. Josh is right, I do feel safer with him around and I can totally be myself. He's seen me at my absolute worst and hasn't resigned yet which is strangely comforting. Max has even been sleeping in the guest room at Mum's while Bridget and I have been staying there. Mum wouldn't let him stay out the front in the car all night.... every night. I think that deep down she feels safer having him around as well. Brock has gone back to Afghanistan for another six-month-deployment so the house is eerily man free. He's refreshing, although he hardly ever says anything. I know he's in my corner and I trust him.

"Natasha, put your seat back up."

I frown as I wake and stretch. "What.... I slept the whole time?" Max gives me a smirk as he nods. "Oww, my legs are asleep," I groan as I seep back into consciousness. My heart starts to race as excitement courses through me. I'm going to see him for the first time in two months, my beautiful Josh. My God, I've missed him, I can't wait to hold him in my arms and kiss his beautiful lips. I know he has been suffering like me. This whole ordeal has been a living nightmare.

"How are we getting to Josh's?" I ask.

"Ben is organizing one of the drivers to pick us up. I rang him before we got on the plane."

"You told him I want it to be a surprise, didn't you?"

He nods. "Yes, don't worry."

Thirty minutes later we are at the luggage terminal and Max sees one of Josh's drivers through the crowd. He nods at me as he walks over and starts to quietly talk in Max's ear. I frown. That's odd. What's he saying? Bit rude, whispering.

"Max, I'm going to the bathroom." He nods and then continues talking as I walk away. This is weird, Max doesn't usually leave me alone at all. He must have really missed his friend the driver, they sure are deep in conversation. I exit the bathroom to see Max waiting patiently outside for me. I smile.

"Natasha, I need to talk to you, honey."

I smile and frown, honey.... he's never called me that before.

He looks uncomfortable, "There has been an accident." I frown. "It's Joshua," he whispers.

"What.... what kind of accident?" I gasp. He grabs my arm and I snatch it away from him. "What's happened, Max? Tell me."

He swallows and looks around as if surveying the situation. "Joshua is in the hospital. He has taken a drug overdose."

My eyes widen, "What? What do you mean? What drug?"

He rubs the back of his neck. "Cocaine, honey."

My face drops and I turn and start to sprint toward the door with him hot on my heels. I look around frantically for the Audi. "Where's the car?" I scream.

He grabs my arm, "Natasha, calm down."

I snatch my arm away from his grip. "Take me to him!" I yell, as I start to freak out. This is all my fault. Dear God, no, not this. The car pulls up and I dive in as I angrily swipe the tears from my face. I have had just about as much as I can take.

Adrian

"I can only speak to immediate family."

Of course, his brother who is also a doctor is in with him now," I reply. He nods and enters the hospital room and I follow. Cameron turns to face us as we walk in. Joshua is in the hospital bed, unconscious and still. He is hooked up to machines in the intensive care ward and nurses are everywhere. I have never been so frightened. Actually, that's a lie. I have, when I was in a hospital ward just like this watching my father lose his battle for life. How did it get to this? I thought he was ok. I knew he was down, but I never thought he would purposely take an overdose. This is my worst nightmare.

"I'm Mark Reynolds. I will be Joshua's doctor."

Cameron nods and holds out his hand to shake the doctor's.

"Cameron Stanton," he replies as he turns back to look at his brother. "What are the stats?" Cameron asks.

Dr Reynolds picks up the chart from the end of the bed. "We have put him in an induced coma to bring his heart rate and blood pressure down. He is suffering Tachyarrhythmia and at this point we are very concerned about him suffering a cerebral hemorrhage or heart failure."

Cameron drops his head and picks up Joshua's hand.

"Christ," he murmurs. "How long until he's out of the woods?"

The doctor shrugs. "Usually about twelve hours, but it could be sooner. If we can just keep his body cool, I think he will make it, but I can't be sure. And then you know of course, depending on how long he went without oxygen, there is a chance he may have sustained brain damage." Cameron nods and drops his head again as I slump into the chair. Why is this happening? "I would suggest you call your family. Is he married?"

Cameron looks at Joshua again. "Yes," he replies softly. "His wife Natasha is on her way."

The doctor rubs Cameron's shoulder. "I suggest you start praying." He gives me a nod before exiting the room.

"Natasha is on her way?" I ask.

Cameron nods, unable to speak past his tears, and slumps onto the floor next to Joshua's bed, his head in his hands. For five hours I sit silently in the corner as I watch Joshua's nurse apply and reapply water cooling blankets directly to his skin and check his vitals and check his vitals. He is hooked up to so many machines but the heartbeat sound echoing through the room is comforting, as long as I hear that beep all is ok. Cameron is a mess. I have never seen him like this. He had to ring his mother and break the news. I feel like I am having an out-of-body experience. I am numb, this can't be real.

"I'm going to get you a drink, Cam." He gives me a weak smile and nods as I walk back into the hall. Ben is waiting patiently with Pete, Joshua's driver, in the small lounge area opposite Joshua's room. They both immediately stand as I walk toward them, their faces anxious.

"He's still ok, no news." I mutter.

"Thank God," Ben blows out a breath.

I rub my head. "I'm going to get some coffee. Do you want some?"

Ben nods, "Yeah, I'll come with you."

"I'm just going to the bathroom. I won't be a minute." I head through the double doors that lead to the bathrooms.

Two minutes later Ben comes into the bathroom after me. "Do you want the bad news or the bad news?" he asks me.

"Dear God, what's happened?" I stammer.

"No, nothing with Josh.... sorry that was put badly.

Vinegar tits just arrived."

My face drops. "Who in the hell rang her?"

He shrugs, "I don't know."

I am not in the mood for this bitch today. I shake my head, wash my hands and head back out to the lounge area.

She storms over to me. "Why in the hell wasn't I rung?" she snaps.

I narrow my eyes. "Hello Amelie, you weren't rung because you are not immediate family or Joshua's girlfriend, that's why."

She scowls at me. "Last time I looked you were neither of those things either."

I roll my eyes. "Go home, Amelie. Natasha is on her way and I know for a fact that Joshua doesn't want you here. I will call you if there is any news."

"I am here because Margaret, Joshua's mother, called me and I am not going anywhere. Why in the hell was Natasha called? She left him if you care to remember," she snaps.

Cameron walks out of Joshua's room and looks up to see Amelie. His face drops and he quickly turns to go back into the room, hoping to escape her.

"Cameron," she storms over to him before he can make

an unnoticed getaway. "Why didn't you call me? I'm furious."

Cameron frowns at her and shakes his head. "I notice you haven't asked me how he is, thanks, Amelie." Cameron's eyes flick to me in disgust. We don't like Amelie. We did at first, but we have watched her manipulate Joshua like a fiddle too many times. She's a conniving two faced bitch but Joshua seems to think she is this gentle pure friend that he has to protect. We decided collectively about two years ago that at least if Joshua spent his weekends with her, he wasn't getting into trouble with Carson. Better the devil you know sort of thing. She is the ultimate player, and she is making a play right for Joshua. Thank God, she's not his type. I think I will kill him if he ever goes there.

Cameron puts his hands in his pockets and glares at her. "Natasha is on her way, so you need to go home. Adrian will call you if there is any change."

"I want to see him," she snaps.

Cameron shakes his head "It's only family at this stage. I will call you when he wakes. Seriously, go home. I promise. Someone will call you."

The doctor walks back up the hall. "Ah, Mrs. Stanton?" he questions.

Cameron's eyes flick to me nervously. "No, this is not his wife. Natasha is on her way." Amelie's eyes widen in shock as the doctor re-enters Joshua's room. Cameron smirks at me and follows him. Oh no.... Great. How am I supposed to explain this shit?

"Joshua and Natasha are married?" she gasps.

I shrug. "Um, yes, not that it is any of your business." Holy shit, she's going to go ape. She shocks me and does the exact opposite, goes deathly pale and slumps silently into the seat. Why in the hell has Cameron told everyone that Joshua is

married? It doesn't make sense. I head back down to the cafe-
teria in the foyer of the hospital to grab our coffee. I am
waiting in line when I see her, Natasha sprinting through the
hospital hysterical, with Max running to keep up with her. I
smile, this is how you act if the person you love is on death's
door. Thank God, she is here.

"Natasha," I call out to her. She sees me and runs over and
crumples into my arms in a fit of tears. This girl is beautiful,
on the inside more than the outside.

"Adrian," she cries. "Where is he? I need to see him."

I wrap her in my arms, even I've missed this beautiful girl.
"I'll take you to him, baby." I nod to my bodyguard to take
care of the coffee and I take her hand and lead her to the lifts
to see him. We approach his room. Amelie lifts her head and
glares at Natasha. My anger rises. I could just knock this
bitch's head off. Natasha doesn't say anything but frowns at
me. I lead her to his room and open the door. The doctor
turns to us.

Cameron nervously looks at Natasha. "Dr., this is Joshua's
wife Natasha."

She smiles and slightly frowns as she holds out her hand
to shake his. "Your husband has taken a cocaine overdose.
We have stabilized him and put him into an induced coma
but he is not out of the woods just yet." She nods as she tries
to hold in the tears. She leans over Joshua and embraces him
as she breaks into sobs on his chest. Both Cameron and I tear
up at her obvious devastation. This is hard to watch.

Natasha

"Joshua. My God, what have you done?" I cry into his chest as
sobs wrack my body. The doctor leaves and I turn to cuddle

Cameron who is just as distraught as me. My eyes flick to Adrian. "What happened, how did this happen?" I sob.

Adrian hunches his shoulders. "We are not sure, but we think it was accidental."

My eyes go back to my broken love. "Does he use cocaine regularly?" I ask as I gently run my hands over his forehead.

Cameron frowns. "No, not regularly. Tash, this was an accident. He has been down lately. He would have just been trying to get through the day."

Realization hits me. "This is all my fault," I sob.

I turn back to Joshua, my beautiful Josh. He is nearly unrecognizable to me. He has tubes coming out of him every- where and is hooked up to machines. He is a lot thinner than when I last saw him and pale, he has no color. He has a beard, probably around two- or three-weeks growth. He's been neglecting himself, as I have. We are as bad as each other, I have never looked like such a sack of shit in my life.

I put my head back down on his chest and sob. "I'm so sorry, Josh. I didn't know what to do. My dad said it was wrong and then he died," I sob out loud. "And then I lost you. I was so deep in grief I couldn't see straight, and now you've done this, and it's all my fault."

Adrian walks over behind me and puts his hand on my shoulder. "Tash, this isn't your fault, and it has been a terrible string of circumstances. Ones that have been out of your control. Josh doesn't blame you, he understands. He is just not handling things well at the moment, but he will get better and now you are here you can work things out together."

I nod as I wipe my eyes and turn back to look Joshua.

"You're right, he has to get better." A sudden burst of anger breaks through. "Do you hear me, Joshua.... don't you dare think about dying. You can't leave me.... not now. You fight this.... do you hear me? So help me God, Joshua Stanton.... I mean it, listen to me." I break back down into a fit of tears. Dear God, let him be ok, this is such a mess.

Cameron walks back over and pulls me into his arms. "He needs you to be calm, Tash. We are trying to regulate his heart-beat, being irrational will not help the cause."

I nod, he's right. Calm.... I need to keep calm. I nod and pull away from Cameron and immediately pull a chair to sit next to the bed. I need to find some inner strength and I need to find it fast. I grab Joshua's hand and kiss the back of it and put my head down and start to silently pray. Please pull through, please pull through. About three hours later I find myself leaning forward with my head resting on Joshua's upper arm. I am somewhere in between sleep and delirium when I jump with a start as the nurse and doctor enter the room. I quickly stand to allow the doctor greater access. He checks Joshua over and reads his chart.

He gives me a warm smile. "Mrs. Stanton, it seems you have a positive effect on your husband. His vitals indicate a promising result and I think he is going to be ok, he has passed the worst of it. It will be a few days, but it seems all is well. We are going to start bringing him out of his sedation." A wave of gratitude washes over me and my face breaks into a huge smile. I run immediately to the door and out into the waiting lounge where I see Cameron and Adrian.

"He's going to be ok," I gasp. They both stand in a rush to cuddle me and the three of us stand embracing each other. We stand still, united and exceedingly grateful. It is then I notice Amelie standing in the corner of the room alone.

I turn to her and smile. "He's going to be okn Amelie." She nods nervously and gives me a weak smile. Cameron then picks me up and twirls me around and I laugh out loud. He carries me back into Joshua's room to see the doctor himself. The doctor smiles warmly at Cameron and shakes his hand and Cameron excitedly grabs him in an embrace, forget the handshake. Adrian walks in behind us.

"It looks as though he is through the worst of it. We are going to keep him lightly sedated for the next twenty-four hours just to keep his vitals down. Mrs. Stanton, do you want to stay the night or are you going home?"

"I will be staying, if that's ok," I smile.

He smiles and nods. "I will organize a bed to be brought in for you then."

"Thank you, Dr.," I reply as he leaves the room.

"Why did you tell them we are married?" I ask Cameron.

He looks sullen. "Because I knew if it got bad and they were going to lose him they would have asked you to leave and you wouldn't have had a say in anything. Joshua would want you with him more than anybody else. I did it for him, not for you."

I give him a weak smile. "Sorry, Cam. I haven't dealt with this shit very well, have I?"

He shakes his head. "No, you haven't and neither has he, he's been a total nightmare."

Adrian must have sensed Cameron's underlying anger at how I've treated Joshua and he butts in. "She's here now and everything is going to be fine. Isn't it, Tash?" He puts his arm reassuringly around me.

I smile and turn to Adrian as he wraps his arms around me. "Thank you for looking after him for me. I appreciate you guys being such good friends to Joshua. God, if anything happened to him." I shiver in horror I can't even bear to think of the consequences. My tears start again. "I'm such an idiot. How could I have treated him so terribly? I just left him and told him I never wanted to see him again, after all we had been through to be together." Guilt fills me, I don't deserve him, but to be fair I could never have predicted what the future was going to hold. I was totally blinded by grief. A nurse re-enters the room and injects something into his drip. "What are you giving him?" I ask.

"Diazepam, this will keep him sedated to keep his body temperature down and even."

"Tash, our mum and dad are on their way with our brothers. Prepare yourself, she's going to be fuming mad and I'm pretty sure it will be aimed at you" Cameron sighs.

"She came to Sydney to see me and asked me to come to Joshua. She was worried about him and it seems she had a good reason to be," I whisper. "This is all my fault."

Cameron and Adrian exchange glances. "She asked you to come to Joshua?" Cameron frowns.

"Ripley's believe it or not." I do wide eyes at him. "What's Amelie's problem?" I ask Adrian.

Adrian's eyes drop to Joshua and he hunches his shoulders. "You, I expect. It's no secret she's in love with Joshua."

"Adrian." Cameron snaps. "Stay out of it."

I narrow my eyes. "It's ok. I already know, you don't have to be a rocket scientist to know that. He loves her as well."

Cameron and Adrian frown. "No, he doesn't. He loves you, Tash," Cameron stammers. My eyes drop to my beautiful unconscious man before me. "I know he loves me, it's ok, boys. I'm ok, I can't blame her for loving him ... loving him is easy. It's the walking away from him that's hard."

They both give me a sad smile and nod. "We will give you some privacy." And with that they disappear out of the room.

To continue this story it is available
On Amazon now.

AFTERWORD

Thank you so much for reading and
for your ongoing support
I have the most beautiful readers in the whole world!

Keep up to date with all the latest news
and online discussions by joining the Swan Squad VIP
Facebook group and discuss your favourite
books with other readers.
@tlswanauthor

Visit my website for updates and new release information.
www.tlswanauthor.com

ABOUT THE AUTHOR

T L Swan is a Wall Street Journal, USA Today, and #1 Amazon Best Selling author. With millions of books sold, her titles are currently translated in twenty languages and have hit #1 on Amazon in the USA, UK, Canada, Australia and Germany. She is currently writing the screenplays for a number of her titles. Tee resides on the South Coast of NSW, Australia with her husband and their three children where she is living her own happy ever after with her first true love.

Made in the USA
Middletown, DE
18 March 2024

51698778R00288